A TAPPING
T MY DOOR

A TAPPING AT MY DOOR

DAVID JACKSON

ZAFFRE

First published in Great Britain in 2016 by

ZAFFRE PUBLISHING
80-81 Wimpole St, London W1G 9RE
www.zaffrebooks.co.uk

Text copyright © David Jackson, 2016

This is a work of fiction. Names, places, events and
incidents are either the products of the author's imagination or
used fictitiously. Any resemblance to actual persons, living or dead,
or actual events is purely coincidental.

A CIP catalogue record for this book is available from the British Library.

Hardback ISBN: 978-1-78576-107-2
Trade Paperback ISBN: 978-1-78576-106-5
Ebook ISBN: 978-1-78576-105-8

1 3 5 7 9 10 8 6 4 2

Typeset by IDSUK (Data Connection) Ltd
Printed and bound by Clays Ltd, St Ives Plc

Zaffre Pub ... Fiction,

In loving memory of my mother

Once upon a midnight dreary, while I pondered, weak and weary,
Over many a quaint and curious volume of forgotten lore—
While I nodded, nearly napping, suddenly there came a tapping,
As of some one gently rapping, rapping at my chamber door.

—'The Raven', Edgar Allan Poe

1

Listen.

There it is again. The sound. The tapping, scratching, scrabbling noise at the back door.

Terri Latham gives it her attention and then, when the sound stops, chides herself for wasting the brainpower. It's nothing. Just the plants, probably.

She laughs at that. Laughs at the way it conjures up the image of an eight-foot Venus Flytrap or some such, banging its leafy fist on her door and demanding to be fed. Like that film – what's it called? – *Little Shop of Horrors*, that's it. Because it's funny. Sitting here alone, getting all jittery over nothing but a plant – well, that's hilarious.

Actually, she has a whole crowd of plants in pots just outside the door, but she's not thinking of them. Most of them aren't capable of knocking for attention.

No, what she's thinking of is the climber that clings to and has seemingly devoured the arched trellis that surrounds her back door. The thing seems to push ahead daily at a rate of knots. She still remembers being reduced to tears of laughter with some girl-friends when they joked that she obviously spends too much time stimulating her clematis.

The problem is, the trellis is old and rotten. Just the other day a section of it collapsed, leaving a mass of tangled fretwork and plant rubbing and knocking against the glass panel of the door. She did her best to tie it back up with string, but wasn't convinced she did a great job of it. Now she's sure of it. The thing has fallen apart again.

Well, it can wait, she thinks. It's late and it's dark and I'm not standing outside on a chair in the middle of the night just to put a stupid clematis back into position. Besides, *Sleepless in Seattle* is one of my favourite films of all time, and I don't want to miss any of it.

So she stays put. Settles into her comfy Ikea sofa in front of her Samsung flatscreen and Tom Hanks. Sips the special-offer Chardonnay that she bought from the off-licence on Derby Lane, and tells herself to relax so that she can look forward to the next soppy scene.

Tap . . . Scratch . . . Tap.

Oh, for Christ's sake, she thinks. She raises her head over the back of her sofa. Beams a thought wave towards the rear of the house that says, *One more creepy noise from you and I'm cutting you off at the root. That'll be painful. Think about it!*

A part of her knows that her anger is forced. It's a mask, a cover for the unease swiftly gaining traction within her. She also knows that this mask won't stay in place forever. It will crack and it will crumble and it will fall away, and all that will remain will be the fear. But if that's not to happen, she needs to make a pre-emptive strike.

'All right, then!' she calls out loud, as though yelling at a naughty but persistent puppy. As though giving into its demands under protest, when what she is really surrendering to is her own craven desire for reassurance.

I'll go into the kitchen, she thinks. I'll go there and I'll see exactly what I expect to see, which is a whole load of leafy crap dangling and scraping at my door, and then I can get back to my film and my wine and a good night's sleep, even though I shouldn't feel the need to check, because I know exactly what this is and I'm being a complete wuss about it.

She beheads the next thought before it can do any damage. The thought that begins, *But what if it's not . . . ?*

She tops up her courage reservoir with a swift mouthful of wine, then abandons the comforting support of her sofa and heads into the kitchen.

She hates this kitchen. Top of her list when she was looking to buy a house was one with a beautiful bathroom and a stunning kitchen, and she ended up with neither because she couldn't afford it. This kitchen has a minimal set of units that must have been cheap even when they were installed. Half of them are falling apart. The washer on one of the taps has failed, there are ugly lengths of gas and water pipes showing everywhere, and several of the wall tiles are cracked.

When she enters, she doesn't put the light on because all it would do is reflect back off the windows and present her with multiple views of the depressing interior. Instead, she forces herself to stand in the gloom and wait with anxiety-tinged impatience for her tired eyes to adjust.

With the gradual emergence of broad angular shapes of furniture comes a slight easing of her tension. She releases a long outbreath and steps further into the room.

Through the grime-caked picture window over the sink she sees a yellowish quarter-moon emerge from behind a solid-looking cloud. As its weak light filters into the room, her eyes seize the opportunity to suck up information.

She moves closer to the back door, her pupils hungrily dilated. Like the kitchen cupboards, the door is cheap and thin, and inspires little confidence in its ability to fulfil its transit prevention role. The upper half contains a panel of frosted glass that could easily be broken and perhaps even used as an entry point by someone small and limber enough.

She should have replaced this door ages ago. But then she should have done many things to make this house more secure. She knows this. Has known it ever since she moved in.

She lives in a small residential area of Liverpool called Stoneycroft, close to the busy dual carriageway that is Queens Drive – one of the city's main arteries. When she explains to people where she lives, they say, 'Oh, you mean Old Swan,' and she says, 'No, it's called Stoneycroft,' because she thinks it sounds posher.

It's not posh, though.

The way she sees things, she has her foot on the first rung of the property ladder. It's not the nicest house in the world, the area has its problems, but at least it's hers. In a few years she'll sell it and move up to something better – maybe in Allerton or Woolton or even over on the Wirral. For now, this will do.

The estate agent described the house as a quasi semi-detached, which was a bullshit way of describing a house that is joined to one of its neighbours on the upper floor but not the lower. Between the two front doors, a brick tunnel runs straight through to the rear of the properties. Some of the houses in this road have lockable iron gates on their passageways. Terri's doesn't, which means that anyone can go for a stroll down it. What's more, her wooden door at the other end of the tunnel doesn't have a lock either. And even if it did, there's another way into her rear garden because it backs onto a small park that anyone can enter and then scale her panel fencing unseen.

All in all, this house is not exactly Fort Knox.

These thoughts have reared up in Terri's head many times. On each occasion she has made a mental note to do something about the situation, and on each occasion she has immediately lost the note in the untidy recesses of her memory.

The reason these thoughts are rushing and cramming into her mind like peak hour traffic right now, though, is because of what she sees. Or rather, because of what she doesn't see.

There is no wayward clematis on the other side of the glass panel of her door.

Although the glass is translucent, and although it is undeniably in dire need of cleaning, the diffused light of the moon makes the absence of leafy matter apparent.

And what that means is that something else has been causing the noise. The noise that goes . . .

Tap . . . Tap . . . Scratch . . .

As the sound starts up again, Terri takes a step back into the shadows. As if their dark embrace is more comforting than whatever denizen of the night might be outside.

It is busily working away on the bottom section of the door. Ground level. Something small, and yet fiercely determined to bore its way into her house. Why? What can it want?

Her first thought is that it's Shit Sue. The yappy little mongrel from across the road. Which, as it happens, is not a Shih Tzu at all. Terri calls it that because, instead of taking it for a walk, its irresponsible owner simply shoos it out of his front door, at which point the mischievous little bitch runs across the street, threads its way through the bars of Terri's front gate, traverses her moss- and weed-infested driveway, scampers up the side passage and then takes a dump that seems almost equivalent in mass to that of the dog itself.

That's Terri's first thought.

Three problems with that. One: inconsiderate prick though he is, Shit Sue's owner never usually lets his excrement generator loose this late at night. Two: even though the wooden door at the rear end of the passage has no lock, it does at least close. And when it's closed, which she is sure it was the last time she looked, even the irrepressible turd machine cannot slide its way under to reach her patio. And three: this doesn't sound like Shit Sue. It doesn't sound like a dog of any kind. The scratching is from feet much smaller than those of a canine. And there's the additional tapping sound, intermixed with the scrabbling. A dog just wouldn't create those noises.

So, what then?

A cat? Possibly, she thinks. Cats scratch at things, don't they? And – yes! – I had tuna for my tea, didn't I? Cats love tuna. It can smell the fish, and it wants some. It—

No. Don't be stupid. Listen to it. Hear that tapping again? Well, cats don't tap, do they? They just don't.

Fuck.

Pull yourself together, she tells herself. This is what you get for living on your own. It's what you wanted. You didn't want to stay in a flat with your mates, and you certainly had no intention of moving in with a bloke again any time soon. You wanted your own space. Well, you've got it. You're a grown-up, so start acting like one.

She takes a deep breath. Covers the distance to the door in one stride. Reaches for the door handle.

You can do this, she thinks. It's not a rapist on the other side of the door. Rapists don't scratch and tap at your door in such a pathetic way. They leap out from bushes and poorly lit doorways. They run up behind you and—

Okay, enough of that. Open the bloody door. It's a squirrel banging its nuts. Or a hedgehog trying to mate with the boot-scraper. Or something else that your pathetic imagination just hasn't conceived of. When you open the door, it'll be more scared of you than you are of it, and it'll almost burst with the shock of seeing you standing there, and its tiny beady eyes will water as it craps itself and scurries away as fast as its stumpy little legs will take it.

She starts to turn the handle.

Tap ... Scratch ...

Turns it as far as it will go.

Scrape ... Tap ...

And ... pull!

She yanks on the handle. The door rattles in the frame but doesn't swing open.

Bollocks, she thinks. It's locked. Of course it's locked. I always lock it when I'm alone at night. Why should tonight be any—

Listen!

The noise. It's stopped.

She pictures the timid little animal, scared witless by the clatter of the door, its marble-sized heart fluttering frantically in its chest.

She considers going for the key, unlocking the door, checking that it's all clear out there. Decides against it.

It's gone. Back to its lair. And if it hasn't gone, then she doesn't want to know about it. If it's still at her door, rolling up its furry sleeves in preparation for a renewed and more vigorous assault, then it's not the kind of foe she wants to face, thank you very much.

She shakes her head. Expels a mirthless laugh. Goes back to the living room, where Tom Hanks awaits.

She sits, crosses her legs, stares at the television without taking in what it's showing her. It's all just pictures and noise. She's not comfortable, either physically or mentally.

She reaches for her wine glass and drains it, then empties the bottle into it and takes another swig. Okay, that's better. Now she can unwind.

She swings her legs onto the sofa. Commands herself to relax and enjoy the film. The kid, the one with the backpack, is in the Empire State Building. This is a good bit. It's getting near the end now. Time to get the Kleenex ready. This is going to be—

Shit!

The scrabbling is loud now. More frantic.

Terri spills wine down the front of her dressing gown. She turns again to look into the adjoining room. The thing – whatever it is – sounds closer. As if it's in there, inside the house, inside her kitchen.

But no, it can't be. That's impossible. She tried the door herself just a moment ago, didn't she? It's locked. The windows are locked, too.

She stands. Grabs the remote and mutes the sound of the television. Stares through the doorway as she listens to that awful racket. The tapping and the scraping and the scratching. But it's different now. Why is it different?

She retraces her steps into the kitchen, accepting that she's moving more slowly now, more cautiously. Like wading through treacle.

She gets through the door. Holds her breath. Eyes darting as she waits.

There it is!

Not at the door now, but at the window.

Not the picture window over the sink – the one through which that moon still beams its skewed, pitying smile at her – but the other window, the one next to the door. The one with the curtains closed over it.

The window is a good three feet off the ground. How did the thing get up that high? No dog or squirrel or hedgehog or whatever could get up there – not unless it's on a pogo stick. A cat, maybe. A cat could leap onto the sill. But hasn't she already discounted the cat theory? Hasn't she already established that cats, while excelling in the scratching department, are somewhat less adept when it comes to tapping skills?

She suddenly finds herself breathing again. But it's fast, ragged breathing. Panicky breathing. It shouldn't be like that. Stop it, she thinks. There's nothing to be afraid of. All the precarious situations you've been in, and you're frightened of a little woodland creature?

Woodland? Where are we now – in a fairy tale? This is Stoneycroft. Which, despite its rustic and idyllic name, is right next to Old Swan. There are no Seven Dwarfs here.

She tells herself that if there is in fact a dwarf or a diminutive person of any kind on the other side of that window, she will shit herself.

Suddenly her mind is racing off in the direction of evil dwarfs. And now all she can think about is *Don't Look Now*. Which is another of her favourite films but for totally different reasons. Scare-the-pants-off-you reasons.

It's not a dwarf, she thinks. It's not a gnome. It's not a fucking gremlin that tears the wings off planes at 10,000 feet. If you want to know what it is, open the fucking curtain and see.

So she does.

She steps closer to the window, her feet dragging even more than they did before. The noise comes in bursts – sudden energetic flurries punctuated by moments of silent exhaustion. She reaches out a hand. Draws it back when the beating on the window seems almost enough to break the glass. Reaches out again. Takes hold of the thick blue material she spent far too much on in John Lewis. Takes a breath. One . . . two . . .

Three!

She yanks the curtain open just as the noise abates once more. Through the glass she can see nothing. No animals, no dwarfs, nothing.

She leans her face into the window. Moves it so close that her breath starts to fog it up. It becomes difficult to see through the mist. She pulls her hand into the sleeve of her dressing gown and begins to raise it to clear a porthole.

And that's when the thing makes its appearance.

It shoots up from below, as if thrown at her face. She gets a glimpse of claws and sharpness and malicious intent and shiny blackness as she screams and leaps backwards, banging hard into a chair behind her but unable to take her eyes off this demonic creature that now opens its mouth and starts to issue eerily deep-throated and human-like calls.

She stares in incredulity, but also with a sense of relief. Why didn't she think of this before?

A bird.

But what a bird. Huge and so very black. Even its beak appears to be fashioned from ebony, and its eyes seem to swallow up the moonlight. Its neck looks muscular and powerful, as if built to help it tear things apart in that vicious mouth. Its wings pound against

the glass as it struggles to maintain purchase with its grasping tal-
ons. And, every so often, it takes another fierce peck at the glass,
threatening to crack it and allow it entry.

A crow, thinks Terri. Something like that. She knows sparrows
and pigeons and robins and starlings, and that's about as far as her
avian expertise goes. She has never seen a bird like this in her garden before.

She doesn't want it here now either. It's big and it's freaky and it's
acting weirdly. It's like something out of that Hitchcock film. *The
Birds*. Where they all turn on the humans and rip them to shreds.

It has to go. That much is certain. She can't go to sleep with a
thing like this hammering to come in. What if it follows her up to
her bedroom window? Starts its tapping in the middle of the night?
How could she sleep with even the prospect of that happening?

So, okay. How do you get rid of a bird like that? Most birds, you
just clap your hands and off they go. Even the stupid, chewing-gum
eating pigeons have worked that one out. But this bird? This one
looks like it's either insanely malevolent or supremely intelligent.
This one looks like it'll take your face off if you go anywhere near it.

I should call someone, she thinks. I should get in a bird expert.
Or someone with a shotgun.

At half past midnight?

Okay, then, the police. No, definitely not the police. The police
are the last people I should call unless I want to be made a laughing
stock for being a total chicken over a stupid bird.

Chicken, bird. That should be funny, but I'm not laughing.

She lets out a growl of furious acceptance that the only one who
can do anything about this ludicrous situation is herself.

It's a bird. Shoo it away or batter it to death. Either solution is
acceptable. Okay, Terri?

First things first. Lights on.

She finds the light switch. Clicks it. Blinks against the brightness.

She decides she needs a weapon. Preferably something that doesn't require her to come within several feet of the creature.

She deliberates for a few seconds, then goes to the cupboard under the stairs. Comes back with a sweeping brush. Then she takes a key down from a shelf and unlocks the back door.

'Okay, birdbrain,' she says. 'Here I come. You have five seconds to get out of my garden before I sweep you to death.'

She opens the door. Sticks her head out into the night. The bird is resting on the sill, cocking its head as it stares a challenge back at her. It reminds her of something. *The Omen*? Wasn't there a creepy black bird in that?

There I go again, she thinks. This isn't the devil in animal form. Not even a dwarf in a costume. It's just a bird.

She steps onto the patio, feeling the cold of the flagstones against her bare feet. She holds the brush out in front of her. Thrusts it towards the bird.

Unimpressed, the creature merely angles its head a little more.

'All right, matey. You asked for it.'

She pulls the brush back. Thinks, Please don't come at me. Not the hair. Don't get tangled in my hair. Bats do that, don't they? They get all tangled in your hair. Please don't do that.

Another thrust. Right up to the bird. She prepares to drop the brush and start running as the creature bursts into action again.

But it doesn't come at her. It doesn't even move away from the windowsill, for that matter.

It doesn't, because it can't.

Terri keeps hold of the brush, but lowers it, like a knight might lower his sword. She takes a couple of small, hesitant steps forward as she squints against the fluorescent light pouring through the window.

The bird is not moving freely. It is caught on something. It can't get its legs free from some kind of thread or wire.

She realises now why it has been acting so strangely. It got tangled up, and now it's panicking. All it wants to do is be free. It's not evil at all. It's frightened. It's—

The blow is as loud as it is painful. Something hard and heavy ramming into her skull. It seems to echo around her garden.

She lets out a yelp and starts to turn. Sees the dark figure of a man behind her, his hand coming up for a second strike. She starts to raise her own arm in defence, but she's too late. The object the man is holding – a brick or a stone – collides again with her forehead with a sickening hollow crunch that sends her reeling backwards. She feels her back slam into the wall and hears a screech that might come from her, the man or even the bird. Her head is swimming and the pain is agonising and her eyes are misting over. She knows she can't allow the blackness to swallow her, she has to get out of this situation, call for help somehow, and so she opens her mouth to cry out, but receives another blow for her effort, this time in the throat. She lashes out blindly, feels her hands connect with something, but also feels him grab hold of her sleeve and pull her towards him, so she uses her feet, kicks low and hard into where his groin should be, and yes, she feels it connect and she hears a grunt of pain and a loosening of his grip. She pulls away and runs to the back gate, because her attacker is preventing her getting back to the house, and she opens her mouth again to scream as loud as she can, please help me, anyone, I don't care who you are, but please come and help me.

She hears nothing and she doesn't know why. She is yelling at the top of her voice and yet nothing seems to be happening. It is as if the knocks to her head have deafened her. But then she trips and falls against the garden fence, and she hears the thin, brittle panels rattle and crack against their concrete support posts, and even in her confused state she wonders how it is that she can hear that and not her own voice. So she reaches up a hand to her mouth to check that it's working as it should be. Only it doesn't get that far.

It doesn't reach her mouth because it feels the hot, sticky wetness that seems to be all over her neck. And when her fingers investigate further, they discover the reason for her silence. They disappear into the huge hole in her windpipe, and she freezes with the horrific realisation that this man has cut her throat.

And then there is no more time for thinking, because he is on her again. He is pulling her away from the fence and dragging her down to the ground, and she sees a smug smile on his face that tells her he knows he has won and that she cannot summon help and that she cannot fight back. Because she is dying. She knows this. Her wounds are too great, too life-threatening. Her mind is going into shutdown, and she wishes it wouldn't. She wishes she could hold on to something. A chance. A possibility. But her mind has decided otherwise. It has weighed things up and decided to cut its losses, to put what is left of its energy into closing down its consciousness and detaching itself from a reality that is too appalling to take in any longer.

And if that were the end, it would be a mercy. But there is more to come.

The man straddles her. Takes hold of her chin and turns her head to face him. She sees his face again, and as the blood continues to pour from her throat she wonders with almost serene detachment what might be going on in this man's mind. She wonders what experiences, what tragedies in his life have led him to this. She wants to know why.

As if in answer, he shows her the knife in his hand. Shows her from a couple of feet away, then brings it closer and closer. Until she knows what he is going to do with it.

She somehow finds it within herself to scream again then. But her pleas never escape her body. They remain locked within, tearing her apart, shredding her from the inside.

On the windowsill, the bird dips its sleek head and watches in rapt silence.

2

All eyes are on him when he enters the room.

There's a little shuffling. A little unrest. A little trepidation, perhaps. But they all watch and wait. Every one of them.

'I did it!' he yells, pumping his fist in the air. 'I bloody well did it!'

The room erupts. Becomes a maelstrom.

He shines his cheesiest grin at them.

'I didn't think I could do it,' he says. 'I thought it would be too hard, you know? I wasn't even sure I'd get over the fence at the back. Not that it was too high or anything. I mean, I could climb it no problem. But I thought I'd back out. I thought I'd end up coming home again with nothing to show for it. But I did it. I actually did it.'

For a moment he can't say anymore. He is too overcome with the emotion of it all. He stands there with tear-filled eyes and pushes his hands through his hair and listens to the chattering around him.

'I need a beer,' he says. 'Wait there while I get myself a can.'

He hurries off to the kitchen. Reaches out a hand to open the fridge. Sees that it is caked in blood. Her blood.

Suddenly he is dashing over to the sink and being violently and copiously sick.

When his retching is over, he turns the tap on full force and washes the mess away. Squirts some Fairy Liquid onto his hands and washes those too.

He heads back to the fridge. Takes a can of Carlsberg from the shelf, pops it open, then takes half a dozen deep swigs before coming up for air.

When he gets back to the room, he has calmed a little. His hands are less shaky as he raises the can to his lips again.

'She deserved it,' he says. 'Bloody hard head, though. I hit her twice with a brick – twice! – and she still didn't go down. Had to use the knife in the end. Got a bit messy then . . .'

His thoughts drift off, and it's a while before he can drag himself back into the present.

'She knew why, though. I told her before she died. I explained to her exactly why I was doing it.'

With his free hand he points at one of his onlookers, then another, then another. 'You all know why I'm doing this, don't you? It's for you. Every one of you. They've got to learn. They've got to be taught a lesson.'

Exhaustion hits him then, and he stumbles across to one of the high-backed chairs.

'I could do with a rest, George, after the night I've had.'

George seems to take the hint, and relinquishes his position.

He slumps heavily into the vacated chair. Takes another long slurp. Scans the faces watching him.

'You'll all get your turn. Every last one of you. Don't worry about that. Tonight was just the start.'

He puts a hand out. 'Well? Is this the best welcome you can give me?'

As if in response, one member of his audience crosses the room and sits on his lap. He strokes her head softly.

'Thanks, Freda,' he says. 'I can always count on you.'

Freda looks up at him. Stares at his face without appreciation, without empathy. Without even a glimmer of comprehension.

Freda is a pigeon.

From every vantage point in the room, almost one hundred pairs of eyes peer similarly at the only human in their midst.

And now he's not so sure this was a good idea.

He didn't give it a lot of thought at the time the request was made. It seemed like it would be a piece of cake. Not a patch on the stuff he used to get up to.

But now Nathan Cody feels the unease building inside him, the pressure in his chest increasing. It seems uncomfortably warm to him, even though it's the middle of October and everyone is wearing dark, drab coats to blend in with the dark, drab days.

Play, he tells himself. Play like a bastard to take your mind off it.

So he does. Starts banging away on his guitar like he's been doing for the past hour. Singing his heart out like it's his only route to a square meal today.

He's standing at the bottom end of Bold Street. He's wearing a ragged, stained coat and greasy denim jeans, and there's a week's worth of itchy stubble on his chin. He hasn't played in public for a long time, but if he says so himself, he's sounding damn good. People have actually been tossing coins into the battered case yawning open on the pavement in front of him.

'Paperback Writer' is what he's singing now. Which couldn't be any more apt given that he's mere feet away from where Waterstones used to stand. Not that many of his passers-by are making the connection. Bit subtle for most of them at this time of the morning. They'll know it's a Beatles song, all right. Cody is trying to maintain a local flavour in his repertoire. Not doing 'Ferry Cross the Mersey', though. He hates that song. He can never resist the temptation to slip into an absurdly exaggerated Scouse accent when he attempts it – so much so that he ends up sounding like Harry Enfield doing his 'Calm down, calm down' sketch.

It's nine o'clock on a Tuesday. Most of the people passing are on their way to work, but some are hitting the shops early. He wonders if any of them miss Waterstones as much as he does, or whether to them it was less about the books and more about being just another place to grab an espresso and a pastry to kick-start their day.

The thought saddens him and provokes him to give extra emphasis to the last lines of the song, but they get carried away on the breeze and nobody notices.

He takes a moment to look around. Opposite is the grand old Lyceum building, originally one of the first lending libraries in Europe, and more recently a post office. Now a homeless man sits hunched up on its otherwise deserted steps, his head resting against a stone pillar.

Farther along the street, a dark-complexioned woman stands at the entranceway to Central Station and tries to sell copies of the *Big Issue*. She is short, but probably not as stocky as her many layers of clothing make it appear. Cody suspects she would never win saleswoman of the year with her timid, mumbling technique. He decides that, when his own stint here is over, he will donate to her the money he has been given.

His gaze shifts up the street. Between him and St Luke's Church at the far end lies an eclectic mix of cafes, coffee houses, art shops and clothing retailers. He has always liked this part of town. He can almost picture a time when the length of Bold Street was employed as a standard measure for ships' ropes, and the surrounding buildings were being erected to house the rich merchants.

He is well aware that the city has its problems, just like any other. A few minutes of travel in almost any direction from the town centre and its tourist attractions leads to areas of dilapidation, decay and poverty. Toxteth, infamous for the rioting of the eighties, is not far from here. Unlike many other cities, though, Liverpool has long been looked down upon, certainly by politicians and the media, and usually by those who have never visited the place. Its people have often been the subject of cruel stereotype, spectacular prejudice, and ill-considered attempts at humour.

Things are changing, though, and rapidly. Following decades of stagnation, the city is being transformed. Money is pouring in. The docklands and shopping areas have been regenerated and revitalised. Liverpool has always had its history and its architecture and its football and the Beatles. But now there is a Debenhams and a Hilton, too. New restaurants and bars are popping up everywhere. Tourists are flocking here like never before.

And what all this brings to the inhabitants of Liverpool is a growing sense of optimism. Despite all the dirt and decay that may still lie on the outskirts, the people can look towards the shiny-bright heart of their city with pride, and with hope that some of the prosperity will trickle their way. But whether that happens or not, it will never deter them from the mission that seems to be written into their genes to make this the friendliest and most welcoming city in the land.

Cody sees and feels this as he looks around now.

But what he doesn't see is what he came here for.

He spends a minute deciding what to play next. Opts for 'Eleanor Rigby'. Gets all the way to the end without making a penny. But then two teenage girls stop in their tracks and smile at him. He smiles back.

'What was that?' one of them asks.

'You don't know it?' he says.

'If I did, I wouldn't be asking.'

The cheekiness amuses him. 'It's by the Beatles. You've heard of them, right?'

''Course. I'm not thick. My granddad is always going on about them. Says he saw them at the Cavern before they were even famous.'

'He's a lucky man. Wish I'd been there.'

'Do you know anything modern?'

'Like what?'

She shrugs. 'I dunno. Something by Beyoncé or Ed Sheeran?'

Cody scratches the stubble on his chin. 'How about "Single Ladies"?'

Her eyes light up. 'You can play that?'

'No. I can do the dance, though, if you want to see that.'

The girls look at each other and giggle. The one who so far hasn't spoken feels emboldened enough to put a question of her own.

'Ever thought of auditioning for *X Factor*?'

A presence. Behind the girls. Cody permits his eyes a swift glance, but doesn't allow them to linger.

He sees a tall man in a long grey overcoat and a beanie, but his view past the girls isn't great.

'Think I'm good enough?' he asks the girls.

'I've seen worse. Who knows? It could make you famous.'

Cody sees the man take a step forward, as if he's just curious to know what's being discussed, or perhaps waiting to hear a song.

Not yet, thinks Cody. Give him the benefit of the doubt.

'If I get famous, will you come and see me on stage?'

'Yeah, deffo. You better get learning something more modern, though, or you've got no chance. You're not much older than us, are you?'

Cody's mind is running on two parallel tracks. Trying to come up with a relevant response to the girls, but also trying to keep his attention focused on what the man might be about to do.

He gets questions like this all the time. About his age. About how he looks barely twenty when in fact he's closer to thirty. In some ways, his boyish looks have been the bane of his life. On the other hand, they're why he's here now, doing this. Being what he's not.

Another cautious movement forward from the man. He's right behind the girls now. He could reach out and touch them. Cody tenses. He's finding it almost impossible to focus on the girls. His eyes want to slide up and lock on to the man, but if he does that it will all be over. He makes nonsense sounds as if in search of a witty reply to the girl's question still hanging before him, but his brain has already given up trying to multitask and is demanding that he stick to one frigging thing at a time.

And then it happens. But not in the way Cody expected.

A second man, as if from nowhere. Suddenly he's there, to Cody's right, but in full view of the girls. He too is wearing a hat – a baseball cap – and he too is wearing a long coat. But it's what he's doing with the coat that makes the difference. Because what he's doing is opening it wide and showing the girls that the only garments he has beneath it are a pair of black shoes and a pair of long grey socks, although these are less noteworthy than the part of his body that could currently be used to hang his hat on if he so wished.

The girls yelp. Cody makes a dive for the man, who turns and starts to run. Cody manages to grab hold of the back of the man's coat. He holds it good and tight, thinking, Got you, you bastard. Got you.

Except that he hasn't got him. Because what the man does then is simply to shuck off his coat and continue running. Naked except for his shoes and his socks and his baseball cap, he launches into a sprint worthy of Usain Bolt.

Shit, thinks Cody. And then he's running too. Swinging his guitar round to his back and chasing down his quarry. He is no longer a busker. He is Detective Sergeant Nathan Cody of the Merseyside Police force, pursuing a suspect and calling into his concealed radio microphone that he requires assistance, and cursing the fact that his plans have all gone wrong and that maybe pretending to be a busker wasn't such a great idea because now he's having to run and his frigging guitar is getting in the way and it's his own guitar and if it gets damaged he will be so frigging upset.

The naked man starts up Bold Street, but quickly jinks left into the entranceway to Central Station. Cody follows him down the slope. Ahead he sees people pointing and laughing at the streaker, but despite Cody's yells, nobody does anything to stop the guy.

Cody decides to save his breath and put his energy into picking up the pace.

He wonders if the man is going to head for the trains. How the hell can he expect to get past the barrier guards looking like that? But instead he takes a left turn at the cake shop, heading back up and towards the other exit. Cody feels he's getting closer, but boy, this bastard can run. And when the man bursts onto Ranelagh Street and hits the pedestrian crossing he doesn't even pause. Doesn't even check what the lights are doing. Just powers straight across the road, seemingly oblivious to the screeching tyres and the honking horns and the swearing taxi drivers. But Cody, being a little more conservative when it comes to risking his life, does slow down a tad, does take a little more time dodging the traffic and gesturing to the taxi drivers not to kill him.

And when he gets to the other side he sees another obstacle in his path. A woman. A huge woman. Wide of girth and about to fill that gap between the fruit stall and the knot of people whose eyes have all turned to enjoy the spectacle of the naked man who has just rushed past them. And despite Cody's calls she does not hear him. Just keeps on approaching that gap like a ship sliding into dock.

He can't stop for this. He hesitated for the cars, but he can't pause for this, even though the woman looks like she could do him just as much damage. And so even as he yells at her to get out of the way he is already trying to overtake her. Already squeezing through a space that he knows cannot accommodate both of them.

When he gets through, he knows it has not been without consequence. He can tell from the cry of surprise and the subsequent crash and noise of tumbling fruit that it was not the most skilfully executed manoeuvre. When he hears the shouting and feels the impact of a large orange as it bounces off his shoulder, he is not surprised.

Ahead, naked guy runs into the Clayton Square shopping centre. Basing his judgement on his luck thus far, Cody knows – he just *knows* – that the automatic doors will choose this moment to close. And close they do. Almost perversely they start to glide together, and Cody also knows that they will be irritatingly unhurried in their reaction to his frantic gestures to reopen.

So he decides not to give them the satisfaction. Instead of slamming on his brakes, he steps on the gas. For a terrifying moment it looks as though it's going to be man versus glass, but still he doesn't stop. At the last instant he makes a huge leap, twisting his body sideways to fit between those jaws.

And forgetting.

Forgetting that he has a fucking guitar on his back. His beloved, cherished instrument. The one he bought with a substantial portion of his first wage packet. The one he has strummed every night in those empty hours when sleep evades him. The one he brought with him today because guitars tend not to be police issue and he didn't anticipate he would end up having to chase a naked fucking maniac through the busy streets of Liverpool.

But it's too late now to reverse his actions. He hears the final discordant crunching and wailing of his guitar as it is ripped from his back and tossed to the floor like a dying animal flung from the blood-stained teeth of a savage predator. He feels the sting of loss that only another musician would understand, but knows he cannot pause and grieve. Instead, he channels his emotions into fierce determination as he zigzags past a bemused woman trying to sell Sky television packages.

Cody issues an unintelligible roar and tries to tap into his energy reserves. He starts to close the distance again as naked man runs through the doors into Boots. Cody enters too, and realises he has more of a chance here. It is less open. The man is corralled because of the aisles, and up ahead there are people. Staff and customers who could help. Cody calls out to them.

'Police! Stop that man!'

But he knows. Knows in his heart that they are unlikely to come to his aid. Most can be forgiven, because they won't understand what the hell is going on. Others will comprehend but be too scared to intervene. A few – the more contemptible ones – will always want the criminal to evade capture and for the police to be seen to fail.

But sometimes there is one.

She steps forward from her station, perfume tester in hand. She takes aim. She fires. A good full spray of the stuff, right into his eyes.

The man issues a high-pitched screech and brings his hands to his face as he whirls away from her. Ironically, he collides with a display of reading glasses, sending them flying across the store, but then somehow manages to recover and resume his run.

Cody issues a breathless thank you as he passes the girl, who looks justifiably proud of her actions. Her gleaming smile renews his faith and re-energises him. You can do this, he tells himself. You can do this.

The flasher manages to get to the far side of the shop and through the other exit. He goes right, then starts up the yellow-edged steps leading to the sweeping curve of Great Charlotte Street. There are a lot of steps, but they aren't steep, and Cody finds himself gaining ground. One last push, he tells himself, and he starts taking the steps two at a time, getting closer and closer to that man who is not offering him the most enticing view right now, and then he is almost within grasping distance but wondering what the hell he is going to grasp. And when the stairs come to an end, Cody realises it's now or never because his lungs are about to burst, and he makes a last-ditch leap, jumping and stretching and snatching . . .

And he gets him. He snags an ankle, which is just enough. His fingers encircle that bony ankle and refuse to let go. They bite into the man's flesh like a manacle. The man falls. A fleshy slap as he smacks into the pavement. And Cody is on him, pinning him to the ground, holding him there while he tries to push words out of his heaving lungs so that he can summon his colleagues, and so that he can swear at this idiot for causing the damage to his precious guitar.

It takes him a while to become aware of his surroundings. A while to realise that people are standing around him, smiling and sniggering and holding up their mobile phones to take photographs and videos.

And he just knows. With a sinking heart, he begins to accept that these images of him sitting breathless astride the buttocks of a naked man are about to go viral.

4

Sometimes people ask Cody what he does for a living. And sometimes, when he can't be bothered to give a more precise answer, he tells them that he's at MIT. The resulting expressions of surprise, admiration or confusion can be enough to brighten his day.

Not that it's a lie. It's just that the MIT he works for is not the one of which most people have heard. He is not at the Massachusetts Institute of Technology, one of the foremost academic establishments in the world. He is instead at a workplace that even he would accept houses a level of brainpower that is somewhat more modest.

Cody works for the Major Incident Team, which is based at Stanley Road police station – a modern, two-storey brick building in Kirkdale, one of the city's most deprived neighbourhoods. As if put there for deliberate comic effect, the station sits right next to a funeral parlour, leading the local wags to comment that it's to give the coppers a fighting chance of finding a dead body.

As Cody approaches the building, he knows she's going to be there. Not just somewhere in the station – this is, after all, where she works. She will be *there*, where he is. It's as if she has some kind of patented Cody detector. As soon as he enters the squad room she will appear, and her attention will be focused on him.

He knows that she has only his best interests at heart, and for that he should be grateful. But sometimes he feels he should take her to one side and break it to her gently that, much as he appreciates the close attention, he would be ever so grateful if she could just back off a little. Just a fraction.

But then he sees her, and all such thoughts run for cover.

Detective Chief Inspector Stella Blunt comes bursting out of the door of the building before Cody even gets to it. A cadre of lesser detectives trailing in her wake, she strides ahead like Boadicea leading her Iceni tribe. She presents an earnest and fearsome aspect, defying anyone to challenge her. She is square and heavy of frame, with a chest like an over-inflated flotation vest, and her greying hair is cut short and parted on one side. No soft flowing locks for this woman. Her clenched jaw matches her body well, being wide and angular.

Spying Cody, she says, 'Morning. Decided to join us, have you?'

'I was—'

'Yes, I know what you were doing. Now you're here, you can come with us and do some proper work.'

She reaches out a stubby-fingered hand to the detective to one side of her. 'Keys!'

The detective lays a set of car keys on her palm, and she tosses them to Cody. 'You're driving.' To the first detective she says, 'You just lost your chauffeur's job. Find yourself another car.'

Cody falls into step with the rushing throng. 'Uhm, you mind if I ask—'

'Murder, sunshine. Our bread and butter. You in my gang or not?'

'Yes, ma'am.'

'Then get in the car. Head for Derby Lane. L13. Unlucky number for some poor cow.'

Cody climbs behind the wheel of a silver BMW and starts up the engine as Blunt wriggles to get comfortable in the passenger seat.

He pulls the car out. Out of the corner of his eye he can tell that Blunt is staring at him.

She says, 'Where the hell did you get that jacket?'

'Charity shop. I thought it would help me look the part. I was pretending to be a busker.'

'Well, I didn't think you were supposed to be an investment banker. Why haven't you changed?'

'I was about to, ma'am. You caught me on the hop.'

'You need a shave, too.'

'Yes, ma'am.'

Blunt sniffs the air. 'And have you had a wash this morning?'

'Yes, Mum.'

She snaps her head towards him. 'What?'

'Nothing, ma'am. Just saying yes.'

But he knows his little joke has hit the nail on the head. In addition to being his boss, Blunt wants to mother him. There's nothing creepy in it. Nothing for which he might need to consider taking out an injunction against her. She just worries about him.

He has never quite figured Blunt out. Not certain he ever will. He has seen her give a vicious tongue-lashing to subordinates that has reduced them to quivering jellies on her office carpet. But he has also come to realise that she will defend any member of her team to the death. He doesn't know what goes on in her private life. Doesn't know if she has been married or had kids. Doesn't even know if she has ever had a boyfriend. But, for whatever reason, she has decided to adopt Cody as her own. He has become her pet project, and something tells him it's wise not to push her protective wing away too hastily.

She says, 'What made you take on that job this morning? The flasher.'

Cody shrugs. 'I was asked. The guy has been appearing every Tuesday, working his way down Bold Street. Seemed almost a cert he'd be there this morning, and he was.'

'Not exactly what I'd call a major incident, though.'

'True. But serial offenders like him often go on to commit worse sexual crimes if they're not stopped.'

Blunt glares at him. 'I do know that, Cody. What I'm saying is that it's not the kind of case we usually handle at MIT. So why did you agree? You haven't got anything else on your plate right now?'

'Like I said, the detectives on the case approached me. They wanted a body who doesn't look like a typical copper, preferably someone with experience of undercover work.'

'And you were happy with that? Doing that type of thing again – it didn't bother you?'

He knows what she's getting at. Knows where she's trying to steer this.

Cody was selected and trained for undercover work right at the start of his police career. The scouts who go looking for candidates are after three things: someone who doesn't stand out from the crowd as an obvious bobby; someone who hasn't picked up all the habits that officers adopt over time; and someone who isn't known to the local criminals. As a fresh-faced young man just coming into the job, Cody satisfied all three conditions. Even more importantly, it was something in which he was eager to get involved. Ever since he was a kid he had wanted to be a police officer. This was even better. This was specialist police work. This was exciting, pulse-racing police work.

He loved it, too. Enjoyed the adrenalin rush, the need to constantly be thinking on one's feet. At school he had always been good at drama, and this was ultimate acting. This was taking the pretence of being somebody else to its limit.

But it can also be dangerous work. As an undercover cop you can be mixing with the most vicious criminals at fairly intimate levels. And such people are naturally suspicious of strangers. It takes a lot of nerve to stick to the script when your audience is testing you with the most searching questions and accusations. When you always need an answer on your lips.

Sometimes even that isn't enough. And that's what Blunt is alluding to. She knows exactly what happened a year ago.

'No,' he answers. 'Doesn't bother me at all.'

She looks at him again, and even without meeting her gaze he knows her eyes are burning with scepticism.

'You're looking tired, Nathan. Sleeping okay?'

She does that sometimes. Calls him by his first name. He finds it slightly disarming. He'd rather the formality was a two-way street. He'd hate to call her Stella. Hate it even more if she quite liked it.

'Sleeping like a baby, ma'am,' he says. Extra emphasis on the *ma'am*, just to hammer home his preference. 'Got a full eight hours last night.'

A blatant lie. He's never sure precisely how many hours of sleep he gets per night, but all told it's probably not more than two or three. He drifts in and out of unconsciousness, and any sleep he does manage never seems to bring him any benefit.

'Good,' she says. 'Glad to hear it.' She goes mercifully silent for a few seconds, and then: 'How are you getting on with that girlfriend of yours? What's her name – Dorset, isn't it?'

Cody feels something tighten in his gut. He wants to snap at her, to tell her to mind her own damn business. He has to clench his jaw to stop the anger spitting forth.

'Devon, ma'am. We're good, thanks.'

'Any chance I'll be needing to buy a new hat soon?'

'Eh?'

'You know. For a wedding?'

'Oh! Er, no. Not just yet. Wouldn't want to rush into things.'

No danger of that. No risk of doing anything at speed as far as Devon is concerned. Even a brief conversation with her is something he'd have to book well in advance.

But Blunt doesn't need to know all that. Let her have her rose-tinted view of things. Let her hear what she wants to hear.

Sometimes a layer of lies acts as the oil that keeps a relationship running smoothly.

5

Cody gets out of the car. Sniffs the air as if sampling it for the aroma of blood, the scent of a murderer. The narrow street is crammed with police cars, marked and unmarked. Blue flashes of light bounce off the windows of the houses. Hung in one of those windows is a Liverpool FC poster, while the next-door neighbour displays one of Everton. Some interesting conversations there on derby day, thinks Cody.

He ducks under the crime scene tape strung between the lamp posts, but while Blunt wastes no time in marching off to engage in battle, he pauses for a minute to study those he has left on the other side of the dividing line. He sees a tattooed man with an ugly muscle-bound dog that looks as though it should also have tattoos. Sees a shaven-headed kid who should be at school. Sees an old lady who seems to have neglected to put her teeth in. The onlookers crane and peer and point and speculate. Cody looks for anyone acting just that little bit differently, that little bit more suspiciously, but sees nothing. These are regular punters, here for the show. He could make a fortune selling hot dogs and popcorn here.

'All right, mate. Which bit of "Do not cross" don't you understand?'

The voice comes from behind him. Female, but not Blunt. He realises her mistake even before he turns around. He's still in his scruffy busker's clothing, and she thinks he's just some idiot who has decided to ignore the instruction written on the police cordon tape. He smiles, thinking he could have a bit of fun here.

He turns, a joke on his lips.

But then he sees her, and the intended mischief dissolves.

The young woman bearing down on him has platinum-blonde hair, tied in a neat ponytail. Dimples in her cheeks. A new suit that sweeps in at the waist. Male heads, and one or two female ones, swivel as she passes by.

All these years, and she hasn't changed a bit.

'Megan?'

Megan Webley halts. Blinks at him. The smile of recognition takes its time arriving.

'Cody?' she says with uncertainty. '*Cody?*'

He shrugs. 'It's me,' he says awkwardly.

'Oh my God. Oh my . . . I-I'm gobsmacked.' She takes a couple of steps towards him. He's not sure whether to throw his arms wide for a hug, or to play it safe and offer a handshake. In the event, he does neither.

She says, 'What the hell are you doing here? Please tell me you're undercover, and that you're not about to ask me if I can spare some change.'

He laughs. 'Are you trying to tell me something about my dress sense? You look fantastic, by the way.'

'Thank you. And you look like . . . shit. What's going on?'

'Nothing. I just came off a job. Now I'm on this one.'

She narrows her eyes at him. In puzzlement, perhaps, but Cody can't help thinking she's bracing herself for unwelcome news.

'You're on this case? How come?'

'It's what I do now. I'm with MIT. The undercover gig today was a one-off.'

'You're with . . . Seriously?'

'Yeah. Why not? I might not be Sherlock Holmes, but I can do homicides. What about you? Weren't you working in Warrington?'

'For a couple of years. Then I was on the Wirral. And now this. Meet the newest member of your team. I started this morning.'

'Really? Wow, that's . . . that's fantastic. Welcome aboard.'

'Yeah. It's, er . . . yeah.' She looks at her feet for a moment, as if desperately trying to find her next line on a script she hasn't rehearsed.

'So,' she says, switching her smile back on, 'what's it like, then –
working with this bunch?'

Before Cody can answer, another voice cuts in.

'He couldn't be happier,' says DC Neil Ferguson. 'We do all the
work, and he takes all the glory. Isn't that right, Sarge?'

Ferguson is a lamp post of a man. Several inches over the six feet
mark, and with a body on which a starving dog wouldn't waste its
time. Never able to shrink into the background, he compensates
by being the classroom joker.

Webley looks into Cody's eyes. 'Sergeant, eh? Going up in the
world.'

Cody isn't quite certain whether she's pleased for him or not.
He is saved from deciding how to respond when Ferguson butts in
again.

'Sorry, but do you two know each other?'

'We were in training together,' says Cody. He sees Webley watching him closely, as if waiting to interject if he strays into territory
she wants to keep private. 'We haven't seen each other for ages.'

Webley appears satisfied with that. 'We must catch up some time,'
she says. 'Talk about the good old days.'

He wonders if she means that, or if she's saying it merely for
Ferguson's benefit.

'Any time,' he says.

'Right,' she says. 'Okay, well, I'd best get suited up. Don't want to
make a bad impression on my first day.'

She walks away. Cody and Ferguson watch her go.

Says Ferguson, 'Small world. You and Wibbly, I mean.'

'It's Webley.'

'Still, bit weird bumping into her after all this time. And you
remembering her so well, considering she was just another copper
in training.'

Cody sees the wry smile on Ferguson's face. He says, 'Don't even
go there, okay? We were just good mates. We had a laugh together.'

'Right,' says Ferguson. 'Right.' And he walks off, still smirking.

Five minutes later, Cody is in his white Tyvek coveralls, experiencing a mixture of emotions. He's feeling the buzz, all right. Always does when he's about to dive into a new case. For MIT to be called in, it has to be something special, something unusual. Otherwise, it would be handled by the local BCU, or Basic Command Unit. At the same time, he's also a little apprehensive. A murder scene necessitates a dead body. A life has been curtailed. A future, with all its promise, all its potential, has been eradicated. Sometimes the acceptance of that fact hits Cody hard, and all the grief and sorrow that is to follow from those who loved the deceased can hit him harder.

But this time there's an added complication. Megan Webley. He's not yet sure how he feels about that. Maybe it's not a complication at all. Maybe he's making too much of it.

'Cody.'

And here she is again. Looking lost and small inside the baggy shapelessness of her protective suit. Her face more serious.

She says, 'I didn't know. In case you're wondering. I had no idea you'd moved. It didn't even occur to me you might . . . You were always so passionate about undercover work.'

He doesn't try to explain. Maybe another time.

'Not a problem. Honestly. I'm fine with it. If you are.'

'Me? Yeah, sure. It was a long time ago.'

'It was. A long time.'

But he remembers it like it was yesterday. Megan Webley – his first true love. Well, his second if you count police work. And that was the problem. She was relegated to second place, and she was proud enough and strong enough not to stand for it. Good for her.

Cody wasn't lying when he told Ferguson that they had met during training. But it didn't end there. They became a tight couple. Managed to stay that way for eighteen months. But the nature of Cody's work took its toll. For the safety of the officer involved, most undercover jobs are carried out at a distance from the home patch. Cody would be out of his girlfriend's life for days, sometimes weeks, at a time. And it was dangerous. Webley wanted him to alter his role in the force. Cody refused. The relationship was doomed.

And now she's back. On his team. They're going to have to work together, in close proximity.

But she's right. It was a long time ago. They've both moved on. They are different people now. It really won't be an issue.

'So,' she says, 'we can keep this on a professional basis, yeah? We work the cases together, and that's it.'

'Of course.'

'Because I really want this job, Cody. I really want to show what I can do at MIT. I don't want . . . *stuff* to get in the way.'

'Absolutely. It's all good. Honestly.'

Her dimples put in another appearance. 'Great. Let's go then.'

She strides off, seemingly recharged by Cody's words. He follows her onto the driveway, where Blunt is waiting. The DCI leads them down the tunnel between this house and the next. Cody finds himself having to duck to avoid hitting his head, since he's having to walk on stepping plates that have been put down to help preserve the scene. God knows how Ferguson managed.

They go through a wooden back door in the fence, and onto a patio that's flagged in alternating pink and beige stones, like a huge piece of Battenberg cake. The rear door to the house is wide open. Beyond the patio is a decent-sized garden. The lawn is in dire need of mowing, and is peppered with weeds. An empty border leads to a stand of bushy shrubs at the far end. Cody notes that somebody could easily hide themselves behind those plants. He knows there is a small park and playground on the other side of the rear fence. From here he can see the top of a small hill. A couple of teenagers are standing there, watching. One of them has a can in his hand. Cody bets himself it's not lemonade.

There are a lot of people here, all jostling for space while trying to avoid contaminating the scene. Some of them are police. Some are CSIs. They used to be called SOCOs – Scene of Crime Officers – but then the television programme arrived and it became more glamorous to be known as CSIs, even though what they do is nothing like that portrayed on the small screen. Systematically and painstakingly they hunt for clues. They sift through the long grass; they photograph; they video; they sketch; they brush; they bag. Busy, busy, busy.

Looming over the body is the pathologist, his presence here another sign of the importance of this case. Pathologists don't attend all murder scenes – often a police surgeon is deemed sufficient, and then primarily to certify death – but they come out when the case looks like it could be a tricky one.

And this one certainly has all the hallmarks of a crime to exercise minds.

The victim is female. Early thirties, probably. She wears only a dressing gown, belted at the waist. There is a lot of blood here. It has soaked into her gown and formed sticky pools on the flagstones around her. There is a smell of urine and excrement, voided from the body at the point of death. Behind the mumblings of the pathologist comes the constant drone of excited flies, drawn hypnotically to the scene by the unmistakable chemical signals of death and decay.

The investigators take all this in as they jockey for position around the body. But one thing above all others keeps vying for their attention. One thing demands to be seen and discussed and puzzled over. It is undeniably the scene-stealer here.

A bird. A large black bird. Its beak is slightly open as if it's about to cry out. Its soft, glossy feathers ruffle slightly in the breeze. The eye facing out stares vacantly at the humans surrounding it.

It's dead. As lifeless as the woman across whose face it lies. Its huge wings have been unfurled and spread across her eyes and cheeks, as if it is embracing her, comforting her, protecting her.

Says Webley, 'What the frigging hell's that?'

Says Blunt, 'I hope that question isn't indicative of your detective prowess, DC Webley. It's a bird.'

'I know. I mean . . . Well, it's bloody huge. And scary. What the hell's it doing there?'

'Well, I don't think it dropped dead in the sky and just happened to land on her, do you? It's been placed there. A message of some kind.'

Webley shakes her head in disgust. 'Gives me the creeps.'

'I think . . .' ventures Cody, 'I think it's a raven.'

'*Boys' Book of Birds*?' says Blunt.

'No, ma'am. Saw some at the Tower of London. Clever rascals, apparently.'

'This one doesn't look too clever.' She turns to the pathologist. 'Can we shift this thing, Rory?'

Rory Stroud is a big man. Gargantuan. Although a medical practitioner, he seems not to acknowledge the health benefits of dieting. However, his bulk has done nothing to diminish his self-confidence with the opposite sex. To Stroud, any female he encounters is fair game, and rumour has it that he enjoys a reasonable amount of success in that endeavour.

Stroud turns his jowly face on Blunt and beams her a lascivious grin. 'For you, my dear Stella, anything is possible. Just bear with me for two ticks.'

She nods briskly, and it seems to Cody that she is blushing slightly. Seems to be a day for it.

They wait while Stroud directs the taking of some more photographs. Close-up shots of the head area, with a ruler laid alongside to show scale. When he's satisfied, he reaches out his blue-gloved hands and begins to lift the bird away.

Cody is the first to react to what's underneath.

'Oh, Christ!'

They all see. They see that the victim has no eyes. Not gouged out, exactly, but stabbed into the back of the eye sockets, as if pecked to mush by the bird.

'Oh, God,' says Webley. She turns, takes a step away, her hand covering her mouth.

'Don't you dare step off the plates,' warns Blunt. She throws Cody a look that asks him to keep things under control.

Cody moves across to Webley. He lowers his voice so as not to compound her embarrassment.

'You okay?'

She nods, but her hand is still over her mouth. And it seems to Cody that there are tears forming in her eyes.

'Hey,' he says. 'Don't worry about it. Sometimes they can be pretty bad. I once had—'

'No,' she interrupts, removing her hand. 'It's not that.'

'Okay,' says Cody. He thinks she's about to make an excuse. Not eating properly or something. Whatever. It's fine with him.

'No. It's not okay. I know her. The victim. I know her. She's one of us.'

'What? What do you mean?'

'Her name's Terri. Terri Latham. She's on the force. She's a bobby.'

6

So this changes everything. And perhaps it shouldn't. In an ideal world, perhaps it should make no difference whether the victim was a police officer or a prostitute. Perhaps it should be the case that exactly the same effort would be put into investigating the murder irrespective of the victim's occupation.

But it does. It does change things. It makes it personal. An attack on a police officer is an attack on all police officers. It's clear from the way the atmosphere suddenly changes that the assembled investigators have digested the new information and can taste the bile it causes to rise in their throats.

Blunt searches the faces around her. 'Why wasn't I told this? Did we know it?'

Nobody owns up. Nobody admits to knowing or not knowing.

'All right,' she announces to the throng. 'We do this by the book, okay? No mistakes. No stone unturned. Bag and tag every blade of grass if you have to. I want the sick bastard who did this.'

'Boss,' says Cody.

He is either unheard or ignored.

'And I shouldn't have to say this, but I will. This story is going to be big. It's going to hit the headlines. Everyone will hear how a policewoman was murdered here last night. What I don't want them to hear is any detail from any of the people at this crime scene. Any leaks, and you will have to answer to me. Got that?'

'Boss,' Cody says again.

She rounds on him. 'What is it?'

He points to the bird, still in the pathologist's hands.

'A message.'

'Yes, I know, Cody. I already said that.'

'No. On the bird's foot.'

Everyone leans forward. They peer at the tiny blood-stained scrap of paper wrapped around the bird's scrawny leg.

'Open it up,' says Blunt.

Stroud looks up at her. 'I'd rather it were done in a lab. I could destroy vital evidence opening it up here.'

Which is a good point, thinks Cody. He watches while Blunt considers this and then reaches a decision.

'I need to know what it says. Any delay might cost us. Do your best, Rory. If it falls apart, you can blame me.'

Stroud places the bird onto an evidence bag, then takes two pairs of tweezers from his kit. Slowly and carefully, he uses them to pull away the elastic band that holds the message in place. He drops the band into another evidence bag. Then he slips off the message and teases it open with the tweezers.

It contains a single line of printed text:

NEVERMORE

The pathologist reads it aloud.

'Never more what?' says Webley.

'Nevermore,' says Cody. 'One word. It means never again.'

'Okay, so never again what?'

Cody feels a crawling on his skin. He looks at the dead bird, half expecting it to jump up at him and start pecking and clawing at his face.

'It's linked to the bird,' he says.

'What do you mean?'

'"Quoth the Raven, 'Nevermore.'"'

'Sorry, Sarge, but I don't know what you're saying to me now. What was that first word?'

'"Quoth". It means "said". The raven said nevermore.'

He can see he's making little sense to Webley, but then Blunt adds a contribution.

'Edgar Allan Poe.'

'Yes, ma'am,' says Cody. He turns back to Webley. 'It's a famous poem by Edgar Allan Poe. About a man who's alone at night. He hears a gentle tapping on his door, but when he opens it nobody's there. Then he hears the tapping again, but it's at his window this time. He opens it, and a raven comes in. It sits in his study, staring at him, and all it keeps repeating to him is the single word "nevermore". Drives him batty in the end.'

Webley's expression is a combination of fascination and fear. She looks down at the dead bird again.

'They can talk, then?'

'Yeah. They sound pretty freaky when they do it, too.'

He follows her gaze to the bird. He can sense Webley's unease. The raven is a bird of folklore and mystery and dark happenings. And it looks the part.

'What does it all mean?' she asks.

The response comes from Blunt. 'That's what we're going to find out. Come with me, you two.'

She leads them back down the tunnel. Gets out of earshot of the others.

'Latham was on the force. Right now we don't know if that fact is related to her death, or just coincidence. There could be a lot of people out there who might be ecstatic to see her dead. It also means there are going to be hundreds of other coppers who want a piece of whoever did this. If they start walking all over our case, they'll bugger it up. This stays with us, with MIT, got it? We're going to solve it, because we're the only bastards around here who know what they're doing. But it means working like we've never worked before. Forget sleeping. Forget eating. Forget seeing your loved ones. This is your main priority right now. In fact, it's your only priority. That a problem for either of you?'

Cody shakes his head immediately. Webley takes a little longer, but gets there.

Blunt looks directly at Webley. 'Tell me about her. About Latham.'

Webley clears her throat. 'We worked together for a while. Over in Birkenhead. This was about three years ago. We only overlapped there for six months or so, but I got to know her quite well. We went out together a few times. Had some laughs.'

'Have you seen her since?'

'Once or twice, but nothing recent. I didn't even know she'd moved here. She was living with a boyfriend in Wallasey when I knew her.'

Blunt goes silent. Cody knows there are other questions that ought to be on her lips. Obvious questions. But something is clearly bothering her.

'Latham,' she says. 'PC Terri Latham. Why do I know that name?'

Now it's Webley's turn to go strangely quiet. She seems unable to hold her superior's gaze.

'Spit it out!'

'The Vernon incident. She was Paul Garnett's partner.'

Cody watches as this sinks into Blunt's mind. He can tell that all the ramifications of this new knowledge are being churned up in her head.

'Oh, God,' she says. 'That's all we need.'

Cody remembers the case well. Most coppers do. Kevin Vernon was arrested when police were breaking up a brawl outside a pub in Birkenhead. As it later turned out, Vernon wasn't one of the trouble-makers. He was just passing by. This was confirmed later both by witnesses and CCTV footage. What they could not attest to, of course, was what was going through the minds of the attending officers at the time.

It's what happened shortly after the police arrived that is the subject of contention. Vernon moved away from the centre of the fracas, out of shot of the security camera. Two police officers – one male and one female – went after him. That's when the timeline split, leading to two accounts that were not merely at variance but in direct opposition. Both plausible, but only one of them could be true.

The first account – the account given by the officers concerned, and the story to which they stuck throughout the whole of the ensuing investigation – is one in which two dedicated coppers were risking their necks as they so often do. In the face of extreme adversity they were striving to restore order and prevent bloodshed. And when someone – they can't remember who, exactly, given that they were in the midst of a pitched battle – told them that Kevin Vernon was one of the ringleaders, they had to take that information seriously. Of course they did. And when that same person – whoever it was, because you have to understand that it was pretty chaotic out there – told them to 'Watch yourselves with him', they had to take that seriously too. Of course they did.

And even though they were armed with all this information, but armed with little else except a baton each, they remained paragons of restraint. They challenged the man, and he ignored them. They issued commands to the man, and he ignored them. And when they became more vociferous, he became more aggressive and threatening. And so they tried to arrest him. Minimum force was what they hoped to apply. But he was strong, this man. And he was large. And then he began swearing at them. Saying things that suggested he was not going quietly. And all around them was violence and hatred and abuse, and people were being hurt, police officers were being hurt, and what were they supposed to do? How could they just stand there having a discussion with this man who might be about to attack them, while some of their colleagues were in such danger? How could they not react to the immediate threat to their well-being? And, in any case, all they did was bring him to the ground. Yes, he hit it a little heavily. Things don't always go to plan. Real life isn't like the textbooks. He banged his head, and unfortunately it turned out to be fatal. But they had to get him under control. Had to bring him down quickly. Anyone else would have done the same. Well, wouldn't they?

That's one version of events.

The other version is one in which the two police officers decided to vent their anger and frustration on a random member of the public. An innocent citizen, just going about his business. They accosted him, they assaulted him, they brought him to the floor. Heavily. So heavily he suffered a head injury that resulted in bleeding into the brain.

And then he died. As a consequence of the unprovoked, brutal attack by two people who are charged with keeping us safe on the streets, this man died.

To be more accurate, it was the male officer who did most of the physical work. He was the one who leapt at Vernon, grabbed hold of his arm and pulled him head first into the unyielding pavement. He was the one who then sat astride Vernon, twisting the man's arm behind his back as he leant on his head and swore angrily into his ear. Doesn't excuse the female officer, though. It was clear whose team she was on. She's as guilty as he is.

That's exactly how it happened. Swear to God and hope to die.

There are other complications. It was later revealed that Vernon had severe learning difficulties. Those who knew him claimed that he was never violent, never aggressive, and that he would not have even understood the situation he was in or what was being asked of him. The two officers begged to differ. They knew nothing of his learning problems. To them, he was an immediate risk. He was where he shouldn't be, acting unpredictably, saying things that were largely incomprehensible but certainly containing some threatening language. He posed a danger that needed to be nullified. In the most controlled way possible, of course.

So there you have it. Two stories stacked against each other. One from witnesses at the scene, who were for the most part profoundly anti-police. And one from upholders of the law with a previously unblemished record. Who are you going to believe?

Those carrying out the investigation knew whom to believe. To be sure, there were a few rumours that proved problematic. Suggestions that Paul Garnett could be a little heavy-handed at times. But these were easily discounted. Especially once the shiny-bright Terri Latham gave her side of things. Her record was spotless. In the interview room she exuded veracity. You couldn't doubt the word of someone as dedicated and trustworthy as PC Latham.

But perhaps someone did.

Perhaps somebody never believed for a moment what came out of the mouth of this woman who might be willing to send her own mother to hell to save herself.

And perhaps this is that particular little bird coming home to roost, excuse the sick pun.

Cody hopes not. And he is certain that Blunt doesn't want it either.

Otherwise, life for the MIT members is likely to get very complicated.

7

He wakes to the sound of birds. Their sound is a joyous one. Bursting with freedom and a sense of being a part of nature. Becoming a taker of human life has not deadened his appreciation of such beauty.

But those birds are outside, in his garden. He can hear nothing from the next room, where his own birds are kept. It's as if they wait mutely in desolate incarceration, like inmates on death row.

But that's okay. This isn't about happiness. It's about the very opposite, in fact. The role of his birds is far more important and profound than they can ever know. Their very existence is highly symbolic. In their own way, they will tell the world what it needs to hear, and it will carry much farther and last much longer than mere birdsong.

He flings off his duvet. Swings his legs out of bed. Smiles.

Last night seems almost unreal now. Like something he might have watched in a film. Did he really do that? Did he really kill that policewoman?

He looks at the clock. A minute to eleven. Late for him, but the sun was already starting to do battle with the clouds before he got to sleep. He was too wired, too full of the night's events.

He switches the clock radio on and watches the seconds count away. At eleven, the news comes on. He listens intently to the headlines. As each brief announcement ends, his heart revs up for the next. Do they know yet? Does the world know what I have just done?

He gets nothing. But that's okay too. The media probably won't have the story yet. It's quite possible that nobody has even discovered the body.

They will, though. Somebody will find her and they will know that this is no ordinary killing. No burglary gone wrong. No accidental

death. Not even a murder of your common or garden variety. This
is special. This means something. People will take notice of this one.
They might not understand the reasons for it. Not yet, anyway. But
that will be made clear later. No point in making it easy for them.
They need to start guessing, to start talking. It needs to become one
of the biggest talking points of the century.

He is not doing this for himself, or even for his parents, although
they deserve this moment too. There are some families that seem
always to have been destined to attain fame or fortune, to be always
happy. And there are others for whom misery and misfortune are a
given – a patent ingredient of every day, every endeavour. He and
his parents were assigned to this latter group. He feels that in his
bones, and it surprises him some mornings that he is still alive. He
never expected to live beyond his thirtieth birthday. Now he knows
he is on borrowed time.

He will make the most of that time.

He stands up. Walks through onto the landing. Carefully he
opens the door into the front bedroom – just a few inches – then
squeezes himself in and shuts the door behind him.

This is the biggest bedroom in the house. He doesn't sleep in
here, but the furniture is still present, including the double bed.
The blinds are drawn – they are always drawn in here. He flicks on
a light switch.

There is some chatter. A few chirrups. Nothing like the cacophony in the rear garden. A kiss of air as a starling flutters past
his face.

It's quite a sight. So many birds. Mostly pigeons, sparrows,
starlings, blackbirds and magpies. But also robins, doves, tits and
finches. A few birds he has paid for, such as the parrots and the
budgerigars. The raven he used last night was stolen from a bird
sanctuary in North Wales. Some of the birds – the ones most
likely to attack the others – he keeps in cages. The rest have the
freedom of the bedroom. They use it, too. Some are on the bed.

Others are perched on the wardrobe or the dresser or the chairs. One of the pigeons stands in front of the mirror, pecking at its own reflection.

There's quite a smell in here too. This many birds create a lot of shit. It's everywhere. It covers the carpet; it covers the bed; it drips down the walls. He used to spend a good portion of each day cleaning it up. Now he doesn't bother. It's too much work, and he no longer has the time. At the end of his mission – if he ever reaches the end – he'll scour the room from floor to ceiling.

To be honest, he doubts that the end will ever be within reach. He's being very ambitious here – he knows that – but there's no point in being half-hearted about this project. He needs to go all out for it, even if it's the last thing he ever does. As it probably will be. The important thing is that he drives his message home. And that will certainly be achieved.

He steps further into the room. He is wearing only the T-shirt and boxers he had on in bed. His bare feet press into slimy wetness as he walks. Birds take flight as he cuts a path through them, their flapping and fluttering startling others into doing likewise, until much of the room is filled with frightened creatures randomly criss-crossing and narrowly avoiding each other.

He scans the area as he goes, checking that all is well. Birds are fragile things. Easily stressed. Occasionally they just keel over and die.

He finds a single dead sparrow. It's under the bed. As though it needed somewhere dark and secluded to abandon its life. He picks it up. Cradles it in the palm of his hand. It's almost weightless. Just a ball of feathers hiding a few scrawny bones. He tips his hand from side to side and watches the sparrow's head loll lifelessly, its feet jutting into the air as if clutching an invisible twig.

It will have to be replaced, of course. The numbers are important – crucial, in fact. He can't go out and buy one. Not any longer. People buying birds will come under suspicion soon. They will be investigated. Offering the police an obvious lead to him this early in the game would be sheer idiocy.

When he is satisfied there are no more corpses, he leaves the room, wiping his bare feet on a dry section of carpet on the way out. Later, he'll have a shower. Right now he needs to sort this out. He won't be able to rest properly until he has a full complement again.

Back in his bedroom, he pulls on jogging pants, a sweatshirt and an old pair of Nike trainers, then carries the sparrow with reverence down to the kitchen. He takes one last long look at the bird. Its premature death saddens him. Dying before one's time always saddens him. Unless it happens to a member of the police force.

He puts the bird into an Asda carrier bag and knots the handles together.

He unlocks the back door, steps into the garden and drops the bag into his wheelie bin. The bag floats to the bottom as though it contains nothing more than air.

He looks around the garden. It is not large, but it is mature and not overlooked. A tall fir tree prevents his neighbours from observing what he does here. Which is a good thing.

In the border beneath the tree sits a cardboard box. Its edges all rest on the soil, which suggests it is occupied.

Was a time he would spend long hours at his kitchen door, gripping a length of string attached to a stick propping up this box. He would wait patiently, staring at the mound of seed and praying for a single bird to allow hunger to overcome its natural caution.

His bird catchers are more sophisticated now. They involve the use of an adapted mousetrap that pulls the box down when it's tripped. He doesn't need to sit and watch.

He leans towards the box. Puts his eye to one of the air holes. A pigeon. It often seems to be the greedy, dumb pigeons who fall for this.

He raises one edge of the box slightly. Slides a hand underneath and grabs the bird, then brings it into the open. The pigeon looks mystified, but not frightened. If only it knew.

He takes it with him, back into the house. He can relax now and have a shower and some breakfast. Order has been restored.

The killings can continue.

8

There is a lot to do, and Blunt makes sure it gets done properly. There is a house to search, neighbours to interview, investigators to receive a bollocking when they make the tiniest mistake. Cody admires her for it. Strange as she is, she knows her job. She knows how to investigate a murder, and God help anyone who thinks they know better.

Cody and Webley are assigned the task of talking to the man who found the body. He's a pensioner. Lives alone next door. Has a glass eye, which Cody finds distracting. Has a hacking cough, too, which Cody also finds distracting, mainly because it sounds like he's about to expel a lung. The man's rambling account is that he heard nothing in the night. Sleeps the sleep of the just, you see. Then this morning he went outside to put an empty cereal box into his recycling bin. Shredded Wheat. Low sugar, because of his diabetes, you see. And high fibre, because of his troublesome bowels. He could tell you some hair-raising stories about those bowels of his. Anyway, over the fence he could see that his neighbour's rear house door was open, but it didn't seem important at first. People can open their doors when they want – why should that be suspicious? But an hour later he went out again. An empty milk carton after making some tea. More recycling. Good for the environment, though, isn't it? Anyway, her door was still open. You start to think then, don't you? A back door open for that long? In October? Bit odd that. So he called out. Just hello – something like that. Not her name, because he couldn't remember her name. Received no reply. So he went out of his door – the one that leads into the tunnel between the two houses. He knocked on her door. Once, twice, several times. Again nothing. He thought he should give up. Go back into his house. None of his business, really. But still . . . So he tried the latch. Opened the door. And that was it. All that blood. The flies – even in October, the flies. Couldn't even see her face because of something covering it. A bag, or a cloth, or . . . something. Well, he knew then, didn't he? Knew it was really bad. Knew this was something for the police.

They get little else out of him. He didn't really know Latham. She hadn't lived here long, and kept herself to herself. Doesn't know what she did for a living. Visitors? Yes, sometimes. Women, mostly. Anybody suspicious on the streets? Yes, of course – didn't you bother to look at the people outside when you got here? – but no more than usual.

Following that, Blunt sends them back to the station, while she stays to keep the investigative machinery operating smoothly. Even though he outranks Webley, Cody doesn't ask her to drive. Driving gives him something on which to concentrate. Stops his mind venturing into areas he'd rather avoid. But he can't help noticing how quiet she is. How the bubbly nature she exhibited earlier seems to have been popped.

He wonders if, despite all Webley's fine words, she still has a problem with the discovery that she will have to work with him.

'You all right?'

'What? Yeah. I'm okay.'

'No you're not.'

'Sorry?'

'You're not okay. Trust me, I can tell.'

'So why did you ask me? If you can tell?'

'I wanted to see if you'd tell me the truth.'

'All right, so I'm a liar. I'm a liar and I'm not okay.'

'Because of me?'

She looks at him. 'What?'

'Is it because I'm here, at MIT?'

'No, Cody. I thought we'd already cleared the books on that score. I'm talking about Terri. I knew her, and now she's dead. That's what I'm talking about.'

And now he feels like a complete egotistical, insensitive fool.

'Sorry. It must have been tough.' Too late, Cody, he thinks. Now it just sounds hollow.

'I've worked a few murders,' she says. 'Seen some horrible sights, just like you have. But this was different. I couldn't detach myself. I couldn't put myself on the outside looking in. Do you know what I mean?'

Cody nods. He knows precisely what she means, but for all the wrong reasons. At least Webley's reaction can be rationalised. His own feelings have become virtually an independent force – a disobedient child doing what it wants and when it wants.

'Blunt's right,' says Webley. 'It'll be all over the news. Police officer murdered. But they won't understand.'

'Understand what?'

'That she was also a person. A human being. People see the uniform. They don't see what's underneath. They think of us as the ones in control, the ones who have power, the ones who can deal with any life-threatening situation. Because that's what we're trained to do. That's our job. What we're paid for. What they won't even realise when they read their tabloid newspapers about Police Constable Latham is that she was also a young woman, living alone. Alone and sometimes really scared ... And when I think about that, I wish ... I just wish ...'

She stops there. Stops because her eyes are glistening and tears are escaping down her cheeks and her lower lip is quivering with the enormity of it all.

The show of emotion hits Cody hard, and he wishes it wouldn't. It grabs at the inside of his chest and refuses to let go. Knocks on a door at the centre of his being. He feels a wave of anxiety building within him, threatening to engulf him. Too much raw feeling in this cramped, claustrophobic space. Hard to breathe.

He pulls the car over. It's as much for his own benefit as for hers, but he tries to act as he thinks he should. He tries to appear concerned and yet in control, when in reality he feels on the knife-edge of panic.

'You okay?' he asks. There is a shakiness in his words that he hopes she fails to notice.

She sniffs. 'If I say yes, you'll make a liar out of me again.'

'Here.' He reaches into his pocket and finds a crumpled pack of tissues. Hands it across.

'Thanks.' She takes a tissue from the pack and dabs at her cheeks, then blows her nose.

Cody watches her and thinks about how ineffectual he is being. He wants to console her, but at the same time he doesn't want to overstep any boundaries.

'I'm sorry,' she says. 'Don't know what came over me. It's just that . . . I remember her, you know? I remember her laughing and smiling and joking. And now she looks like . . . well, like that. It's freaked me out.'

He nods in sympathy again. He knows about being freaked out. Oh, yes, he knows all about that.

'You wouldn't be human if it didn't,' he says.

He wonders how he would react if it were someone he knew lying there on the ground, their throat gaping open and their eye sockets empty. He has a suspicion he would not deal with it as well as Webley is. Has an inkling that he would instantly lose what's left of the thinning cement that is barely holding him together right now.

It's a thought that scares him more than anything the killer has done.

Or might do next.

9

'So,' says Blunt. 'Theories. What's the murderer trying to tell us?'

They're back at Stanley Road. A Major Incident Room has been set up. From now on this will be the hub of all activity related to the investigation of Terri Latham's death. All data relating to the case will be gathered and pulled into this room. It will be sifted, it will be analysed. Actions will be triggered. More data will be gathered. It will build. Connections will be found. Hypotheses will be formed and tested. More data, more connections. Gradually, it will all come together. Like a work of art it will take shape. Detail upon detail, layer upon layer, the components will begin to merge into a whole. Until somebody in this room – Blunt, Cody, the tea lady – adds a brushstroke that makes it what it was always meant to be.

Until that time, questions like Blunt's might as well be in a foreign language.

Blank faces consult other blank faces. This is a mystery beyond the ken of even the most experienced cops here.

'Okay,' says Blunt. 'Let's start with the bird. Any experts on birds here?'

Any other case, the jokes would start to flow. Somebody would say the only type of birds he knows about are the ones without feathers. And then somebody else would tell him that the last time he had a bird was for his Christmas dinner. And then . . .

But not today. Today the assembled detectives are not feeling the humour. They are graver than usual. Their faces are set. They just want to do their jobs and find this bastard.

'I did some research on the internet,' Cody offers. 'It's definitely a raven. Biggest member of the crow family. Can be pretty vicious.'

'Where would our killer find one?'

'They're not rare. You can find them in lots of places. Wales. The Lake District. It's catching them that's probably the hard part.'

Blunt frowns. Cody knows she was hoping for something that would help to narrow down the search.

'Lot of trouble to go to, though. Why not a pigeon or a sparrow? Something more common?'

'Wouldn't go with the message, for one thing. Anything other than a raven would have been a distraction. The killer wants us to understand the message for what it is.'

'Okay, so then let's focus on the message. Nevermore. Never again. Never again what?'

There's a silence while everyone struggles to stay away from the obvious. Webley is the first to dredge up the courage to speak.

'We have to accept that it could be something in Latham's past. Something she did, or that the killer believes she did. And that could have something to do with the Kevin Vernon case.'

Cody feels the ripple of discomfort as it passes through the room. Digging into the past of a police officer – even a dead one – can throw up all kinds of things that might be better left alone. Even the most innocent of events can be made to cast shadows when placed under the probing lights of suspicious minds.

Blunt nods, but Cody can see that she is as troubled as the rest of them.

'Be discreet,' she says. 'Watch what you say and who you say it to. But don't let that stop you digging. If this is related to something Latham got involved with, we need to know about it.'

She scans the grave faces in front of her. 'Bring in PC Garnett. We also need to talk to friends and relatives of Vernon. It's not going to be easy. They already see us as the enemy. They're going to give us a rough time whether they were involved in this or not. But we can't back off because of that. Just be careful, okay?'

'What if they've got nothing to do with this?' asks Ferguson.

'I really hope that's true. That's why we need to know every-thing about Terri Latham. Go through her record with a fine-tooth comb. Look at every arrest she made, every report she wrote, every scribble she made in her notebook. Talk to her boy-friends, her girlfriends, her family, her police colleagues. Somewhere in there is a motive. Somewhere in there is a suspect. Find them.'

Blunt moves on to details then. Assigning specific tasks to specific people. Nothing out of the ordinary. Nothing unexpected. Until . . .

'The PM is scheduled for four o'clock,' says Blunt. 'Cody, I'd like you and Webley to attend.'

She could move on then. Put a name to the task and move swiftly on. It's a mundane job. Standard procedure. No ceremony required.

But not this time. She is asking Cody to attend Terri Latham's post-mortem. Knowing full well what he has been through, she is requesting him to watch a police officer's body being sliced open right in front of him.

So she doesn't move on. She waits, her eyes lingering on Cody's face. Scrutinising him for signs of anguish. Listening for a murmur of objection.

The room is silent. Others know the score. They know how much Blunt is asking of their colleague. Some of them will feel resent-ment or anger towards her because of it.

Cody recognises it for what it is. A challenge. This is his boss say-ing to him, *You tell me you're fine? You tell me you want to be treated exactly like everyone else? Then here's your chance to prove it.*

Cody knows he can refuse. A simple no. A shake of the head. A sentence beginning something like, 'Well, actually, if you don't mind . . .' Anything less than a total positive will be enough. She will seize on that. She won't pursue it, won't press him to take the job. She will simply pass it to somebody else. But then it will be too late. The damage will have been done. Forever after in her eyes he will be less than the detective he wants people to see.

'Yes, ma'am,' he says, and he says it with assuredness.

Blunt's mouth twitches. An approximation of a smile. And then, finally, she moves on.

10

Small world, thinks Webley.

You start a new job. You think everything is fresh and different and exciting. So much to learn, to experience, to discover. New faces, voices. Different jokes and opinions.

But it doesn't last. Not even a day before the ghosts jump out at you.

Terri Latham, for one. Webley can picture her face precisely. Can see the mole on her cheek, the sharp arch of her eyebrows, the tongue touching her upper lip when she was concentrating.

Gone. All gone. As if she was never there at all.

What are the odds? Yes, this is a murder squad and, yes, that means encountering lots of dead bodies, but it's not every day the victim is someone you once knew. Someone you remember laughing and dancing and drinking and swearing, as if it were only yesterday.

She tries telling herself that it can only get easier now. She can't be unlucky enough to go through this again. All the future corpses in her professional life will be complete strangers to her. She can cope with that. She won't go to pieces again like she did in front of Cody. Christ, what a way to start a new job. Cody must already be thinking she's in the wrong line of work.

And there's the other ghost. Cody. Again, what are the chances? It never once entered her head that she might find him here at MIT. Why would it? His top priority was undercover work. It was his life. Becoming a murder squad detective was never an option for him when they were going out. Perhaps if it *had* been . . .

But no, she thinks. Let's not go there. Things change, people change. Cody's life is none of my concern now.

Could be awkward, though, couldn't it? I mean, this is the man I once loved – the man I once believed I might spend the rest of my life with. And now I've got to treat him as just another guy at work. I've got to sit next to him, share cars with him, discuss cases with him, interview people with him, drink coffee with him, socialise with him, listen to his problems, rely on him, confide in him ... and try not to let the past get in the way of any of that.

Is that even possible? Am I crazy for even thinking of staying on this squad?

But she's not walking away, oh no. Despite all her misgivings, Megan Webley is not breaking the golden rule that she has lived by since she was just a kid.

She remembers exactly how it started.

The woman lived on the same narrow street in Walton as the Webley family. Just a few doors down, in fact, although Webley never got to know her name. Still doesn't know it to this day. It occurs to her sometimes to do a little digging to find out more about the woman, but something always stops her. She prefers to remember her simply as the Sad Woman, as though discovering her name would somehow diminish that state of perfect sorrow.

She could never predict when she'd see the woman. Webley would be on her way to school or the newsagent or the chippy, and there she'd be: coming out of her house, or tending to her tiny patch of garden. Even before she could see the woman's expression she would feel the sadness emanating from her. And when the woman did catch sight of Webley's beaming face she would smile back at her, but it would be a false smile, hiding nothing. Even at that young age, it went through Webley's mind to ask the woman what was wrong, but she never did.

The bruises came later. The blues and the yellows and the greens. And then the lumps and bumps and half-closed eyes that make-up could not put right. Webley would slow as she passed the woman's front gate, and she would stare and stare, as children do. And sometimes the woman stared back, and Webley got the impression that she wanted to speak to her, to explain it all, perhaps even to ask for help. But she never spoke, and Webley never asked, and eventually the woman abandoned even the pretence of smiling.

It was on her way home after school one day that she heard the shouting coming from inside the house. Webley had heard shouting before, of course, but this was different. This shouting felt as though its intensity could cause physical damage. It was a male voice doing the yelling. It wasn't the woman. Her answering call was in the form of a scream that almost caused Webley to wet herself.

She ran the rest of the way home. Panting, she told her mother of what she'd heard. Her mother responded that it was probably a television, because some people have absolutely no respect for their neighbours. And when Webley insisted that it wasn't the television, her mother said that it didn't matter what it was, because it was none of their business.

A couple of weeks later, she was walking down the street with her father. Where they were going escapes her now, because it's no longer important. What fills Webley's memory is the image of the woman flying out of the front door of her house, pursued by her furious husband. She was in tears; he was roaring at her to get back in the house. When she refused, he grabbed her by the hair and started dragging her back towards the door.

The young Webley listened to the screams of terror, and knowing that a terrible fate awaited the woman inside the house, she turned to the one person she believed could alter the course of events.

He was a strong man, her father – a plumber by trade. He looked down at his daughter's pleading face . . .

. . . and then he took her by the hand and led her across the road, away from all the trouble.

She asked him what he was doing. She begged him to go back and help the poor woman. When that failed, she shouted across the street, telling the man to leave his wife alone. Her father's response was to yank her arm so sharply it hurt, and to bark her name in that unmistakable tone that meant she was in trouble. And when she persisted, he told her the same thing her mother had said: 'It's none of our business.'

Webley was miserable about it for weeks. Miserable and angry and confused. Her parents were the adults. They were supposed to know right from wrong, and to pass that on to their children. How was this right?

Every day, Webley made a point of walking slowly past the house of the neighbour she didn't even know. She had no idea what she would do if she saw or heard something awful happening to the woman, but she felt she needed to be there for her, because nobody else seemed to give a damn.

When the police showed up one rainy afternoon, Webley knew in her heart that the woman was dead. Her parents refused to let her leave the house, so she stayed cooped up in her bedroom, watching the comings and goings through the rivulets of rainwater on her window. And the more she watched, the more impressed she grew with the uniformed men and women who, unlike anyone else, really did seem to care. She decided she wanted to be just like them, and she made a promise to herself that never again would she cross the road to avoid a problem.

So, Detective Sergeant Cody, I'm afraid you're stuck with me.

I'm not going anywhere.

11

They show Garnett into the interview room. Already Cody can feel a distaste for this man rising within him. He finds it a struggle to appear amiable.

He thinks he might find it easier if Garnett were in uniform. Something that would foster instant respect. But Garnett is in a black leather jacket and jeans. He's wearing a flash watch and huge gaudy rings. He looks like a spiv instead of a police officer. And it goes further than his clothes and ornamentation. There's a cockiness to him. An arrogance. A look on his face that shouts at you that he thinks his time is being wasted.

Cody gestures towards a chair, and while Garnett sits down he tries to talk to him like a member of the same side: 'Thanks for dropping in on your day off. We want to get moving on this case as quickly as we can, so we really appreciate it.'

'Sure,' says Garnett, and the way he delivers it makes it sound almost like 'whatever'. He could say it's not a problem, or that it's the least he can do, but instead he chooses to express his disgruntlement.

Cody exchanges glances with Webley. Her slight rolling of her eyes tells him he's not the only one to have picked up on the attitude problem.

They take their own seats at the table, opposite Garnett. And while their posture is upright and respectful, Garnett is practically slouching. He looks about ready to put his feet up on the table and crack open a beer.

Earlier, Blunt had offered to conduct the interview, suggesting that the presence of somebody more senior might help to head off any antagonism. Cody assured her there would be no antagonism on his part. Now he's not so certain. Garnett hasn't opened his mouth yet, and already Cody wants to close it permanently.

'This must have come as quite a shock,' he says.

This causes Garnett to sit up a little, as though he needed a gentle reminder of what this is all about, and how he might be expected to react.

'Of course it did. She used to be my partner. We got close, as partners do. When they go suddenly and unexpectedly like that, it hurts.'

'Did you see much of Terri before her death?'

'No. Hardly ever since we were reassigned. And maybe if we hadn't been reassigned, I wouldn't be here now.'

'How do you figure that one out?'

'It sent the wrong signals. We did nothing to be ashamed of. And it's not just me saying it; the inquest said it too. They didn't have to split us up, but they did it anyway. That made it look like we were guilty of something. And that's why you've dragged me in here before Terri's body is even cold.'

'Is that what you think we're doing here? You think we're accusing you of something?'

'Not in so many words, but I know what's going through your minds. I haven't worked with Terri for ages, but strangely enough I'm still the first one you pull in for questioning. Tell me, how many of her current team have you spoken to?'

'Webley and I aren't the only ones on this case. We're talking to everyone we can think of, and that includes her most recent colleagues.'

'Yeah, right.'

Cody wants to snap at Garnett, but he knows it won't help the situation. He bites his tongue. Waits for a few seconds before opening his mouth again. But Webley beats him to it.

'Listen, Paul,' she says. Cody notices her use of Garnett's first name. An attempt to tell him that they are all in this together. 'You're right. The Vernon case is on our minds, and there's no point in denying it. But there's no point making it the elephant in the room either. It needs discussing. We're not supposed to reveal details of how Terri was found, but I know how these things work. My guess is that you've already heard some of it. Am I right?'

Garnett looks at her again, but this time the burning has gone from his eyes. Webley has pulled the thorn from the bear's paw.

'I've heard rumours. If they're true, someone did quite a job on her.'

Webley nods slowly. 'They did. It wasn't pretty. I didn't know Terri half as well as you did, but it got to me. God knows what it's doing to you. What I'm trying to say is that I understand how upset you are, and why you might feel we're having a go at you. But we're not, Paul. I swear. The Vernon case is over and done with. We're not accusing you of anything here. All we're trying to do is find out who killed Terri. And if there's anything you can tell us, any direction you can point us in, then we'd really appreciate it.'

Nice, thinks Cody. Certainly a lot more diplomatic than I was about to be.

The approach seems to reach Garnett. He sits up properly now, losing his slouch.

'Terri Latham was one of the best police officers on the force,' he says. 'She stood up for me when others turned the other way. She stuck to the truth when others were trying to put words in her mouth. She did the right thing. She always did the right thing. I've made mistakes in my career, and I'm not ashamed to admit it. Sometimes I could get a bit heavy-handed or a bit mouthy. But Terri knew me for what I am, and she treated me right. I did not do anything wrong on the night Kevin Vernon died. Terri knew that, because she was there and she saw what happened, and she told it like it was. Of course, there are some who think she lied through her teeth. Do I think someone would murder her because of that? No.'

Says Cody, 'Do you still get flak about the Vernon case?'

'Not from those who know me.'

'What about those who don't? Any threats we should know about?'

'Not so much now. At the start, yes. It got so bad I had to move house. Terri did too. Some people always want to believe the worst, especially of coppers.'

'But nothing recent?'

'No.'

'Okay. Because what I'm thinking is that if somebody did kill Terri because of what happened to Kevin Vernon, then they might want to go after you too.'

Garnett shakes his head. 'I don't buy it.'

'You don't?'

'No. It was a long time ago. People have had time to calm down. It's not an issue anymore, even though you seem determined to make it one.'

'It would be wrong of us to overlook the possibility, Paul. You could be in danger.'

Garnett's laugh is mocking. 'Now you're getting ridiculous. What are you planning to do, give me my own personal bodyguard? Besides, you're wrong. Be honest, was there anything about Terri's death that suggested a link with the Vernon case?'

'We can't reveal—'

'There isn't, is there? You're jumping to conclusions because you've nothing else to go on. Whoever killed Terri has probably never even heard of the Vernons. We weren't Siamese twins, you know. Terri had her own personal life, and presumably her own skeletons in her closet. There was more to her than the Vernon story. More to me, too, but you don't seem very interested to hear that.'

He's right, thinks Cody. We've zoomed in on one particular aspect of Terri Latham's life, because it's the one that's most public. Could be, though, that the reason for her murder is totally unrelated.

'Okay,' he says. 'But if there were specific threats that you remember – no matter how long ago you received them – it would be useful for us to know about them. Would you mind making a list for us?'

Garnett leans back in his chair. 'I can do that. Are we finished here?'

Cody thinks they probably are. He looks to Webley, expecting her to nod in confirmation. It surprises him when he finds her still staring intently at Garnett.

'Paul,' she says. 'One other thing, if you don't mind. Just to get everything clear while we've got the chance.'

Garnett locks eyes with her. 'Go on.'

'You mentioned earlier that you hardly saw Terri after you were reassigned.'

'Yep. That's what I said.'

'Do you remember what the last occasion was?'

Garnett runs his tongue over his teeth before replying, as if pre-sifting his answer for potential pitfalls.

'It was a retirement party, at a house.'

'When was this?'

'A while ago. About six weeks or so, I think.'

'You went with her?'

'No, no. I just bumped into her there. I didn't even know she was going.'

'Did you speak to her?'

'Not really. A little.'

'What about?'

'Is it important?'

'I don't know, Paul. Might be.'

'I don't remember. It was just chat. Hello, how are you – that type of thing. Trivial stuff.'

'Uh-huh. How come?'

'What do you mean?'

'Well, this is a woman you once worked with quite closely. This is the woman who backed you up all the way on the Vernon thing. How come all you could find to talk about was the weather? What's wrong with a proper catch-up after all that time apart?'

His gaze becomes a stony glare now, as if to let her know he regards her question as beneath contempt.

'Nothing was *wrong* with it. It just wasn't that kind of night. She was with her mates, I was with mine. We just didn't get to spend much time together.'

'Are you sure about that?'

Cody glances at Webley. She keeps her eyes glued on Garnett, and Cody realises that she knows something.

'What do you mean, am I sure about it?'

Classic deflection technique, thinks Cody. If he was sure, he would have said so without hesitation.

Says Webley, 'There were many other people at that party, Paul. One of them says she saw you and Terri in the garden. Looked to her like the two of you were having a heated argument.'

Garnett gives Cody a look that says, *Can you believe the nerve of this woman?* Getting no support from Cody, he turns back to Webley.

'Don't tell me – you've been talking to Diane Curtis, haven't you?'

'As I'm sure you'll understand, Paul, we're not at liberty to divulge—'

'Yeah, yeah, spare me the small print. For your information, anything that PC Curtis says about me is about as reliable as a paper umbrella. She's had it in for me for years, ever since I turned her down when she came on to me at a Christmas do. She say anything else about this so-called argument?'

'As a matter of fact, she did. She said she heard the name of Kevin Vernon being used.'

Garnett throws his arms up in apparent despair. 'Oh, here we go. Back to that again, are we? Funny how this is all coming out now, isn't it? I mean, now that Terri Latham is dead. It's a wonder Diane didn't say she heard me threaten to kill Terri. You could just lock me up and close the case then.' He yanks up his sleeves and displays his wrists to Webley. 'In fact, why don't you just put the cuffs on me now? Go 'ead. Put them on.'

Cody says, 'Look, Paul, there's no need to get so worked up about this. We're simply—'

The slap of Garnett's hand on the table is like a gunshot in the echoing room.

'No! There's every need. Take a look at yourselves, will ya? We're supposed to be on the same side. We're supposed to trust each other. The Vernon thing was fully investigated, and I was cleared. My record is as clean as yours. So stop treating me like a suspect and start talking to some real criminals. Now, if you don't mind, I've got better things to do.'

He launches himself from his chair and heads out of the room. Cody thinks about stopping him, if only to reprimand him for his attitude, but decides to leave it alone.

When Garnett has gone, Cody turns to Webley, who is gathering her paperwork together.

'Where did that come from?'

She smiles. 'What?'

'That stuff about the argument between him and Latham.'

'Just doing my job. I did some asking around. I like to be prepared.'

'You're full of surprises.'

'Better believe it, mate. That was just the first of many. A few days with me, and you'll be wondering what's hit you.'

'Now I'm worried.' He pauses. 'What do you think of Garnett?'

Webley loses the smile. 'He's a prick. Other than that, I'm not sure. If Terri covered up for him, then that makes him the murderer of Kevin Vernon. And if Diane Curtis is to be believed, Garnett had a heated argument with Terri Latham about that very subject just a few weeks ago. Could be that Terri was threatening to go to the bosses with the true story, in which case that would give Garnett a motive for killing her too.'

'On the other hand,' says Cody, 'he could be telling the truth. Maybe he's just unlucky in getting caught up in two deaths.'

Webley stands up, ready to leave. 'Could be. Doesn't stop me thinking he's a prick.'

12

'You ready for this?' Cody asks.

They are parked up in a car outside a terraced house in Kensington, east of the Royal Hospital. This Kensington is nothing like its London namesake. It is its very antithesis. The divide between the country's rich and poor could be portrayed no more acutely than in a comparison of the two neighbourhoods. Houses in the London district have exchanged hands for more than twenty million pounds. Not so long ago, Liverpool Council sold off a number of properties in its own Kensington for a pound each.

Cody knows this area well. A short walk from here is the library he used to visit as a kid. He still remembers the Francis Bacon quotation above its doors: 'Reading maketh a full man, conference a ready man, and writing an exact man.'

Webley shows him a nervous smile. 'You saw how I dealt with Garnett. Five minutes with me and they'll be offering me tea and cake.'

'If you manage that, I'll give you twenty quid.'

'You're on.'

They get out of the car and lock it up. Cody glances up at the grey sky, and then lowers his eyes to the house. Both look threatening.

There is no bell. Cody raps the tarnished brass door knocker a couple of times. From inside comes the sound of barking. He looks at Webley and states the obvious: 'They've got a dog.'

She shrugs. 'Love dogs, me.'

He thinks to ask her how she manages to stay so chipper, but then the door swings open.

The man before them is large, powerful-looking. His greying hair suggests he is in his fifties. He has sagging jowls and a paunch, but his huge arms look capable of crushing a person to death in their embrace. He examines his two visitors with suspicion and disdain.

Cody holds up his ID. 'Mr Vernon? I'm Detective Sergeant Cody, and this is Detective Constable Webley. Do you mind if we come in for a few minutes?'

Vernon doesn't budge. 'What do you want?'

'We'd just like a brief chat.' Cody nods towards the hallway. 'Can we talk inside? We won't keep you long.'

'The last time police were here it was to call my son a thug. A troublemaker. A no-mark. This was after he was dead, mind you. Only they didn't seem interested in my feelings about losing a son. They just wanted to dirty his name. Right here, in my own house.'

Says Webley, 'We have no intention of upsetting you or your family, Mr Vernon. We just want to talk.'

Vernon continues to fill the doorway, saying nothing.

'Frank? Let them in.'

The voice comes from behind Vernon. Cody tilts his head to see the slight figure of Vernon's wife, standing in the gloom of the hall-way as she dries her hands on a tea towel.

Vernon turns slowly and plods back inside, then enters a room at the front of the house. Cody looks at the wife, who beckons the detectives in with a nod.

As they step in, a scruffy terrier appears from behind the woman's legs.

'Aw,' says Webley. 'Look at him.' She moves towards the animal.

'He's not good with strangers,' warns Mrs Vernon. But it doesn't stop Webley. Squatting down, she allows the dog to sniff her hand, then gives it a good scratch under the chin.

'He's lovely,' she says. 'What's his name?'

Cody watches the woman as this is going on. She reaches her hand out, then withdraws it. It's as if she wants to communicate with Webley, but doesn't want to appear disloyal to her husband. It's a posture that's familiar to Cody. He has seen it in his own mother.

'Frank's waiting,' she says simply.

Webley straightens up, smiles at Mrs Vernon, then follows Cody into the front room.

It's a small room, sparsely furnished. Cody thinks it's not often used. It contains a two-seater sofa, an armchair, a coffee table, and a cupboard in one of the alcoves. No heating on in here. Frank won't want to make his visitors too comfortable. This is the room they use for people they don't want to stay any longer than necessary.

Frank is already in the armchair, waiting to hear what is to be said. Waiting to get this over with so that he can return to his afternoon television and his mugs of tea.

Cody and Webley take their places on the settee. It sinks alarmingly under their weight, as though their arrival has taken it by surprise.

Mrs Vernon comes in behind them. Stands dutifully at her husband's side. Puts her hand on the back of his armchair, as if posing for a family portrait.

And then a curious and unsettling thing happens. The door is pushed open once more and another figure enters. Cody catches his breath. He feels the goose bumps rising on his arms.

It's Kevin. The dead son.

At least it looks like Kevin. Cody saw photographs in the case files before coming here, and this looks exactly like him. Tall and broad, with curly black hair and blotchy skin. Despite his size, he glides silently across the room. His parents seem not to notice, causing Cody to think only he can see this apparition. He watches speechless as Kevin takes up his place behind his father, as if to complete the family with his unseen presence while he forms the subject of their discussion.

Mrs Vernon sees the confusion on Cody's face. 'This is Robert,' she explains. 'Kevin's older brother. He has his own place, but he spends most of his time here now.'

She strokes her son's arm as she says this, expressing her gratitude that the only child she has left has refused to abandon them to a lonely existence.

'You don't need to give them all our private details,' says Frank. 'It's nothing to do with them.'

He returns his attention to the detectives. Returns to his waiting.

'There's been an . . . event,' says Cody, because he's not sure what else to call it. 'No doubt you'll hear about it on the news, but we wanted you to hear about it from us first.'

'What kind of . . . event?' Frank puts the pause in the same place, mockingly.

'A death. A homicide.'

Frank says nothing. His wife's eyes widen as she looks first at him then back at the detectives.

'Who?' she asks when it seems clear that Frank plans not to. 'Who's been killed?'

'A police officer. PC Terri Latham.'

Cody wasn't sure what reaction to expect, but for a long time he gets none. The room is filled with a taut silence that threatens to snap.

'I see,' says Frank. 'Do you know who did it?'

'No. Not yet. Someone entered her property last night and attacked her. Her body was found only this morning. We've just started making inquiries.'

'I see,' Frank says again. 'And you're bringing this news to our door because . . . ?'

And this is where it gets tricky, thinks Cody. Watch what you say here. Choose your words carefully.

'Because we thought you should know. And because . . .'

'Yes?'

'Because we need to know if there's any help you can offer us in finding her killer.'

There. I've said it. Now stand back and wait for the fireworks to go off.

'Jesus Christ,' says Vernon.

'Frank . . .' says his wife.

'You people,' says Vernon. 'You're all the same, aren't you? Why can't you just leave us alone?'

'Mr Vernon—'

'Get out! Get out of my bloody house, the pair of you!'

He rises from his chair. His cheeks have reddened. They're burning now. He's ready to explode.

Robert puts a restraining hand on his father's arm. 'Dad . . .'

Vernon shakes him off. Takes a step closer to Cody and Webley.

'How dare you? How dare you come here looking to accuse us of something we don't know anything about?'

'Mr Vernon, we're not accusing you of anything. We're here because—'

'I know exactly why you're here. You're here for the same reasons you always come here. To blacken our name. To find a scapegoat, because you haven't got the balls to take a look at yourselves in the mirror. Why can't you ever do that, eh? Why can't you drop the holier-than-thou attitude and accept that you've got some bad apples in the cart? You're not perfect. Nobody is. One of your lot killed our Kevin. I don't care what your so-called enquiry said. You told yourselves what you wanted to hear. Kevin was innocent. He was doing nothing wrong, and you murdered him. You want my help? You want information on who might have killed your precious policewoman? Then you try helping us for a change. You try putting yourselves in our shoes for just a few hours. Until you can do that, you can just piss off.'

He storms out of the room then. Takes his anger and his tears and his frustration away with him, leaving only the lasting echo of his outburst.

Cody and Webley stand up. Perhaps Vernon's wife . . .

She turns wet eyes on them. 'Why do you always have to bring it back to us?'

Then again, perhaps not.

Webley tries this time. Woman to woman. Maybe that's best.

'Mrs Vernon. A young woman was killed last night. Yes, she sometimes wears a police uniform. But last night she was at home.

She was wearing a dressing gown, just like you and I might wear. She was watching television and drinking wine, just like anyone else might do. She was being a normal human being. And then somebody came along and took her life. It was brutal. It was violent. I saw her lying there this morning in a pool of her own blood. Her dressing gown was soaked in the stuff. She looked small and weak and vulnerable, just like any other victim.'

Webley has to take a deep breath before she can continue.

'There was a lot of hatred directed at PC Latham when your Kevin died, and it came from many different directions. We're not suggesting for a minute that you would have wished her to come to harm like this, but perhaps you or your husband heard something. A rumour, maybe. A casual remark. Somebody saying they'd sort her out for you. Somebody saying she would get what's coming to her. That kind of thing. You probably wouldn't have taken it seriously at the time, but maybe now, when you think about it, maybe it *was* meant seriously. Is that possible, Mrs Vernon? Could anyone have said something like that to you?'

Bravo, thinks Cody. She should be in the diplomatic corps. Message delivered with minimal force. No collateral damage to report.

Although Mrs Vernon's expression suggests she is not thinking along similar lines.

'I thought you two might be different,' she says. 'You're both young.' She jerks a thumb towards Cody, but keeps her eyes on Webley. 'Him, he looks like he's still at school. I haven't seen either of you before, and because of that I thought you might not have been poisoned by some of the other coppers we've dealt with. I thought you might have come here with open minds. I was willing to give you the benefit of the doubt. When you bent down and stroked Rascal in the hall, I thought, At last, a normal bobby. Someone I can connect with, have a proper conversation with. I should have known better really, shouldn't I?'

'Mrs Vernon—'

She halts Webley with a stern index finger. 'No. Let me finish. Frank's not a well man. He hasn't been well since he lost his son. He's a big fella, but inside he's falling apart. When he said try putting yourselves in our shoes, he meant it. Whatever you believe happened on the night Kevin died, think about how we see it. Put to one side whether we're right or wrong for a minute, and just see it through our eyes. And then see yourselves barging into our house, demanding that we tell you what we know about the death of this policewoman.'

'We didn't exactly—'

'Did you bother to ask us how we are? How we're dealing with things? Did you offer us any sympathy? No, because you're too bloody selfish for that. Come in, get your information, leave. That was your plan, wasn't it? Our feelings don't matter. And then to suggest that we might know who did this murder. Just what kind of people do you think we mix with? I realise this isn't the poshest bit of Liverpool, but we're not all murdering scumbags here you know. And do you know what? Do you know what?'

She is girding herself up for something. The tears are welling in her eyes and her voice is faltering and her lip is trembling and she is about to let fly. Cody readies himself.

'If I did know who killed that bitch, I wouldn't tell you. God help me for saying this, but I'm glad she's dead. There. You want someone who'd be willing to say she got what was coming to her, then here I am. That woman cheated us out of the justice we deserve. She protected a killer. And now she's got the justice *she* deserved.'

She flies out of the room. Robert – or is it Kevin's ghost? – finally steps out from behind the chair.

'I'll show you out,' he says.

'That's not how we meant this to go,' says Cody. 'If you could talk to your parents—'

Robert puts a finger to his lips. 'Shush now. Don't make it worse. Don't start thinking I'm on your side. Let's just go, shall we?'

He ushers them into the hallway. Herds them to the front door. Standing on the front step, Cody turns one last time.

'We didn't come here to upset anyone. I think you know that. We're just trying to find a murderer.'

Robert nods, but it's a nod that says, *Yeah, right.*

'I tell you what,' he says. 'Arrest and prosecute the man who murdered my brother, then maybe I'll start to believe you.'

He closes the door. Cody and Webley head back to the car.

'That went well,' says Cody. 'I love it when we manage to connect with members of the public.'

Webley frowns. 'We made a right pig's breakfast of that one, didn't we?'

'Dog's breakfast. Or pig's ear.'

'Same difference. Either way, we cocked it up.'

'Yup. So it looks like I get to keep my twenty quid.'

'What twenty quid?'

'You said they'd be serving you tea and cake after five minutes.'

'Shut up and get in the car,' she says. Then adds: 'Sarge.'

13

They're striding out of the police station again. Webley and Cody. Normally, this is what Cody likes. Keeping busy. Lots of legwork. Much better than pecking away at a keyboard and staring at a screen. Only this trip is to the mortuary. Not so much fun.

It didn't use to bother him. Like most murder detectives, he became inured to the sight of death, mutilation, dismemberment. Different now, though. Inside, the butterflies are already starting to beat their wings.

He doesn't see the men coming. They seem to swoop down from the sky. Like they have just abseiled into his path.

'Cody!' one of them says. 'Good to see you again, my old mate. How's tricks?'

Cody shakes his head. 'Not now, Dobby. We're busy.'

He takes satisfaction in seeing the man recoil slightly at the use of the nickname. It's a natural enough handle in this city for anyone with the surname Dobson, but Cody is also aware that the man has become very sensitive about it ever since that Harry Potter film came out. The one with Dobby the house elf. Not that he bears any resemblance to the creature. Yes, he has Dumbo-like ears; and yes, his nose projects further from his face than is usual in anyone not named Pinocchio; and yes, his bulging eyes make him appear eternally surprised. But other than that . . .

'Yeah, I heard you were busy. Very busy, in fact. You're on the Latham case, aren't you?'

Behind Dobson, another man pokes a camera lens at them. His hair is blond, but his short beard carries a hint of ginger. He wears a sand-coloured gilet and carries a backpack, and keeps clicking away like he's on safari.

'Who's he?' asks Cody.

'This is Chris. He's one of the best around. He'll even make you look good, Cody.'

Says Chris, 'I also do weddings and parties, if you're interested.'

'I'm not.'

Dobson turns greedy eyes on Webley. 'What about you, Miss . . . ?'

'It's Detective Constable to you,' she answers. 'DC Webley.'

Dobson scribbles it into his notebook with a stump of a pencil. 'So are you also looking into the death of PC Latham?'

'No comment,' she says.

'Come on,' says Cody, and they carry on walking. The reporter and the photographer chase after them.

'Is there any truth in the rumour that Latham's murder is connected to the death of Kevin Vernon?'

Cody doesn't slow down. 'There's no such rumour, and you know it. You're just trying to stir things. It's the only bit of information you've got on Latham, so you're putting two and two together and making five. But I'm sure that a newspaper such as yours wouldn't stoop to printing make-believe just to sell copies.'

'But it *is* connected with the fact she was a police officer?'

'You don't really expect an answer, do you? Come on, Dobby, you know better than that.'

They keep walking. Dobson keeps firing questions at them. The detectives keep dodging them. And all the while, that bloody cameraman keeps shooting images of them.

Stay calm, thinks Cody. Don't let him ruffle your feathers, and especially not while that lens is in your face.

'We hear you've spoken to Vernon's family,' says Dobson. 'What sort of reaction did they give you?'

'A better one than the one I'm about to give you if you don't get out of my way.'

Cody hopes that does the trick. Hopes that Dobson will accept he's getting nothing here and that he needs to try his luck elsewhere.

But Dobson can be a tricky bastard. Oh, yes, his sneakiness knows no bounds. His hack instincts have been honed to the point where he knows exactly how to separate out the weakest member of the herd.

'I don't think we've met before, Miss Webley. Are you new to the team?'

'I joined this morning,' she says. Cody would rather she gave them nothing.

'Oh, really? Then you've never worked with DS Cody before?'

'No. Why do you ask?'

Chris the photographer is right in front of her now, recording every reaction. His camera captures the puzzlement on her face.

'This way, darling,' says Chris. 'That's it. Nice.' He clicks away. For some reason, each shot sounds to Cody like a hammer blow to his skull.

Says Dobson, 'I just wondered what it was like to work alongside someone with his background. Someone who's been through the things he has.'

Cody says, 'That's enough, Dobby.'

Webley tries to mask it, but the confusion is clear on her face. And the camera gets it all. *Bang, bang, bang.*

Cody squeezes his eyes shut to cut out the noise in his head. When he opens them again it's evident to him that the bombardment Webley is getting from both men is designed to throw her off her guard.

'Whatever you're referring to,' she says to Dobson, 'I'm sure it won't be a problem.'

Dobby glances at Cody, a suggestion of triumph in his smile. *Bang, bang, bang . . .*

'You mean you haven't heard? He hasn't told you? You should ask him. It's quite a story.'

Bang, bang. The noises are getting louder. They are hurting now. I need to stop this, thinks Cody.

'All right, Dobby,' he says. 'That'll do. Now go off with your cameraman friend and take some photos of yourselves in compromising positions.'

'A few more,' says the photographer. 'Come on, darling. Give us a smile.'

Bang.

Cody feels his skull split open. And then it's as though he receives an electric shock that galvanises him into actions outside his control. He's hardly even aware of what he's doing as he leaps at the photographer, as he snatches the camera from him, as he wraps his free hand around the man's throat, as he forces him back onto the bonnet of the unmarked police car.

He feels his hand squeezing, squeezing. The man is struggling, going purple in the face, clawing at Cody's unyielding arm.

There is a roaring sound in Cody's head. There are words in there, swimming below the surface, but he can't make them out. He just knows he needs to put an end to things. He needs to squeeze out all the pain. Get rid of it, once and for all. It's that simple.

'CODY!'

Not that simple.

It never is, is it? Life doesn't offer simple solutions. It's always complicated. Always a mess. He decides it will never get easier. He can tell himself it will, but it won't. Every time he imagines things have improved, he gets shown the truth. And it's always a slap in the face. Always another nail in the coffin.

He should have learnt that by now.

He slackens his grip. His eyes see again. See the world as it really is. Reality invades in all its unwelcome colours. The roaring subsides too. He hears Webley shouting at him, the photographer coughing and spluttering.

He blinks. Something weighty in his hand. The camera. Webley tears it away from him and shoves it into the arms of the photographer.

Cody looks over at Dobson. He's smiling. Immense satisfaction on his face. He sees a story here. Maybe not yet, but one day. He will keep coming back. Keep pushing buttons. Keep smiling until he gets what he wants.

'Sarge!' Webley's urgent voice again. 'We need to go.'

She manhandles him to the passenger side of the car. She's not allowing him to drive. Sensible move. He would take them into the nearest lamp post.

She opens the door and feeds him into the vehicle, automatically putting her hand on top of his head, like she would do to a prisoner. Cody sits there, staring straight ahead, feeling numb. He hears her telling Dobson to 'stay away from him'. Nice of her. Protective, just like Blunt.

The slam of a door. The gunning of an engine. A vague sense of motion.

She drives. She mutters. Swears once or twice. Looks his way several times.

He doesn't look back at her. To look back would invite questions. She'll have a million of those.

He thinks it's a pity he can't give her the answers.

14

By the time they find a parking space at the Royal Hospital, he's recovered. Not completely, but enough to present at least a semblance of normality.

Shit!

No, it deserves more than that. At least a dozen 'fucks'.

He went completely over the edge. No excuses, no attempts to dilute what he did. Unacceptable. And all in front of Webley, too – the person to whom he's supposed to be setting an example. Christ, what must she be thinking?

Later, he'll get depressed about this. He knows that. He'll spend hours wondering whether he should still be in this job at all. He would plummet into the blues now if he didn't have something even more worrying jostling for position at the forefront of his mind. And if DC Webley wasn't sitting right next to him.

Okay, now. Deep breath. Act professional. As you were, Sergeant.

'Are you okay?' says Webley.

'Sound as a pound,' he answers. He realises his voice is unnaturally loud. Overcompensating.

'So . . . Do you mind if I ask what all that was about?'

What to say? He can't just dismiss it as nothing of consequence, because, let's face it, that was a bit of a blow-up. It was a totally disproportionate response. On the other hand, he's not about to tell her he's lost his marbles either.

'They pissed me off. The pair of them. Dobson is always pestering me. Always trying to get a story out of me. Press conferences are never good enough for him. He's always got to sneak about, turning rocks over in the hope he'll find something juicy for his scummy rag of a newspaper.'

'It's his job. You know that. I'm not defending him, but that's what they do, isn't it? I just don't understand why it got to you so badly.'

'It just did. They caught me on a bad day.'

She smiles. 'PMS?'

'Something like that. And I didn't like the way that photographer was being with you either.'

Webley flutters a hand in front of her face. 'Why, Sergeant Cody, I didn't know you cared.'

Cody shakes his head at her. 'I don't. I was just defending one of my men.'

She deflates visibly. 'Gee, thanks. In case you hadn't noticed—'

'I'm using "men" in a gender-neutral sense, obviously.'

'Obviously.'

Cody reaches for the handle of the door, but Webley's not done.

'What was that stuff Dobby was saying about your story? The things you've been through?'

Cody pauses for a moment. But only a moment. 'We should get inside. We're already late. The doc'll be having kittens.'

And with that he's out of the car and walking to the building. Glad to be in the open again, sucking in that fresh air and then breathing out his tension. But knowing that his day hasn't finished yet. This day, like most of them, has more up its sleeve.

He leads Webley to the mortuary. They find Stroud in a small anteroom, a sandwich clutched in his sausage-like fingers.

'You're late,' he tells them. 'By nearly ten minutes. When I'm kept waiting, I get hungry. Luckily, I had the means to knock together some sustenance.' He passes a hand over his sandwich, as if about to make it disappear. Which, in a sense, he is.

Webley grimaces. 'What is it?'

'This, not unlike yourself, young lady, is heaven in portable form. A deliciously thick helping of deep-fried root vegetables lovingly embraced between twin layers of baking perfection.'

'You mean a crisp butty?'

'If you wish to be so colloquial about it. May I offer you one?'

'Er, no thanks.'

Cody stares as Stroud takes a huge bite out of his sandwich. The resounding crunch makes him feel sick. In fact, everything about this place is making him nauseated. He can feel the heat beginning to emanate from his body and envelop him beneath his clothing, the perspiration starting to bead on his forehead.

Stay calm, Cody tells himself. Deep breaths. You can do this.

'We had a good one in here the other day,' says Stroud, fragments of crisp dropping from his sandwich as he waves it at them. 'Fellow cleaning the roof of Lime Street station. You know how it's made from all those glass panels? Well, there's one missing. Only our chap didn't realise this. Went to clean the panel, fell straight through. The weirdest thing was the expression of utter surprise that was still on his face when they found him. Priceless.'

Stroud laughs uproariously at this, while Cody finds it a battle to dredge up a smile. He has always thought that coppers have a black enough sense of humour, but it's often beaten into the shade by some of the comments that are traded in this place. Cody still remembers listening to one of the pathologists imitating the sound of a trotting horse by banging the tops of two skulls on a table.

Stroud puts the remains of his snack down and brushes the crumbs from his hands.

'Right,' he says. 'Nutrients restored. I'll just get cleaned up, and then we'll take a look at the body, shall we?'

He goes in search of a sink. Cody looks at Webley, hoping she hasn't yet become aware of his discomfort. It surprises him that she looks even more nervous, biting her lip and not knowing what to do with her hands.

'Are you okay?'

A nod, but not an emphatic one. 'Like I said, this is different. I knew her.'

'Would you prefer to stay out here?'

She thinks for a few seconds. 'No. It's okay. I'll be all right.'

Cody isn't sure he can say the same. He wishes it were the other way round – her asking him if he'd care to skip this one.

Crap, he thinks. We're as bad as each other.

'Come on,' he says. 'Don't look if you don't want to.'

They enter the autopsy room. A long row of steel tables stretches ahead of them. On one of the tables, a naked female figure, white and still. Even from here, the detectives can see that death is on that table. No actor could carry lifelessness off this well.

'Gather round,' says Stroud. 'She won't bite, and neither will I.'

Cody wonders whether Stroud has remembered that Webley was the one who reacted so badly at the crime scene this morning. For a moment he debates telling him, but then decides that Webley probably wouldn't thank him for seeking special dispensation.

Reluctantly, the detectives move closer. From a distance they could kid themselves that Terri Latham was intact – perfect even in death. But as they approach they become aware of her unseeing stare through red, raw holes. And below, the third point of the macabre triangle is the wound in her throat, gaping open as if crying for help. Cody feels his senses being bombarded. The shiny steel and the intense white lights and the man wielding the scalpel and the chemical smells and the cold air and the unmistakable presence of death – all of these things alerting his brain to the fact that this body is about to be torn open to the world in the most gruesome manner imaginable.

And so it begins.

Stroud launches the operation with words he has intoned countless times before: 'The body is that of a well-nourished female . . .'

For Cody, the words quickly fade into a meaningless drone. He can't concentrate on what is being said, because he is trying too hard not to be here. In his mind he is on a beach, then swimming in the sea, then driving along a country lane. Anywhere but here.

The sweating starts up again. He knows it is cool in this room, but he feels like a boil-in-the-bag meal. His blood will soon begin to bubble and his skin will inflate with the steam, and it will balloon out and he will be on the edge of exploding, spreading his insides all over the—

No, he tells himself. Stop that. Don't get all disgusting on me. Think nice things. Think of girls, and of having a pint in the pub with your mates, and going to the match on a Saturday. All the things you used to do before normality was cruelly interrupted.

But he can't help it. Can't help watching Stroud, and the way he's cutting. That big fucking Y-shape of an incision they always make. Right down the body. Look at that. All the way down. Parting. Opening. Opening that fucking body right up. Jesus Christ. Look at that shit. All that stuff inside her. Ribs being parted. Organs being scooped out like the fleshy seedy pulp of a melon. All taken out as if this isn't a human being in front of them. As if this is just some kind of inanimate object to be freely poked and prodded and sliced and damaged.

And if only that were all. The emptying of the cavity. That should be it. That should be enough devastation, enough carnage.

But now this is it. This is the part Cody was really worried about. The bit he dreaded. The bit that is making him hot and nauseated and on the verge of passing out. No, it's more than that. It's the bit where he cries. The bit where he screams his lungs out. Where his very soul is ejected from his mouth and his heart wants to explode with the strain it endures. This is it. Oh, God, this is it.

He would like to ask Blunt why she put him here. Wants to know what purpose it serves. Webley, too. They are the two most unsuitable detectives on the team to be at this particular post-mortem. Blunt knows that, and yet she put them here. What kind of sadist is she?

But it's a test. He knows that. And he's going to pass it with flying colours. Watch me, he thinks. I can do this. I can get to the other side of this.

So he stays put. Forces himself to stare. The beach and the pub and the girls and his mates are all out of reach now. They can't help him any longer. Even Webley has gone, dissolved into the background. There is just the body and the man with the scalpel. It's not even possible to discern the gender of the corpse anymore. This could be a man. Yes, he thinks, that's it. A man. It was a man last time, too. He was there. He saw it all. Saw what happened, just as it's happening now. The scalpel being lowered again. Down, down, down. And then the cutting. The cutting.

And then . . .

Yes.

Oh, Christ.

See what he's doing?

Jesus, he thinks. I see it.

He hears the screams, too. He tells himself they're not there, but he hears them anyway. Why won't they stop? Why won't anybody else in this room do something about it?

But then he looks around and realises the answer. They are not here to help him. They want him to suffer. These sick maniacs with their eternally evil grins are here to do him untold harm. They are coming closer, closer . . .

Cody flees.

He gets out of there as fast as he can. He doesn't even know where he's going. He just has to run, to escape. He knows people are staring at him as he rockets past, but he doesn't care. Getting out of this building is his overriding thought.

He breaks out into the grey light of day. Sucks hungrily on the city air that's probably full of all kinds of crap, but which is at least free of the cloying chemical smells indoors.

And then he throws up. Splashes the contents of his stomach onto the hard cold concrete.

He stands there for a while, bent over, hands on his knees. Wondering if he's got anything left inside. Not just in his stomach, either. Inside, where it matters. This is the second loss of control in a short time period. Things are getting worse. Have I got what it takes, he thinks, or am I just kidding myself? Should I be doing this job? Wouldn't it be better if I just packed it in while I've still got enough of a mind to think straight?

Those are the thoughts that are really eating him up. They keep coming back, time after time, and they never seem any less strong. That's what's so frustrating. That's what—

'Cody?'

Webley has found him. She puts a hand on his shoulder. 'Are you okay?'

He nods. Wipes his mouth with the back of his hand. Webley finds a tissue and hands it to him.

'Let's get out of here,' she says. 'I think we could both do with a drink.'

He allows her to escort him to the car. She's leading him along like he's an elderly patient, telling him he'll be okay. The constable comforting the sergeant.

When did the world get turned upside down?

15

'Are you sure that's all you want?'

Cody nods. The glass of Coke is fine. He doesn't drink anymore. Used to, though. Used to go on many a bender with the lads. He would come home rotten, make some supper he never remembered eating afterwards. He would get up the next morning and there would be soup stains all down the wall and all around his mouth, but for the life of him he wouldn't remember the stuff passing his lips.

But that was then. Before the curtain came down and everything went dark.

He tried drinking afterwards. Hoped it would make things better, if only for a short while. A dram or two of whiskey, just to help him go off. When that didn't work, he tried getting blind drunk, hoping to collapse into unconsciousness and leave the pain behind for a few blessed hours. That didn't work either. He would still wake up in the middle of the night, and the demons would be worse. They would be more fierce, as if fuming at his attempts to suppress them. He decided then that not only was alcohol not the solution, it was an aggravator. It was simplest to shun it totally. And in many ways he is grateful for that outcome. His father has found some solace in drink, and is paying a high price for it.

Says Webley, 'How are you feeling now?'

'Okay, I think. Must be something I ate.'

She nods towards Cody's glass. 'Have a drink. If you're not going to get pissed, at least take the taste away. And your breath. Sitting here with you is like sniffing sweaty socks.'

Cody takes a long draught of the Coke.

'Better?' she asks.

'Better.'

'Want to talk about it?'

'Talk about what?'

'Cody, that was no food allergy. I've seen you knock back several pints and a dodgy kebab, and still wake up fine the next day. Something about that PM got to you. And something about that photographer pushed your buttons, too. You can't keep wigging out like that and tell me everything's hunky-dory.'

Cody shakes his head. 'The two things aren't related. I told you, the photographer just pissed me off.'

'Then be pissed off. Doesn't mean you have to tear the man's head off. That's not like you, Cody.'

'How do you know? People change. How do you know what I'm like now?'

He regrets the way he says those words. Makes him sound bitter.

'You're right,' she says. 'Maybe you're not the man I used to know.'

And love, he thinks. Know and love.

A silence drops in. Webley uses it to sip her wine and soda. Cody uses it to glance around the pub. They are in the Philharmonic, which occupies a corner diagonally opposite the concert hall of the same name. Two of the wood-panelled rooms within the grand old watering hole have signs over the door labelling them 'Brahms' and 'Liszt'. They are sitting at a small table in Brahms.

He remembers the first time he came here with Webley. They were part of a large gang of coppers. Drunk and rowdy. Somebody asked Webley if she had seen the gents' toilets for which the Phil is famous. She made the mistake of saying she hadn't. Seconds later, Cody was one of those carrying her in to get a close-up view of the pink marble urinals, much to the surprise of the customers engaged in taking aim at them.

It was among the best of times. The worst of times was still unimaginable back then.

'So what's changed you?' she asks.

Not letting it go, thinks Cody. She, for one, is the same as ever.

'Dunno. The job, I suppose. Took it out of me. Made me cynical.'

'Is that why you dropped the undercover work?'

'Yeah. I needed a fresh start. Pretending to be other people for so long was doing my head in.'

She mulls this over while she runs her finger up and down the stem of her glass.

'That reporter. Dobby. What was he going on about?'

'When?'

'The stuff about your background, and how fascinating it is.'

Cody waves it away. 'Oh, that. He found out that I'd gone undercover on some major investigations. He's always pestering me about it. I think he wants to write up my life story.'

He laughs, but he's not sure he gets away with it. Webley appears unconvinced.

Still, she leaves it for now.

'And the post-mortem?'

Christ, he thinks. Not out of the woods yet.

'What about it?'

'You still haven't explained what happened. God knows, I was upset enough. It wasn't easy seeing an old friend on the slab like that. But you took it to another level.'

'I don't know, okay? Maybe I've just become more sensitive in my old age.'

'Old age? Cody, you still look like you're about nine.'

'Well, I'm not. I'm not that far away from thirty, but even that doesn't seem enough. I feel like I'm at least fifty. I'm . . .'

He stops. He's about to tell her that he's seen too much, felt too much for the time he's spent on this earth. He doesn't want to go there.

'What?'

'Nothing. Look, can we change the subject, please? I feel like I'm on a psychiatrist's couch here.'

She nods. 'Okay.' But he can tell she is still concerned. He has no doubt that this conversation is to be continued at a future point. That's how well he knows her.

'So . . .' she says. 'What's with the Coke? Gone teetotal, or is that just for tonight?'

'Why would it just be for tonight?'

'I have no idea.'

But she does. He can tell that about her, too. She is thinking that he is avoiding booze tonight purely to stay in control. In case he comes out with something stupid. Something that would complicate matters. But she doesn't want to say so because of the conceit it carries. It would convey her suspicion that he still has feelings for her.

'Well, it isn't. I just don't drink now. I'm trying to look after myself.'

'Good,' she says. 'Good.'

He feels the conversation is becoming ever more awkward. He wants to go home now, where he can be miserable in private. But there's something he needs to clear up first.

He says, 'Can I ask you a favour?'

'Sure.'

'I'd be grateful if you didn't say anything. To Blunt, I mean. Or anyone else, for that matter. About the way I've been acting today. They might get the wrong idea.'

Or the right idea. Which is probably worse.

She rolls her eyes at him. 'Cody, what do you think I am? Of course I'm not going to say anything. Even if I do think you're a complete basket case.'

He smiles. 'Thanks.'

She sips her drink. Says, 'Now can I ask you a favour?'

'It's only fair. Name it.'

'As we're on the subject of keeping stuff under wraps, I'd like you to do the same. About us, I mean. About how we used to be . . . an item. The others don't need to know. Blunt, especially. It could really mess things up.'

'It's a deal.' He holds his glass in the air. She brings hers up too, and they clink a contract.

And that's when he sees it. On her other hand, now resting on the table.

The engagement ring.

He stares, and she catches him staring. She slides her hand away, as if about to hide it, but then changes her mind and leaves it in full view. And why shouldn't she?

He says, 'You're . . .'

'Engaged, yes.'

'To?'

'A man.'

'Okay. I think I might have worked that one out.'

'Took you long enough to spot the ring. Call yourself a bloody detective?'

'Is he a copper?'

'No. Guess again.'

'A soldier?'

'No. And he's not a traffic warden either. Why do you think it has to be somebody in uniform?'

'I don't know. A . . . a window cleaner.'

She bursts out laughing. 'Christ, you're shit at this game. If you must know, he's a hotel manager.'

'Which hotel?'

'The Lansing.'

'Nice. I was in there a few weeks ago. A suspect had stayed in one of the rooms. I talked to quite a few of the staff. What's your bloke's name?'

She hesitates, and he wonders why.

'Parker.'

'What's his first name?'

A longer pause now. 'Parker.'

And now it's Cody's turn to laugh. 'Oh my God. His name's Parker? No, I definitely didn't speak to him. I'd have remembered someone called Parker. Surely he's not from Liverpool?'

'Surrey, actually.'

She says this with a certain frostiness, but Cody presses on. 'Please tell me his surname's Carr. Parker Carr would be a great name for a traffic warden.'

Despite her apparent anger, Webley can't stop a smile breaking out on her lips.

'Stop it. I've already told you he's not a traffic warden. And anyway, enough of my love life. What about yours? Which unsuspecting girl have you got tied up in your basement right now?'

'Nobody. I'm young, free and single at the minute.'

'But there have been others, right? Since we split up.'

'One or two.'

'One or two thousand, you mean. Anyone serious?'

'Maybe.'

'This is like pulling teeth. Spit it out, Cody. Give me a clue.'

'All right. Devon.'

'The whole county, or one specific town? Which bit of Devon?'

'All of her.'

Webley's jaw drops. 'And you have the audacity to make fun of my fella! What kind of name is Devon?'

'I think it's a nice name.'

'It's ridiculous. The next time somebody tells me they spent the weekend in Devon, I'll be crying with laughter.'

'Well, it's not as bad as Parker.'

'Matter of opinion. So, go on then. Spill the beans. How serious was it?'

'Engaged serious.'

She blinks. 'No. Really? What happened? I mean, I'm assuming it's all past history now.'

He's never sure how to answer this. He likes to cling to a hope that perhaps it's not all over with Devon, but the sensible part of him tends to overrule.

'It just . . . fizzled out.'

A lie, of course. It wasn't so much a fizzle as an explosion. But Webley doesn't need to know this.

'Nobody else involved?'

'No, nothing like that. I suppose we just weren't as compatible as we thought we were.'

'When did you break up?'

'Getting on for three months ago.'

'Oh no! That recent? Poor you.'

Webley reaches a hand out and touches Cody on the arm. Then she seems to realise what she's done, and withdraws it again.

'It's fine,' he says. 'Plenty more fish in the Mersey.'

'Don't go looking for them in there, mate. A fish won't be the only thing you'll catch.' She pauses, but seems thoughtful. Then she says, 'Were you living together?'

'Yeah. She's got a house in Hoylake.'

'Nice. So where are you now? Not living with your folks, I suppose?'

He raises his eyebrows at her, reminding her how implausible her suggestion is.

'You're joking, aren't you? I'll have to drop in there this week, though. My mum's birthday's coming up.'

'That'll be fun,' says Webley. 'Let me know when it is, and I'll put Armed Response on standby.'

He gives her a look that tells her he's not amused. 'To answer your question, I've got a place on Rodney Street now.'

'What, *this* Rodney Street?' She points in the vague direction of the well-known city centre street. 'I thought that was all doctors and dentists and stuff.'

'Funnily enough, I do live above a dental practice. I've got a top-floor flat. The dentist is an old friend of mine. He gave me a good deal on rent. Not sure how long he'll let me stay there, though.'

'Those flats must be huge. Lovely, I bet. You'll have to show me around some time.'

He guesses she doesn't really mean this. It's one of those things you say just to be polite.

'Any time.'

But he doesn't mean this either.

'So,' she says. 'Tell me more about the squad. What are they like to work with?'

'They're a great bunch. Footlong's a good laugh.'

'Footlong?'

'Neil Ferguson.'

'Oh, him. The super-tall one. I can see why you call him Footlong.'

'Er, no. I don't think you do. It's nothing to do with his height.'

'What do you mean? Why else would—' Her eyes widened in sudden understanding. 'Oh! Really?'

'So rumour has it.'

'Well, don't look at me to confirm it. Who else is there?'

'Oxo's a good lad. A bit weird, but sharp as a razor. Has a knack of asking the questions nobody else has thought of.'

'Oxo, eh? Let me guess – he likes gravy.'

Cody pulls a face at her. 'Nooo. His surname's Oxburgh. Good job nobody put you in charge of the naming system.'

She laughs. 'What about Blunt?'

'No, that really is her name. It's not rhyming slang or anything.'

'I mean what's she like? She a good boss?'

'The best. I mean that. Get on the wrong side of her, and you'll know about it. But do your job as well as you can, and she'll look after you.'

Webley hesitates before posing the next question. 'Does she look after you?'

Cody knows what she's asking. This is about the way he's been acting. This is Webley trying to find out if Blunt knows something she doesn't.

'Yes,' he answers. 'But no more than anyone else.'

Which is his way of telling her that he doesn't need to be treated as a special case.

Because everything is just fine and dandy.

16

He's lost count of how many news reports he has listened to. As soon as he got home he put on the television and the radio. Kept his attention on both. Flicked from channel to channel in search of something different. A new development. A new take on one of the day's biggest stories.

Because that's what it is. This is big, he thinks. BIG. These head-lines are about *you*. You did this. You are famous, even though nobody knows who you are. This is amazing. Incredible.

And you can't tell anyone.

Nobody can know. Everybody is talking about you and what you did, and you have to keep mum.

The reports contain little detail. Nothing about the bird, but then he knew they would hold that information back. Not a lot about the victim either. An 'off-duty police officer' is what they call her. They say there is nothing at present to indicate that her murder is con-nected with her work in the police force, although this is an 'active line of investigation'.

Active line of investigation. Ha! They haven't got a clue. They don't know where to look, who to talk to, what to do next.

He's happy with that. He could have spelled it out for them. Made it a lot clearer so that their tiny unimaginative brains could cope with it.

All in good time, he thinks. Eventually it will become as plain as the noses on their stupid ugly faces, and they will have to see it for what it is. For now, though, best to keep them confused. Gives me more time. More freedom.

He clicks the remote control again. Cycles through the channels. Nothing at the moment, but there will be soon. The longest he will have to wait until is the start of the next hour. They will talk about him again then. Nothing new, probably, but still . . . He will be the one on everyone's mind for that brief period of time. Sitting in their cosy little houses enjoying their cosy little lives, they will watch the news and they will wonder. About him. About who he is and why he did this. They must all have heard the story by now. He must be on everybody's lips.

He paces the room. Up and down, up and down. He allows himself to enjoy the thrill of knowing what waves he is creating in the world. Such power!

On the television, the news moves on. Sport now. Injuries have ruled out two of Liverpool's key players for Saturday's game.

Weightier matters invade his mind. The excitement fades away. He reminds himself why he is doing this, what it's all for. It's important to remain focused on that, and not to get carried away by emotion.

He presses the red button on the remote, and the television turns black and silent. His thoughts turn fully from the outside world to this one – to what he needs to do next.

He goes out into the hall. Slowly ascends the staircase. Makes his way into the front bedroom. He moves into the centre of the room, the shit-soaked carpet slippery beneath his feet.

The birds seem wary at first. Uncertain. Most remain at a distance, just sitting and staring at him. He closes his eyes. Lifts his arms from his sides until they are straight, turning him into a human cross.

He waits. Still and straight and silent.

And then they come.

One or two at first. Then more. He hears the flapping wings and the chirrups. Feels the currents of air wafting over his face as his companions soar past.

The noise builds until it is a cacophony. The gentle puffs of air become a wind. He senses the excitement of the birds growing to a frenzy. They know. They understand. His eyes fill with tears at the wonderment of their shared knowledge. He takes a deep, shuddering breath. The air is stale and unwholesome, yet it reinvigorates him. Fills his being with purpose and resolve. He knows what he has to do.

His eyes flick open at exactly the moment he snaps his hand to a point directly in front of his face.

He smiles beatifically. The bird in his hand cocks its head at him. He feels its warmth, its pulsating heart. All the other birds beat a hasty retreat to the far corners and shadowy recesses of the room. A reverential hush descends.

'Thank you,' he says to the bird, as it blurs through his tears. 'Thank you.'

Then, slowly, he clenches his fist. Tightens his grasp until he hears the faint popping sound as the bird implodes beneath his fingers.

17

It is said that there are more Georgian properties in Liverpool than in any other city outside London. Cody doesn't know how true that is, but there is certainly a high concentration in the area in which he lives.

Rodney Street is sometimes referred to as the Harley Street of the North. It's crammed with clinics, medical specialists and orthodontists. It even has a hypnotherapist or two. Plaques outside two of the buildings attest to the fact that William Ewart Gladstone was born here and Lytton Strachey lived here. At number fifty-nine, the National Trust has stepped in to preserve the home of the famous portrait photographer Edward Chambré Hardman. Yes, this street is full of history, steeped in character. Plus, it's on the edge of the city centre – an easy drive to work for Cody. He should love it here.

But he doesn't. At least, not as much as he thought he would.

He looks up at his building now. Three storeys above street level, plus a basement below. The facade is grand, elegant. Tall sash windows and shiny black ironwork. It conjures up images of men in tailcoats, women in large dresses, a horse and carriage waiting at the kerb.

But that was a time long ago. All that is left now are their ghosts.

Cody trudges up the stone steps. Unlocks the wide front door and swings it open. Allows the house to swallow him up.

It is dark and gravely quiet in here. During the day there is the constant whirring of drills and electric brushes, the mangled words of patients with mouths stuffed and stretched to their limits, the chatter and laughter of nurses and patients, the occasional cries of pain.

At night all that is gone. The smells remain, of course. The chemical odours of sterility. Sometimes they manage to snake all the way up to his top-floor flat.

But there is no noise. Not right now, at any rate. This is an old building, and often it will creak and it will groan and it will generally complain about its advancing years.

But sometimes there are other sounds too. A banging or a scratching or a rattling. Sounds for which Cody has not managed to find explanations. Sounds that could drive the susceptible mind to imagine all kinds of phantasms and other horrors.

Cody puts on a light. Doors to either side of the huge hallway lead to the reception room and the dental surgeries. They are closed and locked. Behind them lie the reclining chairs and the intense spotlights and the implements for digging and gouging and cutting and scraping. The stuff of nightmares, if Cody's brain didn't already have enough to work with.

And, to make matters worse, there is the brown door.

A featureless slab, it sits towards the back of the house, behind the staircase. It guards the entrance to the cellar, and is always locked. Cody has made the mistake of wandering through this building at night, and the even bigger mistake of putting his ear to that door. There are noises down there – he is sure of it – and he hesitates to guess what might cause them. He tells himself it's just the boiler, the ancient pipework. Possibly mice. He's never entirely convinced by his own assurances.

He ascends the wide staircase, imagining wealthy lords and ladies doing the same long ago. Perhaps their children slid down this polished wooden banister when out of sight of their parents. Perhaps, in the dead of night, they still do.

He reaches the large window at the top of the first run of steps. It looks out on to a long walled yard, now enrobed in blackness. Someone could be out there, looking back at him, and he wouldn't even know it.

He continues on to the first floor. More locked-up surgeries here, plus a small kitchen and toilets. To the left, along the corridor, the door leading to Cody's flat. He finds his key, unlocks the door. When he pulls it open, its squeal is like the final drawn-out moan of a dying old man.

He enters and locks the door behind him, shutting himself off from the rest of the building. Let the ghosts out there cavort and consort and conspire. In here he is alone with his own misery, his own distress. His personal demons are challenge enough without adding to their company.

Ahead is another staircase, narrower and less impressive than the previous flights. He ascends it to the top floor. This is his flat. His space. It's a big space, too. Three huge bedrooms. Tons of storage room.

Far too much for one person.

And that's the biggest problem. That's what's missing. That's what keeps the spirits here.

What this place doesn't have is Devon.

He'd like to think that her presence would change everything. That she would lighten the shadows, silence the voices, banish the spectres.

He misses her so much. Too much. She has made it clear that they have no future, not with things the way they are. Not without drastic changes. Changes to which Cody can't commit. Not that she's being unreasonable or anything. She's being totally reasonable. This is his fault. He's a stubborn idiot. He asked for this.

Time will heal, though. It always does. This is a temporary situation. In the scheme of things, just a hiccup. He can put up with this for a short while. There will be an end to it, and it will all come right. He just needs to do his time, and keep his shit together.

He knows that's easier said than done. When he's alone and he can't sleep and he's seeing things and hearing things and the walls seem to be closing in on him, such words of reassurance aren't so effective.

He decides he should eat. It's getting late and he's hungry. The date with Webley did that.

Although it's wrong to call it a date, he decides. It was just a couple of drinks with a colleague. That's all Webley is now: a colleague. She could just as easily have been Blunt. Or a bloke. It meant nothing, and it'll probably never happen again.

So anyway, back to food.

He goes into the kitchen and opens the freezer. Not the refrigerator, because he hasn't been shopping recently and he knows how desolate it is in there. In the freezer are ice cubes, a pack of frozen peas, some microwave meals and . . . well, that's about it. If she were here, Devon would be appalled. She would slap his arm and yell at him and tell him to sort his life out. And he would love her for it.

But if she were here, it would never get this bad. There would always be food in the fridge and fruit in the bowl and fresh flowers on the table. She would make sure of it.

He used to cook a lot. He enjoyed it. He could knock together a mean stir-fry. A perfect fry-up or Sunday roast. His signature dish was a Moroccan tagine, reserved for special occasions.

Now, though, what's the point? Why go to all that effort when all he's going to do is sit there eating it alone?

So he generally doesn't bother. Eating is just something he does to stay alive. He still tries to get enough fruit and veg inside him, but often it comes to this. Another plastic box of plastic food to nuke in the microwave.

He takes out the first thing that comes to hand. A tikka masala. That'll do.

He heats it up. Empties it out onto a cold plate. Eats it without really thinking about it, without really tasting it.

Afterwards, he washes up. A plate and a spoon don't take long.

He moves into the living room. There's a large flatscreen television in the corner, but he doesn't switch it on. Hardly ever turns it on now. It doesn't hold his attention like it used to. His mind drifts. It finds other images, other sounds. A lot more disturbing than anything his TV shows him.

One of the few things that work for him is reading. Something to do with the mental concentration it requires. No room left for intruders. So he goes over to the bookcase in the alcove and searches it for something diversionary.

A name leaps out at him. An author's name. Cody takes the book down and stares at that name on the cover.

Edgar Allan Poe.

He knows he should replace it. What is in here is not bedtime reading, especially in light of the case he is working on now.

And yet he is drawn to it, hypnotised by it.

He opens the cover. Scans the contents. 'The Raven' is in here. So too are 'The Fall of the House of Usher', 'The Murders in the Rue Morgue', 'The Pit and the Pendulum', 'The Masque of the Red Death'.

All good, wholesome stuff.

Put it back, he tells himself. Slide it back into its space and choose something else. There are books up there by P. G. Wodehouse. How about a Bill Bryson? Something light-hearted. Otherwise you'll regret it. You know you will. The nightmares will come. A curry followed by Poe? What kind of masochist are you? Do you really want to put yourself through that kind of ordeal tonight?

But the killer has referred to Poe. There is method in his madness, and the secret could be here, in this book.

Settling onto his sofa, Cody opens the book and begins to read.

When you're imagining the plaintive screams of a man as he is being sealed in behind a brick wall, the last thing you want is to be shocked into reality by the phone shrieking into the night.

Cody's heart does its best to readjust while he picks up the phone and focuses tired eyes on the display.

Number withheld, of course. This time of night, it usually is.

He's a little early tonight. Or she. Could be a woman. Could be a bunny boiler, like in *Fatal Attraction*.

Good job I haven't got a rabbit, thinks Cody.

He answers the phone anyway. Always does, in the hope that one day he'll get some answers.

'Hello, darling,' he says. 'What's up?'

Silence. Always silence. Not a whisper, not a breath. Just silence.

Says Cody, 'We should get together some time. What do you think? Let me know when you're coming. I'll bake some scones.'

He waits, ear pressed tight against the receiver in the hope of catching something – anything – that might give him a clue to the identity of the caller.

But he gets nothing.

'Well,' says Cody. 'It's been lovely catching up, you little chatter-box, you. We must do it again some time. What's that you say? Looking forward to it? Me too. Take care now.'

He hangs up, knowing there'll be another call in a couple of days. They started a few months ago, sporadically at first, but more frequently of late. He has no idea who they are from or what they are about, but something tells him he will find out one day.

For now, there's no point getting worked up about it.

That's what he tells himself.

And yet somehow he cannot bring himself to return to the man screaming behind the brick wall.

18

It's amazing what noises there are out here.

We don't do it very often. Stand outside in the middle of the night and just listen. Most people are asleep now, especially those lucky or willing enough to be in work tomorrow. The night owls will be watching TV or playing video games or surfing the internet. They won't be out in the cold, just listening. Just soaking up the sounds of the suburbs.

The house is semi-detached. The front door doesn't face the street, but is hidden inside a recently built porch that looks out on to the gravel drive. As you come up the drive, you can't see what is on the other side of the porch. You can't see where he is hiding.

He has been waiting here for hours. He didn't think it would take this long. He thought maybe midnight at the latest, and now it's – what? – after two in the morning. He's feeling the cold now. Needs to get this over with.

He keeps wondering if he arrived too late, but there has been no activity inside the house. No noise, no lights going on or off. Nothing. He's convinced the house is empty. The only flaw in his plan is if it stays that way.

But no. That's not going to happen. Let's remain positive here. Positive mental attitude – that's the only way to a good murder.

So he continues to wait. And to listen.

He has good hearing. Detects the faintest of sounds. The scurrying of a mouse along the fencing. An empty crisp bag rolling across the gravel. The steady drip of a leaky garden tap. He treats the dripping as a metronome, using its beat to accompany the songs in his head. It keeps his mind occupied. Stops the nerves getting the better of him.

Several times he has considered abandoning this mission and going home. What if he's discovered? What would he do then? At one point, the door of the neighbouring house was opened. He had to duck behind the wheelie bin. He squatted there, cowering. Praying that the neighbour wasn't so neighbourly that he would come around and check the security of the property.

But it didn't come to that. The neighbour just closed his gate and then went back inside and locked up for the night.

It felt like a close call, though. Far too close.

There have been other worrying noises too. Cars roaring up the street. People striding briskly along the pavement, talking far too loudly. A police helicopter buzzing ever nearer. He imagined that chopper turning on its searchlight, beaming it directly on him as a swarm of police officers descended angrily. Or perhaps it would have its infrared switched on. He would show up as a white blob of heat on a screen, and there would be no hiding place for him, no escape.

But the cars flashed past. The voices faded. The helicopter became a star in the distance. Luck remained on his side.

Fortune favours the brave, he tells himself. Because this is brave. It takes guts to do this. Too many people whine about the things that are wrong with the world, but don't have the courage to do anything about it.

He sees the cat before it sees him. He watches it sauntering arrogantly up the driveway. He feels like leaping out and scaring it out of one of its nine lives, but he stays hidden in the shadows, thinking how brilliant it is that he can master the night and the silence even more expertly than this dark sinuous feline.

And then something alerts the animal. A sound, a smell – he doesn't know. But the cat suddenly halts and turns its glowing eyes on him. It stands stock still, assessing this unexpected presence in its territory. It raises its head slightly, sniffing the air. Trying to determine whether this is friend or foe.

And then it issues a cry. It's a loud cry for such a small animal. A noise like that could attract attention.

It comes closer and cries again, louder this time. The man looks up at the windows of the neighbour's house. They're closed, thank goodness. But he can't take any chances. He waves his arm, trying to frighten the animal away. But the stupid thing seems to interpret this as an invitation. It meows twice more, pushing its side against the wheelie bin. It seems to have no intention of moving on.

'Fuck off,' whispers the man. 'Go on, piss off.'

His hissing voice has the opposite effect to the one intended. The cat continues its calling and its pacing.

The man is becoming fearful now. He fully expects lights to start going on, doors to be opened. He has never had a cat. Doesn't know what they're capable of. Would its owner know that it has found something suspicious, just from the way it's acting?

He wonders if he's going to have to kill the cat. He doesn't want to. The cat isn't his target. It's a case of wrong place, wrong time. But listen to it! It's going to give me away. It might as well be a fucking guard dog, all that noise it's making.

He reaches inside his coat. Takes out the heavy lump hammer. He has come more prepared this time. A good solid thwack – that's what's needed. No pissing about with a half-brick. Crack the skull, get 'em on the floor, game over.

He shows the hammer to the cat. 'See?' he whispers. 'You want some of this? Do ya?'

The cat cries at him.

He hefts the hammer. Tries to decide what to do.

And then he hears the vehicle. A noisy diesel. Could be a cab. It comes nearer. Slows down as it gets to the house.

His heart thumps. This is it. The target is here. Jesus Christ, this is it.

But the cat . . .

'Get out of it!' he says.

But the cat stays put. And now there are voices.

Voices? More than one? No, don't let there be more than one. That would screw up the whole thing.

But it's only an exchange with the taxi driver. When the engine revs and the vehicle pulls away, the discussion dies with it.

Now there is just the passenger. Alone, coming up the drive, feet crunching on the gravel.

The cat turns its attention to the newcomer. The killer lies in wait, hammer clutched to his chest, trying to control his breathing. It's all happening so fast now. He stood waiting here for hours, and now it's all happening. People hear taxis, don't they? They wake up and look out of their windows. They might be doing that now, watching the drunken neighbour weave to the front door, the door in the porch behind which lurks a murderer. And the cat still stands there, and it's as if it wants to point, as if it wants to warn the house owner about the danger lying in wait. He so wishes he had killed that bastard cat. Mashed its head into the ground before it could give him away. But this isn't about cats, is it? It's about birds, the death of birds. And it suddenly occurs to him that cats kill birds routinely, and he wonders if this is some kind of omen, some kind of serendipitous symbol. Everything is lining up. The signs are there. The time is right.

A voice: 'Here, puss, puss.' And even in those three simple words the slurring can be heard.

That will make it easier, he thinks. A cinch. I could probably do this with one hand, even without the hammer.

But don't get carried away. Never underestimate your enemy. People sober up quickly when their very lives are at stake. Stick to the plan.

But plans go awry sometimes. And right now seems like one of those times. Because the target is closing in on the cat. Moving steadily forward while talking to it like it were a child. And all the while drawing closer, closer. Even through the fog of inebriation it will soon be realised that there is another presence here – an unwelcome presence, waiting, a hammer clenched in its shaking fist. The intruder will be seen, and then there will be no more waiting. The trigger will be pulled.

But the cat has other ideas. It doesn't want to play this game. Its idea of fun is to lash out with unsheathed claws, snagging on a hand that is too slowed by alcohol to escape. And when its victim calls it a 'little shit', the cat simply runs off to find other sport.

And now we're alone, thinks the killer.

He listens to the figure moving into the porch. The jangle of keys. The rasp of one being slotted into the keyhole. The gentle sigh of the door being swept open.

Now. Now. Now.

Time slows. It seems to take an age for him to get around the porch, and he worries he might be too late – that all he will see is a door being closed in his face. But he is not too late. Time has slowed for the victim too, who is still in the doorway, withdrawing the key. Take a good look – your prey cannot move any faster than you. Look at that face. See the awareness of an intruder taking so long to percolate through that alcohol-addled brain. See the confusion in those eyes – a puzzlement that steadfastly refuses to allow alarm and urgency to rouse the body into action. Observe the pitiful inability to duck or bring an arm up to ward off this heavy, heavy lump of wood and metal that is hurtling oh so fast towards that dense skull surrounding its even denser brain. Smile as you realise you have already won this. This is no contest. You fretted so much you almost crapped yourself out there, and for what? This is easy. This is no harder than snuffing out a candle.

It's a sound like no other. A sound to make your buttocks clench and your scrotum tighten. A sound that seems to reverberate around this small enclosed porch.

The victim goes down. Crumples like a marionette released from its strings. Not even a cry as it collapses. It just folds and stays curled up on the tiled floor, whimpering.

This is the way the world ends. A bang, followed by a whimper.

The killer permits himself a smile. He squeezes into the porch, staring pitilessly down at the quivering figure. He closes the door behind him. Now nobody will see. Nobody will hear.

He can take as long as he wants.

19

Déjà vu.

That's what this feels like to Cody.

Groundhog Day.

He's getting suited and booted again. So are Webley and the other detectives. Blunt is striding up and down. A crowd of onlookers has gathered on the street. This is all too sickeningly familiar.

Except for one crucial fact. This time the identity of the victim is known. Blunt tried to make sure there would be no surprises this time.

In that, she failed. A surprise is what they got. A shock, even.

Blunt finally selects a target and bears down on it. Unfortunately for Cody, it seems he's the one in her sights.

She keeps her voice low but tinged with anger. 'Please tell me you warned Garnett. Please tell me you offered him protection. Because if you didn't . . .'

'We did. It's on the interview tape. We warned him. He wasn't interested.'

Thinking back now, Cody wonders whether he could have been a little more forceful in alerting Paul Garnett to the danger he might be in. But how was he to know? The Vernon episode was one of possibly many reasons why someone might want to murder Terri Latham. There was no concrete evidence for making the assumption that Garnett might be in harm's way. Even Garnett himself dismissed the notion as absurd. But still . . . perhaps if Garnett had been a bit more personable. Maybe if he hadn't been such a little . . .

'Shit!' says Blunt. 'The media are going to have a feeding frenzy over this.'

She's right, thinks Cody. He can almost picture the headlines. He can see the smug grin on Dobby's face. The malicious elf will take great satisfaction in recalling how he pointed out to the police that the first murder might have something to do with the Vernon case. He will practically wet himself as he writes the paragraph highlighting the fact that his suggestion went unheeded. He will become irritatingly pious as he emphasises the end result of this negligence on the part of the detectives involved. To wit, the death of another police officer.

The death of PC Paul Garnett.

Fuck it, thinks Cody. I'm not going to feel guilty about this. If anything, the reported argument that Garnett had with Terri Latham pointed to him as a killer rather than as a victim. Nobody could have predicted it. There's only one person to blame. What we need to focus on now is catching him.

In a way, the killer has done them a favour. They know now what this is all about. They have something on which to hang their hats. The two deaths have a connecting thread. It would have been much more worrying if that link was not so obvious. The last thing they want is some psycho who is just running around killing random coppers.

There is nothing random about this. This has been calculated to the last detail. From what Cody has heard, the signs are all there again. Same MO. Same clues left at the scene.

Well, maybe not exactly the same.

Cody moves in to get a closer look at the body. Which isn't easy, given that the eminent Dr Stroud has squeezed his vast bulk into the cramped porch. Cody issues a gentle cough, just enough to make the pathologist aware of his presence. Stroud leans back a little, affording Cody a clearer view of Garnett lying spread-eagled on his back.

'Spot the difference,' says Stroud.

There is a lot of blood in here. Even more than there was with Terri Latham. Streaks of red up the walls, and even on the ceiling.

Thick, sticky puddles of it on the tiled floor. It looks as though Garnett was stabbed multiple times. As with Latham, his eyes have been gouged out. Cody peers uneasily into the dark ragged holes in the man's face.

And that's the difference. Cody can see the eyes. Yes, a bird has been placed on Garnett's face, but this bird is much smaller than a raven. It doesn't cover the hollowed-out eyes, leaving them to stare zombie-like at the porch ceiling.

'What is that?' Cody asks. 'A blackbird?'

'Looks like one to me,' says Stroud.

This puzzles Cody. Why a different bird? Why should Terri Latham be deserving of a huge, imperious raven, while Garnett gets the cut-down version?

Stroud points his gloved finger at the bird's leg. 'There's another message. I suppose you want me to go against protocol and open it here and now?'

Cody turns to his superior. She nods. 'Go ahead, Rory. If it's got the killer's name on it, I'll kiss you.'

Stroud smiles and pushes his bushy eyebrows up and down. 'How could I resist an invitation like that?'

Cody has to chase away the grimace creeping across his face. The scene is gruesome enough without the added imagery of Blunt and Stroud engaged in mutual tonsil-tickling.

Stroud mutters something into his voice recorder, then picks up some steel implements and leans over the body. Standing just outside the front door, Cody and the other detectives can see nothing beyond Stroud's enormous back.

Eventually, Stroud turns his head to the side. 'Ah,' he says. 'There's another slight difference.'

'Rory,' says Blunt. 'This isn't an episode of *Quincy*. Can you cut the drama and just give us the facts?'

Stroud shifts his body mass out of the way. Permits them all a good look at what he has already seen.

Cody hears the intakes of breath. Hears the 'Oh Jesus!' from Webley.

Stroud has removed the bird. What can be seen underneath is undeniably the face of Paul Garnett.

Minus his nose, that is.

It ought to be the start of an absurdly dark joke: *I say, I say, my policeman's got no nose. How does he smell . . .?*

But it's nothing to laugh at. This man has had part of his face forcibly removed, possibly when he was still alive. The protrusion of flesh and bone and gristle has been cut away, leaving a neat, flat triangle of glistening redness.

'Hacksaw job, I'd say,' Stroud offers. 'No sign of the missing olfactory organ.'

Nobody replies. Nobody is quite sure what to say. The silence continues while they gather their thoughts, while they try to come to terms with the horror splashed across their minds.

'All right,' says Blunt, a little shakily. 'Open the message, please.'

But Cody already has an idea what it contains. He has put two and two together, and wonders whether the others have done the same, or whether their brains are just too overloaded to make sense of anything right now.

Stroud teases open the rolled-up paper and reads it out: '*Wasn't that a dainty dish?*'

'What?' says Webley. 'What the bloody hell—'

'The nursery rhyme,' says Cody. '"Sing a Song of Sixpence". Four and twenty blackbirds, baked in a pie.'

Webley nods. 'When the pie was opened, the birds began to sing; wasn't that a dainty dish to set before the king? But what does—'

'Now skip to the last verse. The maid was in the garden . . .'

Webley thinks for a moment as the rhyme comes back to her. 'The maid was in the garden, hanging out the clothes, when down came a blackbird . . .'

She lets it trail, and Blunt finishes it in a solemn tone: '. . . and pecked off her nose.'

Another silence ensues.

'He's playing with us,' says Blunt. 'The bastard thinks this is all a game. I'm not having it. From now on he gets to know how serious we are.'

She looks Webley in the eye, then Cody. 'Pull the Vernons in. I don't care if it upsets them or anybody else. Somebody knows something, and I'm going to make bloody sure they don't keep it to themselves for very long.'

20

They divide the family up. Interview them separately and simultaneously in three rooms. Blunt decides it's prudent to deal with Frank Vernon herself. Another team deals with his wife. Webley and Cody get to talk to Robert, the son who looks so uncannily like his dead brother. He sits across from them in the small, characterless interview room. Very still, hands in his lap, knees together. His face is expressionless, his thoughts unreadable, although Cody gets the persistent impression that Robert is laughing at them inside.

'First of all,' says Cody, 'I'd like to thank you for agreeing to help us with our inquiries.'

'My pleasure,' says Robert. 'I always like to do my bit for law and order.'

Cody searches Robert's face for signs of a wind-up, but finds it impassive.

'I want to stress that you're not a suspect at this present time. You're simply here to answer some questions we have. Are you okay with that?'

Robert considers this. 'I would be . . . if it was true.'

Cody exchanges glances with Webley. 'I'm sorry. If what was true?'

'That I'm not a suspect. Of course I'm a suspect. The two police officers who were involved in the death of my brother have both been murdered. I repeat, it was *my* brother they killed. If I'm not on your list of suspects, then you're not doing your job properly. Now shall we start again, Detective? Only, can we do it properly this time?'

Cody tries to keep his own face as devoid of emotion as his interviewee's. He hopes he is appearing as calm and collected and logical as Robert, but he's not convinced he's managing it. The man is right, of course. Clearly he's a suspect. The only reason Cody told him he wasn't is that the Chief Superintendent handed down a dictum that 'in light of previous events' this family was to be treated with the 'utmost care and respect, and with no finger-pointing unless absolutely warranted by the evidence'.

So much for the softly-softly approach.

'All right, Robert. But you're not under arrest, okay? You're free to go whenever you like.'

Robert looks around at the door, as if contemplating that very option. Cody wonders if this is going to be over before it's even begun.

'I'll stay,' says Robert. 'I've got nothing better to do right now.'

How very kind of you, thinks Cody.

'You're not at work today?' he asks.

'I'm between jobs at the moment.'

'What do you do?'

'I used to be a car salesman. I was good at it, too. Then Kevin was killed. The firm told me to take as much time off as I needed, but my mum and dad couldn't manage without me. I got sacked in the end. To be honest, I don't think they wanted the publicity.'

'You haven't done any work since then?'

'A couple of things, to make ends meet. Some bar work. A short time in a call centre, for as long as I could stand it.'

'You didn't like it there?'

'The people were idiots. Especially the girls. All they talked about was sex, fashion and music.'

'You don't like any of those things?'

'Let's just say that my tastes and opinions aren't as superficial as theirs. I asked one of them what she thought about Mandela, and she thought it was a new clothes shop in town.' He pauses. 'Anyway, why are we talking about this, Detective Cody?'

Cody waves a hand. 'Just breaking the ice. Making conversation.'

Robert stares for a while, then a scornful smile crosses his lips as he shakes his head.

'You find that amusing?'

'Amusing? I find your whole attitude amusing, Detective. Maybe most of the people you drag into this police station are as thick as pig shit, but I'm not one of them. I know exactly what it is you're trying to do with all this small talk.'

'What am I trying to do?'

Robert taps a finger on his temple. 'Trying to get in here. Trying to figure out how I tick. Well, you can forget about it. I have no intention of getting all touchy-feely with you, Detective Cody, so just ask me where I was last night and what I was doing, and then we can both go our separate ways again.'

Cody feels a sizzle of anger. He tries to douse it, but he suspects that Robert Vernon will do his best to pour more fuel onto it.

'Where do you live, Robert?'

'You know where I live. With my parents. They told you that yesterday. I moved back in because they need me. Because of Kevin.' He winks at Cody. 'Just dropping that in again. I assume we'll get back to that subject.'

'And you were there last night?'

'The nights are long. Could you be more specific?'

'Put it this way: were there any times you weren't in your parents' house last night?'

Robert goes theatrical. Puts on a show of wrestling with his memory.

'Last night . . . last night . . . Well, there was— no, hang on, that was just a dream. But what about— no, I changed my mind about doing that. Actually, thinking about it, I'd have to say the answer is no.'

'So you were there all night?'

'That's what I said.'

'And your parents can vouch for that?'

'I doubt it. They do something at night called sleeping. If I went out in the middle of the night – say, to kill a copper – I don't think they'd hear me. Although they don't sleep as well as they used to, not since my brother was murdered.'

Cody notices a slight emphasis on that last word. He doesn't rise to the bait, though. That would be playing into Vernon's hands.

Quiet until now, Webley joins in: 'Robert, can we just get one thing straight? You said before that you want us to do our job properly. Well, this is it. This is us doing our job, talking to the people who might be able to help us. Someone has killed two police officers. Both of them were implicated in the death of your brother. Both were cleared. Now it doesn't matter whether you agree with that decision or not, the point is that these victims have an obvious connection to your family. Like DS Cody said, we're not trying to pin anything on you. We just want to find out if there is any information you can provide us with to help us catch whoever did these crimes.'

Vernon keeps his gaze fixed on Webley throughout her speech. He doesn't move, his hands remaining in his lap.

'No,' he says. 'I'm not convinced.'

Cody sees the flicker of puzzlement on Webley's face.

'Not convinced about what?' she asks.

'You. It just doesn't work.'

'I'm sorry, what doesn't work?'

'Trying to act all superior. Trying to take some kind of moral high ground. You don't pull it off. It might be something to do with you being a woman. You just don't have that same ring of authority that a man has. Now, DS Cody here, he sounds the business. But you . . . No, sorry, you just don't cut it. You're pretty, though – I'll give you that.'

Don't rise to it, thinks Cody. He's trying to rattle you.

'For your information,' says Webley, 'there are a lot of women in the police force, many of them at high levels. My boss on this murder team is a woman.'

'You mean DCI Blunt? Yeah, I've met her. Not exactly the best example of womankind, though, is she? I mean, come on. A guy would have to be pretty desperate to go fishing in that lake, don't you think?'

Cody waits for the eruption from Webley, but she surprises him with how collected she remains.

'You don't really mean that,' she says.

This throws him. Cody sees it in his eyes. He was expecting belligerence, or at least disgust. Not a challenge like this.

'You think?' he answers. A weak riposte.

'I know,' she says. 'I can hear it in your voice. It's an act, and not a very good one either. You don't like us, and you don't like being here, and so you thought you might as well try to be as much of a pain in the arse as you can. Well, that's fine, Robert. If you want to act like a child, go ahead. Your other choice is to be adult about the situation by helping us solve the murders of two police officers. What are you going to be today – a grown-up or a five-year-old?'

Vernon does something odd then.

He cries.

He does it in silence. He stares at Webley for a full minute, and then a single tear beads in his right eye and rolls down the curve of his cheek.

Cody isn't sure he is seeing this at first, but then he notices how the left eye does the same. Vernon breaks contact with Webley. Stares straight ahead at the wall behind them instead. His expression doesn't alter; he makes no sound. But the tears continue to flow down his face until they are dripping softly onto the desk below.

It happens like this sometimes. They walk in acting big. Hard as nails. They mouth off and they swear and they pronounce their hatred. And then, as if by magic, the veneer cracks. Sometimes the trigger is a memory or a photograph or, as in this case, something the interviewing officer has said. It's as if Robert wanted to be himself all along. He just needed to be given permission.

'Robert,' says Cody. 'Are you okay?'

Robert has to open his mouth a couple of times before he can get the words out. 'He was my brother.'

From Webley: 'We know, Robert. We understand.'

'He was older than me. He wasn't all there in the head, but he was still my brother. He was polite and he was caring and he even had a good sense of humour. He would never have hurt a fly. He wouldn't have attacked those two police officers. He might not have understood what they wanted him to do, but he wouldn't have lashed out at them. He didn't have it in him. One time, I caught a load of kids who were teasing him and throwing stones at him. He just laughed, like it was a game. He could have crushed those kids in one hand. But he didn't. He just stood there and took it. That was my brother for you. That was Kevin.'

Says Webley, 'There must be a lot of hate and anger and distrust inside you. The loss of Kevin was a tragedy for your whole family. You needed someone to blame. But whatever mistakes the two officers might have made, they didn't set out with the intention of killing someone that night. They don't deserve to have been slaughtered like this. And believe me, what happened to this man and woman went way beyond straightforward murder. What was done to them was horrific, to say the least. There is a lunatic out there, Robert. Maybe you think he's done you a favour, but that doesn't make him a good guy. If I could go into detail about what he did, I am sure you would agree he shouldn't be on the streets. If you want to look at these killings as putting something straight for your family, then go ahead. But don't leave this killer out there, Robert. If you know anything about him – or even if you have the names of some people we could take a look at – then please help us.'

Cody finds a half-empty pack of tissues in his pocket and hands it across. 'Anything,' he says. 'A threat. A promise to get revenge for your family. Someone who just said weird things about the case.'

Robert pulls out a tissue and wipes his cheeks.

Webley leans closer to him. 'Robert? Is there something?'

Robert blows his nose. Gives a slight nod. Cody tries to hide his excitement.

'There was this guy. In a pub. I didn't know him from Adam, but he came over anyway. I didn't really want any company, but he insisted on buying me a drink. He knew who I was. He started going on about you lot. The police.'

'Saying what, exactly?'

'That you were the scum of the earth. That you were all bent. He said look at all the times the bizzies had shot unarmed suspects, or beaten the crap out of innocent people, and yet you always got away with it. Even when there was an inquiry, you lot always got off scot-free.'

'What did you say to that?'

'Not a lot. To be honest, I don't like talking about it – especially not to strangers. But this guy just kept rabbiting on. Getting on his soapbox. Telling me that something needed to be done about it.'

'But this was nothing specific, right? I mean, it was about the police force in general?'

'At first. But after he'd got a couple of more drinks down him, he brought the conversation back to Kevin. Asked me if I wanted to put things right.'

'Put things right? In what way?'

'Look, he'd had a few pints. I thought it was just the ale talking. People do that when they're pissed, don't they? They try to put the world to rights. Usually, it's all just—'

'In what way, Robert? What was he suggesting?'

'He said . . . He said he knew people. He said he could find things out.'

'What kind of things?'

'Like where the coppers lived. The ones who assaulted Kevin. He said he could find out where they lived and he could make sure they never did anything like that again. Ever.'

'Was he serious? Did you believe he could do those things?'

'No. Not at the time. Like I said, he was drunk. We all say things we don't mean when we're drunk. But now, after what's happened . . . well, I don't know. Maybe he meant what he said.'

Says Cody, 'What did you say to him, when he made this proposition?'

Vernon offers nothing but a stare.

'Robert? What was your reply?'

'You won't understand. You'll think I'm a terrible person. You don't know how I felt back then. My mum and dad, they were full of hate for the police. They still are. They told me what I should think, what I should feel. I didn't really want to hate like that, I swear. But everything they said was against you. Everyone was the same. Aunties, uncles, friends. They all said the same. I always try to see the other person's point of view, do you know what I mean? Sometimes I started to wonder if it was really all just a horrible mistake. Maybe Kevin really was just in the wrong place at the wrong time. Maybe those two coppers didn't really mean to hurt him. I thought that sometimes. But I could never say it. I wasn't even allowed to think it. My mum and dad would have hated me for it. I had to see it their way. Theirs was the right way. The only possible explanation of how things were.'

'Robert, what did you say to the man in the pub?'

'I told him . . . I told him to go ahead and kill them. And if he could kill any other coppers while he was at it, I'd buy him beers for the rest of his life.'

The silence that follows is weighty. Filled with meaning. Filled with shock and regret and the anticipation of where this information is to lead.

'What's his name, Robert?'

21

'His name is Gazza.'

'Gazza what?' says Blunt.

'He didn't know,' says Cody. 'All he got was Gazza.'

'Might not be a Gazza What,' says Ferguson. 'Might be a What Gazza.'

Blunt offers him one of her frostiest looks. 'What are you talking about, Neil?'

'He might not be a Gary. It could refer to his last name. Like Paul Gascoigne.'

'Whatever,' says Blunt. 'I want him found. Start in the pub where he came up to Robert Vernon.' She looks at Cody. 'Got a description?'

'Yeah. It's not brilliant, though. Vernon's excuse is that he was pretty drunk at the time, and can't remember the guy very well.' Cody consults his notes. 'Age about forty-five. Short dark hair, receding at the temples. A large hooked nose.'

'That's it? He has a drink with a man who offers to kill two police officers, and that's all he can recall?'

Cody shrugs. Blunt sighs.

'Well, it's more than we got from the other two,' she says. 'Mr and Mrs Vernon seem to see it as their civic duty to be as unhelpful to this investigation as possible. If nothing turns up on this Gazza bloke, we're going to have to take off the gloves with that family, despite what the Chief Super says.'

'Something about this doesn't ring true, though,' says Cody.

'In what way?'

'A guy comes up to you in the pub and offers to kill two coppers for you? Why would he do that? Some dickhead might say it as a sick joke when he was pissed, but to actually carry it out?'

'We still have to follow it up, Cody.'

'Of course we do. But even if this Gazza bloke was doing it as a favour to the Vernons, why do it in such a weird way? Why not just kill them quickly and get the hell out of there? What's with the birds and the messages?'

Blunt nods and looks around the room. 'Okay, so, theories. What's this maniac trying to tell us?'

No answers. No pearls of wisdom or leaps of the imagination.

Blunt tries prompting them: 'Edgar Allan Poe, and now a nursery rhyme. What's the connection?'

Says Cody, 'Other than the birds, maybe there isn't one. What I mean is, maybe the poems are secondary. Maybe the important thing is the birds.'

'Okay, so what would that mean? A raven, then a blackbird. They're the same colour. Anything else about them? Any other links?'

Another agonising silence.

'Christ,' says Blunt. 'All right, we go with what we've got, which isn't much. We've had no sightings of anyone suspicious at either scene. We've got no fingerprints to work with, no footprints, no fibres, nothing. All we've got is someone called Gazza. So find him!'

'Stay calm,' says Webley.

They are coming out of the station. On their way to track down the mysterious hit man who offers his services to strangers in pubs. Cody glances at Webley, puzzled by her warning and the delicate touch of her hand on his elbow.

But then Webley nods ahead of her, and he understands.

Dobson and his photographer accomplice. Waiting at their car. Dobby perched on the bonnet and sucking on a cigarette, a couple of crushed butts at his feet.

When he sees the detectives approaching, Dobson pushes himself up from the car and affixes an ugly smile.

Cody knows he should have expected this. Dobson is a mutt who doesn't relinquish his bone easily. Especially when he knows he already occupies a higher ground, given what happened yesterday.

'Say nothing,' Webley advises. 'We'll just get in the car and go.'

Cody has no intention of repeating the previous day's episode. He won't react, no matter what Dobson says or does.

But there is something different about the two media men today. They are playing it slow and easy. No snapping of pictures. No rapid-fire questions. They look almost like normal human beings.

Dobson lets his cigarette fall and grinds it into the pavement beneath his scuffed shoe.

'DS Cody. Nice to see you again. And you too, DC . . .'

'Webley.'

'Of course. How could I forget?'

'We're not stopping,' says Cody. 'Some of us have got work to do. And those cigarette butts count as litter. That's an offence.'

Dobson holds up his hands in a gesture of surrender. 'You're right,' he says. 'And you were right yesterday too. We were out of order. I apologise. Chris here apologises too, don't you, Chris?'

The photographer rubs his neck, as if recalling the feel of Cody's vice-like grip on it and debating whether he can find any forgiveness.

'Yeah,' he says, begrudgingly.

Says Cody, 'What is this, Dobby? It's not my birthday. Are you trying to earn a Scout badge or something?'

Dobson dredges up another disturbing smile. 'I'm trying out a new approach. I'm hoping it will prove more fruitful.'

'It won't,' says Cody, 'so don't waste the effort. I can see how hard it is for you to tap into your humanity. It must be buried pretty deep in there.'

Dobson puts a hand to his heart. 'Now you're hurting me, Cody. There's no need for that. I'm just trying to do my job. Just like you and . . .'

'Webley.'

'Webley here. Look, Chris isn't even taking any shots. We're being civilised about this.'

'Civilised,' says Chris, nodding his head. 'Even if you did try to choke me to death.'

Dobson shoots him a glare. 'Shut up, Chris.' Then back on Cody with the happy face. 'Believe it or not, we're on the same side. We can help you. Where would your investigations be without the media?'

This is true. Sometimes the press can be a great help. It just sounds odd coming out of the mouth of this despicable little man.

'What kind of help are you talking about, Dobby?'

'Who knows? We're good at finding things out. It's what we do. A lot of the time, we do it better than the police. I might be able to put some of that information your way.'

'Are you talking about something specific, or is this just hot air?'

'Nothing specific. Not yet, anyway. But think of us as an extra pair of investigators at your service. And don't deny that you could do with the extra manpower. I know how overstretched the force is. Tell us what you want to know, and we'll do our best to find the answers for you.'

'And in return?'

'Insights into the case. Don't worry, I'm not looking for anything top secret. I won't even mention your names. I just want to get a better feel for how your team is responding to these murders.'

Cody turns and looks at Webley. He detects a slight shake of her head, but he's already made that decision.

'I'll bear you in mind,' he says. 'But don't sit waiting by the phone.'

He starts to pull away, but Dobson persists, 'Don't underestimate our power, Cody. We've got a big circulation. How we report this can make all the difference to what people think about you and how you do things. The Vernons have got a lot of supporters. Most of them really don't trust the police. We can tip things one way or the other. We can confirm their prejudices or we can do something to put you in a better light. It's all about tone. We present the facts, sure, but it's how we wrap them up that really influences the impression they make in the minds of our readers.'

Cody halts. Takes a step towards the journalist.

'And you were doing so well, too. I should have known better. One thing you should understand about me, Dobby – I don't respond well to threats. People push, I tend to push back.'

Dobson adopts his surrender pose again, his expression full of feigned innocence. 'No threats. All I'm doing is offering a trade. Your inside story in return for a bit of promotion in our paper. How is that a threat?'

Cody shakes his head. 'You don't need me, Dobby. Do what you always do.'

He walks away now, heading for his unmarked saloon.

Dobson calls after him: 'Meaning what?'

Cody opens the car door. Pauses for a second.

'Meaning make it up. Doesn't matter what I tell you, or what anyone else tells you, you'll make up your own story. You'll write whatever you think will sell papers. It's what you people do. Have a nice day, Dobby.'

And then he gets into the car with Webley and drives away.

22

Cody knows they've been sussed as coppers as soon as they walk through the pub door. This isn't the kind of place that smart, well-groomed people in sharp suits tend to frequent. This is your jogging pants and trainers kind of place. Anything less than the strongest, most impenetrable of Scouse accents is a magnet for trouble in here.

They are in the Armitage. A small, dingy pub in Norris Green. To the uninitiated, Norris Green sounds like a wimpy character in a soap opera. Constantly wears a beige knitted pullover and corduroy trousers. In fact, Norris Green is anything but mild. People have been known to get shot here. If you're looking for someone who wants to kill coppers, this is as good a place as any to start. But Robert Vernon said he was in here just minding his own business when he was approached. Cody wonders what brought him here in the first place.

This time of day, it's not crowded. A few old geezers, reading the papers or watching the television on the wall as they down their pints. But there is a knot of four young scallies gathered at the pool table, and they lost interest in their game as soon as the strangers walked in. One of them issues a wolf-whistle. Cody suspects it's not aimed at him.

The detectives go straight to the bar. The barman – a stocky bloke with rolled-up shirtsleeves showing his Navy tattoos – has his back to them. He dries a beer glass and acts as though he hasn't noticed them. Cody knows it's a pretence: he saw the man glance their way when they arrived.

It's understandable, Cody thinks. Whether the barman has anything against the police or not, he can't risk appearing to be too friendly with the bizzies. Not in front of his customers. Not if he wants to keep running this pub for much longer. Not if he wants the pub to be standing here in the morning.

Cody knocks on the counter. Still the man doesn't turn around. Just keeps polishing his beer glass.

Says Cody, 'You're going to wear through that glass, the way you're going.'

The man turns. Not in any hurry. No welcoming smile. Nothing to indicate he's overly keen to talk.

Cody flashes his warrant card. 'I'm DS Cody. This is DC Webley. We're from Stanley Road police station.'

The bartender glances at the gang of scallies before replying. 'Stanley Road? Did you get lost, then? I've got a map back here somewhere.'

Sniggers from the lads. They start to move closer to the bar. Cody notices that two of them are still holding pool sticks. Another casually flips a cue ball from one hand to the other.

'No, we're not lost. This is exactly where we're meant to be.'

'Oh, yeah? Why's that, then?'

'We're investigating the murders of two police officers. Our inquiries brought us here.'

Cody sees a tinge of worry flash across the bartender's features. Rubbing out two coppers is serious shit, and he knows it.

It's not the barman who speaks next, but one of the pool players. 'What makes you think you'll find anything here?'

Cody turns. It's the man tossing the cue ball who spoke. He's in his early twenties. Dressed in a T-shirt and low-slung jeans, with an Everton scarf knotted loosely around his neck. Hair shaved so close it shows a number of scars and notches in his scalp. He's clearly the ringleader. His mates slowly spread out, surrounding the detectives. Cody sees the unease in Webley. He's starting to feel a little anxious himself, but he keeps calm. The one thing you need to do in a situation like this is maintain the air of authority. Give that up and you're dead meat.

'You look like a bunch of intelligent lads,' says Cody. 'I'm sure you could come up with lots of answers if you tried hard enough.'

Cue-Ball stares at Cody, obviously checking for sarcasm. Cody keeps his face straight.

'That's true. I was on *Mastermind* once. Me mates here were on *University Challenge*. Why? You looking to put a pub quiz team together?'

More sniggers. Sneers filled with contempt for Cody and lust for Webley.

Cody knows there is no reasoning with these men. They see themselves as above the law, and carry no respect for those enforcing it. No fear either. They see being arrested as a mere inconvenience. They know they will be free within a matter of hours. Nobody in this pub will speak against them. They could rip Cody and Webley apart, and everybody here would say the two detectives started the fight.

Webley says, 'Know anyone who'd be good answering questions on murder, do you?'

Cody hears the defensiveness in her tone. He's certain the others notice it too.

Cue-Ball's eyes widen as they turn on her. 'Funny enough, that's my specialist subject. What's yours, darling? I bet there's something you're really good at.'

He grins at her, showing a chipped tooth.

'What's your name, sunshine?' she demands.

Cue-Ball turns to his pals. 'D'ya hear that, lads? She wants to know my name. I think she fancies me.'

Laughter. Another wolf-whistle. Cody is starting to feel the situation slip away from him. He's not comfortable with that.

Slowly, deliberately, he turns his back on Cue-Ball. Faces the barman again. He signals Webley to do the same. Hesitantly, she follows suit.

'As I was saying, we're investigating the homicides of two police officers. I'm sure you've heard about them on the news.'

The barman looks over Cody's shoulder at the young man before he replies. 'Can't say I have.'

Cody smiles. 'Really? Are you certain about that? It's the top headline. You can't turn on a telly or a radio without hearing about it. Ringing any bells yet?'

The barman shifts his gaze again.

'Don't look at him,' says Cody. 'I'm the one asking the questions. Now, would you like to reconsider your answer?'

The bartender keeps his eyes fixed on Cody now. 'I . . . I might have heard about it. Yeah, come to think about it.'

'Good. Now we're getting somewhere. So here's my next question—'

'Hey!' This from Cue-Ball. 'Didn't your ma tell you it's not polite to turn your back on people? Or didn't you have parents?'

Cody continues to ignore him. 'You might have heard that allegations were made some time ago against the two murdered officers. The suggestion was that they were responsible for the death of a man called Kevin Vernon. You've heard this, right? I'm not telling you anything new here?'

Shakily, the barman nods. 'I've heard it.'

''Course he's heard it,' says Cue-Ball from behind Cody. 'Everyone's heard it. Everyone knows exactly what those two twats did to that guy. The poor bastard didn't even have all his marbles. Didn't stop you lot from beating the shit out of him, though, did it?'

Webley says, 'The brother of Kevin Vernon is called Robert. Ever come across him?'

The barman pulls a face and shakes his head.

Webley puts a photograph on the bar. 'This is Robert Vernon. Recognise him?'

Another shake of the head.

'Look again,' says Webley.

Cue-Ball says, 'Give us a flash, darling.'

Webley twists. Holds up the photograph. 'Do you know him?'

'Oh, him. Yeah.'

'Where from? In this pub?'

'Does he say he was in this pub? If he says he was, then yeah, he was in here. But if he says he was somewhere else, then he was there.'

Webley turns back to the bar. Shows a worried face to Cody.

We should cut our losses, thinks Cody. Get out of here before all hell breaks loose.

But not yet.

'Oh, come on, girl,' says Cue-Ball. 'Not you too. Him I can understand, but not you. I thought you liked me.'

Cody opens his mouth for another question, but is cut off by a shriek from Webley. He looks to see her pulling down her skirt. From the way the guy behind her is holding his pool stick, it's clear that he's just slid the tip of it up her leg. He is backing away, laughing. Saying, 'Sorry, love. It was an accident. It slipped.'

Cody sees the fury and the embarrassment on Webley's face. Hears her threaten to arrest the man who has just assaulted her.

But it only just filters through to him.

Things have gone strangely fuzzy. A part of his mind is moving away, stepping outside all this. He struggles to make sense of what is being said or done. He goes to another time, another place. A dark, dark past. The voices change. Images flash of other men surrounding him. Not these wankers, but real hard men. Cody's pulse steps up as he starts to remember the pain. The physical and mental pain.

No, he thinks. Not now. Not here. Get out. Get out of my head.

He returns. Somehow manages to claw his way back into this shithole of a pub. Somehow manages to become conscious again of these four no-marks attempting to justify their pathetic existence, if only to themselves. They are screaming with laughter. The one who assaulted Webley is holding the pool cue at his groin and saying, 'I can't help it. It just pops up when it feels like it.'

Cody knows he should get out of here. He can come back with an army if he needs to. Right now he should just get out.

But still he fixes his attention on the barman. Still he puts his questions. He knows it's a mistake and yet he cannot help himself. Something inside, something stubborn and obsessive within is driving him down this mine-strewn path, and he can't stop it.

'Robert Vernon says he met someone in here. A man called Gazza. Do you know who that might be?'

The barman shakes his head. He no longer wants to speak. He doesn't want to play any part in what must surely come next. His eyes tell Cody to leave him be, to allow him to get on with his simple job of serving beer. He wants no trouble here.

'It's a common enough name,' says Cody. 'Loads of people are called Gazza. Are you seriously telling me you've never served anyone called Gazza in this pub?'

'Look, I don't ask for names, okay? They ask for a drink, I serve it, they pay. That's it. I don't ask who they are, and I don't ask if they've killed any coppers lately. All right?'

'Who said anything about him being the one who killed the officers?'

The barman stares long and hard at Cody. 'Get out of my pub. You're not welcome here.'

And that should be it. Except that Cue-Ball says, 'You're asking the wrong bloke. You wanna know about Gazza, you should be asking me.'

Cody turns. 'You know this Gazza, do you?'

'Yeah. I know him.'

'Regular customer?'

'Oh, yeah.'

'What's he look like?'

'Tall. Good looking.'

Which doesn't chime with Robert Vernon's description. Cody starts to think this is a wind-up.

'Where can I find him?'

'He's right in front of you. I'm Gazza.'

For some reason, the man finds this hilarious. He slaps the white cue ball in the palm of his hand and descends into hysterics.

'My name's Gazza too,' says another of the scallies.

'Yeah, and me.'

'We're the Gazza gang,' says Cue-Ball through his tears of laughter. 'Do you wanna join us? Are you a Gazza? What about your girlfriend there? Is she one?' He calls over to Webley: 'What about it, love? Wanna join the Gazza gang?'

Cody looks across at Webley. She connects with his gaze, nods for them to leave.

She's right. It's time to go. They will get nothing useful here. Not while these four pricks are around to cause interference.

And he thinks he could actually leave now. Despite the mental fog that enveloped him earlier, he thinks he has recovered, and that he has proven a point. He could walk out of here with his head held high.

Except for one thing.

Cue-Ball has other ideas. Cue-Ball has one last set of thoughts to lay out in front of Cody.

The young man stops laughing. He cuts it off suddenly, like nothing humorous was ever there. His mates, too, respond to the new seriousness with deadly silence of their own.

Then he steps forward. Moves right up to Cody. He is tossing the pool ball again. From left hand to right, right hand to left. It's as though it's a metronome for his words as he pours them out at Cody.

Left . . .

'Don't know if you've figured it out in that tiny brain of yours yet . . .'

Right . . .

'. . . but we don't like pigs coming in here.'

Left . . .

'We don't like the way they stick their ugly little snouts in our business.'

Right . . .

'And they smell, too.'

Left . . .

'Well, I suppose if you spend all day digging in shit . . .'

Right . . .

'. . . you're bound to have a bit of a stink on you.'

Left . . .

He continues like this, his language becoming more colourful, more aggressive, more threatening. He starts to warn of what could happen if Cody and his 'piece of skirt' ever come back again.

He doesn't know what he's starting.

He doesn't seem to understand that bizzies don't normally behave like this. Most coppers, they would either ignore him or get all heavy with him. Not this copper, though. This copper just keeps staring at him, without saying a word. This copper just stands there and takes it, the thick bastard.

But Cue-Ball really doesn't know.

He can't see into Cody's head. He can't see the swirling, the unravelling, the craziness. He can't see the horrors flying and screeching out of their dark corners. He can't see what his promises of violence, of mutilation, are doing to his target. What drawers they are opening. What switches they are flicking.

Left . . .

Right . . .

And then no left.

There is no left because the ball has been snatched in mid-air by Cody.

There is a moment of sharing. A fraction of a second during which the reckless, foolish young man is permitted to reflect on what he has just done.

But he's not the most quick-witted of people, this man. Doesn't have the speediest of reactions, either.

Cody proves that to him when he grabs hold of the man's Everton scarf and twists it tightly into his throat. He proves it when he drags the man backwards across the room and throws him onto a table. And he proves it when he raises his other hand – the one still holding the pool ball – and brings it crashing down with all his might . . .

. . . into the table.

'Wanna mess with me, do ya?' he yells into the scally's face. 'Wanna mess with me, you fucking piece of shit?'

And while all this is happening he doesn't care what anybody else is doing. He's not even aware that the scumbag's mates are bouncing up and down and baring their teeth and waving their wooden sticks and shrieking like enraged apes in a zoo. He's not aware that Webley is having to deal with this all on her own by standing in their way and screaming threats of arrest. All Cody knows is that the man in front of him went a step too far, and now he's going to pay for it with his face. It's too late to walk away now. Nothing can stop what is about to happen.

Nothing, that is, except Webley.

Her hand is gentle, warm, as it smothers his fist. There is no tension in her hand, no attempt to match his strength. But somehow the tenderness is a greater force. Somehow it seeps into his arm and robs it of its pent-up energy.

'Cody,' she says. 'That's enough. He's not worth it.'

Things swim back into focus. The object of his hatred turns into a terrified youth with wide eyes and a quivering lower lip.

Cody releases his hold on the scarf. Pats it down on the man's chest as if that trivial gesture might restore order.

He steps away from the youth. Webley stands behind him, her hand on his elbow urging him out of the pub. The bartender and his customers stare at them in silence, their low opinions of the police sucked even further into the mire. One of the pool players is obviously still filled with adrenalin. He rocks on the balls of his feet and clutches his cue in sweaty hands, on the edge of continuing the aggression.

'Catch,' says Cody.

He tosses the ball to the youth, who fumbles it and drops both ball and stick to the floor with a clatter that embarrasses him into inaction.

Webley continues to escort him outside. Once there, she urges him to hurry up.

'Come on, Cody. We need to go. One phone call, that's all it takes. One phone call and we'll have a riot on our hands.'

She pushes him down the street. Gets the car open and crams him inside. Then she jumps behind the wheel and rockets them away from there.

'What the hell, Cody?' she yells. 'What was that?'

'He deserved it. He was wearing an Everton scarf.'

'Not funny, Cody. Not funny at all. I don't know what's going on with you. You could have walked away. You didn't have to stand there, taking what he was dishing out. And you certainly didn't need to start a bloody fight. Jesus! There were four of them. Four! They could have broken every bone in your body. Mine too, for that matter. Not to mention losing our jobs if somebody reports this.'

'Nobody will report it. Those morons aren't going to own up to being made to piss their pants by one guy. And everyone else in that pub is either too scared or too anti-police to open their mouths.'

'And all this went through your head, did it? While that arsehole was having a go at you, you thought all this through, I suppose? Or would it be more accurate to say that you weren't thinking straight at all? You know what, Cody? What you did makes you no better than them. You were a hooligan in there. A Neanderthal. You should know better.' And then she adds, 'Sergeant.'

He wants to smile. Her little nod towards his rank is a cute touch in someone who just tore a strip off him.

But the smile doesn't find its way through his misery. He knows what he did in there was wrong. It went against everything he stands for, everything he has been trained to do. Webley is right: he sank to their level. He lowered himself to become one of the baying, bloodthirsty vermin who live and die by violence, intimidation and anti-social behaviour. He wasn't a policeman in there. He was just another scally.

He realises that Webley has pulled the vehicle into a supermarket car park. She puts on the handbrake and turns in her seat to face him. Her expression and her voice both soften.

'What is it, Cody? What's bothering you? I can help, you know. We might not be together anymore, but that doesn't mean I don't give a toss about you. I'm not that heartless. You need to talk – if not to me, then someone. It's not good for you to keep it all bottled up.'

'You think that was bottling it up?' he asks.

'Well, no. Not exactly. But my worry is there's still more in there, just waiting to be let out.'

'I'm okay.'

'No. No, you're not okay. What you did in that pub wasn't okay. What you did to that idiot photographer wasn't okay. The way you reacted to that post-mortem wasn't okay. You're not okay, Cody. You need help.'

You need help. He wonders how many times has that been said to him. It'll be exactly the same number of times he's ignored it.

'I don't need help. I've just got some . . . some shit going on in my life.'

'Haven't we all? And maybe your pile of shit is bigger than most. But do you really think going around terrorising people is going to reduce the size of it?'

'People need to stop getting in my face.'

He knows it's a piss-poor statement as soon as he utters it. A Neanderthal statement, to use Webley's expression. He braces himself for the response.

'No. That's the job, Cody. You don't need me to tell you that. Our job involves people getting in our faces a million times a day. If you can't handle that, then you should be asking yourself if it's time for a career change.'

The wave of anger hits him before he has a chance to get out of its way. 'All right, Megan, pack it in! I don't need advice from you or anyone else about quitting the job. Do you understand that?'

There is too much force in his words. Webley recoils. Her face reddens.

'I-I'm sorry,' she says. 'I was just . . . I was just trying . . .'

He sighs heavily. 'No, no. It's me. I should be the one saying sorry. I get defensive when people try to tell me I shouldn't be a copper.'

'Why? Why has that started bothering you?'

He shrugs. 'It's all I've got left.'

He doesn't say this to elicit pity, but he sees from her face that he's getting it anyway.

'What makes you say that?'

'Because it's true. I know it's a cliché, but I really am married to the job. You know it's all I ever wanted to do, from when I was just a kid. It's one of the reasons we split up. But lately it's got worse. I've become obsessive about it. It only takes someone to suggest that it might be taken away from me, and I freak out.'

She smiles. 'I'm like that about my clothes. You should have heard the fights between me and my sister when we were little.'

He manages to produce a faint smile of his own. 'I'm really sorry. I mean about the way I've been. I put you in danger in that pub. I should never have done that. I wasn't thinking. That's part of the problem. Sometimes I act before I think. Look, if you want to, I can team you up with someone else.'

Her eyes widen. 'Are you joking? And miss all the fun? Besides . . .'

'What?'

'I'd only end up worrying about you. Wondering if you were okay.'

'Seriously?'

'Of course. Like I said, I'm not heartless.'

He could hug her. He could lean across and hug her tightly for her kindness. But that wouldn't be right. Not right at all.

He stares through the windscreen as he tries to put his head back together. He sees an old man loading up the boot of his Micra with bags of shopping. Every time the man lifts a bag, he puts a hand to his back in obvious pain. Without hesitation, Cody gets out of the car and crosses the car park to help the man load his shopping.

When he returns, he finds Webley staring at him, her expression a blend of surprise and amusement.

'What?' he says.

'You. I'd forgotten about your little acts of charity. Nice to see some things haven't changed about you.'

He shrugs. 'So I've still got some redeeming features, then?'

'I suppose there's still hope for you. You can still be saved.'

'Talking about saving me . . . You know that favour I asked you? Do you mind if it grows a bit bigger?'

'Already sorted. We went to the pub, we asked some questions, we got no answers, and we left. Nothing more to add, is there?'

'No. Nothing more to add. Thank you.'

But he wonders how many more of his misdemeanours he can ask Webley to contain before she snaps.

23

The sight of the house always brings forth a deluge of memories for Cody.

He's alone now, sitting in his own car on the quiet street. It has been a tough day in many ways. Two police officers are now dead, and MIT don't have a whole lot to show for their investigation into such high-profile killings. Cody himself has spent all day chasing down paths that have led him nowhere very useful. He has lost count of the number of people he has spoken to, the number of times he has picked up the phone, the number of reports he has written, read, filed or requested, the number of questions to which he has failed to supply answers.

It would help if they had some forensics to work with. But the killer is proving himself too clever for that. 'Forensically aware' is the term the police use. He leaves behind not even a hair. It's as if he's a ghost.

It might also help if they could locate this Gazza bloke. But then that requires a degree of tact and professionalism that Cody feels a little short of at the moment.

What an embarrassing mess. No, let's get indignant here: what a complete and utter fuck-up.

It depresses him. He feels inadequate. A lousy copper. He handled that situation in the pub about as badly as is possible. If those other three dickheads had decided to pile in, instead of hanging about like demented monkeys, then . . . well, it doesn't bear thinking about. Nobody in their right mind starts a fight against an opposition like that.

So maybe that's it. He's not in his right mind. He's sick and he's never going to get better and he should get out of this business before he or somebody close to him gets hurt.

Webley, for instance. He would hate to see her come to harm. Would hate it even more if it was through some action of his own. Like going berserk in a pub, for instance.

He hates living like this. Hates having to accept that the past is ruling his present and threatening his future.

This is the past. This house. A small end terrace in Fairfield. As with Stoneycroft, the name of this neighbourhood belies its appearance. There are no fields, and it cannot be regarded as being especially fair, rubbing shoulders as it does with Kensington, home of the Vernons. It has no pretensions.

Neither does this house. It could do with a new front door. It's still missing a chunk of wood from when Cody's dad forgot his key and kicked it open. If he'd bothered knocking, he'd have discovered that his wife was inside and could have opened it. But presence of mind tends to evaporate faster than alcohol when the two meet.

To the right of the house is an alleyway, and then a small hill leading up to a weed-infested patch of grass that doesn't seem to belong to any of the houses on the street. It's actually more of a slope than a hill, but when Cody was a kid it felt like Mount Everest. He remembers racing his toy cars down it, and flying down it himself in his plastic sledge when it snowed. That was before he discovered the delights of the much bigger hills in Newsham Park, a short walk from here.

Memories.

Really, he could do without this. He almost wishes he hadn't driven here. It's been such a shit day, and this isn't going to make it any less shit.

And then he thinks, So what? Most of my days are shit. Might as well get it over with.

He sighs. Gathers up the flowers and chocolates from the passenger seat. Carnations and Thorntons, because he knows his mother loves both of those. Gets out of the car.

He stands at the front door for a full minute, just staring at the hole left by that missing piece of wood. Thinking. Remembering.

He knocks eventually. Voices inside. The door opens.

It's Frankie. His sister. Three years younger than him, and as bright and bubbly as ever. She at least is delighted to see him. She pounces on him, crushes him in a hug, asks him how he's been, pulls him into the house, into his past. Familiar sights, familiar sounds, familiar smells. Like he never left. But he did. He had to. And sometimes he wishes he could come back here properly. Just walk in the door, using a key of his own. Throw his bag on the floor and hang his jacket on the peg and put the kettle on and grab some biscuits from the cupboard and just . . . be at home.

Home. Such a lovely warm word. This *was* his home, once.

Frankie calls her mother into the hallway. Cody waits. Feels the apprehension.

But she's alone when she appears. Despite this, her face still betrays her inner conflict. Any pleasure to see him is tempered by anxiety, fear. She smiles, but it looks forced, and her eyes dart constantly to the front door, either in expectation of arrival or in a less-than-subtle hint that he should leave. He knows she loves him – *knows* this – but sometimes it can be hard to believe. Sometimes it is too easy to read her discomfort as a desire to be left in peace. And sometimes he thinks he should do just that. Sever the ties once and for all.

But this is family. Arguably not much of one, but the only one he's got.

He wishes her a happy birthday. Hands over the flowers and chocolates. She smiles, says little. It's left to Frankie to remark on how beautiful the carnations are, and how much she's looking for- ward to scoffing all the pralines. An awkward silence follows, while they stand together in the hallway.

I should go, thinks Cody. This isn't working. Best if I leave now.

But Frankie is having none of it. She speaks the words her mother should be saying. Asking him to come through and have a quick cuppa.

So he does. Hang the consequences. Why shouldn't he have a cup of tea in his own mother's house?

There's a small wooden dining table in the middle of the kitchen. It always amazes Cody how they and a varied selection of relatives all used to cram around it at Christmas time. Not a concern, though. He pulls out a chair and drops into it while Frankie busies herself with making the tea.

She asks about the job, about the murders. He responds as enthusiastically as he can, but reveals only what is already in the public domain. He asks her about her work, her boyfriend, her hectic social life, the latest gossip. He wishes his mother would chip in more, but she says little. Offers a smile now and again, the odd yes or no or non-committal hum, the occasional jump at the slightest sound from the front of the house.

He asks her then. Puts it to his mother directly. He could avoid the subject altogether. That would make life easy for everyone. But why should he? How much worse can things get?

So he asks her how his dad is.

She whitens, and Frankie goes deathly quiet as she permits her mother to deal with this on her own.

She tells him his father is fine. He has put on more weight. Gone a little more grey.

And the drinking?

Yes, well, he still likes a pint. No change there.

She laughs as she says this, but there is no underlying amusement. Cody wishes sometimes that she would just tell the truth – that she hates the way her husband drinks too much, hates the way he spends all his money on booze and cigarettes, hates the way he seems increasingly unable to find time for his own family, his own wife. He wishes she would scream and rant and let the tears of frustration out.

But she doesn't do that. She would never do that. She just carries on with the pretence, even though everyone sees through it.

And, he wants to ask, what about me? Does Dad ever mention me?

But what's the point? He knows the answer already. Why open himself up to yet another stab into his chest?

But it's as if even thinking about it provokes some cosmic prankster into providing him with a definitive reply. Straight from the horse's mouth, as it were.

The bang of the front door is almost enough to give his mother a heart attack. She leaps out of the chair. Starts to come around the table so that she can intercept her husband in the hallway.

Cody grabs her wrist. Smiles into a face that is creased with more worry lines than her age merits. Tells her it's okay, that she doesn't have to keep trying to be the peacemaker. Just let it be.

With a great deal of uncertainty, she sits again. Frankie gives Cody a look that is filled with concern, and again he smiles back.

His father flings open the door into the kitchen and fills the space with his presence. He has always seemed a large, powerful man to Cody. He is obviously no longer as fit as he was, but he still cuts a formidable figure. A cigarette dangles from his lips. He is on the verge of saying something, but then he sees who is at his table and his mouth clamps shut. He stares for a while, as if working out how this has come to pass. The cigarette flares as he sucks air through it, as if he's lighting it with his own inner burning rage. Then he exhales the smoke through his nostrils like a snorting bull. When he finds his tongue again, it is to address his wife, the previous object of his attention now summarily dismissed. He tells her he will be in the living room, and that he'd like a cup of tea in there. And then he's gone, without another glance at Cody.

There's a silence, a coldness, an emptiness. Cody clears his throat and jokes that there's no place like home, but the awkwardness persists and pervades. Frankie, her eyes downcast, looks mortified and on the edge of tears. Cody's mother bears an expression filled with a complex mixture of sorrow and shame and anger and regret and a million other fragments of emotion.

Did he expect anything else? No, of course he didn't. Sometimes, though, there is that tiny nugget of hope. The one that says, *Maybe, just maybe, this time will be different*. It never is. He should consign that nugget to the flames of despondency where it belongs.

It wasn't always like this. In many ways that makes it even harder to bear. If his father had always been so antagonistic towards him, he could handle the atmosphere better. He would have no other yardstick for comparison – no shiny bright ruler marking off the fullness and happiness of a past relationship.

Cody's mistake was in joining the police.

He doesn't know why it should have come as such a shock to his parents. The signs were always there. When he played cops and robbers, he always had to be the cop. His favourite television programmes were the cop shows. His favourite books were crime thrillers. He had toy police cars, police helicopters, police speed-boats – mostly bought with his own pocket money. His folks had seemed okay with that; or at least they never made a fuss about it. Perhaps they believed it was best for him to get it out of his system, and that he'd soon grow out of it.

As he got older, he began to understand their true feelings. At least, they were the feelings of his father. Cody has always suspected that his mother's views are more reasonable, although he knows she would never admit it. He doesn't know where those opinions originated – his dad was never able to provide a direct or convincing answer to that one when challenged – but they overflowed with hatred and distrust of the boys and girls in blue. Naturally enough, the constant berating and condemnation of the police had a profound influence on the young, impressionable Cody. Naturally enough, he chose to walk in the opposite direction to that so emphatically taken by his elders.

Took him a while, though.

Even as an A-level student considering his future, he chose the path of least resistance. He wanted to keep his parents happy. He wanted their support. He wanted their love. And so he chose to sign up for a university degree in English.

It lasted all of a year.

His heart was never in it. And the fact that he spent most of that year unencumbered by the prejudices of his parents pretty much sealed the deal.

He applied to join the police as soon as he finished the second semester.

Breaking the news to his parents was never going to be easy. He knew that. He prepared himself for a certain amount of disapproval. What he did not expect was to be made a pariah in his own family home.

So this is it. This is what he gets every time. A mother who can't show her love, and a father who seems to have no love left to show. His trips here are becoming less and less frequent, because what is the point? Each visit leaves him feeling like he's walked in and told them he's a rapist or a paedophile. Come to think of it, that might not be so bad in their eyes.

His mother gets up from the table and leaves the room. Seconds later, Cody hears raised voices, then full-on yelling.

He looks at Frankie. There are tears forming in her eyes. His mother's birthday, and people are crying and screaming at each other. Happy Birthday, Mum.

He tells Frankie he thinks he should go now, and she doesn't argue the point. She escorts him to the door. Only silence from the living room now. No sign of his mother. His father has won, as he always does.

On the doorstep, Frankie tells him she is sorry, and then she goes back inside. Out here it is starting to rain. Cody turns up his collar and heads back to his car. As he does so, another car pulls up behind his. A white BMW X5. Personalised number plate, but Cody knows who it is. Not many cars like that park in this road.

The man who gets out is taller, broader and more handsome than Cody. At least that's what Cody thinks. He always did look up to his older brother in that way. Now Warren is considerably richer too. Flash car, flash watch, flash everything. But it's how he earns his money that's the problem for Cody. He doesn't know details – doesn't *want* to know details – but it's a career path that's very much at odds with his own. One day they will clash. That seems inevitable, given what they do. For now, ignorance is bliss. Cody has enough problems with his parents without becoming involved in the arrest and imprisonment of their only other son. Their *only* son, if his father is asked his opinion.

The brothers don't shake hands, but they exchange pleasantries. Warren eyes up Cody's rust-bucket of a car. Cody eyes up the massive bouquet that Warren is carrying, along with the bag from Ernest Jones the jeweller's. They both make excuses about getting out of the rain, and it's over. Cody is always left wondering on which side of a police cell door he will next see his brother.

He gets into his car, but doesn't drive away immediately. He keeps an eye on the house.

The front door is yanked open at Warren's knock, and their father is there. There is fury on his face, and he is clearly ready for a fight, clearly ready to tell the visitor that he can go to hell and never come back.

But then his dad sees who it is at the door, and his countenance changes. A smile on his face that Cody has not seen in a long time. A firm shake of his cherished son's hand. A pat on the shoulder as he is welcomed in. Laughter. Words.

Cody watches all this through the veil of raindrops on his window.

Then he puts his heart back together and drives away.

24

More married than a wedded couple.

That's how it often seems to Brian Kearney. Of course, there's no sex. Not even kissing or fondling. It's all strictly platonic.

So, yeah, just like a marriage.

'What are you smiling at?'

Kearney looks at his questioner in the passenger seat. Andrea Whitland is giving him one of her 'don't lie, because I know exactly what you're thinking' looks.

And she probably does, too. God knows, they spend enough time in each other's company. Cooped up in this patrol car for hours on end sometimes. Been that way for years. They know each other intimately now. Okay, maybe not intimately, not in the biblical sense, but there's no way you can work so closely and so long with someone and not get to know pretty much everything there is to know about them.

Kearney knows what Whitland's favourite sexual position is. He knows what schools she went to, and the name of her first boyfriend. He knows she hates coconut but loves cherries. He knows she's good at badminton but lousy at poker. He knows she's allergic to cats and has a butterfly tattoo on her left buttock. He knows she once had a miscarriage. He knows she loves watching *Mamma Mia!*.

Above all, he knows he can trust her and rely on her.

He imagines it's the same for Whitland. The things he must have told her over the years. Some of them he's never even told his wife.

But that's okay. What is said in this car goes no further. That's why it works between them. They both know the other is always there for them.

'I was thinking about me missus,' he says, answering her question.

'You lying hound,' says Whitland. 'You never smile when you're thinking about Debbie. The only times you mention her are when you're having a good moan about her.'

'That's not true. I'm very fond of my wife, I am. In fact, I'm taking her out on the town in a couple of weeks.'

'Oh, yeah? What's that in aid of, then?'

'Halloween. It's the only night I can bring her out of the house without getting funny looks from people.'

Whitland slaps him on the bicep. 'You rotten thing. Just wait till I see Debbie. You're in for a dog's life, mate.'

'Actually, that wouldn't be so bad. You should see the way she treats that stupid puppy I got her.'

'Aw, puppies are so cute.'

'You wouldn't be saying that if you kept finding wet patches on your bed and poo on your kitchen floor.'

'You *have* met my husband, haven't you?'

Kearney laughs. 'Speaking of which, did you hear about that wino that Carney brought in last night?'

Whitland pulls a face. 'Ooh, yeah. Disgusting. What the hell was he thinking, carrying a turd around in his pocket?'

'God knows. Loved to have seen Carney's face when he found it in the search, though.'

'Ha! I hope he handed it in at the desk. Might be the fella's prized possession.'

The radio blares into life: 'Control to Delta Two.'

Whitland takes the call. 'Delta Two. Go ahead, Control.'

'Delta Two, we've had a report of a couple of teenaged lads acting suspiciously near the church on Sheil Road. Can you check it out, over?'

'Will do. On our way.'

Kearney puts his indicator on and waits to do a U-turn to head back towards Sheil Road.

'First bit of excitement for the night,' he says.

'Is that what you call excitement? Telling a couple of kids it's way past their bedtime?'

'I'm easily pleased, me.'

'Hmm. Not according to your Debbie.'

They get to Sheil Road. Many of the houses here have been converted into flats. It's a busy thoroughfare in the daytime, but fairly quiet at this time of the night. The church is small and low and unremarkable. Set back from the pavement, it is barely noticeable from the street. A low wall surrounding the property is surmounted by vicious-looking spiked metal railings.

Kearney parks outside the main gate and kills the engine.

'Looks quiet to me. Suppose we'd better check it out, though.'

The two officers get out of the car. Kearney locks it up. Just in case.

They move closer to the gate. Kearney yanks on it to check it's locked. Then he flicks on his torch and shines it into the church grounds.

'See anything?'

'Nope.'

Kearney spends a few more seconds scanning the area, before nodding to Whitland to follow him. He walks to the corner of the block, then moves up the side street, continually shining his torch through the railings. They come across another set of gates, leading to the church car park. Kearney rattles these too, and finds them also locked.

He moves to the left of the church, where an alley separates it from the neighbouring houses. A big black gate guards the entrance to the alley, one of hundreds installed by the council some years ago to cut down on crime and fly-tipping. Back in the time when it still had some money.

'Gate's open,' says Kearney. He winks at Whitland. 'Fancy coming up this entry with me, darling?'

'You're such a romantic. How could a girl refuse?' She clicks her radio transmitter. 'Delta Two to Control.'

'Control.'

'We're at the church. Nothing to report. The alley gate has been left unlocked, so we'll just take a quick butcher's up there.'

'Roger that.'

Whitland switches on her own torch, then follows Kearney along the alley. Their beams of light pick out a million sparkling fragments of broken glass. Overstuffed black bin bags dot the landscape like unexploded bombs.

The officers move along. Steadily, stealthily. Watching, listening. To their right is the tall, sheer side wall of the church building itself. Its plain glass windows are enclosed in wire mesh. There is no way into it from here. To their left are the much lower walls protecting the back yards of a row of houses. Set into these walls, stark wooden doors are bolted and padlocked against intruders. A few of the walls are topped by vicious shards of broken glass fixed in cement. Most of the houses beyond are shrouded in darkness. Where lights are still on, curtains are tightly drawn. Nobody wants to know what goes on in these alleys in the dead of night.

They reach a junction. Kearney remembers being here before. They are at one corner of a walled courtyard containing garages. Alleys surround the courtyard on all four sides. The last time Kearney was here, kids had been climbing the scaffolding behind one of the sets of flats. The call-out wasn't so much to do with the kids as it was to deal with a nutcase resident who had chased them away with a samurai sword.

'You go round that way,' says Whitland, 'and I'll go up here.'

'And I'll be in Scotland afore ye,' says Kearney.

'I don't think there's anyone here, but we've got them trapped if we do that.'

Kearney nods. 'Those little grey cells of yours are working well tonight.'

'I have my moments. Off you trot. And remember, you only have to call if you get scared of the dark. Don't just stand there and wet yourself, like you did last time.'

'No worries. I've got my plastic incontinence pants on tonight. They're already half full.'

Whitland grimaces. 'Too much information, PC Kearney.'

Smiling, Kearney takes the right turn, heading back towards Sheil Road.

There's nobody here, he thinks. The streetwise kids in this neighbourhood have a nose for trouble. They'll have scarpered ages ago. And even if we do catch them, the most we can do is tell them to go home.

He plays his torchlight over the walls as he walks, studying the graffiti. Someone called 'Robbo' seems to have enjoyed announcing his presence at some point in time. Pity about his lack of artistry though.

Could do better myself, thinks Kearney.

There's a fridge here, with its door hanging off. Reminds him he needs to defrost his own, before Debbie has another moan about not being able to get at the fish fingers without crampons and a Sherpa.

He reaches the corner. A left turn here will take him around the courtyard, to meet up with Whitland. But straight on is a huge mound of rubbish. Not interesting in itself, but was that a noise it made?

He thinks it was. A rustling sound.

He turns the torchlight on it. Starts to walk towards it. Mostly just bin bags, but there's a tall, narrow cardboard box here, standing on its end. It's big enough to hold a person.

Kearney gets closer. He hears a car and a lorry go past on Sheil Road. Not much else. His gaze is fixed on the box.

It's going to be empty, he thinks. Bound to be. Why would someone be hiding in a cardboard box in the middle of an entry at this time of night? That would just be ridiculous.

But then he thinks he hears another noise, accompanied by the tiniest of movements of the box. And so he's withdrawing his baton, getting ready to whack someone if they insist on playing this game, because this is not funny now, this is starting to irritate me and yes, if I'm honest, scaring me a little, so come out now you little bastard before I take your fucking head off your shoulders.

The box is sodden with the rain from earlier. Kearney sees now that it is open, but that the open side has been turned to the wall. Between the box and the wall is a gap of a few inches.

I should say something, he thinks. I should order whoever is in there to come out now. But that would be stupid, because there isn't anyone in there, and even though there is nobody around to see or hear me, I'm going to feel a right dick talking to an empty box.

There is nobody in there, all right? Nobody.

And then he's reaching out. Before he allows his reason to play it safe by countermanding the order, he is reaching out and sliding his fingers into that gap and grasping the box and yanking it away from the wall.

Movement. Lots of movement. Falling and tumbling. A jumping, too. Something not caused by mere gravity. Something that has life and animation. Something that comes directly at him with great speed.

Kearney yells. Leaps back. Legs pedalling furiously to get him away from that thing, that . . .

Cat.

It's a cat. You see that, Kearney, you idiot? That tiny little ball of fluff now doing sixty miles an hour down the jigger? It's a moggie, you div. There wasn't anything in this box other than a cat having its supper. Which you knew all along, didn't you? You said as much, so why the hell did you have to be such a knob?

He shines his torch on the garbage that was hidden by the box. It's clear that one of the bags has been shredded by the cat's claws. Among the crap that has spilled out of the hole is a chicken carcass. Still shiny and wet, it looks to have been left there fairly recently. A nice find for a hungry animal.

Sorry, puss.

He comes away with a smile on his face. Debates whether to tell Whitland about the cat. Decides he will. She will tease him mercilessly, but he quite enjoys it.

The noise of sheet metal is a monstrous roar in the stillness.

He clicks his radio button. 'Andrea. You there?'

She responds immediately. 'Yeah. Stop panicking. One of the garage doors hasn't been shut properly. Just checking it out. Found anything?'

'Nah. Let's call it in and head back.'

'Okay. Give me a minute.'

He resumes his circuit of the walled courtyard, scanning the backs of the houses as he goes. Something squelches underfoot, and he's convinced he's just trodden in dog shit. So that'll be nice in the car on the way back.

Another metallic groan, followed by an almighty clang. He doesn't react this time. It's just Whitland closing the garage properly.

He scrapes his shoe along the floor, hoping to remove at least some of the muck, then continues on his way. He turns the next corner. Whistles a tune through his teeth. Reaches the opening to the courtyard.

Empty.

A row of closed garage doors to the left of him, another to the right, and a whitewashed wall opposite. Nothing else. No kids, no PC Whitland.

'Andrea?' he calls. Then louder: 'Andrea? If this is a wind-up . . .'

But still nothing.

He clicks his radio button. 'Andrea? Are you still on scene? Where are you?'

He gets white noise.

And now his heart is thumping again. This isn't right. He hates practical jokes, but at the same time he hopes this is a prank. He hopes she is about to jump out and frighten the living daylights out of him so at least he can get this over with. But Andrea doesn't do practical jokes. It's not her style.

He spins on his heels, trying to solve this mystery. Wondering where the hell Andrea has gone. Is she giving chase? If she's in pursuit, surely she would have called it in. She wouldn't just—

A noise. To his right. A tap against the metal door of one of the garages. It's very slight, like someone brushing against it by accident rather than trying to attract attention.

Kearney whips out his baton. Steps cautiously towards the door. Someone is hiding on the other side of it. Not a cat this time. Definitely not just a cat.

He's not sure what to do. This is too weird. Andrea wouldn't be hiding in there – she just wouldn't do that. But if she's not in there, then where the fucking hell is she? And if it's not Andrea, then who is it?

He debates calling for backup. Yeah, he could get a vanload of hairy-arsed coppers in riot gear standing alongside him while he opens the garage door. And then he could suffer the teasing and laughter when all he finds there is a pink Fiat Panda with fluffy dice in the window.

Because that's all this is, he tells himself. You misheard. Nobody's in there. So let's just fucking prove it, shall we?

He bends at the knees, his eyes fixed on the door. One of his joints cracks in complaint. His breathing becomes a flutter. Because his left hand is carrying a torch, he has to tuck his baton under his arm while he reaches for the door handle.

He counts to three. Tries to muffle the doubts and fears echoing around his brain.

He twists the handle. Throws the door up with as much force as he can. Takes a backwards leap as he retrieves his baton and readies himself to strike out with it.

There *is* someone here.

But it is someone who presents no danger to Kearney.

His partner lies on the concrete floor, gurgling and quivering.

Kearney knows she is hurt. Knows it is bad. And suddenly he is on automatic pilot, calling on all his experience and training to deal with this. He covers the distance to Whitland in a single bound it seems, and he thinks, but is not sure, that he is calling her name. And when he gets to her he realises to his horror and frustration that there is not much he can do for her. He tells her otherwise, of course, and he wishes it *were* otherwise, but a voice in his head keeps telling him he is too late. He spent too much time chasing after cats when he should have been at his partner's side. He lifts her head and cradles it on his lap and tells her it will be all right, that he will look after her, and after every such faintly believed promise he yells frantically into his radio for assistance, praying that they will get here in time, even though that concept has no meaning here because he knows time has run out. And while the hot blood continues to pump out of her neck at an ever-decreasing rate, and her breathing becomes ragged and her body goes into violent spasm, he continues to reassure her, continues to tell her that she should hang on because help will be here soon and they will fix her up. They will fix her up good and proper.

They arrive quickly and they arrive in force. A call like this takes top priority. Sirens split the night. Lights bring a blue dawn. They descend on the scene with terrifying urgency. And then it is as if they are rendered suddenly ineffectual. Because they see, they recognise, they accept. They do not need the tears of their colleague to confirm the truth so apparent.

It is a while before anyone notices the dead bird lying next to the body of PC Andrea Whitland.

25

The birds seem happy. Delirious, in fact. Their wild fluttering and flapping appears a joyful celebration.

Of course, it could be just a frightened reaction to his own dancing, singing and clapping.

He *did* it.

He took two of them on. Not one, but two.

He wasn't sure he could cope with a pair. Wasn't even sure he could cope with one on duty. They must be more alert then, surely? Walking around in uniform, they must be constantly attuned to signs of trouble.

He almost called it off. When he peered through that alley gate and saw two of them get out of the car, he nearly went home. It seemed too much, too dangerous.

But you didn't, did you? You held your nerve and you went for it. In for a penny, in for a pound. All that research, all that driving around, all that sneaking about to find the perfect location for an ambush – it would have been a waste to throw it all away.

It could have gone so wrong. What if the coppers had stuck together? What if they had both come into the garage? What would he have done then? Wait it out under that tarpaulin, hoping they wouldn't find him? Or leap out at them and hope that the element of surprise would give him enough of an edge to overpower them?

Stop worrying about it. Doesn't matter now, does it? It worked. You got one. Stupid bitch. She had no idea. Didn't even have time to scream. No voice.

Like the songbird.

It'll be singing now, though. In bird heaven. Celebrating. It won't mind now how brief its life was. It will finally understand that it has fulfilled a purpose. It has proved its worth a thousand times over.

The police will be going crazy. It will be as though he has gone up to a wasps' nest and hit it with a big stick. They will be buzzing madly, desperate to locate the source of the attack. They will want to lash out, to sting, to kill.

But they will do it without logic. They don't have enough data to reason about this properly. They don't know what this is all about. They have but a fragment of the whole picture – a square inch of a much larger canvas – and they will be trying to base all of their suppositions and all of their plans on that unrepresentative sliver. They will get nowhere that way.

It's amazing how pathetic and incompetent they are.

Of course, things will become more difficult now. The cops will become a lot more defensive and cautious. They don't know where or when the next strike of the stick will be.

But that just makes it all the more interesting.

All the more fun.

26

There is fear in this room. Fear and confusion and a soul-sucking sense of inadequacy. Cody has never seen anything like it before. Not in his own colleagues.

From Blunt comes the heat of anger. Not at her troops, but at the situation. She takes the loss of another police officer as a personal attack, even though she probably never met PC Whitland. That's just the way Blunt is. The case is hers. She is charged with finding the killer, and yet the killer has just struck again. Cody can understand why she would find that so hard to swallow. He imagines he would feel the same if he were in charge.

'Three police officers dead,' she says to them. It doesn't need saying – they all know this – but she feels the need to hammer it home. 'And we don't seem to be any nearer to catching this guy. Am I wrong? Well, am I?'

She scans the upturned faces. Nobody dares respond. To do so would offer a target to her full wrath.

'Just what the fuck is going on here?'

Again, Cody knows this is not meant as an insult aimed at the assembled detectives. She is not questioning their competency; she is simply expressing her exasperation that progress on the case is slow. At least, that's what Cody hopes she is saying.

She takes a moment. Cody hears her draw deep breaths.

'Okay,' she says. 'What you all need to realise is that the eyes and ears of the world are on us now. Everyone is looking to us to solve these murders, today if possible. We've been promised resources. Manpower and overtime aren't a problem. What is a problem is that I'm not sure we're getting anywhere. If anyone here can convince me I'm wrong, then I'd love to hear it.'

Cody speaks up. 'I thought we *were* getting somewhere. Everything pointed to a connection with the Vernons. But this latest murder . . .'

'There has to be a link,' says Blunt. 'All the signs say this is the work of the same killer. The post-mortem hasn't taken place yet, but Dr Stroud's view is that the method of killing is very similar. A blow to the head followed by a knife attack. Plus, of course, the bird left at the scene.'

'Only one cut this time, though,' says Cody. 'A single slash across the throat. The previous victims had multiple stab wounds. And Whitland's eyes were left intact.'

'Time pressure. Whitland's partner was just around the corner. The killer didn't have time to piss around with the body. He took a big enough risk as it was, and that worries me. This officer was lured to her death while on duty. She had a partner with her and a radio to call for assistance, and still he carried out the murder. He's getting bolder with each killing, and if he hasn't finished yet . . .'

Her words chill the room. The men and women here don't want to contemplate the thought that more of their number may yet die.

'It suggests, though,' says Cody, 'that the mutilation isn't a vital part of the ritual. He's more interested in the killing itself. At least now he is.'

Blunt raises a quizzical eyebrow. 'What do you mean?'

'The first two killings got his message across. He doesn't need to worry so much about that now. It frees him up to just get on with the murder.'

'His message being?'

'That this is the work of the birds. In the first two cases the symbolism was that the birds had pecked out the eyes and removed Garnett's nose. I know that didn't actually happen, but that was what he wanted us to see. Job done. As stupid as he probably thinks we are, he'll know we understand that much. He doesn't need to keep pressing that message home. Given a choice between a successful kill and spending time saying the same frigging thing again and again, he goes for the kill and gets the hell out of there. What *is* important, though, is the bird itself. Even for Whitland's murder he made sure that a dead bird was prepared and left at the scene. If this guy intends to kill again, I'd bet another bird is involved. The question is why?'

Blunt nods thoughtfully. 'All right, let's discuss the bird. Apparently this one was a goldfinch. It's a pretty common songbird. Much smaller and more colourful than the raven and the blackbird. Like the others, though, it had a note attached to its leg.'

Cody didn't attend the crime scene. This is the first he's heard about the latest note.

Blunt picks up a manila folder and opens it. 'The note says, "The sedge has withered from the lake."'

'"And no birds sing,"' Cody continues. 'Keats. "La Belle Dame sans Merci".'

Blunt looks surprised. 'You *are* well read, Cody. I had to consult my friend Google.'

Cody says nothing. He feels a bit like the class swot. He's half expecting to get a Chinese burn at break-time.

'Okay,' says Blunt. 'We go from Edgar Allan Poe to a nursery rhyme to John Keats. All poetry of one form or another, and all involving birds. What else links them?'

Webley speaks now. 'That last one. It's a bit . . . well, sad, don't you think? You said yourself – this was a goldfinch. A songbird. And now no birds are singing. It's . . . I dunno, I just think maybe the killer is saying he's really sad about something.'

'It's a good point,' Cody adds. 'This might be his way of getting his feelings across. There's something he's upset about. It makes him sad, but it also makes him angry. It could be said that the second message was about revenge. A load of blackbirds get baked in a pie, so another one attacks the maid.'

'Yeah,' says Webley, enthused by Cody's support. 'And in the first message, he's saying it's never going to happen again to him. Whatever it was, he's putting a stop to it.'

Says Blunt, 'But why do it with birds? Why not just leave a note on the bodies? If he's got an issue, why doesn't he just come right out and say it?'

'Because he's nuts,' says Ferguson. 'I'm serious. I mean, he's got to be insane to be killing police like this in the first place. The birds are just more confirmation that he's got a screw loose.'

Blunt shakes her head. 'No, there's more to it than that. For some reason, the birds have a profound meaning for whoever's doing this. They're not the easiest creatures to catch. He's gone to too much trouble for them just to be something to tie notes to.'

'Crazy people can be obsessed about things nobody else gives a damn about. Who knows what's going on in his mind? For all we know, these birds might be his friends. He might think they're tiny little assassins, going off to kill the nasty coppers who once gave him a speeding fine. We'll never really know until we get hold of him, and even then it probably won't make any sense to us.'

'For all our sakes,' says Blunt, 'I hope it's not as meaningless as that. It's going to be hard enough catching him if he's following a rational pattern. If it's a totally deranged mind behind these killings, there's little point in us even sitting here and talking about it. We'd have to rely on getting a break with forensics, or on him making a mistake, and right now neither of those looks on the cards.'

She pauses. 'You're right about one thing, though. This is very much an anti-police crusade. Somebody hated these three officers with a vengeance. Let's hope it's only three, and these three in particular, rather than just the tip of an iceberg designed to sink the whole ship. Cody, anything promising in that regard?'

Cody doesn't want to sound too negative. Like Blunt, he is hoping the cold dish of revenge – if that is indeed what this is about – is now regarded as having been served and consumed. Three dead officers is three too many, and the thought of more helpings to come turns his stomach.

'Too early to say, ma'am,' is about as optimistic as he can be. 'So far, I haven't found anything to link Andrea Whitland with either Terri Latham or Paul Garnett. Far as I can see, they were never stationed together, and they didn't do their basic training at the same time. I'm talking to people who knew Whitland, to see if they're aware of a relationship of any kind with either Latham or Garnett. I'm also going through her arrest reports, again looking for a common thread.'

'Good. Keep at it. If you want bodies to help you, just shout. There's got to be a connection there somewhere. It would make life much simpler for us all if a certain family was tied into this latest homicide somehow.'

Both eyebrows fly up this time – an invitation to Cody to brighten her darkness with some good news. But he has to disappoint her.

'I'm looking for that. Believe me, the one name I really want to find in her reports is Vernon. So far, nothing.'

Blunt issues a growling noise. 'Whoever was responsible for last night's attack knows that area well, and it just seems a little odd to me that the location isn't a million miles away from the Vernon house. And the fact that Latham and Garnett were both involved with the Vernon case can't have been sheer coincidence. They weren't picked at random. So Andrea Whitland surely can't be random either.'

'Erm . . .'

The noise comes from Webley, who seems a little reluctant to air her current thoughts.

'Well?' says Blunt. 'Go on.'

'With respect, ma'am, there's a problem with what you just said. Whitland and Kearney were responding to a call regarding kids causing trouble at the church.'

'So?'

'So . . . how did the killer know who would respond? If it was always in his mind to kill Whitland, how on earth could he be sure she would turn up at the scene? And even if he could narrow it down to a certain patrol car, how did he know Kearney wouldn't get to him first? Would he still have killed Kearney? If so, that would suggest it didn't matter to him who he killed, as long as it was a copper.'

Blunt nods, and Cody can see from her expression that she hasn't allowed herself to be checkmated by Webley. 'That thought occurred to me too. If you're right, it could be that all this digging into Whitland's background is a complete waste of our time. On the other hand, this killer is a devious bastard. Maybe he knows who usually patrols that area. He could have encountered Whitland or Kearney there before. He might have even spoken to them directly at some point last night. I don't know. The point is, we have to consider every eventuality. What you just suggested might be exactly what the killer wants us to think. He makes last night's murder look random and spur-of-the-moment precisely so that we don't bother looking at the latest victim too closely.'

She turns back to Cody. 'In fact, pull Kearney's reports too. Maybe he was the intended victim. Maybe they both were. I have no idea. Just find me some answers.'

Cody scribbles a note to himself to check Kearney out. 'There's another possibility, if we're talking about this guy being devious.'

'Go on.'

'A smokescreen. This latest murder is to divert our attention from the Vernon case. To make it look like any cops will do as the victims.'

'Good point. Which is why I don't want us to give up on the Vernons or their associates just yet. Keep looking at them, and keep up the search for that Gazza bloke.'

She pauses for a moment as she scans the faces in the room. 'There's one other thing. We don't know that this killer is finished. Whether it's connected with the Vernon case or not, it's possible that this lunatic might have other coppers in his sights. We need to be careful – all of us. We need to watch each other's backs, because no other bugger will do it for us. I don't want to be at any of your funerals in the near future. Got it?'

She gets nods and murmurs of agreement. Cody stays silent. Being a potential target for murder is as disconcerting as it gets.

27

Cody recognises the voice immediately. There's a certain reptilian quality to it.

'Hello, Sergeant Cody.'

Cody rolls his eyes. He debates putting the phone down, but knows it wouldn't end anything.

'What is it this time, Dobby?'

'Same as it was last time. I'd like to talk to you. Get your side of things.'

'Yeah, well, my answer's the same as last time, too. A big fat no.'

'Come on, Cody. Help out a fellow investigator. This is a big, big story now. A three-time cop killer? This could make you famous. I could help you with that.'

'I don't want to be famous. I just want to do my job. And spending time on the phone with you doesn't fall into that category, so if you don't mind . . .'

'If that's the way you want to play it, so be it. I'll just have to run with the story as it stands. Be nice to check all the facts out with you first, but *c'est la vie.*'

'What story, Dobby? You've been given exactly the same press information as every other hack. Anything you add to it is sheer make-believe.'

A sigh from Dobson. 'There you go again. Underestimating my abilities. I'll have you know I'm pretty good at what I do.'

'I wouldn't go shouting that out if I were you. I don't think it's anything to be proud of. Now is it all right by you if I get back to some proper policing?'

'That's fine, Cody. Just don't say I didn't give you an opportunity to comment on this story before it runs.'

'I'm sure it'll get the reception it deserves, with or without my input.'

'I'm sure it will, too. Pretty freaky, don't you think? Those birds . . .'

Whammo. There it is. Nice one, Dobby. Didn't see that one coming.

For a while Cody doesn't know what to say, but he's aware that every second of silence is being taken by Dobby as confirmation that he's just won the top prize.

'What are you talking about, Dobby?'

That's right – act the innocent. But he can hear the hollowness in his own voice.

'Don't play with me, Cody. If you're going to do that, I'll just go ahead and run my story anyway.'

Cody thinks it over. The big unknown here is how much Dobby has learnt about the case. There's no way he can give his blessing to Dobby to publish without finding out more.

'So what are you asking me?'

'For a friendly chat, that's all. Is that too much to ask?'

'When?'

'How about now? I'm in the Beehive. They do a decent pint here. I'd be happy to buy you one.'

'Now's not a good time.'

'I have deadlines, Cody. If this is to make the next edition . . .'

Cody checks his watch. 'All right. You've got your meeting. But I warn you now that you haven't put me in the best of moods. I'll be there in twenty minutes. Make sure that arsehole of a photographer isn't there.'

'Just me, Cody. I'll do the crossword while I'm waiting.'

The line goes dead. Cody hangs up. Stares into space for a while.

'What was that?'

This from Ferguson, standing there with a large mug of steaming tea in his hand.

'That dickhead from the *Clarion*. Dobson.'

'Old Dobby? He sniffing around for titbits again?'

'Yeah. Only this time he's got a whiff of something. I need to find out what he's dug up.'

Cody stands up and dons his jacket.

'Need some backup?' says Ferguson

'Nah. You drink your tea before it goes cold.'

Ferguson grins. 'I wasn't thinking of me. I was going to look for Wibbly. She'll be pining for you if you leave her here.'

'I'm sure she'll be fine in your capable hands.'

Ferguson winks. 'Don't worry. Five minutes with me and you won't even be in her thoughts.'

'Only because she'll have nodded off.'

Cody leaves the room with a smile on his face. He likes Ferguson. Enjoys his sense of humour and his eternal optimism. Footlong is the guy who, when given a mountain of shit as a present, starts digging into it to find the pony.

The smile fades as he descends the staircase and hears the arguing. He debates turning around and going back. Decides instead that someone needs to deal with the flak.

Frank Vernon rounds on Cody as soon as he sees him coming down the stairs.

'Here he is. Here's one of them. What have you got to say for yourself, eh?'

Cody takes in the sight of the exasperated uniformed officers clustered around Vernon. The desk sergeant looks on the verge of ordering that Vernon be thrown into a cell while he calms down.

Cody beckons to the enraged centre of attention. 'Mr Vernon. Let's go somewhere we can talk.'

Vernon sweeps his arm in front of him, as if imagining that he's flinging Cody across the room. 'No. You're not hiding me away. I've got nothing to be ashamed of. Not like you lot.'

Cody glances at the desk sergeant. Gets a roll of his eyes.

'All right, Mr Vernon. What is it you want to discuss?'

'What is it I want to discuss? I don't want to discuss nothing. I want an apology, is what I want.'

'An apology? And what would that be for?'

'You have to ask? Are you taking the piss? I want you to say sorry for calling us murderers.'

'We never called you any such thing, Mr Vernon, as well you know.'

'No. I don't know that at all. If you had your way, me and my family would be banged up in Walton jail right now.'

'That's not true. The only thing we did was to make inquiries.'

'Inquiries, my arse.' He jabs a finger. 'You thought we had something to do with it. You turned up on my doorstep because you thought we'd killed that policewoman. And when that second copper was killed you were sure of it. You dragged us in here like common criminals.'

His voice is getting louder and shriller by the second. Cody raises his arms to placate him.

'Mr Vernon—'

'We're victims. When will you start to understand that? I lost a son. You've no idea what that feels like. None of you. So now I want an apology. No, I *demand* an apology. Now that you know it's nothing to do with us, you can leave us alone. But not before you've said you're sorry.'

He stands enveloped in his fury, quivering with the force of his emotion. When Cody doesn't provide the words he wants, he concocts his own reason for it.

'I don't believe this,' he says. 'You're not finished with us, are you? You still think we're involved. There's a lunatic out there bumping off your mates, and you're still hanging on to the idea it might be us. Jesus, it's no wonder so many crimes never get solved. You're blinkered. You can't see past your fat lazy arses. How many is it going to take, eh? How many more dead coppers? Five? Ten? Fifty?'

Vernon takes a few steps closer, and Cody braces himself.

'All right,' says Vernon. 'You keep coming after me, if that's the only thing you know how to do. Keep on harassing the innocent ones, the victims. Keep on wasting your precious police time while your buddies lie dying on the streets. Let me know when you're sick of going to funerals. Let me know, so that I can look you in the eye and say that I told you so. Maybe then you'll finally believe me.'

Words fight to escape Cody's mouth. He wants to ask Vernon if he believes there will be more deaths, and if so, then why. But he knows that such questions would be loaded with accusation, and now does not seem the moment to be launching any such missiles at this man.

He decides it's wiser simply to nod. Which takes a lot of effort given that he has developed a tendency of late to speak or act before thinking. In fact, he's proud of himself for exhibiting such restraint.

The compulsion to say something becomes almost unbearable as he watches Frank Vernon leave the building. The man walks out as if his shoulders are draped in a flag of victory, and Cody wants to let him know this isn't over. He wants to tell him that he will do everything he can to stop this killer, and if that means interrogating every member of the Vernon family from now until Christmas, then that's what he'll do.

But he allows caution to hold his tongue in check, because he knows it's the right thing to do.

Doesn't feel as satisfying, though.

28

The traditional frontage of the Beehive somehow looks uncomfortable amidst the big shiny glass and concrete buildings on Paradise Street. It is as though it is refusing to bow to the pressure from the surrounding younger upstarts to accept the inevitable march of progress and to yield the prime position to which it has clung for so long.

Inside, the rows of dusty books lining its walls lend further emphasis to its links with the past – to a time when people actually bothered to read rather than watch television or surf the Web. Cody likes the atmosphere of the place. It's simple and it's unpretentious.

He pushes past a knot of men at the bar. Smiles when he hears one of them say to his mates that Liverpool's latest signing isn't worth twenty pence, let alone twenty million quid.

Seated alone at a small table, Dobson looks up from his paper and returns Cody's smile.

'Good timing. I'm stuck on this last clue. Four down: "One takes flight in a vehicle".'

Cody thinks for a second. 'Avian. But something tells me you knew that already.'

Dobson writes it in, but admits nothing. 'Fancy a pint?'

Cody pulls out a chair and plonks himself down. 'No, thanks. I'm on duty.'

'Sure, sure. But then you wouldn't have one anyway, would you? I've heard you don't drink anymore.'

'Who told you that?'

'A little bird.'

Cody frowns. 'How many more of those are you going to work into the conversation? Next you'll be saying that you were spitting feathers before that pint, and then you'll ask me why the police are in a bit of a flap. Or that maybe we're running around like headless chickens.'

Dobson laughs, but it's a slimy laugh that threatens to curdle the froth on his beer. 'Very good, Cody. You're better at the puns than I am. You'd make a great headline writer for one of the tabloids.'

'If you're going to insult me . . .'

'It was a compliment. Some of those headlines are bloody hard to come up with, you know. Take these murders, for example.'

Cody feels his defences springing up in readiness. It hadn't taken Dobson long to get to this.

'What about them?'

'Well, I'm struggling to come up with a good way of grabbing attention, for when I write my next piece. Obviously the focus will be on the three poor police officers, but now we've got this sinister new twist, haven't we? I'm thinking of including something along the lines of "Birds of Prey". What do you think? I think it puts across the idea quite nicely. Or maybe something about an air strike . . . Yeah, that would be good. And of course I need to work in some references to the film.'

'What film?'

'The Hitchcock movie. *The Birds*. I mean, this could be something straight out of a film like that, don't you think? Birds attacking and killing policemen and women. It's so weird it's almost unbelievable. But then the best stories always are. My editor's going to pee his pants when he hears this.'

Cody picks up a beer mat. Taps its edge on the table. 'What, exactly, are you planning to tell him?'

Dobson raises his eyebrows in feigned surprise. 'Haven't you just been listening to me? About the birds found on the faces of the victims.'

'What birds? What are you talking about?'

Dobson leans back in his chair. Takes a swig of his pint. Wipes his mouth with the back of his hand.

'Nice try, Cody. Acting daft like that – nice try. But we both know I've got a story here. And I'm going to tell it.'

Cody spins his beer mat onto the table. Folds his arms. 'All right then. Go ahead. Tell me this so-called story you're desperate to relate.'

Dobson licks his lips as he considers the challenge. Suddenly he rests his elbows on the table and puts three fingers on display. 'Three police officers. All dead by the same hand. A possible connection with the death of Kevin Vernon, if the first two victims are anything to go by. So far, that's what everyone's got. All of my fellow reporters and journalists, all working with the same material. All speculating, trying to fill in the gaps, but basically all saying the same thing. But I'm a step ahead of them. I know about the calling card.'

'The calling card being?'

'A bird. Left on the face of each victim.'

'What kind of bird?'

Dobson hesitates. Cody can almost hear the cogs whirling in his head.

'Different in each case. But a black one. Always black.'

Mentally, Cody sighs in relief. He realises now that Dobson is on a fishing expedition. He knows little, but is making extrapolations in the hope that Cody will confirm them for him. He wants indignation from Cody. Perhaps a spluttered demand to be told how he came by such privileged information. It's the oldest trick in the book, but it's not working here. Yes, Dobby knows about the birds, but that's the extent of it. In fact, he knows only about two of the birds. Clearly, he is not aware that the third bird was found next to Andrea Whitland's body, and not covering her face. Nor is he aware that the latest bird was a goldfinch. It was a reasonable stab in the dark to suppose that if the first two birds were black, then the third would be too. But the gamble hasn't paid off. Dobson doesn't know about the messages attached to the birds' feet, either. If he did, he would mention it. In fact, the reporter doesn't have very much at all.

What this also tells Cody is that Dobson's source isn't on the job. There's too much detail missing. What's more likely is that he has been talking to the people who found the bodies – Terri Latham's elderly neighbour and Garnett's postman. Probably paid them handsomely not to tell any other reporter too. In the case of Whitland, no civilian was present at the crime scene, and that's why Dobson's information in that regard is so scant.

So, Dobby, you've lucked out. You've gambled on black, and the ball has landed on red. You came to me for confirmation, and you're walking out of here with nothing.

'Dobby, where did you hear this crap?'

An attempt at a smile from Dobson, but it's clear that Cody's reaction has dented his confidence.

'My sources are impeccable.'

'Impeccable. Is that another bird pun?'

'Ha, very good, Cody. Let's see if you and your superiors think it's so funny when this story goes to press.'

It's Cody's turn for a smile now. A big confident grin that will squash Dobson's self-assuredness into the ground.

'There's not going to be any story, Dobby.'

'That's what *you* think. There's such a thing as freedom of the press in this country. You can't stop me printing what I know. In fact, I'd say it was my duty to write it. We have an obligation to our readers.'

'Oh, don't go pretending you're on some kind of moral crusade. You want a sensationalist story so that you can sell lots of papers and earn lots of money. You don't give a shit if your readers are well informed or not, as long as they're handing over their cash for your joke of a newspaper. And in this instance, they won't be well informed at all. You know why? Because you've got fuck all. That so-called information you were given is bullshit.'

'Now who's pretending? My information is legit. Straight from the horse's mouth.'

Cody shakes his head. 'I know exactly where that info came from, and one of those people didn't know what the hell he was looking at when he found Terri Latham's body. You've only got a tiny fraction of the facts, Dobby. Run with that, and your paper will be a laughing stock.'

'Sometimes a fraction is all we need. Anything that gives us an edge over the competition.'

'Yeah, I suppose the complete truth has never been a considera-tion for you before. Why start now? All right then, I'll give you another reason for not printing this garbage.'

Dobson sups his beer again. 'Go on.'

'Can you imagine what a story like that will do to people? A serial killer on our streets, leaving dead birds on his victims? It'll frighten the life out of them. It'll cause panic. Worst of all, it will give the killer the exposure he probably wants. It'll be another reason for him to keep on killing. Is that what you want?'

'Are you saying it's true, then? There is a serial killer leaving dead birds?'

'I'm saying nothing of the kind. I've already told you there are huge chunks missing from your intelligence, and I don't just mean your brain. For Christ's sake, don't turn a few scraps into something that will lead to more deaths.'

Dobson thinks some more, staring at Cody as he does so.

'Okay,' he says. 'So where do we go from here?'

'Don't know about you,' Cody answers, 'but I'm heading back to the station.'

'Not what I meant. We have an impasse. We need to resolve it.'

'We have nothing of the sort. And another thing you haven't got is a story.'

Dobson shrugs. 'Matter of opinion. I'm a risk taker. I've got some-thing here, and you know it. Maybe not all the facts, but enough to suggest that there's more to this than meets the eye. There's nothing our readers like more than a bit of intrigue. See, unlike you, I trust the public. I don't think they'll panic. If anything, they'll demand to know the truth. And why shouldn't they have it? This is a democracy, after all.'

'And the killer? Do you apply the same logic there, too? He should get what he wants? Is that the kind of risk you really want to take? Come on, Dobson. I know there's a heart in there somewhere. I know you've got feelings. Do you want to be the one responsible for egging this guy on to kill again?'

'You know, I never thought you'd stoop to emotional blackmail,' says Dobson. He glances at the spines of the books above his head, then back to Cody. 'But you're right about my soft centre. I like happy endings. Why don't we both make sure there is one?'

So, here it is. What Dobson was after all along.

'And how do we do that?'

'Same deal as before. I hold back on revealing what I already know. In return, you give me full disclosure on the investigation.'

He sees Cody's discomfort, and immediately puts up a hand. 'Don't worry,' he says. 'I don't want it as the case proceeds. I'm talking about afterwards, when there's an arrest. When you've got this guy, I want us to sit down over a beer or a coffee or whatever it is you drink these days, and I want a blow-by-blow account of what happened and how you caught him. If you want to stay anonymous, that's fine, but I want to write up an account of this case that's more detailed than anyone else can manage.'

Cody takes a long look around the pub. He sees an old guy without a tooth in his head, flapping his gums at a woman with a blue rinse. He sees two burly lads showing off their tattoos to the girls at the adjacent table. He sees a man and wife steadfastly ignore each other by burying their heads in their newspapers.

'Why me?' he asks. 'Why not contact our press office, like every other reporter? Or go to someone more senior – someone who has an overview of everything going on in this case?'

'You know the answers to all those questions,' says Dobson. 'The reason I'm good at this job is precisely because I don't do what every other reporter does. I do things my way. And outside of press briefings, the top brass give us nothing. They might as well just hand out prepared leaflets, because they never go off-script. No, I need someone who's in the thick of it. Someone who is doing the legwork, getting his hands dirty. Someone like you.'

'And is that all?' says Cody. But he knows it isn't.

'No. That's not all. I hate to say this, Cody, but I think you owe me one.'

Cody shakes his head. 'I don't owe you anything.'

'Is that right? If it wasn't for me, you wouldn't be on this case. You wouldn't even still be a copper.'

Cody feels the anger bubbling up. He has always known this would come back to haunt him, that it would be used against him at some point. He just hates the fact that now is that time.

'You're saying I should be grateful to you, is that it?'

'Yes, Cody, yes. That's exactly what I'm saying. I could have ended your career with a couple of paragraphs. I chose not to. I chose to help you keep your job. I think that's worth something, don't you?'

'You chose to help me? As I recall, the only reason you got off my back was because your boss told you to.'

Dobson nods thoughtfully. 'Yeah, I still don't know what happened there. Strange the way Ed Kingsley suddenly got cold feet. Maybe I'll get to the bottom of that one day.'

'Maybe it's just that he has a heart capable of being changed. Believe it or not, some people are like that. They're willing to listen to other points of view and act when they realise they're doing a bad thing. You should take a leaf out of his book.'

'I wasn't doing a bad thing. I was following up a story. A fascinating story. About a cop, and how he ended up in a really bad situation, and how it affected him afterwards. Still affects him, in fact.'

Cody knows it's pointless asserting that he is no longer affected by his past. Not after the way he almost choked the life out of Dobby's colleague. But at the same time, he feels annoyed that anyone should think they have the right to make capital out of his life.

'You know nothing about me,' he says. 'You don't know what I went through, or what it did to me. You don't really care, either. All you care about is your story.'

'Actually, I have a very good idea of what you went through. I know about trauma. I know how it devastates lives.'

'Really? How? What big traumas have you had in your life then?'

'I didn't say that I—'

'Exactly. So you're talking out of your arse. You know nothing.'

'You forget what I do for a living. I'm a reporter. I'm in constant touch with people who have been destroyed by what has happened to them. I've . . . I've seen things.'

There is something in the way he says that. *I've seen things.* He is saying not only that he has witnessed them, but also that he has experienced them in some way. Some of this devastation he talks about has brushed against him too.

It crosses Cody's mind to ask about it, but something in Dobson's eyes tells him that too much has been revealed already.

There are things there. Unattractive thoughts hidden behind his unattractive features. Cody is not sure he wants to delve further.

'Then why don't you just go and write your articles about them?'

'Maybe I did,' says Dobson. He pauses for a second, as if reliving a dark history, then snaps back into the present. 'And maybe that's why I didn't pursue your story as much as I could have. I saw what you were, what you are. I know you're a good copper, a decent guy trying to do a decent job. You do what's right. Maybe I was trying to do what's right, too.'

Cody leans back, feeling a little surprised. Nice speech, he thinks. He lets the surrounding chatter wash over him as he looks at this pathetic spectacle of a reporter in front of him, cradling his beer glass, the blank spaces in his unfinished crossword glaring their stark challenge at him.

'Justice,' says Cody.

Dobby blinks at him. 'What?'

'Eighteen across: "Mere cold water will put things right". The answer's "justice". Which is kind of what this should all be about, don't you think? Not what's best for you, or for me, but what's best for the victims.'

He gets up from his chair, pushes his hands into his pockets. 'See you around, Dobson.'

Dobson lifts eyes that look suddenly old and wearied by time. 'Is that a goodbye, or an *au revoir*?'

'It means that you're starting to act like something better than a bloodsucking parasite. Keep it up, and I might just be willing to have a drink with you next time.'

He turns and leaves then. He doesn't check Dobson's expression again. Doesn't want to know if he's just seen a touch of humanity beneath the repellent exterior, or if he's been duped. He'd prefer to believe the former.

That's the glass-half-full kind of guy he is.

At least for now.

29

He waits. And stares.

It should be a simple job. Nothing to get all worked up about. A car vandalised by kids. One copper should be all they send out on a job like this.

But they won't. He knows they won't. And it's driving him crazy. They're too bloody careful now.

They nearly nabbed him earlier on tonight. He was too cocky. After his earlier successes he had started to think this was easy. Make up a trivial crime, call it in, and when some unsuspecting bizzy turns up to check it out, that's when he strikes. A simple and effective by-the-numbers approach.

Only he underestimated the police. Put enough of their single-celled brains together and there's actually sufficient intelligence there to make them realise they need to start being a bit more circumspect.

He should have got wind of it earlier, but didn't. When he made the first call, his story was that he'd seen someone digging up vegetables on one of the allotments near Sefton Park. The switchboard operator asked him a million questions about how he had discovered the crime, what his name and address were, what the suspect looked like and so on. Far more questions than he expected. He gave them nothing, of course. Told them he didn't want to get involved, but that he just thought they should know.

Then he hid, and waited.

Looking back now, he realises how stupid that was. All that questioning should have acted as a hint as to what was to come.

It was a great hiding place, though. Some dense bushes behind one of the sheds. Easy to jump out on one unsuspecting cop.

Except it wasn't one cop, was it? Not a pair either. It was three of the bastards! Three police officers, just to investigate the digging up of a few lousy potatoes. Took them ages to turn up, too. Almost two hours before they got their arses in gear.

Once there, though, they weren't about to make life easy for him. Peering through the foliage, he could see how they were sticking together like they were joined at the hip. No splitting up to search the area. They moved en masse, shining their bright torches into every patch of darkness, and providing constant updates into their radios. For a few terrifying minutes he thought they would discover him. They came within feet of his lair before deciding to abandon their search. Thank God they didn't have dogs with them.

He didn't come out for a good half-hour after they left. He needed to be sure they weren't sitting just yards away in their cars, waiting for him to show himself.

That's when he realised just how spooked the police were, and how much more complicated his mission had become.

He tried several more calls during the night. On each occasion, he was put through a barrage of questions: *Who are you? Where do you live? How can we get in contact with you?* And when they finally responded to his call, it was always in force, always as if expecting an ambush. Of course, he was more careful himself on those occasions, always observing from a distance to avoid discovery.

Just as he is doing now.

He's at the ledge on one of the upper levels of a multi-storey car park on Brownlow Hill. Arms resting on the ledge to steady the binoculars he's holding. This time of night, he's not likely to be disturbed up here.

The binoculars are trained on the pay-and-display car park below, just behind the Adelphi Hotel. Nearly two hours since he phoned up about the car being vandalised down there, and still no sign of any police.

What the hell is taking them so long?

It's as he wonders this that a marked Ford Focus comes up from the direction of the city centre. It slows as it draws level with the car park, then goes past it and turns left onto the deserted road lead-ing towards the old Royal Mail building. It halts, but its occupants seem in no rush to get out. It just sits there.

He would never have chosen this place as a trap. It's too open, and there is too much danger of passing cars and pedestrians see-ing what happens here. But that wasn't the purpose of his phone call. He needed to see how the police would react.

He realises that a message must have been sent out from on high. It has been the same every time. Nobody works alone. They prob-ably even go to the toilet in pairs. That's how careful they're being.

Shit!

Down on the street, his suspicions are confirmed even further when another patrol car pulls up behind the first. Only then do the officers disembark. Four of them this time. Four! Why the hell does it need four bizzies to investigate a vandalised car?

They step over the low wooden fence separating the car park from the pavement, then circle the blue Astra he described in his phone call. Their torches light it up as they study it, warily at first, then more confidently as they acknowledge it presents no danger to them.

There is no vandalism, of course. He made that up, just to get the police out here. And now they realise it too.

But they're not done. Not yet. Now they split up. Two pairs. Moving on to the other cars here. Looking for any signs of some-one lying in wait. They know that this is not a normal call-out. They are prepared for him.

He swallows. His gulp sounds loud in the echoing chamber of the multi-storey. If he were down there, hiding in a nearby car, they would find him. No doubt about it. They would find him and they would discover his weapons and that would be an end to him. They would show him no mercy.

He wonders how he will ever again get close enough to a copper to take another life.

30

'Right,' says Blunt. 'Who wants to hear what our killer sounds like?'

The detectives look at each other, unable to hide the surprise on their faces. Unless Blunt is having them on – highly unlikely in the circumstances – she is actually in possession of a recording of the cop-killer's voice.

'He's been trying to catch us out,' Blunt explains. 'Trying to set traps for us. We got a whole load of calls last night, all apparently from the same man, all refusing to answer any of the key questions put to him by our switchboard operators, and all reporting crimes that turned out not to be crimes.'

'I assume we checked out the scene in each case?' says Cody.

'Thoroughly. He's not stupid. He knows we're on to him, and he knows we're not going to let our guard down. He's looking to see how we operate now. My guess is he's watching us from a distance, checking to see if we make any mistakes he can exploit.'

'Let's hear the bastard then,' says Ferguson. When he gets a fiery glare from Blunt, he adds, 'If you don't mind, ma'am.'

Blunt presses a key on the computer next to her. Immediately, a female voice can be heard over the attached speakers.

'Police, how can I help you?'

'I'd like to report a crime.'

Cody listens intently to the voice. It's little more than a hoarse whisper, as if the man has laryngitis. Overlaid on that is a fairly strong Scottish accent.

'Can I have your name please, sir?'

'What? No. No names or addresses. I'm not getting involved.'

'All right, sir. Can you tell me the nature of the crime?'

'Vandalism. Some kids. They've been wrecking a car.'

'I'm sorry, sir. Could you speak up, please?'

'No,' says the man. 'I've got a bad throat. I was saying about the car. Kids have been damaging it.'

'And where is this car, sir?'

'D'ya know the pay and display car park behind the Adelphi? There. On the side furthest away from the hotel.'

'Can you tell me what type of car it is?'

'Aye. A Vauxhall. An Astra, I think. Are you sending somebody over, or not?'

'We will, sir. I just need a few more details. The vandals you saw, are they still there now?'

'What? No. They're long gone. Someone needs to come and look at this car, though. It's in a bit of a state.'

'What kind of state, sir?'

'Eh?'

'Can you tell me exactly what they did to the car?'

Cody understands what's going on in this conversation. After what happened to Kearney and Whitland, every call to the police is being comprehensively screened. It's partly defensive, to sort out the genuine calls from the dangerous ones. But it's also partly offensive. If this operator recognises the voice as the latest in a series from a possible killer, she will be doing her best to keep him on the line, squeezing any information out of him that might lead to his eventual identification. Cody can picture the scene at the switchboard. The operator wouldn't be the only one listening to her caller. She will have signalled her supervisor to hook into the line as well, and between them they will be doing their utmost to nail this bastard.

'I told you,' says the man. 'They damaged it. They . . . they ripped the tyres, scratched the paintwork – that kind of thing.'

Even without the knowledge of what has gone before, Cody could have worked out that this call was suspect. It sounds exactly like someone making it up as they go along.

'I see. Ripped tyres, scratched paintwork. Is that all?'

'What d'ya mean, is that all? Isn't that enough for ye? Are you gonna do something about this, or am I wasting my time?'

'No, sir, you're not wasting your time. We very much appreciate your call. I just need to know something about the two vandals you saw, to help us catch them. Can you describe them for me?'

Clever, thinks Cody. But he'll spot it.

'I never said there were two of them.'

And he has.

'My mistake. So how many were there?'

'Three.'

'And their ages?'

'I . . . I dunno. I wasn't close enough to see.'

'Right. So can you tell me where you were standing, please?'

'I . . . I was passing. In my car. I was slowing down for the lights, and that's when I saw them.'

'I see, sir. So you only got a quick look.'

'Aye.'

'But long enough to see them rip the tyres and damage the paintwork.'

'Aye. Yes.'

'And when the lights changed?'

'What?'

'What did you do when the traffic lights changed? Did you stay and watch, or did you drive away?'

'I drove away. I didn't want them to see me.'

'Do you think they *did* see you?'

'No. I don't think so. They were too busy.'

'And when was this, sir? How long ago did this happen?'

'Just a few minutes. I pulled over as soon as I could to call you lot. Dunno why I bothered.'

'So they could still be there, then?'

'What?'

'Earlier, you said the vandals were long gone. I'm just wondering how you know that, if they were still there just a few minutes ago.'

'Look, I'm hanging up. I've reported a crime. I've done my duty. You decide what you want to do with it.'

There is a click, some static, then silence.

Silence here in the incident room too. The detectives here believe they have just listened to the voice of the man who has killed three of their colleagues. A sobering thought. But the silence is also borne of frustration, because although they could have closed their eyes and imagined him here in this room, they know next to nothing about him.

Only Webley shows any sign of optimism. 'Jesus, so that's what he sounds like. That should help us narrow things down.'

'Och, d'ye really think so?'

This from Cody. He imitates the voice on the phone. Speaks hoarsely, without any trace of his own tone, and in a mock Scottish accent.

Ferguson joins in, again mimicking the caller: 'Could be Cody there. Could be me.'

Another detective chimes in: 'Could be any one of us, lassie.'

All the voices sound identical. All exactly like the voice on the phone.

'Okay,' says Webley, 'I get the message.'

Cody looks to Blunt for some more positive news. 'Did we manage to do anything with the phone call?'

Blunt shakes her head. 'The calls all came in to different police stations across the region. Nobody realised it was the same man until it was too late. We traced the call eventually, but only hours after the event. It was made in the area from an unregistered mobile. I've put in a request for all CCTV footage recorded there at the relevant time. Same for the sites of the other call-outs. Fingers crossed, we could get lucky.'

The faces around the room don't register much in the way of expectation.

'Look,' says Blunt, 'I know this isn't much to go on, but it's something. I'm getting the voice analysed. Perhaps the experts can pick up something we can't hear. In the meantime, I want each of you to listen to all the calls. You might spot something.'

'And the next time he calls?' says Cody.

Blunt looks down at him. 'We'll be ready. We're making everyone aware of this voice. If he calls again we'll initiate an immediate trace.'

'That's if we recognise it,' says Ferguson. 'Next time he could be Irish. Or Welsh. Or Pakistani. He could even use one of those voice changer devices.'

'Yes, he could, Neil. He could do any of those things. We'll worry about that when it happens. What we need to worry about right now is that he's still after us. He's still out there and still trying to lure us into one of his traps. That means none of us is safe until we catch him. Please bear that in mind.'

With that she is gone. Back to her office.

She leaves Cody deep in thought. Even when Webley and Ferguson amble over to his desk, he finds it difficult to engage with them.

Says Ferguson, 'How's *your* Scottish accent then, Wibbly?'

Webley clears her throat and says, 'You'll nae get any haggis on Balamory.'

Ferguson looks askance at her. 'Who's that meant to be? Jimmy Krankie?' He shifts his gaze to Cody. 'Whaddya think, mate? Reckon she's our prime suspect?'

'Yeah,' says Cody, distractedly. He's not sure what they're talking about, but he suspects it's bollocks. Slowly, he gets out of his chair.

'You all right?' Webley asks him.

He nods. 'Right as rain. Back in a minute.'

He moves off. Behind him, he hears Ferguson saying something about Jimmy Krankie always having that effect on him.

Cody heads over to Blunt's office. Knocks on her door and enters.

Blunt has some paperwork in her hands. She peers at Cody over the top of her reading glasses.

'Cody?'

'Got five minutes?' he asks.

She waves him into a seat. Takes off her glasses and tosses them onto her desk. 'Don't really need them,' she says, as if to protest against the ravages of age.

'What's on your mind?' she asks.

'This guy,' he says. 'He's not giving up. Like you said, he hasn't finished with us. Three's not enough for him. He's going to keep killing and killing. Dead coppers piling up around him for as long as he can keep going. Those calls from him last night show how determined he is.'

Blunt nods. 'That's my feeling too. I don't know what this man's issue is, but I don't see it as a thirst he's ever going to quench.'

'Only now he's got a problem. And so do we.'

'Care to elaborate?'

'We know he's out there, and we know what his tactics are. His first two victims – Latham and Garnett – were different. Somehow he found out where they lived, and so he was able to kill them in their own homes. For whatever reason, his well ran dry after that, and he had to find a way of making us come to him. So he started calling in fake crimes. We didn't know he was going to do that, of course, and so that's how he managed to get to Andrea Whitland. But now we know what he's up to, and we're ready.'

'Which is a good thing. We have to be ready. We have to protect ourselves.'

'Yes, I know. We're making life difficult for him. There isn't a copper out on the streets now who hasn't got another copper watching their back. No single response at all. And if we get a sniff of one of his traps, we respond in force. We don't give him the slightest opportunity to claim one of us as his prize.'

Blunt clasps her hands together, burying them deep beneath her mountainous chest. 'You say that almost as if you disapprove.'

'No, not that. It's just . . . what we've got here is a Mexican stand-off. One slip from either side is the end. Our killer can't do what he wants to do, because we're not giving him a chance. All he can do is keep calling us out and hope we balls it up. And one of these days we probably will. We can't keep operating like this. We can't treat every suspicious call as if it's leading us to an unexploded bomb. We haven't got the resources, and pretty soon the public is going to start wondering why we're taking so long to deal with minor crimes.'

Blunt frowns. 'First of all, Cody, resource allocation and operational strategy are not your problem. Let the powers that be worry about such things. Secondly, we're not treating every call in the same way. You need to give our phone operators some credit. They know what we're dealing with, and they're pretty good at distinguishing between those calls that are genuine, those that are hoaxes and those that come from deranged individuals such as our killer. Trust them to do a good job on that front. And, thirdly, this situation isn't going to last forever, because you and your colleagues out there are going to catch this lunatic very soon. That's me trusting you to do a good job.'

Cody responds not with speech but silence, chewing his lip as if to hold back what he'd really like to say.

'Why do I sense you're not convinced?' Blunt asks.

'It's not that. I know we'll get him, but . . .'

'Yes?'

'I want to suggest a Plan B.'

'A Plan B? You mean, something we try if all else fails?'

'Not exactly. I was thinking more like something that we do in parallel with Plan A.'

Blunt brings out her hands again, now presumably very much warmer. 'Something tells me I'm not going to like this. Go on.'

Cody takes a deep breath. 'This guy likes to set traps. He's hoping we fall into one of them. At the moment he's just studying us, working out how to make his traps even better, or hoping that we make a mistake.'

'Okay. So?'

'What about setting a trap of our own? Instead of being reactive, let's get proactive and create our own trap.'

'And how do you suggest we do that?'

'We let him think we've grown tired. That we've become sloppy. We give him the mistake he's been waiting for.'

Blunt brings the forefinger and thumb of one hand to the bridge of her nose, as though applying them to a pressure point to ease a building headache.

'I'm going to hate myself for asking this, but how do you propose we do that without him smelling a rat?'

'We ease off on the response. Gradually, over the next few nights. We tone down the phone interrogation. We reduce the number of uniforms responding. We cut down on the searches taking place at the scenes. Baby steps, until we're ready, and he thinks his wait has been worthwhile.'

'And then?'

'And then we give him what he wants. A single copper. Alone. No partner in sight. An irresistible target.'

Blunt listens. Thinks. Drums her fingers on the edge of her desk.

'If you're wondering why I didn't say no immediately, it's because I'm desperately trying to remember when I had a more ridiculous suggestion put to me. I can't think of one, so congratulations – you win the Stupidest Idea of the Century award.'

'It's not so ridiculous, and you know it. The cop wouldn't really be alone. We can put cameras and a mike on him, and we'd put unmarked cars in the vicinity. Plus, he'd have the advantage of being ready for whoever came at him.'

'No, Cody. Absolutely not.'

'Why not? Give me one good reason why.'

'I'll give you two. The first is that it would be putting a police officer's life in unacceptable danger. The second is that I know how that brain of yours works. I know exactly what you haven't told me yet, which is that the sacrificial goat you have in mind for this mind-numbingly stupid plan is you.'

'Actually, I was going to suggest Footlong.' He smiles, holds his hands up. 'Okay, it's me. I can do this.'

'You say that like getting yourself killed is a laudable achievement. Well, actually, Cody, I don't want to be congratulating you at your funeral. I don't want to be nailing a medal to your coffin, thank you very much.'

Suddenly Cody is leaning forward, becoming more intense than he knows he should be with his superior.

'Then who else do we sacrifice?'

Blunt appears stunned by the question. 'Nobody. We don't sacrifice anybody, because we're not going along with your stupid plan.'

'I'm not talking about the plan. I'm talking about the other officers who will die if we don't catch this fucker soon. We can hold each other's hands as much as you like, but sooner or later he'll catch one of us alone. He'll find out where one of us lives, or somebody will say the wrong thing in a bar. A mistake will be made, and he will be there, and he will take that person's life.'

'No, DS Cody. That's not going to happen. And the reason it's not going to happen is because of what I said to you all just a few minutes ago. You are going to catch this man. But you are going to do so through good old-fashioned detective work, and not through some hare-brained scheme that sounds like something straight out of a Hollywood movie. My God, haven't you been through enough? And now you want to go undercover again, only this time as a uniformed officer?'

Cody smiles his disarming smile. 'Undercover as a cop. I hadn't thought of it like that.'

'Well, don't think about it any longer. It's not on. End of discussion.'

Cody sits there quietly for a minute, wondering how to come back at her. But he knows her mind is made up. He gets out of his chair and heads for the door, but is stopped by Blunt.

'You do understand, don't you, Cody?'

He nods, but more to keep her happy.

He's not done yet.

31

The roar comes later that afternoon. He's been expecting it, but it's still frightening in its intensity.

'CODY!'

He looks across the room at Blunt. Everyone looks across the room at Blunt. She is the picture of a vengeful queen who has just learnt of treachery and betrayal in her court. She looks capable of breathing fire, turning everything here to crumbling, smoking charcoal.

'My office,' she says. 'Now!'

She doesn't wait for him. She just turns and storms off, expecting – *knowing* – that he will follow, on penalty of a fate worse than death.

'Uh-oh,' someone whispers. All eyes shift to Cody now. All questioning what he could possibly have done to merit a summons like this. There is a deathly silence in the room. They are expecting nothing less than a call to the gallows for this malefactor.

He attempts a smile, as if to say, *It's okay. Nothing to worry about.* But it sits uncomfortably on his lips, and they see it for what it is. And when he trails after Blunt, he hears one of them humming the funeral march.

When he gets to the doorway of Blunt's office, she is at the window rather than behind her desk. Not a good sign. She stares out through the open blinds, obviously troubled.

Cody announces his arrival with a light tap of his knuckle on the glass door panel. She doesn't even turn around.

'In,' she commands, accompanying it with a brief flick of a finger to beckon him inside. 'Close the door.'

He does as he is ordered, but knowing that a closed door will make it easier for her to let rip.

Brace yourself, Cody. Get ready for the hurricane coming your way.

She turns then. Her face is thunderous. Lightning could flash from those eyes.

'What the hell did you think you were doing?'

He forces himself to straighten his spine. Showing her that he's standing up for what he believes.

'It's a good plan,' he says simply.

'It's a fucking stupid plan,' she answers. 'And just because you managed to convince Superintendent Warner to go along with it, that doesn't make it any less stupid. He's as gung-ho as you are. What the hell did you think you were doing by going over my head?'

He thinks about repeating that it's a good plan, but decides against it. Life is too precious.

'I needed a second opinion.'

'Bullshit. You were being pig-headed. You think you know better than I do. You think you're right and I'm wrong. I bet if Warner had turned it down you'd have gone to the Chief Super. You were determined to have your way, because you're so damned sure of yourself.'

'I . . . I just thought we should give it a try.'

'Give it a try? You're not testing out a new recipe, Cody. You're not taking a different route to the pub. You do realise what you're letting yourself in for, don't you?'

He shrugs. 'I'm okay about it. Honestly. It's what I do.'

She shakes a finger at him. 'No. It's what you did. When you worked undercover. You don't do stuff like that anymore because of what happened. You work at MIT now. You work for me. And the boys and girls who work for me don't go running off to the headmaster when they don't get their own way. What did Warner say, anyway?'

'He . . . He said he thought it was an excellent idea. He said this is the kind of thing he's looking for in his officers. Innovation, originality, fortitude—'

Blunt puts a hand to her mouth. 'Stop, stop, I'm going to be sick. He said that? In a one-on-one chat? Jesus Christ, does he ever stop rehearsing for his next move up the ladder?'

Cody isn't sure Blunt should be saying these things about her boss in front of him, but right now she seems too upset to care.

She shakes her head in despair. 'I thought we had a better working relationship than this, Cody. I thought we could trust each other. I know I give you a hard time sometimes, but only when you need a kick in the pants, for your own good. Of all the people in this team I would trust with my life, it's you. You're a damn good copper. I know my saying all this is embarrassing you, but you're going to hear it anyway. I see great things in your future. You went through one of the most traumatic events an officer can possibly experience, but you fought back. You got back in the saddle. That takes guts. And now I'm starting to sound like Warner.'

Cody smiles at her to let her know how much he appreciates what she's saying to him, even though a part of him is denying most of it. If he's back in the saddle, then it's on a stallion that's galloping away with him.

'What I'm trying to say,' continues Blunt, 'is that you have damaged something today. You could have come and spoken to me again about it. My door is always open, you know that.'

'Would you have changed your mind?' he asks.

'The truth? No. Certainly not. I would have suspended you from duty rather than authorise this reckless action.'

'And now?'

'What do you mean?'

'Now that it's got the green light. Will you run it for me? The operation?'

She stares at him, and for a brief moment he is convinced he sees the glint of wetness in her eye.

'You want me to oversee the operation, the one in which you could possibly be killed?'

'Yes. Only I won't be killed. You won't allow it.'

She stares some more. Nods. 'Damn right I won't allow it. And Warner will have to put me in a strait-jacket to keep me away from this one.'

Cody straightens his back again. Less standing up for himself this time; more a coming to attention. A gesture of respect.

'Thank you, ma'am.'

A silence ensues. The two look into each other's eyes. Unspoken messages pass between them. A pact to deny death and to affirm life. Two very different people, with different backgrounds and different experiences, but both acknowledging what they share.

'Now get out,' says Blunt. 'And if you do get killed out there, don't come running back to me.'

When he has left, DCI Stella Blunt lets out a long sigh. She grabs a tissue from the box on her desk. Dabs at the corner of her eye.

Stupid, she thinks. Not Cody. Me. I'm the stupid one for allowing my feelings to get the better of me.

He's a copper. A brave one at that. One of the bravest I've ever known. He's doing what he believes is right. I respect and admire that.

And I wish he weren't going on this mission.

God help me, I wish it were somebody else putting their life on the line like this.

That's wrong. I shouldn't be showing any favouritism. But I can't help it. Sometimes I just can't stop myself.

Cody has noticed. Of course he has. Doesn't say anything, though. Doesn't ask for an explanation.

Best if he doesn't know. Best if he just thinks I'm a menopausal old fool.

Stay safe, Cody.

Webley. Marching along the hallway. Thinking, I'm going to nail his balls to the ceiling.

She catches up with Cody as he comes out of the men's toilets. In her fury, she doesn't even notice that he's wiping his hands down the sides of his trousers.

'What the hell do you think you're doing?' she demands.

He shows her his palms. 'It's not what it looks like. They're washed, honestly. The dryer wasn't working.'

'I'm not interested in your urination rituals, Cody. I'm talking about your fucking stupid plan.'

'Not you, too. You know, I'm beginning to think I should call this Operation Fuckwit.'

'Actually, I think that would be pretty apt. How the hell did you get a green light to go and throw yourself on a grenade?'

He shrugs. 'Cutbacks. It's cheaper than a redundancy package.'

She slaps his arm. 'Stop being a dick. You need to call it off.'

'Why?'

'Why? Because turning yourself into an easy victim is not recommended in the police manuals as a way of catching murderers.'

'You won't be saying that when he's in a cell.'

'I will be saying that if he's in a cell and you're in a coffin. Call it off, Cody.'

'I can't. The operation has already been approved.'

'Then get it unapproved. You don't know what you're doing.'

'Megan, I know exactly what I'm doing. Trust me.'

She lowers her voice. She didn't want to do this, but . . .

'Did you know what you were doing in the Armitage? What about at the post-mortem? And how about the photographer? How do I know this isn't just another of your moments?'

'They were different. They were knee-jerk reactions. I've thought this one through for a long time.'

'Really? Suppose I tell Blunt how you've been freaking out? Do you think she will still regard this as a carefully considered course of action?'

He looks at her sharply. 'You promised you wouldn't say anything. You said—'

'That was before you decided to go one-on-one with a vicious killer. Cody, this is your life we're talking about. I want you to stay alive.'

Cody reaches out and touches her arm. 'You almost sound like you care.'

She looks him in the eye, in a way she thought she'd never do again.

'I always cared, Cody. But you never listened. It never bothered you that I cared. So you know what? I'm not caring anymore. If you want to throw your life away, go ahead. I'm done with allowing you to keep hurting me.'

She turns then. Turns and storms away before she gets really angry with him.

And before he sees how hurt she really is.

32

It's killing him.

The waiting. He has waited four whole nights, and it's torture. He hasn't called them, he hasn't watched them. Above all, he hasn't killed.

The birds are getting desperate. He can tell just by looking at them. They seem more agitated than before. They are squabbling and pecking at each other. More than usual have died, for no apparent reason. They need him to do something. Now.

'ALL RIGHT!' he yells at the birds. 'I'm doing my best, aren't I? What good will getting caught do? These things need careful planning.'

He paces the room. Squelches through the bird shit.

Planning, yes. That's what's needed. And a little lateral thinking. Something different. Something they won't be expecting.

A thought occurs to him. He goes out onto the landing. Looks up at the hatch set into the ceiling. Thinks about what he's got stored up there in the loft. Smiles.

That'll do it.

Cody is starting to think this is one of the dumbest ideas he's ever had.

For one thing, he's had to change his work patterns. The killer does his thing at night. That means Cody has to be here at night, ready to go. Not that he's missing out on his sleep – he never gets much of that anyway. But it does mean he can't be here in the day, too – Blunt wasn't prepared to let him live in the station around the clock – which in turn means he's missing out on all the investigatory work.

The only consolation is that he doesn't appear to be missing out on much. The investigation has hit a dead end. No eagle-eyed witnesses; no telltale forensics; no Gazzas just dying to sign a confession.

In his more confident moments, Cody tells himself the case has stalled because the other detectives are missing his insight and perception and downright determination. Most of the time, though, he doesn't believe that. Most of the time he is worried that they are never going to catch this guy, with or without Cody's involvement. And it's when he starts thinking that way that he wonders if his scheme to trap the killer is as hare-brained as Blunt said it was.

Blunt herself is tucked up in bed. Probably. Cody knows nothing about her nocturnal activities. Doesn't really want such thoughts entering his head. Blunt is needed here during the day. She's not as dispensable as he is.

He accepts it's his own fault. Sitting here at – what time is it now? – two in the morning is what he asked for. He wonders how many more lonely nights he's going to spend in this room before he abandons this ridiculous undertaking.

He thinks the killer might have smelled a rat. He doesn't appear to have called the switchboard once in the past four nights. He could have ended his killing spree. He could have left the country. He could be at home, fast asleep like the sensible majority of the population.

Cody wishes he could go to sleep himself right now, here in this deserted incident room. He wishes he could close his eyes and drift off, to be awakened only when the call comes in. But it's hard enough sleeping in his own house, his own bed. Here it's impossible. It's not the noise: this part of the building is deathly quiet right now. It's the anticipation that's the problem. Cody finds himself running ceaselessly through scenarios in his mind. What if the killer does such-and-such? What if this happens, or that goes wrong?

All to no avail, of course. He has no idea what the killer has planned. He doesn't know if he will strike tonight, tomorrow night, or never again. This could be a complete waste of time.

The phone on his desk rings.

It's nothing, he tells himself. Don't get excited. Somebody is checking up on you, or a call has been put through to the wrong extension. Save the adrenalin for another time.

'Detective Cody?' says a male voice.

'Yes?'

'It's Inspector Mostyn in the control room. I think we're on.'

'I'll be right over, sir,' Cody answers.

He puts the phone down, his expression grave in the knowledge he's about to go fishing for a cop killer.

Cody makes his way to an annexe connected to the main control room. This separate area is used for communications during special operations, and right now is bustling with officers handling calls, issuing orders and making plans.

He is led over to a table covered in maps, while a member of tech services fastens miniature cameras to him, then checks their operation on a portable monitor. Cody feels weighed down by the uniform, the stab-proofs and all the equipment. He's not used to wearing anything more substantial than a suit and tie. With the paraphernalia hanging off him now he feels like an overdecorated Christmas tree.

A door swings violently open, and Blunt comes bustling in. She is red in the face, and panting. Cody imagines it's the swiftest she's ever jumped out of bed and high-tailed it into work.

'Is this it?' she asks of nobody in particular. 'Is it him?'

From where he has been directing conversations with his men at one of the consoles, a uniformed officer breaks off and comes over to Blunt. Inspector Mostyn offers his hand, and she takes it.

'Stella,' he says.

'Nick,' she replies. 'Is this it?'

'Looks like.'

'I want to hear the call,' she says.

Cody glances at her. Normally unflappable, she now looks anxious.

Mostyn turns to the comms officer. 'Can we replay it over the speakers?'

The officer nods, flicks a couple of switches. The wall speakers burst into life.

'Police, can I help you?'

'I want to report some trespassers.'

Cody watches as Blunt listens intently to the voice. It's a harsh whisper again, just like the other calls. This time, however, the accent is Irish.

'Certainly, sir. Can I have your name and phone number, please?'

'No names. There's an old empty office building on Porter Street, close to Waterloo Street at the docks. The sign outside says "Emerson Printing Supplies". A couple of young kids keep going in there. I think they're planning to set fire to the place.'

The line goes dead then.

'That's it?' Blunt asks.

Mostyn nods. 'He didn't hang about. Obviously he's become a lot more cautious about his calls being traced.'

'And was it? Traced, I mean?'

'No. There wasn't time.'

Blunt turns to Cody. 'What do you think? Same guy?'

Cody shrugs. 'Could be. Seemed to me like he was trying too hard to sound Irish.'

Blunt looks uncertain about the whole thing. Like she needs someone in the room to provide her with some reassurance. She turns to Mostyn.

'This could be anything,' she says. 'It could be an ex-IRA member with a thing about Brits, for all we know. There could be a bomb in that building.'

Mostyn nods. 'I didn't authorise this op. I was just asked to coordinate it. If somebody tells me to pull it, I'll pull it. Do you want to make some calls?'

Cody can tell she is tempted, and feels the need to head her off at the pass. 'Ma'am, it's fine. We can't miss this opportunity, and we're running out of time.'

She opens her mouth to say something, but Mostyn beats her to it. 'There are other options.'

Blunt's eyes are greedy for the alternatives. 'What options?'

'Well, for one thing, we don't have to send anyone in alone. We could just surround and storm the place.'

Blunt's gaze flicks back to Cody, as if to ask if that will satisfy him.

But Cody has to disappoint her: 'No. This guy isn't stupid. He might not even be in there. He might just be observing from a distance, the way we think he probably was the last few times he called. If he sees an army go in, he'll just disappear, and then he'll change tactics. If he does that, we might never catch him. And if he *is* in there, he's probably got an escape route planned. Through the next building or over the roof or something. No, the whole point of this is to draw him out, and the only way we'll do that is if he thinks I'm a soft target.'

'You *are* a soft target,' says Blunt. She looks to Mostyn again. 'You said options, plural. What else?'

'Doesn't have to be young Cody here. We could send in an armed officer.'

Cody is already shaking his head. 'Nope. Any thought that it's not just a normal beat copper in there, and the guy will run. You can't send in someone with a Heckler & Koch and expect our killer to hang around.'

Mostyn gives a smile. 'I was thinking more of a concealed sidearm.'

More head-shaking from Cody. 'There would still be an element of risk to the officer. Correct me if I'm wrong, but Armed Response probably aren't used to walking into threat situations without guns at the ready, knowing they have to be prepared to whip out their weapons like it's *High Noon* or whatever.'

'Well, that's true, but—'

Blunt finishes Mostyn's sentence: 'But you're not accustomed to situations like this either, Cody.'

'I was an undercover officer for years,' he says. 'I'm used to being surrounded by people who would slit my throat without a second thought if they found out what I did for a living.'

'That was then, Cody. Not now! Now you're a member of a murder squad. You're not Batman.'

There's a desperation in her voice that is becoming more evident. It's the tone of a worried parent, not of a superior officer. Cody senses that it's making Mostyn uncomfortable.

'We need to make a decision,' Mostyn says. 'This guy has become used to waiting for us to show up, but he won't wait forever.'

Cody's answer is directed at Blunt. 'I'm fine with it. Let's go and catch this bastard.'

Blunt says nothing, but Cody sees the challenge in her eyes. She wants him to back out, and he can't.

'Okay,' says Mostyn. He nods to the technician. 'Explain the set-up.'

'Pretty straightforward,' says the tech. 'Miniature cameras on the shoulders, looking front and rear. We'll see what you see, Sergeant Cody, plus anything that might come up behind you. We've got infrared too, so we can see in the dark, even if you can't. You're also fitted with a microphone and earpiece. If the target is in there, you won't be able to give us a running commentary or he'll know something's up, but you can call us in if you need to, and we can warn you if we see anything.'

'Okay,' says Cody.

Mostyn directs everyone to look at the maps on the table. 'Here's Waterloo Street, and here's Porter Street. We've already stationed armed officers in several unmarked vehicles. They're here, here and here.'

He gestures towards the other uniformed officer standing by the comms man. 'Inspector Hewison here will direct the men if we need to send them in. Your job, Cody, is just to be our eyes and ears, okay? No acts of heroism, please. This man carries a knife and he is willing to use it. If you see him, you yell. Don't be subtle about it. Make it clear to him that you're calling in backup. That's it. Leave it to us to come in and take him down. If he's got any sense he'll try to run, but if he comes at you, be ready with your baton. Okay, Cody? Have you got all that?'

Cody nods his understanding, but not his assent. He has no intention of shouting for reinforcements unless it becomes absolutely necessary. He wants a piece of this sick maniac for himself. And it's not about heroism or glory-seeking. It's about getting some kind of revenge for the deaths of three other police officers. He wants to be the one to slap the cuffs on their murderer. He wants to be the one to issue the caution, and perhaps one or two other messages to this bastard. He wants that sense of closure.

'Then off you go, Sergeant Cody,' says Mostyn. 'And good luck. Just remember we're right behind you.'

Mostyn moves away, leaving Blunt to have the final word.

'One thing,' she says quietly. 'I'm staying here in the ops room. I'll be watching and I'll be listening to everything you do. Listen out for my voice, okay? I don't care what these men here might say to you, if you hear me shout then you do what I say, even if it's the opposite of what they want. If I tell you to get the hell out of there, then you do it. Do you understand me, Cody?'

He smiles. He feels like a kid being sent into his first day at school. He half expects Blunt to wet a handkerchief with saliva and rub the dirt from his face.

'Say it!' she commands.

'I understand,' he says. 'But I'll be fine. In an hour's time you'll be congratulating me for nabbing this guy.'

She nods, but without conviction.

Nothing like a bit of faith to boost your confidence, he thinks.

33

Cody drives slowly and steadily. Nothing to indicate haste. He doesn't want to arouse the suspicions of the target, who could be watching him right now.

Which is an eerie feeling in itself. The eyes of a killer fixed on you. Studying you. Thinking about the best way to dispatch you, to mutilate you, to use your corpse as the bearer of his next sinister message.

But Cody has already decided it's not going to come to that. He's going to put an end to such shenanigans. He's going to arrest this maniac. And, in the process, he might even administer a couple of whacks with his baton for good measure. Might even turn off his cameras while he rams his boot into the deviant's groin a few times.

And yet . . .

The feeling is growing. The doubt. Creeping into Cody's gut. Sitting there with its poison and making him want to retch it up. It always returns at moments like this. The thing is not to let it win.

He finds Porter Street. Parks up at the dockland end. In the port's prime this area would have been bustling during daylight hours. Now much of it sits forlorn. Crumbling buildings staring longingly at the grey river, as if waiting for the ships to return. At night it's even worse: it seems haunted by its past, just as Cody himself is.

He notices a blacked-out people carrier parked opposite, and knows instinctively that it's filled with police officers armed to the teeth. It seems so conspicuous to him, but he tells himself that it's only because he's on the job. He hopes that it hasn't even registered with the killer.

'On scene,' he says. 'Getting out of the car now. You reading me?'

'Loud and clear,' says Mostyn over his earpiece.

Cody gets out. Locks up the car. Starts up the street.

It's a narrow road. Dark and forbidding. A few cars, parked tightly against the walls to allow traffic to pass.

Cody walks slowly. Tries to look as though he's on just another routine call-out. A normal, unsuspecting copper checking out a call that he thinks will amount to nothing.

He wonders if he's being watched right now. If he is, where will the observer be? At one of the mesh-covered windows above? In one of the shadowy doorways, waiting to pounce as he passes?

He lowers his hand to the grip of his baton. Just in case.

His shoes click loudly on the cracked pavement. If the killer is up ahead, he will know exactly where his prey is. He will know exactly when to strike.

Cody's fingers caress the baton. Just in case.

It gets darker the further he walks. Not much in the way of street lighting up here. He pulls his torch from its holder on his belt. Switches it on and plays it over the buildings. The shadows dance and sway and bend as if coming to life.

Most of the walls are bare, but Cody catches sight of a faded and cracked sign above one of the doorways. He moves closer to it. Raises his torch to get a better look.

Emerson Printing Supplies.

He's here.

And now that gremlin in his stomach is really starting to make its presence felt. Pinching and twisting Cody's insides.

Cody lowers the cone of light from his torch. The painted red door below the sign looks secure enough, but Cody is guessing it's not.

'I'm going in,' he says.

'Be careful, Cody,' says a voice. Blunt, this time.

Cody smiles. He can imagine Mostyn frowning at her interference. But she won't care about that. She would make her voice heard even if she didn't outrank Mostyn.

He steps up to the door. Pushes on it. It doesn't budge. This puzzles him. Is this the only way in?

He tries again, harder this time. And now the door moves, its bottom edge scraping along the floor. He continues to push, all the while shining his torchlight into the blackness beyond.

When the door is as wide open as he can make it, he steps over the threshold.

One step. Just one. He's not going charging in like a rhinoceros. No. Softly, softly. Scan the area. Take your time.

He's in what used to be a lobby area. Ahead of him is a counter and, set into the wall alongside it, a shuttered reception window. Corridors run along either side of the lobby, both tunnelling into impenetrable darkness. A few items of furniture are still here, but only because they are broken or unusable: a chair with only three legs, an overturned filing cabinet with a massive dent in its side and a drawer missing, a bookcase with no shelves. There are alcoves here – places where someone could lie in wait.

Cody thumbs the button on the radio at his shoulder, then speaks loudly. 'Echo One to Control. I'm in the building. No sign of occupants at present.'

The radio blares back at him: 'Roger that, Echo One. Keep us apprised.'

It's all show, of course. He needs to look, act and sound like a real uniformed plod investigating a minor crime.

He raises his voice and shouts into the room now: 'All right, lads. I'm a police officer. Show yourselves before you get into any more trouble.'

Convincing, he thinks. I should be on the stage.

Getting no response, he makes sure he shines his light into every nook and cranny before moving further into the room.

'Check behind the counter,' says Mostyn.

Good idea. Why didn't I think of that?

He steps towards the counter. The floorboards squeak beneath his shoes. He is reminded of a comedy film in which it turns out it wasn't the floorboards but the character's own feet that were making the noise. Seemed hilarious at the time. Not so much now.

If somebody jumps up from behind that counter, he thinks, I am so going to scream like a girl.

He gets to the counter. Nothing so far, but then he cannot see over the top of it. He leans forward. Further, further. Shines his torch into the space behind. Appears to be nobody there, but then he still cannot see what might be lurking underneath the countertop. You could squeeze a person beneath it quite easily – several people, in fact.

The noise is sudden, and belonging to something of substantial weight. Cody leaps back, whips out his baton.

'Cody!' Mostyn cries. 'What is it?'

Cody says nothing. He's not sure what to answer, because he doesn't know the source of the noise. But something moved underneath that counter. Something definitely moved.

And then before he even knows what he has in mind, he is using the overturned filing cabinet as a stepping stone to leap onto the counter and then down into the area beyond. He stands there, baton resting on his shoulder in preparation to strike, while he frantically throws light into every inch of the space underneath that countertop.

Books. A large pile of books had toppled over. Shit. He can breathe again.

'Cody. What happened?'

Cody keeps his voice low now as he talks into his collar mike: 'Some books. They fell over. It was just . . . books.'

A pause from Mostyn. Cody wonders what the man is thinking. Probably that Cody isn't the right man for this job if he's going to crap his pants every time some paper rustles.

'Okay. You ready to continue?'

In other words: *Get a move on. We haven't got all night.*

'Affirmative.'

Affirmative. He doesn't often use that word. He thinks he's using it now only because it sounds more militaristic, more macho. He needs a dose of machismo right now. He needs to be Bruce Willis or Liam Neeson or whoever. Not a lily-livered bobby with a torch and a stick.

There's a door on this side of the counter, leading to the room with the shuttered window. He tries the handle, but it's locked.

He hops back over the counter, then goes past the window and into the mouth of the left-hand corridor. He aims his torch along the passageway. Not much there, but doors opening to left and right, and a staircase at the end. And more shadowy alcoves, of course. Lots of places where somebody could be waiting, hammer in one hand, knife in the other. Or maybe a shotgun.

He thinks, A shotgun? Who said anything about a shotgun? Since when does this guy use firearms?

Well, how about tonight?

No, he thinks. Not tonight. Not ever. He doesn't use guns. That's not in the script. And if he does have a gun, then, well . . . I have this stick.

He orders himself to focus. There are no guns here. Probably not even another human being here. Just him and the rats. Because there are bound to be rats. They'll be as big as cats in a place like this. That's guaranteed.

'Okay, Cody,' says Mostyn, 'you need to be methodical here. One floor at a time. Clear the whole floor before you go up to the next one. Check each and every door. We need to be sure.'

Cody looks at all the doors ahead of him. There are a lot of them – and these are just the ones he can see. Clearing this whole building with just one man could take all night.

He wonders if his nerves will be able to hold out for that length of time.

But no point worrying about it. It has to be done.

So here goes.

The patience of a saint. A curious phrase. Why are saints so renowned for their patience?

Whatever. He's got that amount of patience. He will wait here for as long as it takes.

And it will be different this time. He has a secret weapon. Something they won't be expecting.

It was a tough decision. A difficult thing to give up. The thrill of getting up close was so exhilarating. To feel the crushing impact on a human skull, to experience it travelling through his hand and up his arm. And then the work with the knife. Oh, yes! The cries and the pleas and the whimpers and the gurgles.

Hard to abandon all that.

But, like everything in life – and death – sometimes you have to compromise. The end result will be the same: another police scumbag wiped from the face of the earth. It is only the execution that is different. Ha – execution! A most appropriate word in the circumstances.

But if the mission is to continue, then it has to be like this. He has to protect himself. He has to be able to do the job and then walk away, free to move on to the next victim.

So now it's distance work. No more close and personal. Shame, really, but there it is.

Come and get it, sucker.

He smiles. This is still pretty damn cool. It will be fun.

Sitting there quietly in the dark, he brings the stock of his weapon to his shoulder, peers along the sights, and rests his finger lightly on the trigger.

And then he waits.

With the patience of a saint.

34

By the time Cody gets to the top floor he is exhausted. Not physi-cally, but mentally.

It's the strain of remaining alert, of forcing himself to expect the unexpected. After checking room after desolate room, it starts to become tempting to think that the next one will be just as devoid of threat as all the others. It's a dangerous urge – one upon which the killer might be relying. Knowing that fatigue and inattentiveness will set in, he may well have chosen one of the final rooms in the search in which to secrete himself.

So Cody needs to keep vigilant. Needs to tap into a new reservoir of adrenalin for each of the last few rooms. He's nearly at the end. Mustn't become careless now.

When he gets there, he finds that the layout of the top floor is different from the others. The fire door at the head of the stairs opens into a huge area, with just a couple of doors leading from it into what must be tiny offices. Cody wonders whether this floor was used mainly for storage. Or perhaps there were workbenches here at one time, staffed by people putting together items for shipping.

Not much furniture here now, which makes it easier to search. Two rows of pillars stretching from floor to ceiling. Several piles of old packing crates. Some large pieces of board resting against one of the pillars. Other than that, not too many places to hide.

It smells damp up here. Cody shines his torch up at the ceiling and finds a couple of large holes where the rain has come in. The holes are easily big enough for a man to climb through into the roof space above.

There's nobody up there, he thinks. There's nobody in this entire building. I should just finish the recce and get out of here. It's looking like our man has brought us out on another wild goose chase, so I should just confirm that and go.

Cody advances into the room. It reminds him of something. A place he's been before.

No, he tells himself. No, it doesn't. Erase that thought. It's nothing like it.

More creaking floorboards. And they feel slightly spongy underfoot. The rain has rotted them, probably. He wonders if he's about to go plummeting like a stone through the whole building.

He takes a few more steps. Just those two doors at the far end to investigate. Check those out and he's done.

Another step and . . .

Something moves. To Cody's left. He's sure of it. Okay, maybe not sure. There was no sound. But something seemed to flicker in his peripheral vision.

He turns his torch in that direction. Sees nothing, of course, because there's nothing here. Not another soul.

'If you're in here, lads,' he says, 'then come out now. We need to get you out of here.'

Nothing at first, but then a noise. To his right this time. He whirls round. Stands stock-still while he wills his beam of light to seek and discover. He can almost feel his ears twitch with the effort of trying to capture more sounds.

What was that noise? A laugh? It sounded like a laugh. A low, muted snigger.

But if that were true, there would be somebody standing there right now. And there isn't. Look. Nobody there.

His ears pick up the thudding of his own heart. It feels like it's bouncing around his ribcage like a rubber ball.

Mostyn's voice bursts in again: 'Okay, Cody. This is starting to look fruitless. Finish up, but keep your wits about you.'

Cody moves on again. Mostyn is right. It was another prank call. The killer didn't fall for Cody's plan.

Another noise. Like the shuffling of a wooden chair on the hard floor. Cody spins again.

There *is* a chair there. Right in front of one of the pillars. Was that there before? He doesn't remember it. But what he does remember is . . .

No. Stop it.

But it's exactly like it. A little darker in here, but this could almost have been the place. The pillars, the musty dampness. The old chair. Only difference now is that he's not sitting in it. He's not tied to it like he was that other time. And of course there are no—

A cry! From somewhere behind Cody. He definitely heard that. A whimper of pain.

He advances quickly, baton in strike position again. Past a stack of crates. Around a pillar.

Nothing. There's nothing there. Stop this!

From Mostyn: 'Cody? Are you okay?'

Cody puts a thumb up in front of his chest camera. But he doesn't feel okay at all.

'All right,' says Mostyn. 'Then clear those last two rooms and come back in.'

Two rooms, thinks Cody. That's all. We're almost there. Concentrate. See those doors at the far end? And the tiny window between them? The window with the face grinning out at you?

What?

The pale face. See it? Staring. Laughing. Waiting.

'NO!' he yells.

Mostyn responds: 'Cody?'

He ignores Mostyn. Concentrates all his attention on that window. It's gone. Whatever was there has gone now.

Or perhaps has just dropped down from the window.

Perhaps he's still in there, just waiting for you to enter.

No, he thinks. I'm being ridiculous. I didn't see anything.

'Cody!' says Mostyn. 'What are you doing? Clear the rooms.'

He wants to follow orders. Wants to complete his task. But it's dark in here. The bloody torch is useless. He can see only a small part of the room at any one time. Things could be moving around, shifting from shadow to shadow, and he wouldn't even know it. And it feels hot in here, too. Middle of October, no heating on, and yet it's bloody boiling.

'Cody.'

His name being uttered again. But not by Mostyn this time. This is lower in tone. Gruffer.

And it didn't come over the earpiece.

Cody spins on his heels. Does the same again and again, each time urging the yellow light to tell him he's not going mad.

Another menacing laugh.

'Please.'

A single word in a voice he recognises. A single word encapsulating all the begging for mercy that could possibly be imagined.

This cannot be happening. It's not real. Not real.

'Cody, what the hell's going on?'

This from Mostyn. At least he thinks it is. He's not sure anymore. Too many voices, too many things going on.

A scream, suddenly cut off. Cody himself yells in fear.

'Cody? Do you need backup? Repeat, do you need backup?'

'Negative.'

He starts back towards the stairs. There are noises behind him. They are building to form a more complete picture. A scene in which human beings are perpetrating the most horrific acts he has ever witnessed.

'Cody, where are you going? You haven't finished clearing the building.'

'It's clear.'

He doesn't know why he's lying. The officers back at base are fully aware that he didn't check those last two rooms. All he knows is that he has to get out of here. He thought he could cope, and he can't. Can't even manage a simple job like this. He needs to get out. Needs to run for his life.

And he does run. Even though the only light he's got is from his torch, and even though a single wrong step could send him hurtling to his death, he runs. He needs to be as far away from this place as possible.

He hears the babble of voices in his ear, Blunt's among them, all clamouring to be heard. But he's not paying them any attention. He is on the edge of blind panic, and he just needs to flee.

He races down the staircase. He hears it creak and groan and occasionally snap in complaint, but he flies down it nonetheless. The threat of death on these steps is immeasurably preferable to the fate awaiting him back there on the top floor.

And even as he thinks this, he is telling himself there is nothing on that top floor. This is his sick mind playing its sick games, causing him to run away from his own shadow.

But rationality has surrendered. It speaks to him without conviction, knowing it has lost. His primitive instincts have taken over. It is fight or flight, and he has chosen to save his hide to live another pitiful day. It sickens him, and he knows he will regret this, and he is crying with the mental anguish of it even before he gets to the ground floor and goes full tilt towards that door back on to the street, back into the glorious fresh city air. Back to safety.

This is safer.

Wait for the police to come to you. No sneaking up on them. No trying to catch them by surprise. Just sit and wait.

Here, in your car. Out on the street.

If it all goes wrong, you can start up the engine and drive away. Just sit and wait. Window slightly open. Enough to get a shot out.

And he's a good shot, too. A little bit rusty, perhaps, but he got some practice in earlier. He won't miss.

He's had to be patient, though. Those saints – well, he bets they were never this patient. His arse has gone numb and his joints have stiffened up with all this hanging around in a car. Had to pee into an empty plastic milk carton earlier. The indignity of it. The things he has to go through just to kill a few coppers.

Still, it'll be worth—

But wait. Here he comes. An honest-to-goodness policeman. In a bit of a hurry, by the looks of things. That'll make the shot more difficult, but he appreciates a challenge.

So here goes . . .

He shoulders the stock again. Grips the weapon firmly. Takes aim. Blinks to clear his eyes. Wait for it. Wait for it. Hold your breath. Caress the trigger. And . . .

Fire!

Bingo. A bullseye. Right smack in the forehead. Probably dead before he hits the ground. Nice.

He starts up the engine. Edges the car past the still twitching body. Tosses out the usual parting gift before he steps on the gas.

He takes a deep lungful of air as he drives. It smells sweet. It smells of success.

In the ops room pandemonium breaks out. Their recent view on the monitors has been a dizzying whirl of flashing light as Cody sped them down through the building. Their rapid-fire questions were ignored, their instructions disobeyed. Cody's only responses came in the form of panting and grunting – nothing intelligible. They heard the pounding of his feet as he ran towards the door, then an almost panic-stricken fumbling and banging as Cody worked seemingly in desperation to fight his way through it. And then, once he finally managed his exit, their glimpse of the street was short-lived before the sudden guttural cry from Cody accompanied the crazy tilt and pan of the camera. They watched the world spin, and then the hard pavement rush up to meet them, and they all flinched as the lens smacked into its unyielding surface. And then . . .

Stillness.

Mostyn calls out to Cody. Blunt does the same, but with more of an emotional edge to her voice. And when they get no response, Mostyn is barking orders to others, urging them to get in there without delay, and amongst the words he utters are the words that no police officer, least of all DCI Blunt, wants to hear.

Because what he is saying is that there is a possible man down.

35

DCI Blunt remains frozen, staring at a screen that shows her only blackness, listening for sounds that do not come.

And when sounds do finally reach her, they do not harbour the voice of Cody, strain as she might to hear it. They are the squeals of tyres, the thuds of car doors, the pounding of boots, the barking of orders – all carried over Cody's microphone, but apparently not heard by him directly.

Because he does not move, he does not speak, he does not respond.

She believes he is dead. She does not know how or why, but something awful has happened tonight. Something she dreaded from the very inception of this damned stupid operation.

'Sergeant Cody! Sergeant Cody, are you all right?'

This from one of the armed officers on the ground. But Blunt knows in her heart it will not be answered, because Cody is far from all right. Cody is—

'Unnh.'

Her heart leaps, because it sounds like . . . But no. It must be the other guy, perhaps straining to lift Cody and get him away from the danger.

'Unnh, yeah. Yeah, I'm okay.'

And that is Cody. That is most certainly Cody. And now she is filling up, and she can't help it, and she doesn't care who knows it.

'Cody!' she yells. 'Talk to me. Tell me you're okay.'

'I'm okay. I . . . I fell. I was coming out of the building and I fell. I think I banged my head.'

Blunt looks at Mostyn. 'Get him out of there.'

She sees Mostyn's expression of puzzlement and dissatisfaction with all that he has just witnessed, and she answers it with, 'We can dissect this later. Please, can we just get him back where he belongs?'

She knows there is too much pleading in her voice, and she can tell that Mostyn is making a mental note of her lack of objectivity. Well, stuff him, she thinks. This isn't about me. It's about my officer. He needs to be safe now.

Mostyn turns to Hewison, in charge of the armed response officers. Nods his head. More commands are issued.

Blunt moves away from the comms station. Away from the chatter. She tries to settle her thoughts.

She closes her eyes for a few seconds, her back to everyone else in the room. Cody is alive. The crisis is over. She can go back to being the gruff intimidating DCI. Be the professional they are used to seeing.

A voice filters through to her. She is not sure to whom it belongs, but someone is demanding her attention. Okay, she thinks. About face. Show them what they're expecting.

But then she sees their expressions. All of them the same. Grim. Funereal. And all she wants to do is crumble.

'What is it?' she asks weakly.

It is Mostyn who responds: 'A policeman has been killed. PC Tony Stebbins. He was coming out of Hoylake police station, on his way home after finishing a stint of overtime. Somebody fired a crossbow bolt into his head.'

36

They will come, of course. The questions. He is dreading them, but they will come.

Before that, he spends several hours in the A & E Department of the Royal while he gets his noggin checked out. And when he finally gets the news that his skull is still intact and his brain is none the worse for wear, he receives an order that he is to go home and rest for several hours more.

He gets no rest. He hardly ever sleeps anyway, but the knowledge that he will need to explain himself to the bosses keeps him edgy all day.

When the phone rings, he ignores it. His colleagues will be back on duty. They will have heard rumours of what happened to him last night. They will want to know the full story. And a story would be what he would have to deliver if he answered their calls. A tissue of lies to explain his erratic behaviour.

He doesn't want to do that to his friends, but he certainly can't hand them the truth. So, better to evade the questions.

But that can't last forever. When it gets to the middle of the afternoon, he decides he needs to face the music. Head throbbing, he gets into his car and takes himself over to the station.

As he enters the incident room, he is surprised by the expressions on the faces of the other detectives. They seem somehow darker than he expected, and that causes him to worry. What has been said about him?

Webley is first out of her chair. She steps right up to him, blocking his way.

'Are you okay?' she asks.

He points to the lump on his head. 'Other than looking like the Elephant Man, yes, I'm fine.'

'I . . . I tried to call you. Several of us tried.'

'I know. I couldn't get to sleep because of you lot.' He laughs as he says this, but the humour doesn't rub off. Something else is bothering Webley.

'Why?' he asks. 'What have I missed?'

She doesn't get a chance to answer before Blunt calls out Cody's name. He looks over Webley's shoulder and sees his boss filling the door frame.

'Gotta go,' he says. 'Fill me in later, okay?'

He moves away from her, but still with the feeling that he's the only one not privy to a vital piece of news.

When he gets into Blunt's office, she signals him to close the door. Here come the questions, he thinks.

He jerks a thumb behind him. 'What's going on? They're acting like it's the day of my funeral.'

She narrows her eyes for a second. Then they widen again, as if in astonished realisation that he really doesn't know what everybody else knows.

'I'll get to that in a minute,' she says. 'First of all, we need to talk about last night.'

'Yes, ma'am.'

'So? What happened? It was all going fine until you got to the top floor, and then you seemed to freak out. What the hell was going on?'

'I thought I heard something, ma'am.'

Which is true, he thinks. I heard my name and I heard laughter and I heard screaming and . . .

'You heard something? What kind of something?'

'A person. On the stairs. That's why I went running down. I was convinced I heard somebody else in the building.'

'I see. And did you catch a glimpse of this person?'

'No, ma'am.'

'You ran out of the room, and all the way down the stairs, and you didn't once see this person you were chasing?'

'No, ma'am. It was dark. All I had was a torch.'

'Didn't stop you running hell for leather, though, did it? I mean, one could be forgiven for thinking that you were the one being chased.'

'I . . . I suppose it could have looked like that. I guess I was moving pretty fast down those stairs.'

'Yes, you were. And when you got to the bottom?'

'Ma'am?'

'When you got to the bottom of the stairs, what happened then?'

'I . . . I couldn't see anyone, so I thought he must have gone through the front door. So I went that way too.'

'How?'

He pauses, shakes his head. 'I don't . . .'

'How did you go through the door? Cautiously?'

'No. Not really. In fact, I just burst through it. I thought I was hot on his heels.'

'You did? Even though you couldn't see this person? You thought you were right behind him?'

'Yes. That's what it sounded like to me.'

'That's what it sounded like? So you could hear two sets of feet on the stairs – yours and his?'

'I thought so. I mean, that's how it seemed at the time.'

This is crap, he thinks. This is so much bullshit, and she knows it.

'We couldn't hear anything. On our speakers. We could only hear you.'

'Well, with respect, ma'am—'

'We switched your cameras to infrared, too. We couldn't see any other person in that building, at any time.'

'I . . . I didn't have the benefit of those cameras, ma'am. I couldn't see as well as you could.'

She shakes her head, as if with some sadness. 'No. I suppose not. You knew we were there, though. Why didn't you call for backup?'

'I didn't think I needed it.'

She sits back in her chair, her face a picture of incredulity. 'Really? You're chasing a suspected murderer through a building in which you have almost zero visibility, and you don't think you need assistance?'

He realises his leg is shaking with nerves, and he has to put a hand on his knee to steady it.

'I thought I could handle it. I thought it was one-on-one. He was running from me. He was scared. It seemed to me I had the upper hand.'

'But this guy is a master at setting traps. We know that from past experience. We made it very clear when you were briefed how you should handle this. Mostyn told you in no uncertain terms: you find someone, you holler, that's all. Do you remember that?'

'Yes, ma'am, I do. I guess I got a little carried away.'

She nods gravely. 'Carried away. Yes, that's a good way of putting it.'

She squares up some papers on her desk while she squares up the thoughts in her head.

'Armed response searched every inch of that building. They didn't find anyone, or any sign that anybody else but you had been there. They also report that nobody came out of that building ahead of you.'

'That doesn't alter what I believed I heard, ma'am.'

'No, it doesn't. Because that's what's at the heart of this, isn't it? What you believed.'

'Ma'am?'

'The suggestion has been made, Cody, that you lost it in there. That you panicked, went to pieces.'

Cody wonders who made the suggestion. Most likely Mostyn, but it could have come directly from Blunt herself.

He shakes his head emphatically. 'That's not right. I was in control at all times. Well, until I banged my head.'

Blunt's sigh is a heavy one. 'Nathan, I want you to be honest with me. We both know what you've been through. One of the reasons I objected to your plan to draw out our killer was precisely because of your history. I wasn't sure you were capable of handling it. Mentally, I mean. What I saw last night – well, that looked to me like someone having an anxiety attack. Don't get me wrong – I'm not blaming you in any way – but I need the truth. I need to know what kind of state you're in.'

He wants to tell her. She is asking calmly and with genuine warmth and interest, and he wants to tell her everything. Open up to her about what a basket case he really is, and how he proved that to himself and everybody else last night. He needs rest, he needs help, he needs somebody to talk to.

'I'm absolutely fine, ma'am,' he says.

She stares at him for a long, long time. Penetrates his skull with her staring. She can read the truth, he thinks. She can see the messages of desperation and anguish passing across my brain like a ticker tape.

'Then that's what I'll put in the report,' she says finally. 'An honest mistake. You put yourself into what was potentially a highly dangerous situation, and when you heard what you believed to be the suspect, you set off in pursuit without even a thought for your own safety. That's how I'll write it up, Cody, because of what you've just told me. Who knows, you might even get a commendation for this.'

He realises she is deliberately making him feel uncomfortable. Letting him know he could be in line for an accolade he hardly deserves. That's her punishment for his lies, and she's right to dish it out.

He stands up, anxious to get the hell out of here.

'Sit down, Cody. We're not done yet.'

So, what else? What additional mental persecution does she have planned for me?

Says Blunt, 'From the way you acted when you came in, I got the impression you haven't yet been fully briefed about the events of last night.'

'Er, no, ma'am. I went to get checked out at the hospital, and then I went home. This is the first proper discussion I've had about it.'

'Nobody called you?'

'They tried. I switched off my phones. I was shattered.'

Another lie, but what the hell difference does another drop in that murky ocean make?

'And you haven't seen the television news?'

Oh, crap. What is this? What was Webley trying to tell me out there?

'No, ma'am.'

'Well, Cody, I hate to be the one to tell you this, but our killer struck again last night.'

No. This can't be happening. I had a trap set. He was meant to fall into my trap.

'Where? When?'

'Just outside Hoylake police station. PC Tony Stebbins, walking back home after doing some overtime. He was murdered at just about the same time you were searching the building at the docks.'

Shit, shit, shit.

Cody puts his head in his hands. 'Oh, Christ. The bastard. The devious, sneaky little bastard.'

She could try to make him feel better about things. She could tell him that his idea was a good idea nonetheless, that the murder would have taken place even without the attention and resources diverted on to his admirable operation. But she does none of this. She leaves him in torment, and again he knows he deserves it.

'What happened?' he groans. 'Same MO as the others?'

'Actually, no. This time the killer played it safe. He did it from a distance. Used a crossbow. Good shot, too. Hit Stebbins right in the forehead. The pathologist says he would have died instantly.'

'Jesus. The guy was wandering the streets with a crossbow? And nobody noticed?'

'We assume he drove there. Fired from his parked car.'

'Do we know that for certain? Any CCTV of the car?'

Blunt looks glum. 'It was out of sight of the station's cameras, but we're going through other footage from cameras in the area. I'm not hopeful, though. Chances are the car was stolen just for this job. And this is Hoylake we're talking about. It's not exactly a hotbed of crime. Nobody was expecting something like this to happen there. Our killer has changed his pattern yet again. He's moved out of the city, almost certainly because it was getting too hot for him here. He's wise to us. He knows we're trying to trap him. Hence the diversionary tactics involving you last night.'

Cody says nothing for a while. Tries to let all this horrific information percolate through his exhausted brain. When it does, it brings with it another question.

'Was there a bird this time? A message?'

Blunt nods. 'His method of execution might have changed, but he still wants to tease us. He left a dead robin this time. The note on its leg said, "Who'll dig his grave?"'

Cody thinks about this, but Blunt answers it for him.

'We've beaten you to it this time. It's a line from "Cock Robin": "Who killed Cock Robin? I, said the sparrow, with my bow and arrow". Then, later on, it goes: "Who'll dig his grave? I, said the owl". Okay, it wasn't exactly a bow and arrow that was used, but near as damn it.'

Birds again. Always birds. Why? What is this man trying to tell us?

Cody is anxious to get up to speed on this case. He needs to talk to his colleagues, find out what they know about these latest developments.

'I want you to go back home,' says Blunt.

He blinks. 'What? Why? Because of last night?'

'Because you look like shit, if you want the honest truth. You haven't slept today, have you?'

He ignores the question. 'You need all the personnel you can get on these murders. This guy is really clever. He's making fools of us.'

Blunt slams her palms on the desk. 'Yes, I know he's making us look like amateurs, Cody. And it's not going to get any better by putting people on the team who aren't awake enough to think straight.'

'No,' he answers. 'This is because of last night's cock-up, isn't it? This is your way of punishing me for an operation that didn't work out as well as we hoped.'

The blaze in Blunt's eyes tells him he should have remained silent.

'For one thing,' she says, 'it was an operation that had very slim hope of working in the first place. For another, if you think that I'm so petty as to go handing out red cards to officers just because they have ideas that don't pan out in the way they'd like, then you don't know me very well. I'm ordering you home, Sergeant Cody, because you are no use to me in the state you're in right now. Go home, get some rest, get your act together, and then come and see me again in the morning. Got it?'

He's got it. Only too well. Okay, so maybe it isn't about the operation. But it *is* about her perception of him as someone who doesn't allow her into his confidence. He refuses to let her into his head – that's what she cannot abide.

He jumps angrily to his feet, clicks his heels together as he adopts a military posture. 'Permission to be excused, ma'am.'

She raises an eyebrow. 'Don't be a dick, Nathan.'

He slumps a little. She's right – he is being a complete toss-pot. Doesn't stop him being annoyed, though.

He leaves her office and strides along the corridor. On the way out, he almost collides with Webley.

'Cody? Where are you off to in such a rush?'

'Home. Apparently I'm surplus to requirements.'

Her mouth drops open. 'Surplus to . . . Cody, what are you talking about?'

He realises then how petulant he is sounding. He shouldn't take this out on Webley.

'Nothing. Forget it. I'm taking some time off, okay? Good luck with the case.'

He leaves then, not wanting to get into a prolonged discussion. He meant what he said about taking time off. Maybe more than just today. Maybe a lot more.

37

The first thing he does when he gets home is take his frustration out on the gym equipment in one of the rooms at the front of the flat. He does a lot of jogging, a lot of rowing, a lot of weights. He accompanies this with a lot of sweating. Then, before hauling his exhausted frame into the shower, he lumbers into the bedroom and collapses onto the bed.

It's at least ten minutes before he can bring himself to reach for the phone on the bedside table. He knows he has to make this call – it would be unforgivable if he didn't – but he also worries about how it might be received.

He speed-dials the number. It rings eight times before it's answered.

'Hello, Cody.'

Her voice is flat, monotone. No cheery notes permitted. The type of response that is intended to make you wish you hadn't bothered.

'Hi, Devon. I thought I should just give you a quick call. Make sure you're all right. You know – because of the murder last night.'

He gets a few seconds of silence, and can picture her trying to decide if there might be more to the call than this. His cynicism is a measure of how badly things have deteriorated between them.

'Well, thanks,' she says. 'It's good of you. To tell the truth, it did shake me up a bit. I mean, this is Hoylake, for God's sake. Things like that don't happen here. It's awful.'

She sounds sincere. Chatty, even. He feels less edgy now.

'I know. It's bad enough anywhere . . .'

'Of course.'

'. . . but Hoylake police station is so quiet.'

'Not anymore. There are police everywhere now. Reporters, too. The place hasn't had so much television coverage since the Open. The poor man. He was local, you know.'

'I know.'

'Yes. I was forgetting. You must know a lot more than I do. Was he . . . Is it . . . ?'

'What?'

'They're saying . . . that it's connected to the other killings, the ones in Liverpool. Is that true? I mean, I suppose it must be. Four police officers in such a short time – that can't be coincidence, right?'

He pauses. He can't confirm her suspicions directly, but at the same time he doesn't want to irritate her by being obviously evasive.

'What else are they saying?'

'Who?'

'People. In the area.'

'Loads of stuff. To be honest, I think much of it is just rumour. You know how these things get all blown out of proportion. Not that it isn't a big enough story already, mind. There is one thing that keeps coming up . . .'

'What's that?'

'They say he was killed with a crossbow. Even on the news they're saying that. Is it true?'

Cody thinks about this one. It's a simple enough question. Yes or no is all it needs. If he was there, sitting next to her on the sofa, he would answer it. He knows he would, even in the absence of official confirmation. But right now he feels he has to hold back, and it shocks him to realise that such a substantial piece of his trust in Devon has been eroded.

'To be honest, I haven't been very involved with this latest killing. I have no idea. It would be an unusual way to kill someone, though.'

He waits out the silence from the other end, knowing that she is fully aware of his evasion. He's a Liverpool copper, she'll be thinking.

Working with the murder team. Of course he knows what's going on. He just doesn't trust me enough to say. That's how much of a gap there is between us now.

'Yes,' she says, but it's just to fill the space. 'So, anyway—'

He cuts off what is obviously meant to lead to a termination of the conversation: 'Yeah, so, what I was trying to ask you was if you're okay. I mean, with this murder being so close to home for you.'

'Well . . . You kind of already asked me that when I answered the phone.'

'Did I? Yeah, okay. So you're fine, then.'

'That's not exactly what I said. I said I was shaken. This was practically on my doorstep, Cody. And it wasn't just anyone. It was a policeman. One of the people who are supposed to protect us.'

Cody wonders whether that's a small dig at him, then decides he's being too defensive. She's upset and she's scared. Why would she be scratching at old wounds at a time like this?

'Oh. Sorry. That's what I thought – that it might have got to you. So I just wanted to say . . . if there's anything I can do . . .'

'I don't know. Like what?'

'Well, I'm not sure. Like, do you want me to come round? Or do you want to come over here? I could even come and get you if you—'

'I . . . Cody . . .'

He can hear her struggling for the best way to reject his offer, and it was only what he expected, so he lets her down gently.

'Just a suggestion, that's all. Didn't want you to think I didn't care or anything. Didn't want to think of you sitting there scared of every noise outside and wishing someone would do something to help you.'

'Is that how you see me? As a frightened little mouse?'

'Well, not exactly. I just—'

'I can look after myself, Cody. I'm a big girl. Like I said, I'm just a bit shaken. Besides, I've got someone coming round to keep me company.'

So. There it is. The thing he always dreaded hearing. But wait. It might mean nothing. Could be a female friend. More than probably is. He can't ask, though. Can't come right out with it and demand to know if it's a bloke.

'Yeah? Anyone I know?'

Say it's Aileen, he thinks. Or that one with the annoying laugh – what's her name? – Philippa, that's it.

'No. Just a friend.'

He hears this, and despite its neutrality believes immediately that it's a man.

'Right. So . . . you and your friend . . . you'll both be okay?'

'We'll be fine. I've got a nice bottle of wine in the fridge. Soon take the edge off.'

He wonders what else will come off. When they're both pissed and in need of each other's company and . . .

No, he thinks. I'm being stupid. It's none of my business.

'Great,' he says, but it comes out practically dripping with sarcasm. He tries to brighten up. 'Then I'll leave you to it.'

'Thanks, Cody. It was good of you to check on me. Really, it was thoughtful.'

Thoughtful is my middle name, he thinks. I can put a lot of thought into things. I just can't convert them into any actions worth a damn.

'No problem. Hope you didn't mind me calling.'

'No, but as you can tell, I'm really okay.'

Yes, he thinks. So it would seem. You're right as rain. You and your anonymous friend there, sitting in my spot on the sofa, knocking back the rosé. Lovely.

'Good. Well . . . goodbye then.'

'Goodbye, Cody.'

'Devon—'

But she's gone. Couldn't get off the phone quickly enough.

He lies back on the bed. His sweat-soaked neck feels clammy against the cold cotton pillowcase.

He tells himself it doesn't matter. He was right to make the call, to show he hasn't stopped caring about her. And Devon is under no obligation to tell him what's going on in her life. They have separated. She has a right to privacy.

But still he snatches up the phone when it rings, in the hope that she regrets her previous coldness and is calling him back.

'Devon?'

But of course it isn't. And now he feels idiotic and needy and angry.

He says, 'I don't know who you are, but I will find out. And when I do, I will rip your fucking eyes out of your skull. That's a promise.'

And then he hangs up.

38

When the intercom buzzes, he looks up from his book and checks the clock on the wall. It's just after eight o'clock. He's not expecting anyone, so he returns his attention to his book. He has showered and put on a fluffy bathrobe and has finally managed to lose himself in the pages of Thomas Hardy, so no thank you, he does not want to talk to anyone who just might pull him back into the snapping jaws of the real world.

Another buzz. The electronically generated noise is so at odds with the world of *Jude the Obscure*. The magic has been broken.

He sighs. Slams the book shut. Pads across the carpet to answer the call.

'Who is it?'

'Cody? Is that you? You might have put your frigging name on the doorbell. I've rung at every flat above every dentist on Rodney Street. I don't even like dentists.'

'Megan, what do you want?'

'To persuade you to change your electricity provider. What do you think I want? I want to talk to you.'

'What about?'

'Liverpool's chances against Southampton next Saturday. Stop fannying about and open the frigging door, will you?'

Cody sighs again. Presses the button to release the door lock.

He knows that as soon as she pushes open the front door she will be faced by a wall of eerie blackness on the ground floor lobby. Even if she can find a light switch, she won't know where to go, and will be stymied by the locked door leading up to his flat. So he slides his feet into a pair of slippers and heads downstairs, flicking lights on as he goes.

When he gets to the top of the final flight of steps, he finds Webley staring up at him and grinning.

'What's so funny?' he asks.

'Slippers,' she says. 'I can't believe you're wearing slippers. And a dressing gown. Have you taken up smoking a pipe, too?'

'If you've come here just to have a laugh at me, you can leave now.'

She shakes her head. 'I haven't. Honest.' But she's still grinning.

He beckons her with a flick of his head. 'Come on up.'

She starts up the wide staircase, her fingers sliding admiringly along the polished wood of the banister.

'Nice place you've got here. Like being in a stately home. You should have stags' heads on the walls. Or maybe paintings of your ancestors, all looking like you but dressed in silly clothes.'

'Sillier than a bathrobe and slippers, you mean?'

'That's what you could wear in *your* portrait. I expect to see it next time I'm here. Pipe and all.'

'I'll see what I can do.'

He leads her up to the first floor, then along the corridor to the door leading up to his flat.

'Blimey,' she says. 'This place is huge. Do you have this whole building to yourself?'

'At night, yes.'

'Doesn't it get scary?'

'Only when the resident ghost comes out, but he never appears until after eight o'clock. What time is it now? Oh, ten past eight.'

She slaps him playfully on the arm. 'Pack it in. You know I don't do ghosts and scary stuff.'

He steps aside, allowing her to go up the stairs ahead of him. She is wearing a short quilted jacket and tight jeans, and from here he gets a wonderful view of her rear end. The rear end upon which he once wrote a love message, all those years ago.

She pauses at the top of the stairs, her eyes darting from door to door. 'I'm spoilt for choice. Where to next?'

'Do you want a coffee?'

'I wouldn't say no.'

'In here then.'

He opens the first door on the right, and shows her into the kitchen. She takes a quick look around, then jumps onto a stool at the breakfast bar.

'I've only got instant,' he says. 'That okay?'

'Fine. Can't be any worse than the stuff I'm used to.'

Cody switches the kettle on. 'So, what brings you here at this time of the day? Not got enough going on in your life?'

'I was worried.'

'Really? Then you've come to the right place. Dr Cody's surgery is open for business. What troubles you, young lady?'

'I'm worried about *you*, soft lad.'

'Me? Why?'

'Because things haven't exactly been normal with you, have they? Ever since we started working together you've been like a puppy on springs. You never seem to relax. And then today you just go walking out of the building, like you've had enough of the place.'

Cody fills two mugs, passes one across to Webley.

'Maybe I *have* had enough. Don't get me wrong, MIT is great most of the time, but every job has its rougher side too. Maybe it's finally got to me.'

She sips her coffee. Doesn't grimace, so it can't be too disgusting.

'What happened last night?' she asks, out of the blue.

'Oh, so they've been talking, have they? The rumours have started already.'

'No. No rumours. Just . . . Okay, yes, there are rumours. They're saying it all went a bit weird last night. That something in that building spooked you. Something nobody else could find.'

'Uh-huh. Okay, fine. If that's what you want to believe, then—'

'No. Cody, no. I don't believe anything yet. Not until you tell me what I should believe. You were there. Nobody else was. Only you know what really happened in there.'

'Nothing happened in there, okay? Nothing *weird*, as you put it. I thought I heard someone, I chased after him, but I was wrong. I was mistaken. End of story.'

He hears the increased volume in his own voice, the touch of bitterness.

She puts her hands up in surrender. 'Okay. Fine. I didn't come to interrogate you.'

He lets out a deep sigh. Hopes his anger will float away on his breath. Then he goes to the fridge and takes out one of the few things left on the shelves.

'Here,' he says. 'Have a chocolate roll.'

'Wow, you really know how to spoil a girl.'

But she opens it anyway and takes a bite. A fragment of chocolate clings to her lip, and she stretches out her tongue to collect it. Cody has to tell himself not to get distracted by manoeuvres such as this.

He's not sure what to say to her next, but she has no trouble filling the gap.

'Look, I really didn't come here to wind you up. If you want me to go, I'll go. I just thought you might want somebody to talk to. It must get pretty lonely up here.'

He shrugs. 'I'm used to it. I've learnt to like my own company.'

She shakes her head. 'I couldn't do it. It'd drive me bonkers. How do you let off steam?'

'I've converted one of the front bedrooms into a gym. A good workout does wonders.'

'Yeah, but . . . everyone needs to talk sometimes, don't they? We all need to have a good moan now and again.'

'Not me.'

She nods, but he can tell she doesn't believe him.

'Cody,' she says, 'can I give you some advice?'

'What kind of advice?'

'Helpful advice.'

'Narrows it down. Go on.'

'Promise you won't get mad?'

'I won't get mad.'

'I don't want you to think I'm interfering or anything.'

'I won't think you're interfering.'

'Just tell me if you think it's none of my business.'

'Megan, stop pissing about and just tell me.'

He sees her take a deep breath, getting herself ready. This is going to be a biggie.

'All right . . . well . . . I just think . . . I think you need to see a doctor.'

'A doctor.'

'Yes, a doctor . . . of some kind.'

Meaning not your everyday GP. A head doctor, is what she's saying. A shrink.

And now, yes, he's starting to feel annoyed. A tad irritated. No, more than a tad. A whole barrelful of irritated. A roomful of the stuff. He's had this so-called advice from Devon, lots of times. But she was engaged to him. She had a right to offer such opinions. Webley hasn't been on the scene for years. She doesn't know him anymore. She needs to keep out of his personal life.

He wants to let rip. Wants to roar at Webley to get the hell out of his flat. He glares at her, feeling the heat rising in his cheeks and burning in his eyes. As if from a dragon, his words will be fired at her like a stream of flame, incinerating her on the spot.

'I'm sorry,' she says.

It takes him by surprise, confuses him enough to stifle his wrath temporarily.

She continues: 'I shouldn't have said anything. It's none of my business anymore. I just wanted to . . .' She pushes her half-full coffee mug back at him. 'Me and my big mouth. I'd better go now.'

She slides off the barstool. Cody can see how filled with remorse she is. His expression told her in painful clarity how affronted he was by her suggestion, and now she is suffering its sting.

'Megan,' he says.

She turns her eyes on him. They scan his face for meaning.

He says, 'It's okay. What you just said . . . It's probably good advice. I've got a lot of shit in my life at the moment, and I'm not handling it very well. I probably should go and see someone about it.'

'But you won't.'

He smiles. ''Course not. I'm a bloke. Blokes don't talk things over.'

She finds a smile of her own, and it swamps his with its beauty.

'Then we'll have to settle for the next best form of therapy.'

'Which is?'

'A drink. Alcohol. Come on – my treat.'

He looks down at himself. 'I'm not exactly dressed for it.'

'Then hurry up and get your glad rags on. I'm gasping here.'

39

He's in a pub. Again. With Webley. Again.

The Cracke is a tiny little place on a dark and narrow back street. It's famous as being one of the places where John Lennon used to drink. At that time, the Liverpool Institute High School for Boys stood on the next block. Both Paul McCartney and George Harrison attended the grammar school, and McCartney later helped to convert the building into the Liverpool Institute for Performing Arts.

Seated at a quiet table in the rear of the pub, Cody thinks about why he's here. Especially given that he doesn't drink. Well, not normally.

Tonight is not normal. Tonight Cody has decided that the apparent speed-up in the disintegration of his life is not going to be held in check by the simple expedient of avoiding alcohol. Tonight he is thinking, Fuck it; it can't get any worse. Let's live a little before we die a lot. *Carpe diem*, and all that.

He's practically drooling at the sight of the pint glass carried over by Webley. Its contents look rich and foamy and delicious. Truly an object of desire right now.

'Flippin' heck,' says Webley. 'Your eyes are on stalks. I could have carried this over naked, and you'd still have been more interested in your pint.'

'I've gone without for a long time.'

'I hope you mean drink. Go on, then. Get it down your neck.'

Cody lifts the glass. Dips his face into the foam. Allows the fluid beneath to slip down his gullet. It goes down easily, too easily, and he doesn't stop until the glass is half empty. Or half full, depending on your outlook.

'Steady on,' says Webley. 'I'm not carrying you home, you know.'

'I was ready for that.'

'So I can see. Makes me wonder why you gave it up in the first place. Do you turn into a werewolf or a Chelsea fan or something?'

'Nah. I just decided it wasn't doing anything for me. Made me moody.'

She laughs. 'Right. Because until now you've shown no mood swings whatsoever.'

He doesn't rise to that one, but finds it difficult to end the ensuing silence.

'Sorry,' she says. 'I didn't bring you out so I could piss you off again. I just thought you could probably do with some company.'

'What about Parker? Won't he be feeling lonely?'

'He's working late at the hotel. Says he'll be too knackered to do anything tonight. You'll have to meet him some time. You'll like him.'

Cody's not so sure. He already has an irrational distrust of the man.

'Is he posh?'

'He sounds posh. I feel like I'm in *Educating Rita* sometimes. But he's just a normal bloke, really.'

'Got a date set yet? For the wedding.'

'Not yet. He doesn't like to rush into things.'

'Am I invited?'

'Sure, if you want to come.'

He smiles. He doesn't really want to go to the wedding, and he's certain he won't be invited anyway.

'So,' he says. 'This is weird. Out drinking with you again.'

'It is. Nice weird, though. I mean, there's no reason why we should fall out, is there?'

'Definitely not. Just do whatever your sergeant tells you to do, and we'll get along fine.'

She shows him her dimples. 'Yes, Sarge. Whatever you say, Sarge. How many gobfuls of phlegm do you want in your tea, Sarge?'

'Charming. But you're okay about working with me, right?'

'Of course. If you are.'

It strikes Cody that each of them seems to be constantly checking that the other is happy with the working arrangements. But what the hell? The way things are heading, he's not likely to be at MIT for much longer.

He nods to reassure her. Sups his pint. She sucks amber liquid through a straw. Cody's not sure what's in it, but he suspects that alcohol is a major ingredient.

Says Webley, 'I really want to make a go of this, you know.'

'You said. I won't muck things up for you, I promise. Look, you're engaged, I'm getting over an engagement, and we're older and more mature than we were back then. We'll keep it purely professional. No fraternising after work. No going to pubs together. No running up and down Rodney Street, ringing every bell in a desperate attempt to find your lost prince.'

She stares at him, eyes twinkling.

'Oh, piss off, Cody,' she says. 'And get the drinks in, you miserable skinflint.'

So this is unexpected.

He's back home. Had a couple of drinks – well, three pints to be exact – and some great conversation, mostly about old times, and now he's back in his flat.

And he's not alone.

Webley is here with him. She of the platinum hair and the dimples and the infectious laugh and the ability to transport him back to days of happiness has accompanied him to his abode.

He's not even sure how it happened. It was certainly never on his mind to invite her back here, but here she is nevertheless, criticising his choice of supermarket coffee granules as she cradles a mug of the stuff.

He gives her a proper tour of the flat. Shows her the makeshift gym and the bedroom and the bathroom, all the while wondering what's going through her head, what signs she might be looking for.

In the living room, she scans the wall-to-wall bookshelves.

'Still a big reader, then? And I bet you've read every page of every book.'

He nods. Books have always been his friends.

She spies his guitar in the corner of the huge room.

'I remember that old thing. Where's your other one? The good one?'

'It got mangled in the automatic doors at Clayton Square when I was running after a naked man. Don't ask.'

She chuckles. Sips her coffee.

'Play something for me.'

'*Misty*?'

She looks at him. Says nothing to that. He knows that she remembers watching *Play Misty for Me* with him on one of their first dates. She will remember what happened when the Roberta Flack song came on in the movie.

He says, 'I've been drinking. My fingers are about as useful as sausages when I've been drinking.'

'Try.'

So he does. Webley sinks onto the sofa, and he sits opposite her. He plays 'Blackbird' by the Beatles.

A beautiful song, but also a sad song. And it's only when he is several bars in that he realises how reflective it is of recent events.

When the final bars fade into the night, her smile is beaming, but at the same time she seems a little wistful.

'You can still do it, Cody. You've got a great voice.'

He puts the guitar down, leaning it against the side of his armchair.

'Megan, what's this about?'

'What do you mean?'

'This. Why are you here, in my flat, alone, late at night?'

She blinks, as if caught out. Then she puts her coffee down carefully, the cup not making the slightest noise as it touches the glass surface of the table.

'You have to ask, Cody? I was in love with you once. I thought that—'

'Megan.'

'Don't worry. I'm not about to jump your bones, Cody, so don't get any bright ideas. Just let me finish.' She takes a deep breath. 'We were good together. Fantastic. And when we split up, I was devastated.

Don't get me wrong – we had to do it. It would have been disastrous to pretend everything was okay when it wasn't. But you had a . . . a calling. It was like a religion to you. You had to follow your faith. I couldn't see what you could see. I just wanted you, Cody. Just you.'

'Megan . . . I . . .'

'I'm happy now. With Parker. We'll be getting married soon, and that's the best thing ever. Since you and I broke up, I've always hoped that you found happiness too, in whatever way you choose to define it.

'When we met again, at Terri Latham's house, it was a big shock to me. I thought you'd still be off working in other cities. I never dreamt you'd be at MIT. I won't lie, but part of me hated the prospect of teaming up with you. I just didn't think it could work. But I'm getting off the point here. The point is, once I saw you again, I wanted to find out how happy you were. Maybe you were loving the job, or maybe you were married. Kids, perhaps.

'But you're not happy, are you? Something is deeply wrong with you, Cody, and it's tearing me up inside to see what it's doing to you. You've changed. Something has changed you. So, to answer your question, the reason I'm here in your flat, just you and me, is because I think you need someone. You need to talk. Because if you don't do it now, you never will, and I think that will be the end of you.'

He stares at her. She knows me so well, he thinks. She sees through me. Sees what others don't.

He acknowledges that if he were completely sober, he would turn down her offer of a listening ear. He would perhaps even make a joke of it, as he often does to camouflage the pain beneath. In fact, she probably wouldn't have got past the front door this time if it hadn't been for the booze.

But the alcohol has worked its magic. It has loosened his tongue, stirred up his emotions, punctured his inhibitions. And this is Megan Webley, the woman who cried along with him as they made love to the sound of Roberta Flack singing 'The First

Time Ever I Saw Your Face'. She, too, is under the influence of that damnable potion, and perhaps she wouldn't be saying all these things if that were not the case. But here she is, watching and waiting and willing him to be honest with her.

He says, 'You really want to know?'

'Yes.'

So he opens up.

Not with words, but with actions.

He knows how absurd they must seem to her. He sees the puzzlement on her face as he removes first one shoe, then the other. He sees the twist of her mouth as she tries to decide whether this is something she is supposed to find humorous.

But then he pulls off his left sock. He hears the intake of breath. The short, sharp expression of shock. She raises her eyes to meet his. He stares the truth of it back at her. He thinks she understands, at least to an extent. When he slips off the second sock, he thinks he detects a tiny slump of sorrow in her. Her eyes now are moist as she lifts them again. She puts a hand to her mouth, but a sob explodes through her fingers.

She goes to him.

She crosses the room. Looks again at his feet. At the fiercely pink scar tissue where the two smallest toes on each foot used to be.

'Oh, Cody,' she cries. 'Oh, Cody.'

And then she is on him. Hugging him close. He feels her hot tears on his neck. He cannot stop himself. The emotion bursts out of him. It comes from deep inside, under immense pressure. There is no stopping it now.

When it dies down, when the torrent becomes a trickle and the room is almost silent again, she strokes his hair and asks him the question.

And he answers it.

40

Where are the sirens? There ought to be sirens.

A bit like the beginning of a song, but the song is about clowns and he's got enough of those right now, thank you very much. One clown is a clown too many, and he's got four of the supremely unfunny bastards.

What he wants is sirens. This is when they are supposed to sound. It happens in all the movies, all the television dramas. Just when our hero is about to meet his demise, the sirens announce the arrival of the cavalry. In the nick of time they rescue him and round up the bad guys. That's the way it's supposed to go. There's a law about it somewhere.

They're not coming.

He tells himself to accept that, in the hope that somehow it will give him an extra burst of initiative to extricate himself from this mess.

The clowns seem to have other ideas. They are not real clowns – as if it even makes sense to talk about reality and clowns in the same sentence – but men wearing clown masks. There will be no slapstick here. He suspects that these men are planning something infinitely more sinister. Perhaps even involving unbearable levels of pain.

That thought causes him to realise how scared he is. No, not just scared. Indescribably terrified would be closer to the mark. His legs are shaking. He wants to appear calm and in control, but he knows he's not succeeding. He is giving off all the signals he has seen in those he has confronted in police interview rooms.

He has no idea who these men are. They are not the men he has been trying to entrap for the past three months. He and his partner Jeff Vance arrived at the docks fully expecting just another meeting with the members of the gang with whom they had been doing business. And at first that's what they got. It all seemed to be going to plan. No reason to suspect they'd been rumbled.

But then the clowns walked in. Four burly figures in overalls and masks – one of them carrying a sawn-off shotgun. It was clear that the gang members were expecting them, but even they seemed wary of the newcomers. And when they abandoned Cody and Vance to their fates, they appeared almost relieved to get out of there.

So now here they are. Cody and Vance seated on hard chairs, their arms bound tightly behind them, their legs tied to those of the chairs, being circled by clowns who refuse to talk.

Cody wonders about the reason for the silence, and his answer sounds a note of optimism. Since the men are keeping on their masks and not allowing their voices to be heard, that is presumably because they are afraid of being identified, either now or later. Which in turn suggests that it's their intention to let at least one of their captives walk out of here alive.

Or perhaps it's just to be more scary.

Because if there is anything more menacing than clowns, it is clowns who walk around and around you in deathly silence. Their muteness suggests they have no interest in engaging in conversation, and therefore no willingness to listen to reasoned arguments. They have already made up their minds as to how this scenario will play out, and there is no stopping them.

Yes, that's an alternative explanation, thinks Cody. I'm so glad I thought of that one.

'What's this about?' he asks, his voice echoing around the cavernous warehouse.

The clowns look at each other, as if enquiring the meaning of words spoken in a language foreign to them. But none of them makes a response. They simply continue to circle, at an almost slow-motion pace.

'Who are you?' Cody asks. 'What's going on?'

Still no reply, no change in their actions.

'Look,' says Cody. 'I don't know what you're trying to do, but this is obviously some kind of mistake. We're here on business. Get Barry back in here. Let us talk to him.'

Barry Duffy. A vicious bastard. The main man in the gang, and the one they hoped could lead them to even bigger fish. But apparently even he is unwilling to soil his hands with whatever is about to happen here.

Cody looks to his left at Vance. His face is white, nearly as white as those of the clowns. His eyes are darting almost at random, as though he can't permit them to settle on anything for fear of missing something crucial, such as a way out of this. He's a big man, overweight, and quite a bit older than Cody. He doesn't look well, doesn't look as though he will be able to cope with this stress for much longer.

The clowns stop walking. If there was a signal to halt, Cody missed it, but everyone seemed to know exactly when to stop. The tallest one, straight ahead, steps closer to the two undercover officers. He stoops slightly to examine Vance first, then Cody, as though he is trying to choose between them. Then he straightens up, still gazing down at Cody.

Cody gives this one a name. Undoubtedly the principal joker in this circus of the macabre, this clown has a face that is even more nightmarish than the others. Its smile is that of a man who has had fish hooks inserted into his cheeks and then the lips pulled away from his teeth, which are mottled in yellow and brown. He is not suited to a light-hearted name such as Bobo or Coco or Charlie.

Cody names him Waldo. Waldo isn't a funny name. Waldo is the name of someone who hides in the dark recesses of your bedroom, waiting to steal your breath.

'What? What do you want?'

His eyes fixed on Cody, Waldo points to the colleague on his right, then curls his finger to beckon him over. When his assistant arrives, Waldo points down at Cody's bound feet.

Cody narrows his eyes. Wonders what he's trying to intimate.

The assistant does not seem clear about that either. He continues to look up at his boss, seemingly mystified.

To help the message sink in, Waldo smacks his subordinate on the side of his head, then jabs a finger once more towards Cody's feet. The second clown seems to catch on. He gets down on one knee, starts untying the laces of Cody's left shoe.

The shoe comes off, then the sock. Then the same for the right foot. Cody finds himself wishing his legs weren't tied to the chair. He would love to lash out right now, to punch the ball of his foot into that mask, crumpling it into the face beyond. It would be so satisfying. But also, he acknowledges, so stupid. What would it accomplish? It's hardly likely that the retaliation would be proportionate.

So he does nothing except live through his mounting fear, knowing there is worse to come.

Waldo doesn't disappoint. He clicks his fingers, and another minion brings something across to him. As soon as Cody sees the object, he feels his heart begin to race, his breathing becoming a pant. He hears a murmur of anguish from Vance.

What Waldo is holding is a pair of garden loppers. Unlike simple shears, these cutters can chop through narrow branches with ease.

Toes shouldn't be a problem.

Because that's what's about to happen here, Cody thinks. I'm about to have my toes cut off. It's as plain and simple and terrifying as that. And still there are no sirens. Nobody is coming. Nobody can stop this. Unless . . .

Unless this is merely a ruse. A threat. Waldo wants information or something. This is his bargaining tool. He's about to make an offer in return for not carrying out this mutilation. That must be it, thinks Cody. He's at least going to give me a chance.

But when Waldo approaches, still without uttering a word, let alone any merciful trade-off, Cody begins to suspect he may be wrong. And when Waldo tries to position the blades of the lopper around the smallest toe on Cody's left foot, Cody accepts his error of judgement fully and unequivocally. This is actually happening, he thinks, and then the panic takes over and he starts moving his foot, as much as he can, dodging it one way and then the other, making the target as unsteady as possible, until Waldo loses patience and demands tacitly that his assistant makes himself useful by holding Cody's foot rock-steady, which he does, and now Cody's foot can no longer shift, can no longer escape, and Cody cannot look as the cutters slip around his toe, but he can feel it, he can detect the coldness of the sharp steel of those new, well-oiled loppers, and he knows that he is mere seconds away from actually losing a part of his body, a part that is irreplaceable, that will not grow back . . .

'No! Stop it! What the fucking hell is this about?'

The outburst is from Vance. Cody snaps his gaze towards him, warning him not to say too much. If they offer up everything now, then they will lose everything. They will lose more than a toe.

Because that's all it is, Cody tells himself. A toe. Your smallest one, too. It has no practical use. What do you ever do with it? It's tiny, and it's not particularly attractive, and you can easily manage without—

Snip!

He changes his mind when he hears that noise and feels the excruciating pain that shoots up through his leg, and finds himself enveloped by the echoes of his own screams bouncing around the massive chamber.

He's done it. My God, the lunatic has actually gone ahead and done it! He has taken away a part of my body, and there is no reversing that fact, there is no way we can just step back in time and undo that deed.

'Jesus Christ!'

This from Vance again. He is on the edge of desperation. Cody is the one feeling the pain, he is the one being chopped to bits, and yet it is Vance who is about to lose all control.

And perhaps he is right, thinks Cody. Perhaps Jeff has a better grasp of the hopelessness of the situation. Because there is only one end in sight. This is torture for torture's sake. This is being done because these men – or at least the one in charge – enjoy administering pain. Which in turn means that Cody's persecutor is, by any definition, undeniably unhinged.

This realisation does little to help matters. In agony, Cody is unable to look down. He has no desire to bear witness to the fact that he is now in two parts, no matter how unequal in size. He can do pain. He has suffered it before, and he will no doubt suffer it again. But pain is usually transitory – he knows it will eventually subside. The loss of his toe is somewhat more permanent, and so correspondingly more difficult to accept.

Through the tears clouding his vision, Cody stares his defiance at Waldo. He tries to peer beyond Waldo's eyes, straining to know the man behind the mask, but those eyes have the coldness and hardness of granite.

'You're making a mistake,' Cody says through his tears, his voice unnaturally high and wavering. 'A big one. Whoever you think we are, you're wrong. Before you go any further, you need to know how wrong you are about us.'

But Waldo isn't interested. The only thing concerning Waldo right now is getting the cutters positioned properly around the next toe on Cody's foot. There is no stopping him. He has made his mind up. And, yes, here he goes, putting his energy into bringing those two long green handles together to the accompaniment of a lovely snipping, crunching sound and Cody's long drawn-out wail.

When Cody's screams subside and he opens his eyes to the sting of the sweat running down his brow, he tries telling himself that this cannot be happening, cannot be true. How can it possibly be the case that he is being torn apart like this? When will enough be enough for this monster?

And he wonders where the sirens are. Where in God's name is the help he needs?

Not here. No help here. Only pain and destruction. This is a scene from Dante, from Bosch, from Milton. This is a hell.

And so it goes on. As if merely for a touch of variation, Waldo turns his attention to Cody's other foot.

Snip goes the little toe, scream, scream, scream. Crunch goes the next toe, cry, cry, cry.

And Cody has given up. His mind has resigned itself to the fact that the body it controls is doomed. It has stopped formulating plans for escape, because it acknowledges that escape is impossible. The only light at the end of an increasingly suffocating tunnel is the promise of sweet relief in the form of death. That is where this is leading, and it will be welcome.

The fingers now. Cold hard pincers pressing into the flesh of the little digit on his left hand. Maybe back to the toes later. Who knows? Who cares? Not much point fighting it now. He needs to accept that it's over. Let it be.

'Let It Be'. A beautiful Beatles song. Sing it now, he tells himself. In your head, sing it while you journey to your death.

'Police! We're police officers!'

He hears the yell, and it should be a wonderful announcement. It should herald the arrival of a dozen or more boys and girls in blue, piling into this den of despair and meting out instant and severe punishment.

But it is not that. He is being teased. This shout is from Jeff Vance, who needs this to end, for Cody and for himself.

It's not that easy, Jeff, thinks Cody. These men know what we are already. They plan to kill us no matter what we say. But first, they want their fun. They're clowns, see. Fun is what they're all about. Laugh with me, Jeff. Enjoy the moment, because it's the last you'll have.

But something does change in Waldo. It's almost as if he is only now aware of the other captive, and his gaze drifts menacingly in Vance's direction.

'We're police,' Vance continues. 'Okay? That what you want us to say? There, you have it. We're working undercover, trying to build evidence against Barry and his gang. Not against you. I don't even know who you are. This is just about Barry Duffy. You can walk away from this right now.'

Cody hears the desperation in Vance's voice and thinks, No, stop it. You don't know what you're doing. You're making it worse.

But Vance keeps on jabbering, spilling information about the operation in the hope of getting something in return. And what Cody sees is that every word he utters is another tug on Waldo's consciousness, dragging Vance further and further into the forefront of this deranged mind.

'Jeff! Shut up, Jeff!'

But the way that Jeff interprets this is as a warning not to reveal police secrets, rather than as an attempt to save his life.

'It's too late, Cody. We need to stop pretending now. Look at you. Look at the state you're in.'

Cody doesn't need to look. He feels the pain, the loss of his flesh and bone. He knew what was coming next and he had accepted it. Jeff hasn't reached that point yet. There is still a chance for him. The longer that Waldo remains preoccupied with Cody, the greater the possibility of fellow officers getting to the scene before Vance becomes the next victim. Those are the stark and clinical terms in which Cody views it, and Vance is about to mess it all up.

Vance turns his attention back to Waldo. Tosses out a few more choice nuggets of confidential information. Waldo is captivated now. He shuffles inexorably towards Vance, and although Cody can no longer see the clown's eyes, he knows they are gleaming with anticipation.

'Jeff! Enough! He's not listening to you. You're just making your-self a target. For the love of God, stop!'

The words reach home, then. Finally, they sink in. Vance's gaze switches back and forth between Cody and Waldo. Conviction gives way to uncertainty, then fear, then abject terror. He stares up at the figure looming over him, takes in the gruesome smile, realises what he has brought down on himself. His mouth, previously so exercised, now simply quivers without sound.

Waldo lets the loppers fall to the ground with a clatter. He stands for a while, studying his prey, then reaches under his blue boiler suit and produces his next prop.

A knife. A big bastard of a knife. Seven- or eight-inch blade, wide and shiny and bellowing its sharpness. Something that belongs in the hands of an expert chef.

'No,' says Cody. 'He's talking crap. Don't listen to him. Leave him alone.'

But Waldo seems oblivious to Cody now. His focus is entirely on Vance. He steps closer to his new victim. Closer.

'No. Please. Leave him. Please.'

But it's done. In Waldo's head the decision is made, the act is irrevocable. Cody knows this, and can only watch, only listen, even though he finds himself wishing his own eyes and ears could be ripped from his skull.

What he witnesses is worse than anything he could have imagined, and at times seems beyond belief. An ordeal that seems to last longer and to be more terrible than any of the torments of hell envisaged by all those famous artists and writers of so long ago.

And Cody knows even then that, should he survive this, he will never be the same man again.

41

He is sobbing again now. It's difficult to drag air into his lungs. Webley is hugging him, stroking him, whispering calming words to him. And she is crying too. She tells him what a poor, poor thing he is, and that it's over now. It's all over.

Except it's not over. He lives with the images and the sounds constantly. They run around his brain at all times of the day and night.

He has to tell her, has to finish the story.

'They . . . they . . . they cut his fucking face off.'

He sees her shock, but there is no way of playing this down.

'While he was alive. Jeff sat there in the chair, crying and pleading while that insane clown sliced the face from his skull. It was the worst thing I have ever seen in my whole life. And I couldn't help him, I couldn't move. Nothing I said was making any difference. How could they do that, Megan? How could one human being do that to another?'

Webley has her hand to her mouth again, looking as if she is ready to vomit. It is some time before she can bring herself to speak again.

'Oh my dear God. What happened to him, to Jeff?'

'It was too much for him. He died. Heart attack. And you know what? Terrible as it might sound, I think he would have welcomed it. God knows what they would have done to him next.'

She takes this in, tries to come to terms with it.

'And then? Didn't they turn on you again?'

'They were about to. Waldo picked up the loppers again. After what they'd just done to Jeff, I knew there was no hope for me. And that's when it happened. Backup finally arrived. I heard the sirens I'd been praying for. A little late for Jeff, but at least they saved me. I thought Waldo would just finish me off then, but he didn't. He bent forward and stared into my eyes, then he blew me a kiss and got out of there. He didn't even seem in a hurry, like he wasn't worried about being caught at all.'

'Did they ever catch them?'

Cody shakes his head. 'Not as far as I'm aware. Waldo and his cronies are still out there somewhere.'

'That's a scary thought.'

'Tell me about it.'

She studies his face for a moment, then slips to the floor. She traces a finger over the scar tissue on his right foot.

'Does it hurt?'

'Not physically.' He taps his temple. 'Not sure about up here, though.'

She smiles at him. 'You were never right up there, Cody. Seriously, though, you've got to do something about it. Your behaviour is all over the place. You're becoming a danger to yourself and to others. Didn't you get counselling, after what happened?'

'I had a psychological assessment. I told them I was okay.'

'Cody—'

'And actually, I was okay then. I felt a little numb about things, and I had nightmares, but other than that I didn't feel too bad. The psychologist told me there is sometimes a delayed reaction when it comes to traumatic events. She said it could be weeks or months before it really hit me.'

'And that's what happened?'

'Yes. My sleep pattern became even more disturbed. The nightmares got worse. Sometimes I would hallucinate. I started getting angry at the most trivial of things. One time, I hit a guy for jumping into a parking space I was about to take.'

'What about Devon? Did you take it out on her, too?'

Cody goes silent. He knew this question was coming, but he's still not sure how to answer it.

'Cody?'

'I, er, yeah, I did.'

'Cody.'

'Okay. If you want the truth, I tried to kill her.'

'You did what?'

He finds it hard to believe he's just told her this. He's never mentioned it to anybody before now.

'We were in bed. It was the middle of the night. I woke up, feeling that something was very wrong. My hands were clammy and my heart was going like the clappers. I turned to look at Devon. It was almost pitch black in there. All I could see was a vague outline. My brain filled in the rest. It told me it was Waldo lying next to me.'

'Oh, shit.'

'Yeah. I lost it. I went for Waldo. I put my hands around his throat. I was going to choke him to death, and nothing was going to stop me.'

'Cody, please tell me that something *did* stop you.'

'She struggled. We fell out of bed. She started screaming at me. That's when I realised it wasn't Waldo.'

Webley is silent while she tries to get her head around this information.

'Shit, Cody. That's . . . that's awful.'

'She kicked me out the same day. She'd been going on at me for ages to get help. This was the final straw. She couldn't live with me the way I was, and I don't blame her.'

'So, why not just get help? Why allow it to destroy your relationship? I don't understand the logic.'

'Because I can't risk it, Megan.'

'Risk what?'

'Losing my job. I can't have some quack saying I'm unfit for work. It's all I've got left.'

'They won't sack you. They'll get you the proper treatment.'

'They won't let me do what I'm doing now, though. Not until I'm fixed, and who knows how long that could take? At best they'll stick me behind a desk. At worst they'll suspend me. I can't cope with that.'

'You don't have to see a police shrink. Go to your GP. Get a referral. Go private if you have to.'

He shakes his head. 'Not that easy. We're supposed to be mentally and physically fit for police duties. If I get diagnosed with a mental health problem, I'm under an obligation to disclose it to the force. And if I don't, they'll find out anyway, and I'll be sacked on the spot.'

'Why will they find out?'

'Come on, Megan. Every case of ours that gets to court leads to some hotshot defence lawyer looking into the background of the officers involved for a reason to get the case dismissed. And then there are people like Dobby on my back, constantly looking for stuff to write about me. No way could I keep it under wraps. Far as I'm concerned, if it's not diagnosed, then I haven't got it, and nobody can say otherwise.'

'I see. The old head in the sand approach. Fat lot of good that's done you, Cody. You've lost your fiancée because of it. Was that really a price worth paying?'

'It wasn't an either–or, Megan. If I'd been unable to carry on doing the work I love, Devon and I wouldn't have lasted anyway. At least this way, there's still hope. Maybe she'll have me back when this is all over.'

Webley gets to her feet. Goes and sits back on the sofa.

'How, Cody? How is it going to get any better if you don't do something about it?'

'I don't know. They say time is the great healer, don't they? And there's one other possibility.'

'What's that?'

Cody gestures towards his mutilated feet. 'They catch the bastards who did this to me. If I had that, if I knew they were behind bars for the rest of their miserable lives, unable to hurt anyone else, then I really believe my problems would disappear.'

'And how likely do you think that is?'

He shrugs. 'Not very. But stranger things have happened.'

'And if it gets worse? If you go completely off the rails?'

'Then I'll lose my job anyway. I just have to hope that doesn't happen.'

She nods. Checks her watch. 'I'd better go home. We've got work in the morning. Both of us.'

He says, 'Megan, about that favour. The one that keeps growing . . .'

'I know. You don't have to say it. It just got a million times bigger, right?'

'What I've just told you – about the way it's affected me, I mean – nobody else knows about it. Nobody. You mustn't tell anyone. I'm not even sure why I told you.'

'Come off it, Cody. Do you really think you had a chance of keeping it from me?'

'Not really.'

She stands up. 'I left my stuff in your kitchen.'

He leads her back there. She picks up her bag, rummages around in it, brings out her phone.

'Damn!'

'What?'

'Nothing. Parker's been trying to get hold of me for the past hour. Listen, I've really got to go.'

'No problem. I'll take you downstairs.'

He escorts her to the front door.

'Thanks,' he says. 'For everything.'

She gives him a hug, and a peck on the cheek.

'Take care of yourself, Cody.'

Then she flies out of the door.

As she disappears into the night, Cody realises it's the first time he's allowed anyone else into his apartment.

And certainly the first time since Devon that he's allowed anyone into his life.

42

He wonders where Webley is.

Despite the beer, he got a good night's sleep. Best he's had in a long time, actually. He reckons that it probably had something to do with his opening up to Webley. Maybe he should start paying her to act as his therapist.

At his desk now, he finds it hard to concentrate. Webley is too keen to be late like this.

She flies in a few minutes later, obviously aware that she's not punctual. She looks harried, and perhaps in need of a bit more sleep herself.

Cody watches her, hoping to catch her eye. But for some reason she seems determined not to look his way. When she finally relents, and he shines a smile at her, she declines to reflect any warmth.

Cody turns back to his work, but again fails to engage with it. He starts replaying the events of last night, trying to analyse where things might have gone wrong. Did he say or do something out of line? Should he have kept his problems to himself after all?

Half an hour later, he hears Webley on the phone.

'Yes,' she is saying, 'I know you don't live near to Hoylake police station, but your car was seen in the area and . . . What? No, we're not being intrusive at all. This is a murder inquiry, and we're just trying to eliminate . . . No, we haven't got the number plate wrong because it was caught on camera. Now if you could just tell me what you were . . . Look, you're going to have to account for your movements one way or another. I'm trying to make this easy for you . . . Fine. If that's how you want to play it, I'm sending a car round to pick you up and drag you into the police station . . . Yeah, well, same to you!'

She slams the phone down. Says, 'For fuck's sake!' Gets up and storms out of the room.

Cody watches her go. When the door closes, his eyes shift to Ferguson, who indicates his puzzlement with a shrug.

Cody leaves his desk and goes after her. He sees her striding down the corridor like she's on a mission to throttle someone.

'Megan,' he calls, but she doesn't slow down.

He has to break into a jog to catch up with her. When he gets in front of her, he sees the wetness in her eyes, the redness in her cheeks.

'Megan, wait. What's wrong?'

She halts then. Flips him the finger. Except that it's not the middle digit. This is her ring finger. Without a ring.

'That's what's wrong.'

She starts marching off again. Cody overtakes.

'Wait. Talk to me. In here.'

He opens up the door to an interview room. Bundles her inside.

'What are you doing, Cody? I don't need to be interrogated right now. And those cameras had better be switched off.'

'They're off. Now calm down and tell me what the hell's going on.'

'Nothing's going on. My engagement isn't going on. My wedding won't be going on. And it's all your fault.'

'My fault? Why is it my fault?'

'Because you had to go and be more in need of my company last night than Parker did. Or at least that's what I thought. Turns out, though, that Parker was very much in need of my company. So much so that he turned up at my house after work. So much so that he tried ringing me, and then texting me, and then panicking about me. Only I didn't know all this because I was too busy listening to your bloody problems.'

'Well . . . it's nice, though. That he was worried about you, I mean.'

She stares at him like he's just landed from space.

'Nice? Nice? No, it wasn't nice at all. Not when he heard I was with another man. Not when he found out that the man in question was only the frigging ex-boyfriend I used to live with.'

'Ah.'

She stares again. 'Is that all you've got to say? Parker was basically accusing me of having an affair. Me! An affair! I felt like punching him. I did the next best thing instead, and threw his frigging ring back at him. And now . . . and now . . .'

Tears are streaming down her face. As he did the other day in the car, Cody finds a tissue in his pocket and hands it to her.

'Jealous type, is he?'

She sniffs. 'I tried to tell him. I tried to explain to him that I was just helping you out. But he didn't want to listen. Said he wasn't interested in some other bloke's mental health problems, especially when it's a bloke I went out with for eighteen months.'

'Wait,' says Cody. 'You told him? About me?'

'Cody, haven't you been listening? That's what the argument was all about. That's what I'm—'

'No. I mean, you told him about the difficulties I've been having? You told him about what I went through?'

'Well . . . yes. I had to.'

'No, Megan. You didn't have to. We had an agreement. You promised you wouldn't say anything about it.'

'To the force. I'm not going to tell anyone on the job. But this is Parker we're talking about.'

'I don't care if he's the fucking Pope. I don't know this guy from Adam. He might be best mates with the Chief Constable for all I know. Do you know everyone he speaks to in his bloody hotel?'

Yet another stare. But this is a third strike. This one is long and hard and sharp enough to pierce flesh and bone.

'You know what, Cody? Fuck you. I tried to help you. I saw what you were going through, and I listened to you, and I consoled you, and I covered up for you. I didn't ask for anything in return. But what I've just been trying to tell you is that everything I've done for you has cost me my engagement. And what do you do? You turn it back to poor old you. Well, fuck you, Cody, because, believe it or not, not everything in life is about you and your problems.'

And then she's running out of that room, in tears again. And all Cody can do is stare helplessly at the door.

His day gets no better.

He spends most of it away from the station, mainly because Blunt is piling the pressure on her team to get answers. She doesn't want to see them sitting at desks; she wants to know that they are out on the streets, posing incisive questions and uncovering promising lines of investigation. Cody realises it's because Blunt herself is under intense pressure to find the killer. This is a national story. An international one, even. Dobby is the least of the nuisances to be encountered whenever Cody steps outside the building. Now he has to fight his way past bodies working for every major newspaper, radio station and television broadcaster in the land.

What makes it even worse is that the MIT detectives are in danger of becoming marginalised as other, higher-ranking officers become involved. The top brass want an end to these killings, but they also scent the opportunity for personal glory and media coverage. There are so many fingers being dipped into this pie that it's in danger of being turned into mush. And the frustrations that Blunt is feeling are being vented on her team.

On the few occasions that Cody finds himself back at Stanley Road, there is little sign of Webley. She is as busy as everyone else, but she has obviously chosen to be busy on things that do not involve Cody.

He's not sure how he feels about that. He is still angry with her, but he also understands why she is angry with him. It's not black and white, because real life never is. It would be complicated enough without the fact that they used to go out with each other.

In a way, he's glad he's so busy.

Sometimes dealing with a murderer can seem preferable to dealing with personal relationships.

The killer observes, and his frustration becomes unbearable. He is close to breaking point now. The end has come much earlier than he hoped.

He watches the news reports throughout the day. He sees the politicians frittering away the taxpayers' money in trying to stop him. He sees the masses of extra police officers spreading out onto the streets, searching every nook and cranny for him. He sees the Chief Constable at a press conference, promising that the heinous killer will be caught very soon. He sees the television reporters similarly opining that his time at large is coming to an end.

He would love to be able to laugh all this off. He would love to act the arch-villain, scoffing at the antics of the idiot law enforcers.

But the problem is that he believes them. He believes they will come knocking on his door soon. He has nowhere to go, nowhere to hide. And what is worst of all is that it has become virtually impossible to kill. They are expecting him. They are waiting for him. They have set traps for him. He is the bird, and they hold the string attached to the box, just waiting for him to wander into its shadow.

Ah, yes. The birds. He watches them now, flying and eating and shitting and fighting and dying. They are restless too. They have their demands, and they wonder why he is not satisfying them. They are here for him, offering up all that they have, and yet he is not delivering them from their pain. Why is that? they ask. Why are we being cheated? Where is the destiny you promised us? You brought us here, elevated our status. And now you deny us.

He knows they are right. He is failing them. This is far more difficult than he ever imagined.

But he cannot surrender yet. The birds won't allow it. They have one huge collective message to send to the world, and this time he will be their carrier pigeon.

He is not quite certain yet what form the delivery will take. But it will come to him, and it will be spectacular. He will shout it loud and he will shout it clear.

And then they will finally understand.

43

He shouldn't be here. He should have gone home, like a normal person. Webley flew out of the station hours ago, as soon as she was able to get away from the place. He can't blame her. He'd blackened her day into one of utter misery. Which in turn only made himself even more miserable.

He's not here to cheer himself up. He's not even supposed to be here at all. Blunt would have a fit if she knew. And she might find out, especially if this backfires.

But he needs to know. He needs to do something that will make some kind of mark on this case. He needs to redeem himself after the fiasco in the old printers' building.

Now is the time. He has sat in his parked car for the past hour, watching and waiting. Mr and Mrs Vernon left their house two minutes ago. He doesn't know when they'll be back, so he needs to make his move.

Here goes.

He gets out of the car. Locks it up and strides across to the house. Nobody on the street. Just a lone white cat, staring at this intruder on its territory.

He knocks on the door. It is answered within seconds.

Robert Vernon displays surprise, then indignation. 'You're not supposed to come here. You're supposed to leave us alone. We were told you were going to leave us alone.'

'I need to talk to you, Robert.'

'I've got nothing more to say. I've told you all I know.'

Cody doesn't waver. He gives Robert his most determined stare. 'I'm not going away. I'll stand here all night if I have to.'

'Then stand there. My mum and dad'll be home soon. See what happens then. Or what about if I call the cops? Or the newspapers?

No, you don't like that, do you? I bet your boss doesn't even know you're here. I'm right, aren't I?'

Cody realises he's on the verge of having the door slammed in his face. He also realises that getting heavy-handed right now is going to be counter-productive. Robert has the upper hand, and he knows it. It's time to be honest. Time to be real. Time to act less like an arsehole and more like Webley.

'Listen to me, Robert. I haven't come here to cause trouble for you or your family. I'm here because people are dying out there. Yes, they are police officers, and yes, two of them were not your most favourite people on earth, but now other coppers are dying, coppers you've never even met or heard of. You can't have a grudge against them just because they wear a uniform or carry a badge. That last copper who was murdered – the one in Hoylake – he left behind two little kids. Are you being fair on them? Are you being fair on the next young man or woman to die, and the one after that?'

'You can't blame me. I had nothing to do with it. My family had nothing to do with it.'

'I believe you, Robert. I'm not blaming any of you. I'm simply asking you to help me. Five minutes of your time, that's all I want.'

Robert stands in silence for a while, his hand gripping tightly to the edge of the door. If he closes it now, Cody thinks, then I may as well goes home.

'Five minutes,' says Robert. He steps aside, motioning Cody in, then scans the street for onlookers before closing the door.

He leads Cody into the front room. The cold, uninviting room. The one for unwelcome guests.

He sits where his father usually sits, as if temporarily adopting the role of the man of the house. Cody gestures enquiringly towards an empty place on the sofa, and gets a nod of consent to occupy it.

Robert sits back, like a judge waiting to hear evidence before passing judgement. 'Say what you've got to say.'

Cody hasn't rehearsed a speech. He knows he just needs to give from the heart.

'You were absolutely right,' he says. 'From the outset, you and your family were prime suspects for murder. And after PC Paul Garnett was found dead, you became even more of a favourite.'

'And now?'

'To be honest, there are many who still think you bear responsibility. Some think you want to take revenge on all coppers, and some think the latest two victims were murdered just to divert us from the real targets.'

Robert seems slightly taken aback by Cody's frankness. As if honoured that he should be permitted an insight into the thinking process of the police investigators.

'What about you? What do you think?'

'Me personally? I don't think you had anything to do with it. You or your family.'

Robert rolls his tongue around the inside of his lips while he mulls this over.

'You could be just saying that, to catch me off guard.'

'I could be, but I'm not. I believe you're innocent. At least of the murders.'

A flash of irritation in Robert's eyes. 'What do you mean by that?'

'I'm putting my cards on the table here. I don't think you killed any of those police officers, but I think a part of you is glad someone did. You regard it as some kind of justice. An eye for an eye, a tooth for a tooth.'

Cody waits for the backlash, but none comes.

'So what if I do? Is that so wrong?'

Cody shakes his head. 'Not at all. It's human. I'd probably feel the same in your position.'

'Okay ... so, if I haven't done anything wrong, why have you come to see me?'

Cody pauses a second before answering: 'Gazza.'

A few rapid eye blinks. A lick of the lips. He's rattled.

'Gazza. The guy in the pub. Okay, what about him?'

'He's giving us problems, Robert. Based on what you told us, he could be the key to all this, so it's really important that we find him as soon as we can. We're devoting a load of resources to tracking him down – resources that could be used elsewhere.'

Robert nods along to this, but Cody senses his discomfort.

'I told you what I know about the man,' says Robert. 'If I could remember any more, I'd tell you. It was just a brief chat in a pub. I'd been drinking. It's difficult . . .'

'I understand that. It's just that . . . well, we can't find anything about this guy. Nothing whatsoever. We've tracked down every Gazza we can who might have visited the Armitage recently. Not one of them seems to be a likely suspect.'

Robert shrugs. 'What can I say? Maybe he only went there once. He might have even followed me in there. Just because nobody knows him, it doesn't mean he wasn't there.'

'No, you're right about that. Trouble is, they don't remember you either. We showed your photo to a lot of people who go to that pub on a regular basis. Nobody recalls seeing you in there at any time.'

Robert is becoming more restless now. Twisting in his chair to get comfortable.

'No, they probably wouldn't. I went in there just once, for a few drinks. I never went there before or since. Why would they remember me? What are you trying to say?'

'I'm trying to ask you to give us a little bit of help. A tiny bit of assistance so that we know where to focus our efforts. I'm asking you to be straight with me.'

'I *am* being straight. I've been straight with you all along.'

'You could really help us, Robert. Just a word from you to make sure we stay on the right track instead of chasing shadows. You don't need to play with us anymore.'

Robert jumps to his feet. Cody resists the impulse to do the same. Stay calm. Be the voice of reason in this room.

'What are you talking about? I *have* helped you. I told you what I know about this Gazza bloke. If you can't find him, that's your problem. I can't do your job for you.'

'Like I said, Robert, I didn't come here to make trouble for you or your family. I'm not going to arrest you or drag you into the station. Just be honest with me, and I'll get out of here. Help us. Isn't that what Kevin would have wanted?'

Cody hears the name coming out of his mouth and realises too late that it's a mistake. Robert's eyes practically fluoresce at the mention of his dead brother.

'Don't you dare! Don't you fucking dare! What do you know about what my brother wanted? Your lot killed him. Your lot destroyed our family. And now you've got the nerve to come here and ask for my help. You want to know what you did to us? You want to know what you've put my mum and dad through?'

He turns his back on Cody. Marches over to a cupboard in the corner of the room. Cody tenses. It occurs to him that, in his agitated state, Robert Vernon might be going for a weapon.

Robert flings the cupboard doors open and stands aside to let Cody see inside. Cody isn't sure what he's looking at. He can just see shelves full of folders and box files with labels on them. Robert grabs one, seemingly at random, then brings it across to Cody and flings it onto the sofa next to him.

'Take a look. Go on, open it up.'

Cody opens up the box and looks inside. On the top is a newspaper report about an investigation into allegations of corruption in the Metropolitan Police. Cody flicks through the other cuttings in the box. He sees one about institutional racism in the force, another about how a member of the armed response unit was put on a charge of manslaughter, another describing an incident in which a teenager was killed by a policeman driving his vehicle too fast.

'My dad collects these. Every day he scours the papers, looking for articles on how terrible the police are. It's an obsession. You should see his file on the Plebgate affair. And as for Hillsborough – that gets a shelf of its own.'

Cody continues to riffle through the reports. He finds it impossible to comprehend how someone can become so obsessed with a topic that is so filled with sadness and violence and hate and immorality. But then he has never lost a child at the hands of police officers. Cody is only too aware how fragile a thing the mind is.

'Here,' says Robert, 'take a gander at this . . .' He tosses another box file onto the sofa. 'That's where it all started.'

Cody can guess what's in here, but he opens it up anyway. He's right. Dozens of articles on the death of Kevin Vernon. He pulls out some of the cuttings and finds himself in the midst of the investigation into the officers involved: Terri Latham and Paul Garnett. Some of the reports are accompanied by photographs of the two officers, usually in police uniform.

'Do you see now?' Robert is saying. 'Do you understand what my family has been going through? What I've been going through? Do you?'

Cody doesn't know why, but he finds himself picking one particular article out of the box.

'Every day my mum and dad tell me how evil the police are. I've got my own house, you know. I should be living my own life. I moved back in when Kevin died, so I could help my parents. And ever since then they've shown me examples – articles like these – proving what evil bastards you lot are. What am I supposed to believe, eh? What am I supposed to do?'

Cody doesn't answer. He is too busy reading the article.

'So you want the truth then, eh? You want to know if I lied to you? Well, yes I bloody well did. I lied, okay? This bloke Gazza – I made him up. He doesn't exist. I don't know who killed those bizzies, and I don't care. But it wasn't me, and it wasn't my mum or dad. And if you hadn't come round here, throwing out your accusations at us, I wouldn't have lied to you. An ounce of respect – that's all we want. Why can't you just leave us in peace?'

Something about this article is troubling Cody, niggling him. What is it? He quickly scans to the end, then back to the beginning. What is it about these words?

'Are you listening to me? Have you heard one word I've said?'

But Cody has stopped listening. What seemed so important when he came here has just paled into insignificance.

He has identified what was bothering him. Perhaps he saw it straight away and it didn't properly register the first time. But now it is staring him in the face. Not just the content of the report, but its originator.

A journalist called Martin Dobson.

44

Cody drives away from the Vernon house leaving Robert not a little bemused by the fact that his confession seemed of such insignificance to the detective. Cody made him a deal: he would overlook Robert's deceit if he could take with him the newspaper article he had just read. It was too good an offer for Robert to turn down.

Cody gets less than a mile from the house before having to pull the car over. He's not concentrating on the road. There are too many thoughts buzzing around his head. Too many questions. He's not sure what any of it means, exactly. Not at the moment. There is still plenty of work to be done here.

And yet . . .

There are too many coincidences as well. Think about it. Latham and Garnett are killed. There's an obvious connection between them – the Vernon case. That's what everybody believes is at the root of it, until the other two officers are slain. Then the focus shifts, widens. The connection becomes murkier.

But there is another connection, it seems. Dobby, who has been putting his nose into these killings from the outset, was a key reporter on the death of Kevin Vernon and its aftermath. There was not just one article by him in the box that Robert showed him, but a whole host of them.

What does that mean? Does it mean anything at all?

Cody remembers what Dobson told him about the investigative powers at his disposal. He can find things out, he said – things even the police can't discover.

Like, for example, the home addresses of Latham and Garnett?

See, that's another thing differentiating the first two killings from the later ones. In the cases of Andrea Whitland and Tony

Stebbins, the killer lay in wait, like a spider might wait for a fly to venture into its web. There was nothing to indicate that Whitland and Stebbins were deliberately targeted. It was a question of wrong place, wrong time.

But Latham and Garnett were killed at their homes. The killer knew precisely where they lived. He went to them, rather than the other way around. How did he know the addresses? Police officers are usually extremely guarded about giving out their contact details, because you never know what lunatics might turn up at your door. Most of the bobbies that Cody knows don't even have their home phone numbers listed in the directory. How the hell did the killer find out where Latham and Garnett lived?

Cody pulls the newspaper article from his pocket. His eyes jump straight to the first of the relevant paragraphs:

'When confronted outside his semi-detached house in Grassendale, Mr Garnett refused to comment on the investigation into his part in the death of Kevin Vernon.'

Then, further down:

'PC Terri Latham, who assisted Garnett in tackling Vernon on the night he suffered fatal injuries, also declined to answer when questioned outside the Wallasey flat she shares with her police boyfriend.'

So, Dobson managed to find out exactly where the two officers lived at the time. The furore surrounding the case led to both officers having to move house after they were cleared. But if Dobson could locate them once, he could do it again.

Maybe he did exactly that.

Wait a minute, thinks Cody. If Dobson had anything at all to do with the murders, why didn't he simply use his investigative powers to locate the other victims too? Why didn't he go directly to their homes, just as he did for Latham and Garnett?

Answer: because it would have been far too obvious. Not many people would have been capable of tracking four police officers to their homes before killing them. Far safer to start using a different approach to finding them, even if it makes life for the killer more difficult.

Cody tosses the possibilities around in his mind. Dobby? A serial killer? A strange man, yes, but *that*?

Cody knows full well that killers don't conform to type. They come in all shapes, sizes, colours and personalities. But still – Dobby?

He decides he needs to go in search of some answers.

45

After a few phone calls, a few promises, a few threats, Cody finds his quarry in the London Carriage Works. Which, despite its name, is neither in London nor specialises in repairing horse-drawn vehicles. It's actually a swanky restaurant on Hope Street.

Forced to abandon his dessert after only a mouthful, Edward Kingsley seems less than pleased to be called out to the desk.

'It's a crème brûlée,' he tells Cody.

'What is?'

'My dessert. Crème brûlée. One of the best I've ever tasted. And I've just forsaken it to talk to you, so I expect some scintillating conversation.'

Cody looks around. The staff are studiously attending to their business, but he's not convinced they're out of earshot.

'You mind stepping outside?'

'Are you planning to punch me?'

'Have you done something to deserve it?'

'Probably. But not to you, as far as I know.'

'Then I'll restrain myself. Anyway, you look like you need a ciggy break. Must be at least two minutes since you last lit up.'

'Is it that obvious? Come on, then. My body is a temple to the god of nicotine, and I need to pray.'

They go outside. While Kingsley digs out a cigarette, Cody checks out the cathedrals at either end of the street, bathed in an ethereal glow. Each is so different from the other, yet each is so beautiful in its own way. Hope Street is aptly named, and Cody wonders if his own hopes can be fulfilled tonight.

He turns his gaze back on Kingsley. Light spilling from the restaurant bounces off the man's distinguished silver hair. In other respects he does not look his advancing years, and has done remarkably well to weather a lifetime of journalistic excess. Many of his younger colleagues were consigned to the knacker's yard years ago.

'So,' says Kingsley, 'are you bringing me a scoop, or are you here to accuse me of something? FYI, I've never authorised a phone hacking in my life.'

'Neither. I'm looking for a story.'

'What? You thinking of going into journalism now? Good. I'm glad you've seen sense. Come over to the dark side.'

'Thanks, but no thanks. I have standards.'

'Really? Then there's no hope for you. Come back when you've put a price on your soul. And keep it realistic. In this economic climate, you've got a lot of competition out there.'

'To be honest, I don't think my soul is worth very much at the moment. That's not why I'm here.'

'Okay. Give me the who, where and what.'

'The who is Martin Dobson.'

Kingsley sucks hard on his cigarette, then blows a huge cloud of smoke into the crisp air.

'Jesus! Come on, Cody. He's just doing his job. You know that. I can't keep calling him home every time he gets on your nerves.'

'I don't expect you to. That's not what I'm asking.'

Kingsley's eyes flare into life, almost as brightly as the tip of his cigarette. 'What then?'

'I want you to tell me his history. Why you hired him, where you found him – that kind of thing.'

'That's an unusual request, Cody. Where did this come from?'

'From me. I'm interested.'

Another puff of smoke, followed by a shake of the head. 'No. You need to give me more than that. Something has provoked this.'

'I can't tell you. Not yet. It might be nothing.'

'Which also means it might be something. So what's up?'

'I don't know. I'm just fishing. But the longer I talk to you, the more I'm starting to think there's a prize catch in the lake.'

Kingsley laughs. 'Are you certain you don't want to work for me? You've got a reporter's nose.'

'Does that mean there's a story here?'

'It means you're able to come up with one, even when there isn't one there.'

'Is that what I'm doing? You still haven't told me anything about Dobson.'

Kingsley sighs. Looks back through the restaurant window at his friends in all their finery, laughing and joking and knocking back expensive bottles of bubbly.

'Look at what you're keeping me from.'

Cody shrugs. 'They don't seem to be missing you.'

Kingsley smiles. Nods. 'Too true. I'm not the life and soul of the party that I used to be. Too old now. Did you know I'm thinking about retiring?'

'I didn't, no.'

'Yep. I've seen it all in my time. You wouldn't believe some of the things I knew about but never printed.'

'Because you didn't have the evidence to back them up?'

Kingsley laughs again. 'When did a lack of evidence ever stand in the way of a good story?'

'Now you're starting to sound like Dobson.'

'Maybe. He's not all bad, you know. I wouldn't have hired him if I thought otherwise.'

'But there's something there? Something you're not telling me.'

Kingsley drops his cigarette to the pavement. Grinds it into the ground beneath his shiny black shoe.

'I should get back.'

But he doesn't move immediately. Cody knows he's expecting the next card to be played, and so he plays it.

'You owe me one.'

'Aha! I was wondering when you'd try that one. As I recall, the last time we spoke I said we're straight now, and you agreed.'

'Well, I've thought about it, and we weren't. It wasn't a fair deal.'

'I pulled Dobson off your back. Kept you out of my paper. It would've been a pretty big story.'

'And your daughter's death would've been an even bigger one.'

He sees Kingsley wince at the mention of his daughter's possible fate at the hands of her abductors. If it hadn't been for Cody, he might never have got her back safely.

'Okay,' says Kingsley. 'You're right. I owe you. I'll owe you for the rest of my life. But you can't keep using that to interfere with press freedom.'

'I told you, I'm not asking you to put a muzzle on him. I just want his story. Where'd you find him?'

Kingsley looks skywards, then back at Cody. He sighs again.

'All right, Cody. But this guy is one of my best reporters. If I lose him because of this, I'll come looking for you.'

A half-hour later, Cody is standing outside Dobson's house in Woolton Village. He obtained the address from Kingsley.

But that's not all he got.

We all have secrets, but it seems that Dobson's are darker than most. He has a past, but he's hidden it well. He had to – especially here of all places.

Christ, thinks Cody. What irony! How does Dobby live with that? How does he put that behind him?

Well, maybe he doesn't. Maybe the pressure of living with what he did finally got too much to bear, and he snapped.

Or maybe that's not what happened at all.

Cody now knows something about Dobson he never would have suspected. But it's not enough to label him a murderer. More answers are required.

He hoped to find them here, by confronting Dobson directly. But the house seems empty. Not a light on anywhere, and nobody answering the doorbell.

Cody steps back on the street and looks up at the house. Its dark windows stare back at him, defying him to discern their secrets.

I can wait, thinks Cody. For once, my inability to sleep comes in useful. You'll be back home soon, and then the shoe will be on the other foot. You'll be the one having to answer the questions.

And then we'll know.

46

'Fickle lot, readers,' says Dobson. He knows he's slurring his words, but he doesn't care. He's lost track of the number of pints he's supped, but he doesn't care about that either. It's his birthday, for Christ's sake. It should be celebrated, and what better way than with a load of mates at a pub?

Well, one mate. Okay, a colleague.

Opposite him, Chris is probably bored stiff. He probably wants to get off home. Take some selfies, or whatever photographers do in their spare time.

Fuck him, thinks Dobson. My birthday, my rules. We'll do whatever he wants when it's his birthday. I'm not sitting here on my own. I'd look like a right saddo then, wouldn't I?

Just like all the other times.

Bastards. They're all bastards.

What was I saying? Oh, yeah . . .

'Really fickle. Slag us off constantly for the stuff we put in the papers. Say we're trading in misery, or that we glamorise violence, or that we have no empathy for the people we write about. Well, you know what? Fuck 'em. Who buys the sodding papers anyway? They do. In their millions. They lap it up. They love it. Bit of titillation – wonderful stuff. Bit of gossip – can't get enough of it. *You* know what I'm talking about, don't you? A celeb jumps out of a car with no knickers on and you snap a picture – shocking! How dare you! Sells copy, though, doesn't it? They all want to see that, the dirty pervs, and yet you're the one who's being intrusive! It's not as if you go around shoving your telephoto up women's skirts now, is it? Well, at least I hope you don't. Although put me down for some snatch shots of that one from the last Bond film if you manage to get hold of any. And that's another thing – what are they doing going commando at a media event anyway, especially if they're going to get out of a car like they were doing the can-can? What the bloody hell do they expect to happen?'

He realises he's doing nearly all the talking tonight. But he's got a lot on his mind. He's feeling the stress. So much going on right now. He needs the release. Get a few things off his chest, even if it all seems complete garbage to his drinking buddy. Okay, not a buddy. Companion, then.

He has no buddies. Nobody he can really call a friend. He blames it on the work. He's dedicated to his job. Married to it. No time for friendships, let alone more serious relationships. In his darker moments, he toys with the idea that his commitment to the job might not be the real reason for his loneliness. But he always sees sense in the end. Sometimes one has to make sacrifices, painful though they might be.

'Still no word from Cody,' he says. Then he wonders why his mind suddenly leapt to that topic. He had been thinking about friends, so where did that come from? Cody's certainly not a friend. He's interesting, though. Fascinating. Damaged goods like him always make a compelling story. Dobson wishes he could tell it, and maybe one day he will. A part of him knows it's the real reason he's pestering Cody for his insider knowledge on the serial killings going on right now. He could have approached other coppers, but Cody is like a magnet. A man of inner turmoil and drama. His view on life is unique. Annoying, then, that he refuses to respond to Dobson's overtures.

'I reckon he's not interested,' says Chris.

'Then he's an idiot. He should be interested. I told him what I can do for him. He needs me more than I need him.'

'Why? Why does he need you?'

For a fleeting moment Dobson is tempted to pitch his beer into Chris's face. The question seems loaded with the suggestion that nobody could possibly need such a loser. But then he narrows his alcohol-troubled eyes at Chris and realises that the man is making no such insinuation. He's just filling a gap with another mindless sequence of words. Good job he can take photos, because he'd make the world's worst reporter.

'Because I can find stuff out. I have contacts. I know people. People in high places. People with knowledge and power. I said all this to Cody, and he still isn't taking the hint. He still insists on doing things his own way, which is why he'll never solve these bloody murders.'

'Why don't you solve them, then? If you know so much.'

There he goes again, thinks Dobson. Sounds ever so much like an insult to me. But look at his face. Guileless. Lucky for him. If there was so much as a smirk there, I'd soon wipe it off his clock.

'Not how it works, mate. Not how it works. For me to start getting information like that, I have to pull in some favours. I can't be wasteful about it. It's taken me a long time to build up the IOUs I've got. I need to be sure I get something in return. Tit for tat. Cody knows this. He just doesn't want to be in my debt.'

Chris nods, but he seems to have lost interest. Dobby isn't sure he's been interested in anything that's been said all night. He feels an impulse to demand to know if Chris is listening, but what's the bloody point?

Jesus, he thinks. Happy birthday to me.

He follows Chris's gaze, which has drifted to the occupants of another table. Two young women, both attractive and bubbly and giggly.

Well, if that's what it takes to get his attention . . .

'I might have to try another copper,' he says. 'Maybe that Webley woman. You know, the bit of stuff who's hanging round with Cody now.'

When Chris's head snaps back into line, it comes as no surprise to Dobson. Predictable, see. Everyone's so bloody predictable.

'Yeah?' says Chris. He tries to keep the salacious curiosity out of his voice, but it's there all right. Pathetic.

'Yeah. What do you think? Worth a try?'

Chris takes a swig of his drink, which is only a half-pint of lager because he's a complete lightweight.

'Sure. Not certain Cody would stand for it, though.'

Dobson offers him a smug smile. 'Well, maybe Cody wouldn't have to know. I told you, I can find things out. Maybe I know how to get to Webley when Cody's not even around.'

There is a definite light of interest in Chris's eyes now, but Dobson decides he's already said too much. He's satisfied that he's managed to impress Chris. That'll do. No need to give away everything. Better to keep your cards close to your chest.

He can tell there are questions on Chris's lips. Well, tough shit, he thinks. I'm leaving you on a cliffhanger, mate. Maybe you'll be a bit more attentive from now on. It's my frigging birthday, for Christ's sake.

'Get the beers in,' he orders, even though Chris bought the last round. 'I'm dying for a slash.'

And then he's up and away from the table. Not even looking back, but knowing that he's left Chris desperately wanting to know more.

At the urinals, he starts to feel more regretful. He shouldn't have said anything about Webley, or about what he has the power to do. Nobody's business but his own. It was the beer talking, which is always a dangerous state to get into. If there's anything he has learnt in his line of work, it's not to reveal your plans. Some bastard will always steal them and claim them as their own.

He returns to the table without washing his hands. He's decided he is going to change the subject, although finding something else that this dickhead of a photographer might be willing to discuss could be something of a challenge.

Idly, he picks up his mobile phone, which he'd left on the table. Worth a quick check. Maybe he's received some birthday greetings from an old friend. Or maybe from that girl in accounts – the one with the enormous . . .

He sees that a text came in while he was taking a pee.

Not a welcome one, though.

It's from his boss. Edward Kingsley.

It's short, but definitely not sweet. It starts with, 'Cody came to see me. Very interested in you. Had to tell him about . . .'

And then there's one more word.

Dobson stares in disbelief at it. That single word that represents so much to so many people. Why the fuck did Kingsley have to say anything about that? And to Cody, of all people?

Shit!

A thought crosses his mind: that Chris might have seen the text on his phone when its arrival was announced. But when he looks across the table he sees that Chris once again has his mind on the girls across the room. He seems oblivious to anything going on elsewhere in the pub, including at his own table.

But that's of small comfort.

Cody is asking questions about me, thinks Dobson. Why? What led him to do that?

And now Cody knows. He knows!

This changes everything.

47

Cody turns the car radio off. He's getting bored. He has flicked through a dozen radio stations, and none of them are playing anything worth listening to. The news breaks provide no relief, because all they do is drone on about the lack of progress on the murders.

He glances at the dashboard clock. Almost eleven, and still no sign of Dobson. He doesn't seem to Cody like somebody who would hit the nightclubs, so surely he will be home soon. But then it strikes Cody that he knows nothing about Dobson's private life. The man might be anywhere from a strip joint to his darling mother's house. Who knows?

Give it another hour, he thinks. If Dobson comes home pissed I won't get much sense out of him anyway. Another hour. If he's not here by then, I'll leave it until morning.

It's not like I can pin anything criminal on him. Not yet, anyway.

He turns his thoughts to other things. To Webley in particular.

He's starting to think that maybe he handled it all wrong. No big surprise, because when it comes to matters of the heart, he feels he normally gets it wrong.

It was a knee-jerk reaction, blowing up like that. He has always been so terrified of others finding out how he ticks. Or fails to tick, because he's not exactly running like clockwork right now. And that's the point, isn't it? He's falling apart anyway. How can he last much longer in this job? What difference is it going to make that one random guy knows his secret? Who's he going to tell?

So, yes, screaming in Webley's face was probably not the wisest thing he's ever done. Especially after what she had done for him. And especially the way she was feeling at that moment.

All of which makes him think it's probably time to man up and apologise. Webley deserves so much better.

He takes out his mobile phone. Clicks into the contacts. Scrolls down to Webley's number. Hovers his finger over the call button.

But it's getting late, he thinks. After eleven now. She'll be asleep. Or crying her eyes out. Or trying to patch things up with Parker. Whatever, not the best time to call.

In the morning. Yes, that would be better.

He'll call her in the morning.

Definitely.

She should get into bed. Lord knows, she's tired enough. Drained. Not that it's been a hard day physically. But emotionally – well, that's another story.

Last night was bad enough. She went through enough turmoil then to last her a lifetime. How dare Parker accuse her of cheating on him? How dare he suggest that the only reason she moved to MIT was to be near to Cody?

She remembers it now as a maelstrom of tears, fury and words that should have been left unspoken. She can't see how the relationship can ever be repaired.

He could try, though, couldn't he? Parker could at least try.

She must have checked her phone a thousand times today. She needed to see a missed call, or a text. She's not sure how she would have responded, but at least there would have been something to set things in motion again. As it is, it seems he doesn't care.

Of course, he could be thinking along exactly the same lines – wondering why she doesn't call him. But why should she? She's done nothing wrong. She's the one who is the victim of unfounded allegations.

And then, just to put the top hat on things, there's Cody.

What kind of reaction was that? Where was his compassion, his sympathy? All he could think about was himself, and he's the one who caused all this in the first place.

Well, perhaps that's not strictly accurate. Cody didn't ask her to worry about him. He didn't invite her to bang on every door in Rodney Street in an effort to find him.

So, she thinks, why did I do that? Why didn't I keep my distance and let him sort out his own problems?

She understands now why the force has regulations about getting involved with colleagues. Not that she is involved with Cody. That's well and truly over. But it doesn't stop her caring about him, worrying about him. That can't be wrong, surely?

It can get in the way, though. Of work, of objectivity. And, patently, of relationships with partners who should know better. It's for all those reasons that she thinks she'll have to talk to Blunt tomorrow. See if she can do something about getting her reassigned. It might not look good on her record, but what choice does she have? Cody is never going to be merely her sergeant. They know too much about each other, and that will always lead to friction.

Ding-dong.

The doorbell startles her. She glances at the clock on the wall. Close to eleven thirty. There's only one person who would come to her door this late at night.

Parker.

He's come to apologise. He realises how idiotic he's been, and now he's come to make it up to her.

She jumps to her feet, re-energised by the prospect of sorting out this whole stupid mess. In the hallway she checks herself in the mirror. She's looked better, but maybe it's a good thing that he sees what effect his hurtful remarks have had on her. He needs to be made to feel at least a little guilty.

She heads towards the front door.

Halts when she gets to the porch.

Stupid.

I should know better, she thinks. I've been working on the damn cases, for God's sake. There's a lunatic on the loose, knocking off coppers. What if that's him now?

She is suddenly less sure that she wants to answer the door. She is instead responding to the adrenalin surging through her blood, causing her to wonder if she ought to be making an emergency phone call.

Ding-dong.

No, she thinks. Can't be him. Our killer doesn't just turn up at the door and ring the bell. That's not his approach. He wouldn't expose himself like that. Wouldn't take such a risk.

But better safe than sorry.

So she puts the chain on the front door before opening it. Flicks the switch that puts on the porch light too. Only then does she open the door as far as the chain allows.

The man appears much less self-assured than usual. Worry lines further distort his already unattractive features.

'Dobson. What the hell are you doing here? How did you even find—'

'It's complicated. I was given your address. By Cody. He said if I wanted info on the murders you're investigating, I should talk to you.'

New-found rage bubbles up inside her. 'He said what? The cheeky bastard!'

'You make it sound like he's not in your good books at the moment.'

'He's not. And you turning up at my door this close to midnight doesn't help either. I'm sorry, Dobson, but Cody's sent you on a wild goose chase. I've got nothing to tell you.'

She makes a move to close the door, but Dobson puts a hand out.

'Wait. Please. There's more. I . . . I think I've found something.'

She notices a change of tone in his voice. A hint of unease.

'What kind of something?'

Dobson looks behind him, as if checking for eavesdroppers. 'A link. Between the four officers that were killed.'

'Are you serious? What link?'

Dobson moves in closer. He looks almost afraid as he speaks in a conspiratorial whisper. 'The problem is . . . I think it involves Cody. I think that's why he tried to divert me on to you, to get me off his back. But I didn't come here because he suggested it. I came because I need to talk to someone about this, and I can't do it in front of Cody.'

Webley goes quiet. She still can't believe the gall of Cody. Sending Dobson to talk to her, just to get the reporter out of his hair? Cheeky sod. But this other thing, about the murders – that could be some really serious shit. It can't wait till morning. Plus, she wants to hear this before anyone else. This could be big. This could be a career maker.

'Hold on,' she says. She pushes the door closed. Slides off the chain. Pulls the door open again.

'Come in,' she says.

Dobson takes a step forward. His head is bowed, so that she can't see his face. His slumped posture puzzles her. When he slowly raises his head again, she can see that there are tears in his eyes.

'I'm sorry,' he says. 'I'm really, really sorry.'

She doesn't get it. What does he mean? What's he sorry about?

And then the shadows move. From behind Dobson, another figure slides into view. The porch light hits his features, and she recognises him. She knows the face and she knows the power of the weapon that he rests gently on Dobson's shoulder and points between her eyes.

And then she understands.

48

When it gets to 1.30 in the morning, Cody decides to call it a day. He's not going to sit here all night. He doesn't really know for sure that Dobson is up to anything bad. Yes, he's a pain in the arse, and yes, he's got some questions to answer, but that doesn't make him a killer.

I should go home, he thinks. Try to get some sleep. Talk to Dobson in the morning.

Oh yeah, and keep my promise to sort things out with Webley.

There is madness in those eyes. Desperation. Webley judges that it would take only the slightest provocation to convince him to tighten his finger on the crossbow trigger and send that lethal missile spearing into her body.

They are seated in her living room. She is next to Dobson on the sofa. He is blubbering softly. The man who has the blood of four police officers on his hands sits in an armchair directly opposite.

'Why, Chris?' she asks.

She had completely forgotten his name, but now it springs back to her almost violently. She had consigned him to the set of non-entities who had entered her life fleetingly and departed it without distinction, but he has suddenly become the prime focus of all her conscious thought. All of her faculties are concentrated on the man in front of her, the deeds he has perpetrated, the atrocities he might still commit.

And yet, behind the weapon, the man looks so innocent, so normal. But that's always the way. She knows this. Knows that the most dangerous criminals are the ones who are able to keep their evil hidden from view until they choose to unleash it. She shouldn't feel such surprise.

Chris tilts his head as he regards her, as if finding her speech difficult to understand. She can tell from this that he views her as less than human.

'Why what?' he asks in return.

'What do you think?' she says, a little too loudly. 'Four people dead. You killed four human beings.'

He shakes his head. 'Wrong. I killed four scumbag coppers. Not human beings at all.'

There is no wry smile on his face as he says this. He is not trying to provoke a reaction with trivial insults. That is what he believes. That is how he sees police officers – as a separate and insignificant species, undeserving of any right to life. And Webley is a member of that species.

'So what happened?' she asks. 'Get arrested once? Put in a cell for a night? Get a parking ticket? What momentous event in your life convinced you that all members of the police force need to be exterminated like vermin?'

He shakes his head in pity. 'You really don't know, do you? You're one of them, and you don't even know what you did. How sad is that? Don't you see how pathetic you are?'

'No, I don't, Chris. Tell me.'

'Why don't we just see if you can figure it out for yourself, eh? We've got all night for you to think about it.'

She wonders what he means by that. All night? Why? If he has come here to kill her, why wait? In a way she is grateful for the stay of execution, but at the same time she dreads to think what else he might have in store for her over the next few hours.

She decides to try a different tack. 'How did you find me?'

Chris nods towards Dobson. 'I didn't. That piece of shit did all the work. He wasn't joking when he said he could find things out. He's got good contacts. Knows some very shady people. Getting your address was just as easy as getting the addresses for Latham and Garnett. His problem is that he can't keep things to himself. He likes to talk, especially after a pint or two. Can't shut him up when he gets going. Boring bastard most of the time, but occasionally he says something useful. Isn't that right, Dobby? Hey, Dobby, I'm talking to you.' He puts the emphasis on the nickname, knowing how hurtful it is to the reporter.

Dobson looks directly at his tormentor. He sniffs wetly, then turns flickering eyes on Webley. 'I'm sorry,' he says to her again. 'I really am.'

Webley ignores the apology. There are still too many holes in this story.

'Okay, so he told you how to find me. But why bring him here? Why not come on your own?'

'Because he's just as bad as you. He played his part, just like you did.'

'What are you talking about? What part?'

'Ask him. Ask him what he is. I saw it, on his phone. Cody knows too. Cody's on to him. He thought he was safe, but he isn't. Cody found out, and now I know, and now it's almost time. I knew I couldn't do this much longer, but I didn't know when it would end. But now I've had the sign. It's all fallen into place. I have him, and I have you, and it's almost time to tell everyone.'

He's rambling. Making no sense at all. What sign? Time to tell everyone what? And what does Cody know about Dobson?

'Cody? What's he got to do with this?'

'Everything. Ironic, really. He provided the sign. Told me what Dobby is. Don't you see? It's all come together tonight. Without Cody, this probably wouldn't be happening. I would have waited, maybe for too long. But we need a climax, a big finale. The message needs to go out. The birds demand it.'

'The birds? What about the birds, Chris? Tell me about them.'

Chris's eyes roll in his head, and for a second Webley thinks he's about to lapse into some kind of trance state. She braces herself to make a move, but suddenly he snaps back into the here and now.

'The birds are everything. They have been calling to you, to all of us, and we've been ignoring them. They want the world to know what happened to them. They want us to hear about their pain. The pain that people like you caused.'

He thrusts the crossbow forward as he says this. Webley winces, fearful that it might go off accidentally.

'I don't know what you mean, Chris. How are they in pain?'

He barks a laugh that carries no humour. 'You know. And if you don't, you should be ashamed of yourself. You brought the birds down. You brought them crashing to the ground and you left them there to die.'

She doesn't know how to continue the conversation. It makes absolutely no sense to her. It's as though they are walking along two parallel bridges, and she just can't make the leap across to his. But whatever he's fixated upon, it means everything to him.

'Me personally, Chris? Or police officers in general? Because we're not all the same, you know. Some of us—'

'Yes! You *are* all the same. You think the same and you act the same and you lie for each other, even when you've done really bad things.' He jabs the crossbow at Dobson now. 'And he's no better. I thought he was one of the good guys, I really did. The way he spoke, I believed he was interested in exposing police corruption. I almost trusted him. But he's a liar, just like you. He wanted the birds to suffer. He enjoyed it.'

The birds again. What's the significance of the damn birds?

'And what about the suffering *you* cause the birds, Chris? You killed four of them. Maybe you've killed even more?'

Chris isn't swallowing that one. He shakes his head again. 'You don't get it, do you? These are the same birds you hurt. They're already dead. They're trying to tell you their story, but you're too stupid to listen. They are messengers. You just need to open your minds to their message.'

'Then help me do that. Tell me about their messages. That first one – what was it? – "nevermore", right? Tell me about that.'

He studies her, as if checking to see that she's not just stalling for time or trying to distract him. But she genuinely wants to know. If she's going to die, then she wants to know why. Surely he can see that in her face.

'Isn't it obvious? It means "never again". That's the most important message. But you can't even see it, can you? You need to have it spelt out for you.'

'You're right, Chris. I'm just a dumb copper. Please explain the—'

'They're about loss, about grief, about death. Surely even you could see that? The birds are crying. They need all of you to understand. Don't you hear them? Nevermore, nevermore, nevermore.'

'But, Chris, if you kill us we will never understand. Tell us what the birds are saying in simple, plain English. That's all you have to do.'

His laugh is scornful now. 'No. I have to make sure. I have to teach you all a lesson, and sometimes lessons have to be painful. Sometimes a child has to be smacked. Sometimes people have to die, so that everybody else understands. I have to make an example of you. Both of you.'

Dobson brings his hand to his face and begins sobbing again.

'This isn't going to teach anyone anything,' says Webley. 'We'll just be two more victims of a deranged killer. And when they catch you – because they *will* catch you, Chris – nobody will understand why you did it. They'll just lock you up and throw away the key, and there will be nobody left to speak for the birds. The message will be lost forever.'

Chris smiles at her. 'That's where you're wrong. Because this is the end. This is the grand finale. And you two will be the stars of the show. You will treat your audience to a spectacle they will never forget. We're going out with a bang.'

For the first time this evening, Chris's face is shining with glee.

And suddenly Webley is even more afraid.

49

Three o'clock in the morning, and Cody is wide awake.

Nothing unusual in that, he thinks. But the cause is different this time. The cause is Webley.

He decided earlier that he would call her to apologise, to explain. Then he put it off, telling himself he would ring her in the morning. Only, he knows that was a lie. He had no intention of making that call. Truth be told, it would have got to morning and he would have used delay tactics again. He would have looked at Webley and said to himself something along the lines of, *Hey, she doesn't seem so upset now. She's over it. We can move on. Big intense conversation no longer required.*

It would have been the coward's way out. A despicable stomach crawl away from the line of fire. That's not how he lives his life.

So, he thinks, it's time to grow a pair. Call her.

But it's three in the morning.

So what? he thinks. You need to talk to her. If she doesn't want to hear it, she'll let you know. But you need to try. If you don't, you'll never be able to live with yourself.

So call her.

He reaches for the phone on his bedside table.

She doesn't understand the waiting. She has tried asking him, of course, but he seems to have lost all interest in talking. He just sits there, staring. Sometimes his eyes are on Webley, sometimes on Dobson, but most of the time there is a blankness to them, as though he is seeing nothing except the pictures conjured up by his troubled brain.

She had hoped he would grow careless as the hours drifted by, but everything he does suggests he is still very much at the helm.

Earlier, when Dobson insisted he needed to pee, Chris herded them both into the bathroom so he could keep an eye on them. She had to stand there while Dobson relieved himself in a stuttering stream.

She oscillates between making a move and resigning herself to whatever fate awaits. Each impulse to be courageous is speedily quashed when she looks at that steel-tipped crossbow bolt and imagines the pain as it tears through her soft tissues – through her heart, maybe. She sees herself falling to the floor before she has even fully left her seat, and then lying there in her own blood and agony and despair. And as those pictures enter her brain she is already chiding herself – telling herself that it's too late now, that she has talked herself out of it and missed her chance.

But now another wave of optimism strikes. I can do this, she thinks. I can cover that space in one dive. He won't be expecting it. Even if he gets off a shot, he won't be able to aim properly. He will be firing wildly. And if he gets lucky, the likelihood is that I will be only injured. And he will be unarmed then. I will have him, and I will be like a tigress, and I will tear the shit out of him.

All right, she thinks. I'm going. This is it.

She experiences a surge of adrenalin that gives her a sick feeling in the pit of her stomach and a compulsion to crap herself. She tenses. She plants her feet squarely on the floor, her hands on the edge of the cushion.

She thinks, Go now! Do it!

And then the phone on the sideboard bursts into life, and a page in everybody's mind is turned.

'Who's that?' says Chris. He shuffles to the edge of his seat, his eyes moving feverishly between the phone and Webley. His voice becomes more demanding: 'Who's that?'

'I . . . I don't know,' says Webley. 'My boyfriend, maybe. Or it could be work. Or a wrong number. I don't know.'

'Don't answer it,' he orders. Which seems redundant, because she was hardly about to get up and saunter over to the phone without seeking permission.

'Fine,' she says.

But still her mind works furiously on the possibilities. For the first time tonight she doesn't want this to be Parker. Apologies are no good to her now. She wants this to be somebody from work. A cop. Someone who might be able to save her life, if only he or she can be made aware of her plight. A single word is all it would take. A single plea for help.

But she cannot even do that. She cannot move out of her seat. She has to let the phone ring until her caller gives up, and her hopes wither with that surrender.

This caller is persistent, however. When the ringing stops and Webley's own curiously business-like voice cuts in with its invitation to leave a message, there are more words to follow.

In a male voice.

Cody's voice.

Despite the depth of anger that Cody has managed to foster in her today, the sound of his voice is, at this moment in time, the sweetest thing she has ever heard. Yes, he is infuriating, and yes, he has no end of problems that desperately need fixing, but there is one thing she knows about him: when it comes to policing, he is more dedicated and courageous and stubborn than anyone else on the force. And that's what she needs right now.

But he hasn't rung to tell her that he is saddling up his white steed and donning his armour. He has rung to do what he is so, so good at. To wit: breaking her heart.

He says, 'Hi, Megan. Sorry for ringing you up at stupid o'clock. I don't blame you for not answering, especially if you saw it was me calling. I just wanted to say . . . to tell you how sorry I am for the way I acted today. I was a total dick. I overreacted, and I completely understand why that pissed you off. Anyway, I just want you to know that I still think you're wonderful, and that I enjoy working with you, and to say thank you for listening to me, and to ask if you'll forgive me, and – what was the other thing? – oh, yeah, to say that I hope you and Parker sort things out, because he's a lucky man to have a girl like you, even if he does have a stupid name. And . . . wait . . . Just in case he's there with you now, listening to this – Parker, I take back what I just said about your name. It's different. And what Megs – I mean Megan – said to you last night is the truth. There's nothing between us now. What we had was a long time ago. I got engaged myself since then. Megan and I just talked last night – nothing more. Anyway . . . so, that's it. Megan, I hope I see you tomorrow at work. Okay, well, goodnight.'

The message ends then. Tears are running down Webley's cheeks, and she tries to work out why she is so sad. It would be understandable if the message had been from Parker. They would probably have been his final words to her. He would have been trying to rebuild a future that is already doomed, and that would have been heartbreaking. But Cody? He's only a colleague now – a man she barely understands anymore – saying he's sorry about a pathetic little argument. How can that carry such weight?

'Well, well,' says Chris. 'You and Cody, huh? I had no idea. But that makes things so much better. He attacked me – I thought he was going to kill me. And now I'm going to take revenge on him by killing his ex-girlfriend. That's pretty cool. I like that.'

He glances at the clock. 'Just a few more hours, and then Cody will get his comeuppance, and the world will hear the birds. Nice how things work out, sometimes.'

50

He sleeps a little after leaving a message for Webley. No clowns, no faceless people, no screaming. A short but blissful period of unbroken sleep.

He awakes refreshed and looking forward to work. Looking forward to seeing Webley again. She must have listened to the message by now, and she's not heartless. She will give him a chance to redeem himself.

Yes, today is going to be a good day.

'It's time,' says Chris.

Webley's stomach lurches. The announcement can mean only one thing: it's the appointed hour of her execution. And yet she wonders why he has waited this long. What difference can it possibly make?

So this is her last chance to do something about it. Her last opportunity to save the lives of herself and Dobson. Knowing this, she is suddenly alert again, despite not having had an ounce of sleep. She fixes Chris in her sights, eager for any sign of a lapse in his concentration. She will seize upon such a slip. She will take that fucking crossbow and fire it up his rectum, the insane twat.

'Time for what, Chris?' she asks innocently. 'What exactly do you have in mind?'

'We're going for a little drive.'

This comes as a huge surprise. But, on reflection, it makes sense. If Chris wants to put on a show, he can hardly do it here. He waited until morning because it needs to be visible to an audience. And perhaps also because the location he has in mind is available only during the day.

'What? A drive? Where are we going?'

'You'll find out. Everyone will find out. You're gonna be a star.'

Chris reaches into his pocket, pulls out a key and tosses it across to Webley.

Cody catches the car key that has just been thrown to him by Blunt.

It's déjà vu. This whole thing started with the MIT gang marching towards him from the station and with Blunt ordering him to drive, and now it's happening all over again.

He falls into step alongside his boss, but she speaks before he can put his own questions.

'Where've you been?'

'Following a lead.'

Which is shorthand for saying that he's been to Dobson's house again, hammering on his door to no avail. Where the hell is that ugly little squirt?

'And did it lead anywhere?'

'Not yet.'

'Well, don't get your hopes up too much, Cody. Our man's decided not to hang about waiting for you to find him.'

Cody feels a tightening in his abdomen. Not another murder? And with Dobby out of his house all night, isn't that too much of a coincidence? Could I have prevented it?

'Ma'am?'

'He's taken matters into his own hands. We've got a situation.'

'Another victim? One of ours again?'

'Not yet. The perp's decided to call his own little press conference. We're specially invited guests, along with most of the country's media. But that's not the worst of it.'

'No?'

'No. He's got hostages.'

They are at the car, but Blunt pauses to stare meaningfully at Cody. A sudden sense of dread strokes his spine.

'Who?'

'DC Megan Webley for one.'

For a moment he cannot speak. Webley? In the clutches of a serial killer? That cannot be true. Cannot be real.

'Ma'am . . . If I can ask . . . Is she with Dobson?'

Blunt narrows her eyes at him. 'How did you know that?'

His breath catches. He was too late. If he had managed to track down Dobson earlier, he could have averted this. He could have kept Webley safe.

'Long story,' he says, knowing that Blunt doesn't have time for it now. It doesn't seem the best moment to reveal that he went to the Vernon house without permission.

'Well, we need to get going if we're to keep either of them alive. Get in.'

She opens her door and stoops to climb in, but Cody stops her. 'What do you mean, keep Dobson alive?'

She straightens again, irritation on her face now. 'What do you think I mean? I know you two aren't exactly bosom buddies, but the last time I checked it was still police policy to get hostages out alive if possible. Now get in the bloody car and drive!'

His mind is swirling with questions, but he decides it's prudent to do as he's been told. He gets in, starts up the engine, gets on the road before daring to unleash the foremost of the queries on his list.

'Ma'am, you said that Dobson is a *hostage*?'

'That's the intel I was given.'

'So . . . so do we have an ID on whoever's taken the hostages? Do we know who our killer is?'

'We do. Dobson's mate, apparently. Chris Davies. The photographer bloke.'

Cody glances at her. Chris? It's not what he expected to be told. But then he didn't expect to hear that Dobson had been taken hostage. If he'd had to place bets, he'd have put Dobson on the other side of the line between victims and criminals. It doesn't make sense.

But then he thinks about it some more. And as he does so he realises that, actually, it makes perfect sense. The connection between Dobson and the police officers who were killed is just—

'Cody!'

He is suddenly aware of his surroundings again.

'Ma'am?'

'Two questions. One: are you even looking at the road ahead? And two: are you at some point going to ask where we're going?'

'Sorry, ma'am. Lost in thought. Where are we going?'

Blunt eyes him with suspicion. 'The Pier Head. I'm sure we'll see the media circus from a mile off.'

He nods, then moves the car into the correct lane. He tries to stay focused, but his mind soon switches into a more contemplative mode.

Why the Pier Head, of all places? What kind of stunt could the killer possibly be planning to pull at a location like that?

But then he gets there. Blunt was right about the media hubbub, although the word she used was 'circus', and he doesn't like the use of anything that has such a strong association with clowns. A uniformed officer directs them to a parking spot at the centre of the melee. They climb out of the car. Cody follows the gaze of everybody else, which is very much pointed in an upwards direction.

And then he understands.

It's the missing link. The connective tissue between the three individuals now alone on the top of this most iconic and distinctive of buildings on Liverpool's waterfront.

They are staring up at the Royal Liver Building. Perched atop each of its two clock towers is a verdigris-coated copper sculpture.

Each sculpture is of a Liver Bird – a creature resembling a cormorant, and carrying a sprig of seaweed in its beak. It is hugely symbolic to the city and the people of Liverpool.

Birds and symbols. That's what all this has been about.

The whole tragic story could have ended nowhere else but here.

51

It's cold up here. Webley is dressed as she was in the house. Jog pants and a thin sweater. Chris didn't allow her to pick up a coat, and now she's shivering in the brisk wind, her skin pimpling. Although that might have more to do with fear. She's certainly afraid. Up here, looking out across the Mersey and to Perch Rock on the northern tip of the Wirral, she feels so removed from everyone. So alone.

She is on a paved walkway running along the north-facing side of the building. At each end of the walkway stand cupolas that can be used as small meeting rooms. Next to them, at the east and west ends of the building, are the clock towers supporting the imposing Liver Birds. A similar walkway runs down the south side, but Webley couldn't get to it even if she wanted to. She is separated from it by long banks of air-conditioning units, and beyond them, in the centre of the building, two huge atria leading down to glass-roofed reception areas below. Along the other edge of the walkway is a low ledge topped by a simple black rail – the only thing hindering a person from stepping into oblivion.

She still doesn't know exactly what Chris has in mind. But she guesses it won't be pleasant. You don't force someone up onto a roof at the point of an arrow just to show them the view. And just to complicate the puzzle, he's brought a length of rope with him too. She doesn't want to think about what plans he might have for making use of that rope.

It was surprisingly easy to get them up here. Straight into the building just after the doors were opened and the security guards were occupied. Then, as soon as people became aware that here was a deranged man wielding a weapon of death, they kept their distance. Even the security personnel weren't about to risk losing their lives for the sake of preventing the intruders getting to the top of the building. Hell, let them get up there and then call the cops. Isn't that *their* job?

Well, yes, it *is* the job of the police to deal with situations like this. Except that Chris isn't about to make it easy for them to do that job. On his mobile phone he has already told the negotiators that any sign of a cop trying to get onto the roof, or of a helicopter approaching, will result in instant summary execution of a hostage.

She believes it, too. Murder is his ultimate aim here. Has been all along. The only thing she can hope for is that her death can be postponed long enough for somebody, somewhere, to take some action. But what she is also beginning to come to terms with is that such action may have to come from her. Dobson is a wreck, incapable of doing anything spontaneous and physical. And Chris will be aware of that. When it comes to the slaughter, it's likely he will cull the most threatening of the pair first.

So, she thinks, the only person with the remotest chance of getting me out of this situation is me.

Great.

Cody can hear the impatience growing in Blunt's voice as she demands answers from a uniformed inspector called Haynes.

She says, 'What do you mean, you don't know what's happening up there?'

'Just that,' says Haynes. 'We can't see anything. There's no building around here tall enough to look down on them, and Davies has already warned us what will happen if we send in a chopper.'

'What about the CCTV? Place like this, occupied by a bank among other things, must be bristling with security cameras.'

'It is. Everywhere but the roof.'

Blunt sighs. 'So I suppose that means we can't shoot the bastard either?'

Haynes shrugs. 'Same problem. If we can't see him, we can't shoot him. Might be a different story if he comes to the edge of the building.'

Blunt looks up again, and Cody wonders if her gaze is directed beyond the building's roof edge and on to the heavens above.

She says, 'How'd he get up there anyway? Don't you need keys?'

'The doors are controlled by card scanners. Davies grabbed an ID card from the woman at reception. We've disabled the system now so that our guys can go where they need to.'

'Has he told us what he wants?'

'Nothing solid. We're in communication via his mobile phone, but all we can get out of him is some nonsense about speaking for the birds.'

Cody knows he ought to make a contribution. He has information they don't, but something tells him he needs to keep it to himself for the moment. It could prove to be his only way of getting to Webley.

And, to Cody, that's the nub of it. Webley is up there, and although that's not his fault, he somehow feels it is. Besides, he can't let her die like this. He has already reached a decision that he will do everything in his power to prevent it.

He moves away from the crowd. Finds a quiet spot. He doesn't know Chris's mobile phone number, and he's certain that the hostage negotiators won't hand it over to him. But he does have Webley's. He dials it. Waits. It rings several times and then goes to voicemail. He tries again, with the same result. Either she doesn't have her phone with her, or else Chris isn't allowing her to answer it.

He takes out his wallet. Fishes out a scrap of paper and tries to decipher his own handwriting. The note contains a hastily scribbled name, address and phone number. He got them last night from Ed Kingsley.

Dobson's boss.

* * *

To Webley, it's a surreal moment when Dobson's phone comes to life. His ringtone is the theme music from *The Good, the Bad and the Ugly*. It could almost be a direct reference to herself, Chris and Dobson, respectively.

Interrupting his own call to the cops below, Chris clicks off his phone and strides across to where his captives have been made to kneel on the paved walkway.

'Who's that?' he demands.

Dobson gives him a fearful glance. 'I don't know.'

'Fucking well have a look, then.'

Dobson reaches into his coat and takes out his mobile. Checks the screen.

'It's . . . it's Cody.'

Something leaps inside Webley as she hears mention of Cody's name. It fades when she notices the sly smile on Chris's face.

'Give it here,' says Chris.

He snatches it from Dobson's grasp. Stabs the call answer button.

'Cody! Good to hear from you. Are you here, watching the show?'

Go and take a look for yourself, thinks Webley. Go to the edge and look over it so that a police marksman can blow your fucking brains out.

But he doesn't. He merely turns to face Webley and Dobson again, that hateful grim smile still contorting his features.

She wishes that Cody could see this killer's expression. He is wily, this man. Clever. Do not stray into his web, Cody.

Keep yourself safe.

'I'm here,' says Cody. 'We need to talk.'

'We're talking now. What do you want to say?'

'I'll tell you in person. Face to face.'

'Piss off, Cody. You're in no position to make demands. This is *my* show. You do what I say. All of you.'

'No demands, Chris. An offer.'

There's a pause. A brief one, but at least he's not rejecting it outright.

'What kind of offer? What could you possibly have that I might want right now?'

Here goes, Cody thinks.

'Me. I'm offering me. As a hostage.'

The laugh is deafening in Cody's ear. 'What? Are you serious? You're taking the piss, aren't you, Cody?'

'No, I'm not. But it's conditional. I'm talking about an exchange. Me for Webley.'

'I knew there'd be a catch. Forget it. I've got a copper already, and she's better looking than you. Why would I replace her pretty face with your ugly mug?'

'Two reasons. First, I'm the one who assaulted you. Have you forgotten about that already? My fingers around your scrawny neck?'

Another silence. Cody pictures the man on the other end of the line fingering his throat and contemplating the only opportunity he'll ever get to wreak revenge on the policeman who attacked and humiliated him.

'I remember. What's the other reason?'

'I understand why you're doing this. I know the reason. I know why you killed the police officers, and I know why you've got Dobson up there with you. You don't need Webley. She knows nothing about what you've been through – what you're still going through. She doesn't understand why the birds are so important in all this. I do. You want to broadcast a message to the world? Then at least do it with a copper who has some idea of what you're trying to say.'

Cody stops talking then. There's no more to say. Either it has worked or it hasn't. It's all up to Chris now.

'You can come up,' says Chris. 'Alone. No weapons, no body armour, no radio.'

'I'm on my way.'

He clicks the phone off.

And wonders what he's done.

52

He finds Blunt in discussion with Haynes again. His mouth dries up as he approaches her. She's not going to like this, he thinks. Actually, that's putting it mildly. She's about to go ballistic.

'Ma'am,' he says. 'There's something I need to—'

It's clear from the way she rounds on him that she is already aware of what has just taken place without her authorisation. Chris must have made another call.

Blunt glares at Cody. Haynes glares at him. It feels as though the whole crowd is glaring at him.

'Well, well. Detective Sergeant Cody. It seems you've got explaining to do.'

'Er, well, ma'am. I've been talking to Davies, and—'

She holds up a palm. 'Stop right there. You've been talking to Davies.'

'Yes, ma'am.'

'The killer of four police officers.'

'Yes.'

'The man now standing on top of the Liver Building with a crossbow and a pair of hostages in tow.'

'Yes.'

'The man at the centre of delicate and complex negotiations that, if they are not handled in a sensitive way by appropriately skilled and experienced people, could easily result in the deaths of everyone up on that roof.'

Cody says nothing in reply. He is getting the feeling that she is not entirely impressed with his efforts. In fact, she looks ready to burst into flames.

'What the hell do you think you're playing at?'

'I . . . I think I can help. I know this guy. I know what makes him tick.'

'*What makes him tick?* Cody, the man is a deranged killer. He loves nothing more than to take the lives of police officers. Even you, with all the mental anguish you've been through in your past, don't know what makes a lunatic like that tick.'

Cody is taken aback at the reference to his history. Blunt wouldn't normally fire off such a below-the-belt punch, especially in front of others. It's another indication of how upset she is at the moment.

He decides to try another tack.

'I've had dealings with this guy in the past. He knows me. He'll talk to me. He's not letting anybody else up there, but he's willing to make an exception for me. Surely that's a way in we should exploit?'

Cody knows he's being disingenuous here. The only real dealings he's had with Chris are when he cut off the man's air supply. But he's not about to tell Blunt that. He's also not about to reveal that, for the time being, he alone knows why Chris is doing this. Chris will undoubtedly announce that himself soon enough. Until that time, it's the only thing giving Cody the edge he needs to get Webley out of there, and he's not about to pass that advantage on to anyone else, police negotiators included.

Blunt aims a stubby thumb at Haynes. 'These chaps are the experts, but one thing I do know about hostage situations is that you do all you can to reduce the number of hostages. The one thing you never do is increase that number.'

'That's not going to happen. I'm going up there to talk to him – that's all.'

It's a lie, of course. He just hopes that Blunt can't read his mind.

'That's if Davies plays ball. What makes you think he will? He's a psycho, Cody. Don't forget that. He might just decide to keep you too.'

'I won't let it come to that. I'll stay close to the door. If things start to get hairy, I'll be out of there in a flash.' He pauses. 'Look, if it's a choice between letting those people up there be killed or sending in someone who might be able to make a difference, then why are we even wasting time discussing it? And if he does start anything, there'll be three of us against one. He's got a crossbow. He's got just one shot. The odds are pretty good that we can take him down.'

'One shot is all it takes to kill one human being, Cody. Don't underestimate this guy.'

'I'm not. But we've got to try something. This is our only chance to send someone up to talk to this guy face to face. We shouldn't throw that away. And if he won't listen to reason and I have to come back down, then at the very least I'll return with a good appraisal of what the situation is like up there.'

Blunt mulls it over. She looks to Haynes, who simply shrugs. Cody figures that the officer knows exactly how the discussions have gone with Chris. He will know that Chris has been unwilling to accept any offers in return for the release of his captives, and that time is running out for them.

'Come here,' says Blunt.

She drags him away from the crowd, out of earshot of other police officers.

'What is this, Cody? I mean, really? This is confidential, off the record. Tell me what's going through your head right now.'

He sees how earnest she is, how desperate to know the truth. There's a pleading in her eyes that touches him deeply.

But he doesn't think she really wants to know what's going on in his head. Doesn't believe that she would like to be made privy to the terrors that parade regularly through his mind, or the fact that, right now, he doesn't care whether he lives or dies when he gets to the top of this building.

'Ma'am, I—'

'Stella. My name's Stella. For this one brief moment there are no ranks, no badges. We're just two friends discussing something important to both of us. Now talk to me properly. Tell me why you were so desperate to go into that building on the docks. Tell me why you came running out of there like you'd just seen a ghost. Tell me why you now want to put your life in danger yet again. That man up there will kill you as soon as look at you. Maybe he does have only one shot, but if I were him, I would use that shot wisely. I would take out the biggest threat first. And if I let you go up there, I might as well paint a bullseye on you before you go. So come on, Nathan. Talk to me. Tell me why you might want to throw away your life like this.'

He wishes she wouldn't keep doing this: offering him the chance to ask for help, offering him a way out. He doesn't need a way out. At least not the way she envisions.

'I'm not throwing away my life,' he says. 'It'll be okay, I promise.'

He watches her mull this over. When she opens her mouth to speak again, he swears there's a slight tremble in her lower lip.

'I could put a stop to this, you know. Order you not to go up there.'

He looks directly into her eyes. Not with anger but with empathy.

'You could. But only if you stop being Stella and go back to being DCI Blunt. And that would be a shame.'

She has no answer to that, and she looks away. Cody moves past her before he can see what might be in her eye.

53

It feels to Cody like a walk to the guillotine. The corridors and stairs are lined with police officers, many of them wearing body armour and carrying semi-automatic weapons. They stand in silence, their eyes on this lone man in a suit, slowly passing them by on his way to the roof door, step by solemn step. Cody reckons that the necessary orders have already percolated down. These officers will have been commanded to allow him through, but they will not have been made privy to all the details. They will be wondering what the hell this unarmed, unprotected young fool possibly thinks he will be able to accomplish other than the discarding of his remaining years on this earth.

Cody is starting to think along similar lines. He has no plan, but he does have a straightforward objective, and that is to get Webley off this roof alive. If necessary, he will end Chris's life and he will sacrifice his own; and if he is to be frank with himself, Dobson's fate can go one way or the other. Webley is all that matters. Anyone else that lives will be a bonus.

And then he's past the last man. He's on his own. Nobody to shield him from harm. He pauses for a few seconds behind the last door separating him from a confrontation that might mean his death. Then he opens it.

A gust of cold wind hits him hard as he steps out, as if giving him a final warning of the violent forces he will face. Ahead, Chris is watching his every move. Webley and Dobson have been made to kneel in front of him, and he is pressing the crossbow tight against the nape of Webley's neck. Cody is painfully aware that all it will take is one wrong move from him to provoke Chris into pulling that trigger.

'Hello, Cody,' says Chris. 'Good of you to join us. Close the door and come a bit nearer.'

'We made a deal. You need to let Webley go now.'

He notices Webley raise her head slightly, then widen her eyes at him. The suggestion of a hostage exchange is news to her, and she's not receiving it with enthusiasm.

'D'you think I'm stupid?' says Chris. 'Let's get you sorted first, and then the bitch can leave.'

'How do I know you'll stick to your end of the bargain?'

'Oh, fuck off, Cody. This was your idea. If you've changed your mind, then piss off now and let me get on with it. We do this on my terms or not at all. I don't really give a shit one way or the other.'

He's right, thinks Cody. There's no point in arguing about what is, after all, your own suggestion. Do you want to help Webley or not?

He closes the door. Slowly traverses the walkway.

'That's close enough,' says Chris. 'Don't want you attempting any heroics now, do we?'

Cody shows his empty palms. 'No heroics. I would like to talk to you, though.'

'Talk to me? What about?'

'About the birds.'

Chris falls reverently silent. As if he needed the reminder of his reasons for doing all this. He chin-points at a pair of pigeons strutting across the floor.

'Look at them. Not a care in the world. Just doing their own thing. That's what we were like. Thousands of us, just enjoying life.' Fury crosses his face as he looks back at Cody. 'Your lot ruined it. You had to go and destroy everything.'

He turns his face upwards now. Towards one of the Liver Birds.

'You don't realise how important the birds are. These two in particular. They protect us. They watch over us. Believe it or not, a lot of Scousers don't even know what these birds represent. They don't know the legend, about the bad things that will happen to their city if these two birds ever decide to leave. And they will leave, you know. You lot will see to that. You don't realise how badly you've hurt them.'

He lapses into silence again, staring up at the huge copper creature, its massive wings outspread in demonstration of its power. It's why the Liver Birds aren't covered in excrement, for no other bird will dare go near them.

For the moment Chris is distracted, but he still has his crossbow against Webley's neck. The time is not yet right, but Cody knows he has to build trust, has to remain patient. Chris will make a mistake. It will happen.

'Tell me about it, Chris. Tell me how it all started for you.'

Chris lowers his head slowly. He has the vacant eyes of a man who is stoned on drugs or alcohol.

'What do you want to know?' he asks.

'Tell me about it,' Cody says again.

'What?'

And then Cody utters the magic word. The name that can send a shiver across the whole of Merseyside.

He says: 'Hillsborough.'

54

Fifteenth of April 1989. The Hillsborough football stadium in Sheffield. Liverpool are playing against Nottingham Forest in the FA Cup semi-final. The Liverpool fans arriving at the Leppings Lane end of the ground are excited, keen to take their places so that they can watch and support their heroes. What they don't know is that the pens here are already full to bursting point. But the police let them in anyway. The crowds are allowed to surge into a space that cannot possibly accommodate any more bodies without inviting disaster.

Ninety-six people die in the ensuing crush. Hundreds more are injured.

Afterwards, the police cast blame on the fans, claiming that they had rushed the gate. But subsequent inquiries and panels came to different conclusions. Not only did they absolve the supporters of all blame, they also found that the main reason for the tragedy was the failure of police control. Bad enough, but what made things much worse were the findings that the police covered up their culpability by altering statements made by themselves and witnesses, and that attempts were made by the police to malign the reputations of the victims.

'I was there,' says Chris. 'With the other birds. We were there because . . . we just wanted to enjoy ourselves. We were *alive!*'

'The other birds, Chris?'

Chris looks sideways at Cody, studying him with one eye. An avian-like gesture of his own as he tries to work out what Cody fails to understand. With his free hand he pulls down the zip of his jacket to reveal a plaid shirt. Then he begins to unbutton the shirt. After the first couple of buttons, he loses patience and rips the shirt open.

And then Cody sees it.

The crest of Liverpool Football Club, starkly tattooed in red on the left side of Chris's milky-white chest. Exactly where it would appear on the shirts of the team players. It depicts a shield containing a sideways-facing Liver Bird. What makes this particular emblem different, though, is that it has the characters 'JF96' running beneath it – a reference to the 'Justice For the 96' campaign for the victims of Hillsborough.

It's the final piece of the puzzle. Cody understands it all now. He sees the relevance of the birds. They were there, at the game. Emblazoned on scarves, shirts, banners, flags and programmes. Huge numbers of those birds carried by supporters crammed into a minuscule space at one end of the ground, like they were factory-farmed chickens.

'You squeezed the birds into tiny pens,' says Chris. 'You crushed us. We couldn't breathe, and still you forced more and more of us into the space. I was a kid, just ten years old. My dad was with me. I tried to keep hold of his hand, but we got pulled apart. I had never felt so alone, so afraid. People around me were crying. Some were screaming. I saw injured people on the floor, and others were trampling on them because they couldn't avoid it. And you lot just stood on the other side of the fences, yelling at us and hitting us with sticks and telling us to behave, even though you could see we were dying in front of you. You could see the birds dropping to the ground, all broken and still and no longer singing, but you did nothing to help. You just made it worse. You kept on letting us die, like we were nothing to you. Like we were vermin.'

Tears are streaming down Chris's face now, and even Cody is finding it difficult to swallow the lump in his throat. What went before, and what is happening now, is sheer tragedy for all. There are no winners or losers, no good or evil. What Chris was as a child was ripped from him forever during those few hours of what should have been one of the happiest occasions of his life. It broke his spirit and it broke his mind. Cody understands this. There is a resonance for him here in this telling of a past trauma that can never be exorcised and that continues to wreak devastation.

'Chris,' he says, 'I'm really sorry for what happened to you, and I'm not going to make any excuses for what happened on that day. But it's for others to decide who was to blame. It's not my job to do that, and it's not yours either, no matter how much you were hurt by it. Yes, I'm a police officer, but that doesn't mean I think like every other member of the force. It doesn't mean I have to agree with or support every act committed by other coppers. Sometimes what is done is a disgrace. I have no trouble in saying that. But what you have to realise is that we're not all the same.'

Chris emits a scornful laugh. 'No? Then where was the truth immediately after Hillsborough, before the inquests started tearing down all the shields you were putting up? How many of you came forward to say that, actually, no, it didn't happen like that, it happened like this? Where was the honesty, the breaking of ranks back then? It didn't happen, did it? What we got was the opposite. What we got was police reports being falsified, witness accounts being altered, police scum at the highest levels lying through their teeth. So tell me, Cody: how many of these decent, virtuous coppers you claim exist were raising their heads above the parapet back then?'

Cody takes another step forward. Stops when he sees Chris tighten his hold on the crossbow.

'You weren't the only one there, Chris. You weren't the only one affected. Some lost wives, husbands, sons, daughters. It didn't turn *them* into killers. It didn't make *them* think that the only good copper is a dead copper. What makes you so special that you should act on their behalf? What makes you believe that it's what those grieving family members would want?'

'Family? You want to talk about family? I'll tell you about family. Yes, my dad and I walked out of Hillsborough alive. But that didn't mean we came out unscathed. We were damaged. We saw and heard and felt things that no human being should have to experience. My dad was never the same after that. He lost his sense of humour. His love of football turned to utter hatred of the game. Every time a match was mentioned on the telly, he would swear at it and change the channel. He became morose, depressed. He wasn't the dad I knew and loved anymore. About ten months after Hillsborough, his car broke down on the M62. He was in the vehicle alone, but he was being filmed by the roadside cameras. He managed to get the car onto the hard shoulder, but then he just sat behind the wheel for about five minutes, doing nothing. Finally he opened the door and got out. Walked straight onto the inside lane of the motorway and into the path of a truck carrying frozen food.

'It didn't end there, either. We all suffered. My mum, especially. She had to go on tablets for her nerves. She cried endlessly. She suffered that way for years. Then, the Christmas before last, she took an overdose of her tablets. She died in her bed, covered in vomit and holding a wedding photo of her and my dad.'

Chris wipes away his tears with the back of his free hand. 'You see, Cody? There weren't only ninety-six victims. There were hundreds of them. Thousands. Victims like my mum and dad. And it hasn't come to an end. The fallout will carry on claiming lives. And what's important is that people get to hear about them too. They need to hear the calls of the birds. That's why I'm doing this. I'm speaking for the birds, because nobody else will.'

Cody is silent for a few seconds. He finds it difficult to counter much of what Chris has said, not least because it contains more than a grain of burning truth. What happened at Hillsborough devastated many families, and voices speaking on their behalf have too often gone unheard. Sometimes they have been deliberately silenced. Chris has found a new way to make his words heard. The problem lies not with his message, but in the way he has chosen to convey it.

'Chris. Listen to me. This isn't the way to do things. You need to talk to someone. You've been through a lot. You've had some awful experiences. You need to discuss them, the way you're doing with me now. There are people who can help you.'

It occurs to Cody that words very similar to his own have been thrown at him before now. He experiences a pang of guilt at not having practised what he is now preaching.

'Little late for that, don't you think? Four coppers are dead already. I'm going to prison for life. Whatever I do now will make no difference.'

Cody gestures towards Webley and Dobson. 'It'll make a difference to them. Come on, Chris. You've got *me* here now. You can still make your point with me. Why don't you let them go?'

Again Webley tries to catch his eye. 'Cody, no.'

Chris prods her with the tip of the crossbow bolt, and she winces. 'Shut up.' Then, to Cody: 'She can go. That's what we agreed. But not him. Not this two-faced, lying gobshite.'

'He's not a copper, Chris. He didn't do any of the things we've talked about.'

'No. He didn't do those things. In some ways what he did was worse. I saw it on his phone, Cody. I saw what you found out about him. Didn't take me long to get the full story out of him after that.'

Cody can imagine the threats of violence, and Dobson caving in quickly. Dobson might be a good investigator, but a fighter he's not.

'He was a lot younger back then, Chris. He was trying to make a name for himself.'

'We were all younger then. We didn't need to be called thieves, pickpockets, looters. We didn't need to have those lies told about us. We didn't need anybody reading that we urinated on the bodies of the dead. That's what he did, Cody. What this bastard did. He made up the most evil lies imaginable about us, just so he could sell his stories.'

He wasn't called Dobson back then, and he was with a different newspaper. That's what Ed Kingsley had told Cody. When the reporter's name became mud because of the Hillsborough coverage, he changed it, not least because Kingsley offered him a good job at his paper here in Merseyside, where there is no shortage of Liverpool supporters who would gladly tear him limb from limb if they knew what he had written about them.

Sticks and stones may break my bones, but words can never hurt me. That's how the saying goes. But Dobson's words can certainly hurt. His words can be fatal. What he let slip to Chris about the whereabouts of Latham and Garnett led to their being selected as the first victims. And now the words that Dobson wrote about the Liverpool fans all those years ago have come back to bite him with serrated-edge fangs. He too will die because of what he chose to say.

'It's funny,' says Chris. 'If it wasn't for you, I wouldn't be here now, on this roof. I knew I couldn't go on for much longer. You would have caught me in the end. But I didn't want to just fizzle out. I needed a show-stopper. You gave it to me. You lit the fuse that led to Dobby. And now I have all the ingredients I need. The police and the media. Representatives of those who did their best to make that day in 1989 such a dark one. It's time to bring it to an end, Cody. Time for the world to sit up and listen to birdsong.'

Cody hears the tone of finality. Something is about to happen. Something awful. He tries to stall it with further talk, but he can hear the panic in his own voice.

'So that's it? This is how you choose to commemorate the deaths of those football fans? With further violence, further killings?'

For a few moments Chris doesn't answer. He raises his head. Looks at the Liver Bird as if seeking an answer from it.

'Listen,' he says. 'The birds are singing.'

His movement is sudden. Too fast for Cody to react. Since he got up here he has regarded the crossbow in front of him as the item to fear most, a single trigger pull being all that is required to release a bolt of terrible power, speed and deadliness.

He didn't account for other weapons. He didn't reckon on the knife. He didn't imagine for one second that he'd be standing here helpless while a blade is thrust into Dobson's neck and yanked out again, not straight out, but in a twisting, dragging motion that tears open a huge ragged wound and causes a geyser of crimson to spurt onto Webley's face and hair.

Screaming. Yelling. Shouting. None of it making any sense, but everyone reacting with sheer emotion to the scene of devastation being played out as a man keels over and kicks and shakes and struggles vainly to staunch the life force gushing from his severed arteries.

Cody wanting to move. Webley wanting to move. Chris panning his crossbow from one to the other as he tries to keep them in check. More shouting. Cody feeling powerless and horrified and incensed and distraught, all at once.

And then the maelstrom collapses into something more stable. Cody and Webley resume their subservient status while Dobson's thrashing diminishes to become the quivering and twitching of a body in the final stages of shutdown.

Cody lets out a long, shuddering breath, in synchrony with Dobson's last. The situation has been taken to the next level. The time for talking is over.

He starts backing towards the door.

'Hey!' says Chris, his voice betraying panic. 'What are you doing?'

'I'm leaving, Chris. If you don't let Webley go right now, I'm going to open the door and I'm going to tell the cops inside that you've started killing all the hostages. They won't hold back any longer then, Chris. They'll think they have nothing to lose. They will come for you in force.'

'Stop! I'll shoot.'

'Can you hit me from there, Chris? Stop me in my tracks? Are you sure? Because even if I'm wounded I can make it through that door.'

He keeps moving. Keeps putting distance between them. Every step is a hammer blow to Chris's carefully constructed plan.

Chris's words tumble out. 'Then I'll kill her. You won't let me do that.'

'You give me no choice, Chris. If you want to complete your mission, if you want to put your message up there in neon lights, you have to let Webley go.'

He knows he's playing with Webley's life now, and it's tearing him up inside. But the situation is spiralling out of control. He has to resort to desperate measures.

He says, 'I'm at the door now, Chris. What's it going to be?'

Give him no time to think. Force his hand.

He reaches behind him for the door handle.

'Wait!' Chris yells. 'Okay. Okay. Get back here.'

'Let her walk, Chris.'

Chris prods Webley in the back with the toe of his boot. 'Get up. Start walking. Slowly.'

With great uncertainty, Webley gets to her feet, but hesitates before moving.

'Get the fuck out of here,' says Chris. 'Now!' Then he raises the crossbow and calls over to Cody: 'Start moving, Cody. Or I shoot your girlfriend.'

Slowly, Cody and Webley walk towards each other. Cody tries to keep his attention on the killer, to be ready to act if he makes a move. But he can't help but be pulled in by Webley's fearful eyes as he gets closer to her.

She shakes her head, and the motion dislodges another tear.

'Not for me, Cody,' she says. 'Don't do this for me.'

He tries to dredge up something profound to utter. All that poetry he has read, all those great works of literature, and yet the best he can manage is, 'I owed you one.'

As they pass, he puts a hand out and brushes his fingers against hers.

And then she is behind him, and the exchange is made.

'Here,' says Chris. 'Down on your knees. Hands behind your head.'

Cody steps around the growing pool of blood surrounding Dobson's unmoving form, then lowers himself onto the cold grey paving slabs. He looks across to Webley, who is now at the door. She meets his gaze in a final, lingering look, then flings open the door and disappears inside, safe at last.

And then the only hearts still beating up here are those of Cody, Chris and the pigeons.

55

Something has happened. Blunt can tell from the expression on the face of Haynes.

'What?' she asks. 'What is it?'

'A hostage has been released. DC Webley.'

Blunt wants to celebrate the moment. Wants to experience hope and optimism. It's a good thing, she tells herself. One hostage out already. That has to be good, right? Letting Cody go up there must have been the correct decision. He's doing a great job. Pretty soon everyone will come off that roof alive. That's what will surely happen.

'Sir?' This from one of the uniformed officers watching the building through binoculars. 'We've got some movement up there.'

Blunt looks up as Haynes spins away from her and lifts his own binoculars to his eyes. She can see a figure climbing over the rail at the roof's edge, as if preparing to jump.

She says, 'Who is it?'

'It's your man,' Haynes answers. 'Cody.'

No, she thinks. What the hell is he doing? What the fuck is going on?

'Tell your men,' she says, 'as soon as that bastard Davies shows his face, I want him taken out. I want that fucker shot dead.'

She doesn't care that she isn't running this operation. Doesn't care whether Haynes resents her interference or not. All she cares about is getting Cody out of there alive. And right now the chances of that are starting to look pretty remote.

'Sir. Another IC1 male getting onto the ledge.'

'That's our suspect,' says Haynes.

'Take him,' says Blunt. 'One of your men down here must have a clear shot now. Do something!'

'Sir, he's waving something. It's . . . It's a rope.'

'A what?' says Blunt.

'A rope,' Haynes echoes. 'He's holding a rope, and the other end is tied around Cody's waist. If we bring down Davies now, we bring down both men.'

So here he is. Trying not to look down. Trying to hold back the dizziness. Trying to resist the wind wanting to pull him into its embrace so that it can fling him to the ground all that way below.

And he wonders whether in fact this is what he really wants. He wonders whether the reason he is following Chris's instructions so readily is that he has already given up on life. He is to die now, but Webley is alive, and that's all that matters. That is what is fair and just.

He risks a brief downward glance at the people-dots, and imagines that he can see the horror and anticipation on their faces. Perhaps it's right that they are not cheated of what they now expect.

To his left, Chris holds on tightly to the rope. For good measure he has coiled it several times around his lower arm. His other hand still grasps the crossbow. He is not stupid, this man. He has thought everything through. He has left Cody no escape route.

Says Cody, 'So you still think this is the right thing to do? This is what you want to be remembered for?'

Chris smiles serenely. He seems almost at peace up here.

'It's not about me. It's about letting the world know what people like you and Dobson did, and are still doing. It's about telling them it has to stop.'

'You really think they'll understand? You think they'll be interested in that side of the story? Or do you think they'll just put it down to a nutter who goes around killing coppers?'

'Oh, they'll understand. I made a video, explaining exactly what all this is about, and while we've been up here I've put it live on YouTube. I don't trust your girlfriend to pass the message on. After all, she's police, and we all know how much they lie, don't we,

Cody? Your lot can't hide this one away, Cody. You can't falsify it or pretend it didn't happen. The world will hear the message and it will understand.'

Cody nods. 'Okay. Then your point is made. You can stop now. Job done.'

Chris's smile broadens. 'Almost. One task remains.'

'Which is?'

'We fly. Like the birds.'

56

She runs. Faster than she has ever run in her life.

They wanted to take her down. Away from the roof. But first they needed to check her over. She was covered in blood. Dobson's blood, but they didn't know that.

When she got inside and collapsed, they hastened the paramedics through to check her over. She told them she was all right, but still they insisted on assessing her.

And it was while they were doing this that the thought came crashing in.

He's going to kill Cody. Cody has given up his life for mine. He's going to die.

She knew this with more certainty than she had ever known anything before.

Cody is going to die, she thought. Any second now.

And so when the medics had done their job and stepped away and allowed her to get up, she looked at the outstretched hands of all the uniformed officers ahead of her . . .

. . . and she chose to go back.

She did it quickly, before they could grab her and stop her. Ignoring the protests of her colleagues, she turned and she retraced her steps and she went back onto that roof. She had no idea what she would do when she got there; she knew only that she had to go back.

Which is when she saw that Cody and Chris were already on the other side of the rail separating life from certain death. Their backs were to her. They couldn't see her.

So now she is running, straight across to them, praying she can get there before either can turn and spot her. She may have only seconds. Fractions of seconds.

I will kill him, she thinks. I have no choice. To save Cody, this man has to die.

So she runs.

This is it, this is it, this is it . . .

She doesn't know about the rope.

It takes but a moment of time, but it also takes an age. So much compressed into so short a period.

It is Chris who unwittingly gives him the signal that something is wrong. It's in the way he twists away from Cody. The way his mouth drops open and his body tightens in readiness for action.

And then Cody is aware of Webley. The last person he expected to see up here. She is flying in from left field. Entering his vision in a blur of motion that seems to be propelled from the paved roof and straight at Chris. He hears yells, both from Chris and from Webley. He starts to shout himself, but it is all happening so fast in front of him. He sees Webley's arms stretch out in front of her, and Chris trying to dodge away from the speeding bullet into which she has turned herself. He thinks for a moment that Chris will be successful – that he will manage to evade this human missile, leaving her to soar past, jettisoning herself from the building.

But she connects.

She hits him. Hard. Chris has no chance. He goes sailing over the edge.

Cody spins. Manages to grab the rail with both hands before the rope goes taut and he is yanked backwards.

He feels like he's been tied to two horses galloping in opposite directions. His whole upper body is suddenly stretched to breaking point. He is convinced his arms have left their sockets and that each of the vertebrae in his spine has parted company with its neighbours. The rope tightens to an impossibly tight circle around his waist and hitches on his pelvis. The pain is excruciating.

But it will not last, because his fingers are slipping. No matter how much his feet scramble on the wall for purchase, no matter how tightly Webley clutches his wrists, he cannot continue to support this weight while in this amount of pain.

When he looks down, all he sees is Chris's face. The killer has lost the crossbow, and has both hands on the rope. He can hang there for as long as it takes. And that won't be long now. Chris knows this, and he is smiling.

And then his head explodes.

A single shot, from the car park below. Chris loses his grip as he loses his life. And in spite of all his fine words about the birds and what they meant to him, his fall is nothing like flying. Instead, he bounces off a ledge and spins into the void. His descent has no grace, no beauty, no wondrousness, no control. It is the sad plummet of a man for whom all of those things were irretrievably lost, and the cries that well up from the onlookers below are not of mourning and sadness as they might be for a rare bird shot from the sky, but of horror and repulsion.

Grunting with the pain, Cody clambers back to safety. He slumps over the rail, next to Webley in a similar bent-over position.

'That was a stupid thing to do,' he tells her.

She manages to find a laugh. 'Not as stupid as you swapping yourself for me. Why did you do that?'

'I told you. I owed you one. You were the first person to listen to me.'

'Guess I should have known better. I knew there was trouble brewing when I clapped eyes on you again. You were never good for my heart, Cody.'

She coughs. Spits onto the floor.

It's bright red.

'Megan? Megan?'

She pushes herself away from the rail then, turning to face Cody. As she does so, her legs buckle and she collapses onto the paving stones. And then Cody sees it.

The crossbow bolt. Buried deep in her chest.

After that, he doesn't know what happens. Noises overwhelm his senses. The pounding of boot-clad feet behind him. Voices calling. Radios squawking. The vicious chopping of helicopter blades as they get nearer and nearer. His own voice crying into the wind that carries past the ears of the Liver Birds staring steadfastly across the city and its river.

Everyone wants a piece of him.

His superiors, his colleagues, the media – they all want to talk to Cody about exactly what happened up there.

All except Blunt. She takes one look at him and seems to understand something. As far as he knows, she is not aware of his past relationship with Webley, and she certainly has no idea he almost gave up his life for the young detective constable. And yet she seems to sense his need to be by Webley's side.

'Go,' she tells him.

And so he does. He travels with Webley to the hospital, holding her hand and telling her it will be okay, and saying lots of things that he won't even remember later, because he knows she needs a friendly, comforting voice at the moment, and that's all he has to offer now to the woman who once believed she would become his wife.

And even as he tells her to be strong, he feels his own strength waning. He can't hold back the tears, and he can't keep his voice from breaking, and he can't stop himself wishing that Webley hadn't come back for him on that roof. He had already made his pact concerning who should live and who should die, and she had to go and mess it all up.

At the hospital the intimacy is ended abruptly. She is whisked out of his hands. Wheeled off to an operating theatre by a professional-looking team who have only the welfare of the patient on their minds. Cody is quizzed briefly but efficiently. The medics extract only the information they need about the background to Webley's predicament. And when they have drained him of his data and he informs them that he is not family, he seems to be relegated in their estimation of his further usefulness. He becomes a mere bystander, peripheral to the whole situation.

He paces. He sits. He drinks coffee. Occasionally he asks for news. Time drags.

At some point he glances up and sees familiar faces at the desk. Webley's parents. Accompanying them is a tall, handsome man in an expensive suit. Parker, presumably.

Cody decides it's best to make himself scarce. He's not sure how any of them will feel about him being there, and he doesn't want to make a scene. Webley wouldn't wish that.

He sneaks off. Finds a cafeteria. Drinks more coffee.

He returns to the ward when he feels it might be safe to do so. Standing at the desk, he looks along the corridor. There is no sign of Webley's parents, but Parker is there, alone on a chair. He has his head in his hands, and he is shaking slightly. Cody thinks he might be crying, but he's not sure. He wants to go over to him. Try to console him, or at least talk to him. But again he's not sure that's a good idea.

He turns to the woman behind the desk. 'I, er, I came in with Megan Webley earlier.'

'Oh. Yes.'

'I . . . I was just wondering if you had any more information for me. About her condition.'

The woman looks to her left, as another woman strolls over. This one is wearing hospital scrubs.

'Hello,' she says. 'I've just been talking to the family members. And you are?'

'I'm Detective Sergeant Cody. Megan Webley is my colleague. I brought her in.'

She nods. Cody steels himself. There is news. If this doctor has been talking to the family, there is news.

His eyes flicker again to Parker. Look at him, he thinks. This can't be good. This must be the worst news possible.

Says the doctor, 'She's a strong girl. Looks like she'll be making a few more arrests yet.'

Cody feels tension flood out of him. He almost collapses on the spot.

'She's okay?'

'We think so. The crossbow bolt didn't hit her heart or any major blood vessels. It nicked her lung, but we've managed to patch that up. Right now she just needs rest. She can be seen later, but really we want to keep that to a minimum. Close family members only, for the moment. Perhaps tomorrow?'

He nods. 'I understand. No problem. Could you just . . . maybe later, when the family have gone . . . could you just tell her I was here? And tell her I said thank you.'

The doctor smiles. 'Thank you?'

He smiles back. 'Long story. She'll understand.'

The doctor disappears. Goes back to saving lives, fixing disabilities, mending bodies. Little things like that.

Cody takes one more look at Parker. He understands now that the man's tears are there through sheer relief. And the intensity of his relief is due to his unbounded love for Webley.

And that's all Cody needs to know.

She suspects.

Cody can see it going through Blunt's head. She knows that more went on than Cody is telling her.

He spins her a story, of course. Tells her what her official head wants to hear. Says that he had to intervene when Chris decided to kill Dobson, and that's when Chris got the drop on him.

He leaves out the bit about offering himself as a substitute for Webley. Doesn't seem relevant, somehow.

Blunt doesn't care. She wants to write this up as a success story, not as a suicide mission. She's more than happy to polish this to a high gloss.

And so she tells Cody how brave he was, and how committed he was to stopping the killer. She congratulates him on discovering the truth about Dobson's background and the link to Hillsborough that would surely have led to an arrest before long. She tells him that officers have already gone into Chris's house – a simple semi-detached property near the old student residences in Mossley Hill – and found there a room full of birds of all shapes and sizes. When counted up and added to the four already left with the initial police victims, the birds total ninety-six – exactly the same as the number of Hillsborough victims. Cody's efforts, she assures him, helped to prevent a much greater proportion of those creatures being found dead alongside police corpses.

Cody nods along. Feels the accolades hitting him, but not being absorbed. In his opinion this is not a time for triumph, for celebration. He knows only too well about trauma and the effects it can have on the mind. How much more devastating must those effects be on the mind of a young child? You have watched people die all around you. You have heard the screaming and seen the terror on the faces of those having the very breath squeezed out of them. And even when you get out of there, your ordeal is not over. Not by a long chalk. Because then you are told that it is all your fault. The responsibility for those ninety-six deaths is yours.

The trauma, the overwhelming sense of guilt, and then the deaths of both of your parents. How much worse can it get? Why is it surprising that a mind can snap under such strain?

And how many others are still suffering not only because of what happened at Hillsborough, but also because of the lies that were told about it so brazenly?

The self-questioning continues when Cody finally goes home. He experiences a whole cocktail of emotions. He is happy that Webley is alive, of course, even though she was so badly injured. There will be scars – physical and mental. But he is also reminded of how he felt when he was up there on that roof with her.

He was ready to die. It's something that he could easily convince himself was an act of heroism to save others. But that would be

kidding himself. The painful truth is that he *wanted* to die. End-
ing his own life to save Webley's was just a matter of expediency.
Killing two birds with one stone – ho, ho.

He doesn't think he can carry on like this. Talking things over
with Webley helped, but he knows it's transitory. She can't risk
alienating her fiancé again. Cody can't allow her to do that. And so
the pain will return. The nightmares will start up again. At some
point he will crash and burn.

He dwells on this for the next couple of hours. Tries to decide
what to do about his future, and reaches no conclusions.

Later, he is almost surprised to find himself in bed, staring up at
the ceiling. Eventually, he drifts into a sleep that, if not disturbed,
is deep enough to keep him blessedly unaware of reality for much
longer than usual.

Except that it *is* disturbed.

The phone on his bedside table. Calling to him so loudly and
urgently that its ensuing silence will be disorienting. The usual
thing.

But no. Not the usual. Not this time.

He thinks he is dreaming at first – that he hasn't really answered
the phone, and is still living one of his many nightmares. That
would make more sense. He could cope with that.

But this . . .

The screaming. Coming over the earpiece. Powerful and raw
enough to stop his breathing and punch at his heart. What is this?

What it is, he realises, is himself. That's *his* voice he can hear. *His*
screaming. *His* pleading for the ordeal to end. He remembers it like
it was yesterday, because it bursts into his mind every single day.

But this can't be real. It has to be another hallucination. Like those
in the building at the docks. It's his mind toying with him again
because he stubbornly refuses to get it fixed. Yes, that's what this is.

And yet it seems so real.

And if it's real . . .

Well, that means someone made an audio recording of what he was put through in that warehouse a year ago. It means they must have been there.

And it means that, for whatever unfathomable reason, they have finally decided to make themselves known to Cody.

That's a link to past devilry that he thought had been severed for eternity.

That's a beginning, just when he thought things were coming to an end.

What was it he told Webley about the men who had hurt him?

If I knew they were behind bars for the rest of their miserable lives, unable to hurt anyone else, then I really believe my problems would disappear.

Could this be the first step towards making that happen?

Nathan Cody has to hope so.

Acknowledgments

I would like to offer massive thanks to the following people for their part in making this book what it is:

My agent, Oli Munson, for believing in me, for letting me know when the words work and when they don't, for getting me the fab deals, and for being a really nice guy.

Oli's wonderful assistant, Becky Brown, for her perceptive editorial notes and all the other help she has given me since joining the agency.

Joel Richardson, my editor at Zaffre, for wanting the book, for being so passionate about it, and for doing such a fantastic job of whipping it into shape.

Steve May, and Rob and Mandy Callander – ex-police officers who provided me with a wealth of information about how the police do things, and who I hope will forgive me for the occasions on which I sacrificed that reality in the name of story.

Mario De Cabo Ramos, for allowing me such a close look at the amazing Royal Liver Building; and Terry McNamee, for being such a superb guide.

And, of course, my wife Lisa. Mere words don't work here.